THE WORLD OF
THE DIFFERENCE ENGINE
1855

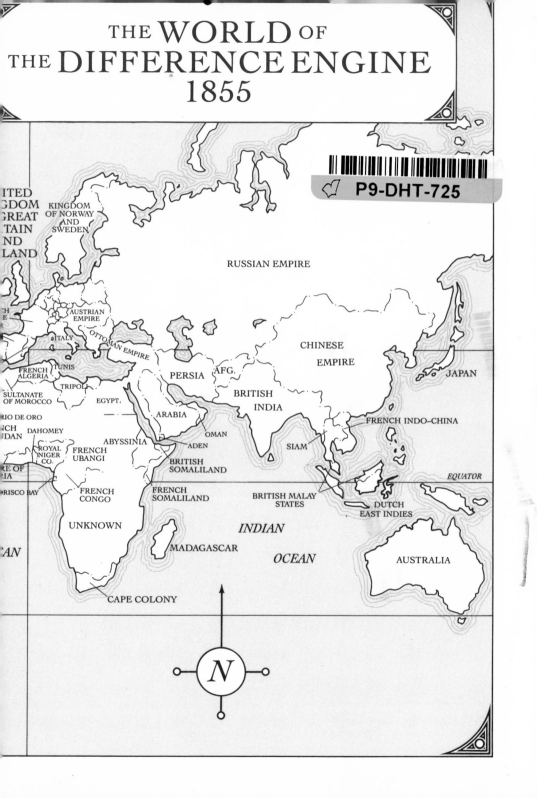

P9-DHT-725

ITED
GDOM
GREAT
TAIN
ND
LAND

KINGDOM
OF NORWAY
AND
SWEDEN

RUSSIAN EMPIRE

AUSTRIAN
EMPIRE

ITALY

OTTOMAN EMPIRE

CHINESE

EMPIRE

JAPAN

FRENCH
ALGERIA

TUNIS

PERSIA

AFG.

SULTANATE
OF MOROCCO

TRIPOLI

EGYPT.

BRITISH

INDIA

FRENCH INDO–CHINA

RIO DE ORO

ARABIA

NCH
UDAN

DAHOMEY

ABYSSINIA

OMAN

ADEN

SIAM

ROYAL
NIGER
CO.

FRENCH
UBANGI

BRITISH
SOMALILAND

EQUATOR

RE OF
IA

RISCO BAY

FRENCH
CONGO

FRENCH
SOMALILAND

BRITISH MALAY
STATES

DUTCH
EAST INDIES

UNKNOWN

INDIAN

MADAGASCAR

OCEAN

AUSTRALIA

AN

CAPE COLONY

N

THE DIFFERENCE ENGINE

Books by William Gibson

NEUROMANCER
COUNT ZERO
MONA LISA OVERDRIVE
BURNING CHROME

Books by Bruce Sterling

INVOLUTION OCEAN
THE ARTIFICIAL KID
SCHISMATRIX
ISLANDS IN THE NET
CRYSTAL EXPRESS
MIRRORSHADES (ed.)

THE
DIFFERENCE
ENGINE

WILLIAM GIBSON
BRUCE STERLING

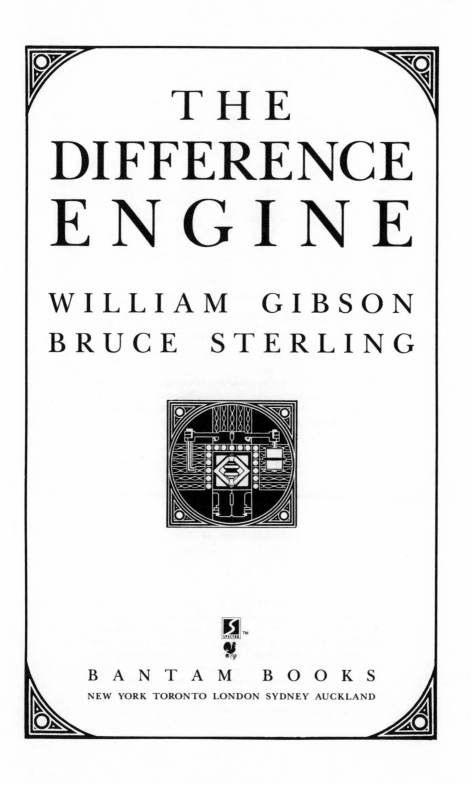

SPECTRA™

BANTAM BOOKS
NEW YORK TORONTO LONDON SYDNEY AUCKLAND

THE DIFFERENCE ENGINE

A BANTAM SPECTRA BOOK / APRIL 1991

All rights reserved.

Copyright © 1991 by William Gibson and Bruce Sterling.

Book designed by Jaya Dayal

Endpaper map designed by G DS / Jeffrey L. Ward

No part of this book may be reproduced or transmitted in any form
or by any means, electronic or mechanical, including photocopying,
recording, or by any information storage and retrieval system,
without permission in writing from the publisher.
For information address: BANTAM BOOKS.

LIBRARY OF CONGRESS CATALOGING-IN-PUBLICATION DATA

Gibson, William, 1948–
The difference engine / William Gibson, Bruce Sterling.
p.   cm.
ISBN 0-553-07028-2
I. Sterling, Bruce.   II. Title.
PS3557.I2264D54   1991
813'.54—dc20   90-42761
CIP

PUBLISHED SIMULTANEOUSLY IN THE UNITED STATES AND CANADA

Bantam Books are published by Bantam Books, a division of Bantam
Doubleday Dell Publishing Group, Inc. Its trademark, consisting of the
words "Bantam Books" and the portrayal of a rooster, is Registered in
U.S. Patent and Trademark Office and in other countries. Marca Regis-
trada. Bantam Books, 666 Fifth Avenue, New York, New York 10103.

PRINTED IN THE UNITED STATES OF AMERICA

BVG 0 9 8 7 6 5 4 3 2 1

THE DIFFERENCE ENGINE

FIRST ITERATION

The Angel of Goliad

COMPOSITE IMAGE, OPTICALLY encoded by escort-craft of the trans-Channel airship *Lord Brunel*: aerial view of suburban Cherbourg, October 14, 1905.

A villa, a garden, a balcony.

Erase the balcony's wrought-iron curves, exposing a bath-chair and its occupant. Reflected sunset glints from the nickel-plate of the chair's wheel-spokes.

The occupant, owner of the villa, rests her arthritic hands upon fabric woven by a Jacquard loom.

These hands consist of tendons, tissue, jointed bone. Through quiet processes of time and information, threads within the human cells have woven themselves into a woman.

Her name is Sybil Gerard.

Below her, in a neglected formal garden, leafless vines lace wooden trellises on whitewashed, flaking walls. From the open windows of her sickroom, a warm draft stirs the loose white hair at her neck, bringing scents of coal-smoke, jasmine, opium.

Her attention is fixed upon the sky, upon a silhouette of vast and irresistible grace—metal, in her lifetime, having taught itself to fly. In advance of that magnificence, tiny unmanned aeroplanes dip and skirl against the red horizon.

Like starlings, Sybil thinks.

The airship's lights, square golden windows, hint at human warmth. Effortlessly, with the incomparable grace of organic function, she imagines a distant music there, the music of London: the passengers promenade, they drink, they flirt, perhaps they dance.

Thoughts come unbidden, the mind weaving its perspectives, assembling meaning from emotion and memory.

She recalls her life in London. Recalls herself, so long ago, making her way along the Strand, pressing past the crush at Temple Bar. Pressing on, the city of Memory winding itself about her—till, by the walls of Newgate, the shadow of her father's hanging falls . . .

And Memory turns, deflected swift as light, down another byway—one where it is always evening. . . .

It is January 15, 1855.

A room in Grand's Hotel, Piccadilly.

One chair was propped backward, wedged securely beneath the door's cut-glass knob. Another was draped with clothing: a woman's fringed mantelet, a mud-crusted skirt of heavy worsted, a man's checked trousers and cutaway coat.

Two forms lay beneath the bedclothes of the laminated-maple four-poster, and off in the iron grip of winter Big Ben bellowed ten o'clock, great hoarse calliope sounds, the coal-fired breath of London.

Sybil slid her feet through icy linens to the warmth of the ceramic bottle in its wrap of flannel. Her toes brushed his shin. The touch seemed to start him from deep deliberation. That was how he was, this Dandy Mick Radley.

She'd met Mick Radley at Laurent's Dancing Academy, down Windmill Street. Now that she knew him, he seemed more the sort for Kellner's in Leicester Square, or even the Portland Rooms. He was always thinking, scheming, muttering over something in his head. Clever, clever. It worried her. And Mrs. Winterhalter wouldn't have approved, for the handling of "political gentlemen" required delicacy and discretion, qualities Mrs. Winterhalter believed she herself had a-plenty, while crediting none to her girls.

"No more dollymopping, Sybil," Mick said. One of his pronouncements, something about which he'd made up his clever mind.

Sybil grinned up at him, her face half-hidden by the blanket's warm edge. She knew he liked the grin. Her wicked-girl grin. He can't mean that, she thought. Make a joke of it, she told herself. "But if I weren't a wicked dollymop, would I be here with you now?"

"No more playing bobtail."

"You know I only go with gentlemen."

Mick sniffed, amused. "Call me a gentleman, then?"

"A very flash gentleman," Sybil said, flattering him. "One of the fancy. You know I don't care for the Rad Lords. I spit on 'em, Mick."

Sybil shivered, but not unhappily, for she'd run into a good bit of luck here, full of steak-and-taters and hot chocolate, in bed between clean sheets in a fashionable hotel. A shiny new hotel with central steam-heat, though she'd gladly have traded the restless gurgling and banging of the scrolled gilt radiator for the glow of a well-banked hearth.

And he was a good-looking cove, this Mick Radley, she had to admit, dressed very flash, had the tin and was generous with it, and he'd yet to demand anything peculiar or beastly. She knew it wouldn't last, as Mick was a touring gent from Manchester, and gone soon enough. But there was profit in him, and maybe more when he left her, if she made him feel sorry about it, and generous.

Mick reclined into fat feather-pillows and slid his manicured fingers behind his spit-curled head. Silk nightshirt all frothy with lace down the front—only the best for Mick. Now he seemed to want to talk a bit. Men did, usually, after a while—about their wives, mostly.

But for Dandy Mick, it was always politics. "So, you hate the Lordships, Sybil?"

"Why shouldn't I?" Sybil said. "I have my reasons."

"I should say you do," Mick said slowly, and the look he gave her then, of cool superiority, sent a shiver through her.

"What d'ye mean by that, Mick?"

"I know your reasons for hating the Government. I have your number."

Surprise seeped into her, then fear. She sat up in bed. There was a taste in her mouth like cold iron.

"You keep your card in your bag," he said. "I took that number to a rum magistrate I know. He ran it through a government Engine for me, and printed up your Bow Street file, rat-a-tat-tat, like fun." He smirked. "So I know all about you, girl. Know who you are . . ."

She tried to put a bold face on it. "And who's that, then, Mr. Radley?"

"No Sybil Jones, dearie. You're Sybil Gerard, the daughter of Walter Gerard, the Luddite agitator."

He'd raided her hidden past.

Machines, whirring somewhere, spinning out history.

Now Mick watched her face, smiling at what he saw there, and she recognized a look she'd seen before, at Laurent's, when first he'd spied her across the crowded floor. A hungry look.

Her voice shook. "How long have you known about me?"

"Since our second night. You know I travel with the General. Like any important man, he has enemies. As his secretary and man-of-affairs, I take few chances with strangers." Mick put his cruel, deft little hand on her shoulder. "You might have been someone's agent. It was business."

Sybil flinched away. "Spying on a helpless girl," she said at last. "You're a right bastard, you are!"

But her foul words scarcely seemed to touch him—he was cold and hard, like a judge or a lordship. "I may spy, girl, but I use the

Government's machinery for my own sweet purposes. I'm no copper's nark, to look down my nose at a revolutionary like Walter Gerard—no matter what the Rad Lords may call him now. Your father was a hero."

He shifted on the pillow. "*My* hero—that was Walter Gerard. I saw him speak, on the Rights of Labour, in Manchester. He was a marvel—we all cheered till our throats was raw! The good old Hell-Cats . . ." Mick's smooth voice had gone sharp and flat, in a Mancunian tang. "Ever hear tell of the Hell-Cats, Sybil? In the old days?"

"A street-gang," Sybil said. "Rough boys in Manchester."

Mick frowned. "We was a brotherhood! A friendship youth-guild! Your father knew us well. He was our patron politician, you might say."

"I'd prefer it if you didn't speak of my father, Mr. Radley."

Mick shook his head at her impatiently. "When I heard they'd tried and hanged him"—the words like ice behind her ribs—"me and the lads, we took up torches and crowbars, and we ran hot and wild. . . . That was Ned Ludd's work, girl! Years ago . . ." He picked delicately at the front of his nightshirt. "'Tis not a tale I tell to many. The Government's Engines have long memories."

She understood it now—Mick's generosity and his sweet-talk, the strange hints he'd aimed at her, of secret plans and better fortune, marked cards and hidden aces. He was pulling her strings, making her his creature. The daughter of Walter Gerard was a fancy prize, for a man like Mick.

She pulled herself out of bed, stepping across icy floorboards in her pantalettes and chemise.

She dug quickly, silently, through the heap of her clothing. The fringed mantelet, the jacket, the great sagging cage of her crinoline skirt. The jingling white cuirass of her corset.

"Get back in bed," Mick said lazily. "Don't get your monkey up. 'Tis cold out there." He shook his head. " 'Tis not like you think, Sybil."

She refused to look at him, struggling into her corset by the window, where frost-caked glass cut the upwashed glare of gas-light from the street. She cinched the corset's laces tight across her back with a quick practiced snap of her wrists.

"Or if it is," Mick mused, watching her, " 'tis only in small degree."

Across the street, the opera had let out—gentry in their cloaks and top-hats. Cab-horses, their backs in blankets, stamped and shivered on the black macadam. White traces of clean suburban snow still clung to the gleaming coachwork of some lordship's steam-gurney. Tarts were working the crowd. Poor wretched souls. Hard indeed to find a kind face amid those goffered shirts and diamond studs, on such a cold night. Sybil turned toward Mick, confused, angry, and very much afraid. "Who did you tell about me?"

"Not a living soul," Mick said, "not even my friend the General. And I won't be peaching on you. Nobody's ever said Mick Radley's indiscreet. So get back in bed."

"I shan't," Sybil said, standing straight, her bare feet freezing on the floorboards. "Sybil Jones may share your bed—but the daughter of Walter Gerard is a personage of substance!"

Mick blinked at her, surprised. He thought it over, rubbing his narrow chin, then nodded. " 'Tis my sad loss, then, Miss Gerard." He sat up in bed and pointed at the door, with a dramatic sweep of his arm. "Put on your skirt, then, and your brass-heeled dolly-boots, Miss Gerard, and out the door with you and your sub-stance. But 'twould be a great shame if you left. I've uses for a clever girl."

"I should say you do, you blackguard," said Sybil, but she hesitated. He had another card to play—she could sense it in the set of his face.

He grinned at her, his eyes slitted. "Have you ever been to Paris, Sybil?"

"Paris?" Her breath clouded in midair.

"Yes," he said, "the gay and the glamorous, next destination for the General, when his London lecture tour is done." Dandy Mick plucked at his lace cuffs. "What those uses are, that I mentioned, I shan't as yet say. But the General is a man of deep stratagem.

And the Government of France have certain difficulties that require the help of experts. . . ." He leered triumphantly. "But I can see that I bore you, eh?"

Sybil shifted from foot to foot. "You'll take me to Paris, Mick," she said slowly, "and that's the true bill, no snicky humbugging?"

"Strictly square and level. If you don't believe me, I've a ticket in my coat for the Dover ferry."

Sybil walked to the brocade armchair in the corner, and tugged at Mick's greatcoat. She shivered uncontrollably, and slipped the greatcoat on. Fine dark wool, like being wrapped in warm money.

"Try the right front pocket," Mick told her. "The card-case." He was amused and confident—as if it were funny that she didn't trust him. Sybil thrust her chilled hands into both pockets. Deep, plush-lined . . .

Her left hand gripped a lump of hard cold metal. She drew out a nasty little pepperbox derringer. Ivory handle, intricate gleam of steel hammers and brass cartridges, small as her hand but heavy.

"Naughty," said Mick, frowning. "Put it back, there's a girl."

Sybil put the thing away, gently but quickly, as if it were a live crab. In the other pocket she found his card-case, red morocco leather; inside were business cards, cartes-de-visite with his Engine-stippled portrait, a London train timetable.

And an engraved slip of stiff creamy parchment, first-class passage on the *Newcomen*, out of Dover.

"You'll need two tickets, then," she hesitated, "if you really mean to take me."

Mick nodded, conceding the point. "And another for the train from Cherbourg, too. And nothing simpler. I can wire for tickets, downstairs at the lobby desk."

Sybil shivered again, and wrapped the coat closer. Mick laughed at her. "Don't give me that vinegar phiz. You're still thinking like a dollymop; stop it. Start thinking flash, or you'll be of no use to me. You're Mick's gal now—a high-flyer."

She spoke slowly, reluctantly. "I've never been with any man who knew I was Sybil Gerard." That was a lie, of course—there was Egremont, the man who had ruined her. Charles Egremont had known very well who she was. But Egremont no longer mattered—he lived in a different world, now, with his po-faced respectable wife, and his respectable children, and his respectable seat in Parliament.

And Sybil hadn't been dollymopping, with Egremont. Not exactly, anyway. A matter of degree. . . .

She could tell that Mick was pleased at the lie she'd told him. It had flattered him.

Mick opened a gleaming cigar-case, extracted a cheroot, and lit it in the oily flare of a repeating match, filling the room with the candied smell of cherry tobacco.

"So now you feel a bit shy with me, do you?" he said at last. "Well, I prefer it that way. What I know, that gives me a bit more grip on you, don't it, than mere tin."

His eyes narrowed. "It's what a cove *knows* that counts, ain't it, Sybil? More than land or money, more than birth. *Information.* Very flash."

Sybil felt a moment of hatred for him, for his ease and confidence. Pure resentment, sharp and primal, but she crushed her feelings down. The hatred wavered, losing its purity, turning to shame. She did hate him—but only because he truly knew her. He knew how far Sybil Gerard had fallen, that she had been an educated girl, with airs and graces, as good as any gentry girl, once.

From the days of her father's fame, from her girlhood, Sybil could remember Mick Radley's like. She knew the kind of boy that he had been. Ragged angry factory-boys, penny-a-score, who would crowd her father after his torchlight speeches, and do whatever he commanded. Rip up railroad tracks, kick the boiler-plugs out of spinning jennies, lay policemen's helmets by his feet. She and her father had fled from town to town, often by night, living in cellars, attics, anonymous rooms-to-let, hiding from the Rad police and the daggers of other conspirators. And sometimes, when his own wild speeches had filled him with a burning elation, her father would embrace her and soberly promise her the world. She would live like gentry in a green and quiet England, when King Steam was wrecked. When Byron and his Industrial Radicals were utterly destroyed....

But a hempen rope had choked her father into silence. The Radicals ruled on and on, moving from triumph to triumph, shuffling the world like a deck of cards. And now Mick Radley was up in the world, and Sybil Gerard was down.

She stood there silently, wrapped in Mick's coat. Paris. The promise tempted her, and when she let herself believe him, there was a thrill behind it like lightning. She forced herself to think about leaving her life in London. It was a bad, a low, a sordid life, she knew, but not entirely desperate. She still had things to lose. Her rented room in Whitechapel, and dear Toby, her cat. There was Mrs. Winterhalter, who arranged meetings between fast girls and political gentlemen. Mrs. Winterhalter was a bawd, but lady-like and steady, and her sort was difficult to find. And she would lose her two steady gentlemen, Mr. Chadwick and Mr. Kingsley, who each saw her twice a month. Steady tin, that was, and kept her from the street. But Chadwick had a jealous wife in Fulham, and, in a moment of foolishness, Sybil had stolen Kingsley's best cufflinks. She knew that he suspected.

And neither man was half so free with his money as Dandy Mick.

She forced herself to smile at him, as sweetly as she could. "You're a rum'un, Mick Radley. You know you've got my leading-strings. Perhaps I was vexed with you at first, but I'm not so cakey as to not know a rum gentleman when I see one."

Mick blew smoke. "You *are* a clever one," he said admiringly. "You talk blarney like an angel. You're not fooling me, though, so you needn't deceive yourself. Still, you're just the gal I need. Get back in bed."

She did as he told her.

"Jove," he said, "your blessed feet are two lumps of ice. Why don't you wear little slippers, eh?" He tugged at her corset, with determination. "Slippers, and black silk stockings," he said. "A gal looks very flash in bed, with black silk stockings."

From the far end of the glass-topped counter, one of Aaron's shopmen gave Sybil the cold eye, standing haughty and tall in his neat black coat and polished boots. He knew something was up—he could smell it. Sybil waited for Mick to pay, hands folded before her on her skirt, demure, but watching sidelong from beneath the blue fringe of her bonnet. Under her skirt, wadded through the frame of her crinoline, was the shawl she'd nicked while Radley tried on top-hats.

Sybil had learned how to nick things—she'd taught herself. It simply took nerve, that was the secret. It took pluck. Look neither right nor left—just grab, lift her skirt, stuff and rustle. Then stand quite straight, with a psalm-singing look, like a gentry girl.

The floorman had lost interest in her; he was watching a fat man fingering watered-silk braces. Sybil checked her skirt quickly. No bulge showed.

A young spotty-faced clerk, with inkstained thumbs, set Mick's number into a counter-top credit-machine. Zip, click, a pull on the ebony-handled lever, and it was done. He gave Mick his printed purchase-slip and did the parcel up in string and crisp green paper.

Aaron & Son would never miss a cashmere shawl. Perhaps their account-engines would, when they tallied up, but the loss couldn't hurt them; their shopping-palace was too big and too rich. All those Greek columns, chandeliers of Irish crystal, a million mirrors—room after gilded room, stuffed with rubber riding boots and French-milled soap, walking-sticks, umbrellas, cutlery, locked glass cases crammed with silver-plate and ivory brooches and lovely wind-up golden music-boxes. . . . And this was only one of a dozen in a chain. But for all of that, she knew, Aaron's wasn't truly smart, not a gentry place.

But couldn't you just do anything with money in England, if you were clever? Someday Mr. Aaron, a whiskery old merchant

Jew from Whitechapel, would have a lordship, with a steam-gurney waiting at the curb and his own coat of arms on the coachwork. The Rad Parliament wouldn't care that Mr. Aaron was no Christian. They'd given Charles Darwin a lordship, and he said that Adam and Eve were monkeys.

The liftman, gotten up in a Frenchified livery, drew the rattling brass gate aside for her. Mick followed her in, his parcel tucked under his arm, and then they were descending.

They emerged from Aaron's into Whitechapel jostle. While Mick checked a street-map he took from his coat, she gazed up at the shifting letters that ran the length of Aaron's frontage. A mechanical frieze, a slow sort of kinotrope for Aaron's adverts, made all of little bits of painted wood, clicking about each in turn, behind leaded sheets of bevel-glass. CONVERT YOUR MANUAL PIANO, the jostling letters suggested, INTO A KASTNER'S PIANOLA.

The skyline west of Whitechapel was spikey with construction cranes, stark steel skeletons painted with red lead against the damp. Older buildings were furred with scaffolding; what wasn't being torn down, it seemed, to make way for the new, was being rebuilt in its image. There was a distant huffing of excavation, and a tremulous feeling below the pavement, of vast machines cutting some new underground line.

But now Mick turned left, without a word, and walked away, his hat cocked to one side, his checkered trouser-legs flashing under the long hem of his greatcoat. She had to hurry to match his step. A ragged boy with a numbered tin badge was sweeping mucky snow from the crossing; Mick tossed him a penny without breaking stride and headed down the lane called Butcher Row.

She caught up and took his arm, past red and white carcasses dangling from their black iron hooks, beef and mutton and veal, and thick men in their stained aprons crying their goods. London women crowded there in scores, wicker baskets on their arms. Servants, cooks, respectable wives with men at home. A red-faced squinting butcher lurched in front of Sybil with a double handful of blue meat. "Hallo, pretty missus. Buy your gentleman my nice kidneys for pie!" Sybil ducked her head and walked around him.

Parked barrows crowded the curb, where costers stood bellowing, their velveteen coats set off with buttons of brass or pearl.
Each had his numbered badge, though fully half the numbers
were slang, Mick claimed, as slang as the costers' weights and
measures. There were blankets and baskets spread on neatly
chalked squares on the paving, and Mick was telling her of ways
the costers had to plump out shrunken fruit, and weave dead eels
in with live. She smiled at the pleasure he seemed to take in
knowing such things, while hawkers yelped about their brooms
and soap and candles, and a scowling organ-grinder cranked,
two-handed, at his symphony machine, filling the street with a
fast springy racket of bells, piano-wire, and steel.

Mick stopped beside a wooden trestle-table, kept by a squint-
eyed widow in bombazine, the stump of a clay pipe protruding
from her thin lips. Arrayed before her were numerous vials of
some viscous-looking substance Sybil took to be a patent medicine, for each was pasted with a blue slip of paper bearing the
blurred image of a savage red Indian. "And what would this be,
mother?" Mick inquired, tapping one red-waxed cork with a
gloved finger.

"Rock-oil, mister," she said, relinquishing the stem of her pipe,
"much as they call Barbados tar." Her drawling accent grated on
the ear, but Sybil felt a pang of pity. How far the woman was from
whatever outlandish place she'd once called home.

"Really," Mick asked, "it wouldn't be Texian?"

" 'Healthful balm,' " the widow said, " 'from Nature's secret
spring, the bloom of health and life to man will bring.' Skimmed
by the savage Seneca from the waters of Pennsylvania's great Oil
Creek, mister. Three pennies the vial and a guaranteed cure-all."
The woman was peering up at Mick now with a queer expression,
her pale eyes screwed tight in nests of wrinkles, as though she
might recall his face. Sybil shivered.

"Good day to you, then, mother," Mick said, with a smile that
somehow reminded Sybil of a vice detective she'd known, a sandy
little man who worked Leicester Square and Soho; the Badger,
the girls had called him.

"What is it?" she asked, taking Mick's arm as he turned to go. "What is it she's selling?"

"Rock-oil," Mick said, and she caught his sharp glance back at the hunched black figure. "The General tells me it bubbles from the ground, in Texas. . . ."

Sybil was curious. "Is it a proper cure-all, then?"

"Never mind," he said, "and here's an end to chat." He was glancing bright-eyed down the lane. "I see one, and you know what to do."

Sybil nodded, and began to pick her way through the market-crowd toward the man Mick had seen. He was a ballad-seller, lean and hollow-cheeked, his hair long and greasy under a tall hat wrapped in bright polka-dot fabric. He held both his arms bent, hands knotted as if in prayer, the sleeves of his rumpled jacket heavy with long rustling quires of sheet-music.

" 'Railway to Heaven,' ladies and gents," the ballad-seller chanted, a veteran patterer. " 'Of truth divine the rails are made, and on the Rock of Ages laid; the rails are fixed in chains of love, firm as the throne of God above.' Lovely tune and only tuppence, miss."

"Do you have 'The Raven of San Jacinto'?" Sybil asked.

"I can get that, I can get it," the seller said. "And what's that then?"

"About the great battle in Texas, the great General?"

The ballad-seller arched his brows. His eyes were blue and crazily bright, with hunger, perhaps, or religion, or gin. "One of your Crimea generals then, a Frenchy, this Mr. Jacinto?"

"No, no," Sybil said, and gave him a pitying smile, "General Houston, Sam Houston of Texas. I do want that song, most particular."

"I buy my publications fresh this afternoon, and I'll look for your song for you sure, miss."

"I shall want at least five copies for my friends," Sybil said.

"Ten pence will get you six."

"Six, then, and this afternoon, at this very spot."

"Just as you say, miss." The seller touched the brim of his hat.

Sybil walked away, into the crowd. She had done it. It was not so bad. She felt she could get used to it. Perhaps it was a good tune, too, one that people would enjoy when the ballad-man was forced to sell the copies.

Mick sidled up suddenly, at her elbow.

"Not bad," Mick allowed, reaching into the pocket of his great-coat, like magic, to produce an apple turnover, still hot, flaking sugar and wrapped in greasy paper.

"Thank you," she said, startled but glad, for she'd been think-ing of stopping, hiding, fetching out the stolen shawl, but Mick's eyes had been on her every moment. She hadn't seen him, but he'd been watching; that was the way he was. She wouldn't forget again.

They walked, together and apart, all down Somerset, and then through the vast market of Petticoat Lane, lit as evening drew on with a host of lights, a glow of gas-mantles, the white glare of carbide, filthy grease-lamps, tallow dips twinkling among the foodstuffs proffered from the stalls. The hubbub was deafening here, but she delighted Mick by gulling three more ballad-sellers.

In a great bright Whitechapel gin-palace, with glittering gold-papered walls flaring with fishtail gas-jets, Sybil excused herself and found a ladies' convenience. There, safe within a reeking stall, she fetched the shawl out. So soft it was, and such a lovely violet color too, one of the strange new dyes clever people made from coal. She folded the shawl neatly, and stuffed it through the top of her corset, so it rested safe. Then out to join her keeper again, finding him seated at a table. He'd bought her a noggin of honey gin. She sat beside him.

"You did well, girl," he said, and slid the little glass toward her. The place was full of Crimean soldiers on furlough, Irishmen, with street-drabs hanging on them, growing red-nosed and screechy on gin. No barmaids here, but big bruiser bully-rock bar-tenders, in white aprons, with mill-knocker clubs behind the bar.

"Gin's a whore's drink, Mick."

"Everybody likes gin," he said. "And you're no whore, Sybil."

"Dollymop, bobtail." She looked at him sharply. "What else d'ye call me, then?"

"You're with Dandy Mick now," he said. He leaned his chair back, jabbing his gloved thumbs through the arm-holes of his waistcoat. "You're an *adventuress*."

"Adventuress?"

"Bloody right." He straightened. "And here's to you." He sipped his gin-twist, rolled it over his tongue with an unhappy look, and swallowed. "Never mind, dear—they've cut this with turpentine or I'm a Jew." He stood up.

They left. She hung on his arm, trying to slow his pace. " 'Adventurer,' that's what you are, then, eh, Mr. Mick Radley?"

"So I am, Sybil," he said softly, "and you're to be my 'prentice. So you do as you're told in the proper humble spirit. Learn the tricks of craft. And someday you join the union, eh? The guild."

"Like my *father*, eh? You want to make a play of that, Mick? Who he was, who I am?"

"No," Mick said flatly. "He was old-fashioned, he's nobody now."

Sybil smirked. "They let us wicked girls into this fancy guild of yours, do they, Mick?"

"It's a knowledge guild," he said soberly. "The bosses, the big'uns, they can take all manner of things away from us. With their bloody laws and factories and courts and banks. . . . They can make the world to their pleasure, they can take away your home and kin and even the work you do. . . ." Mick shrugged angrily, his lean shoulders denting the heavy fabric of the greatcoat. "And even rob a hero's daughter of her virtue, if I'm not too bold in speaking of it." He pressed her hand against his sleeve, a hard, trapping grip. "But they can't ever take what you *know*, now can they, Sybil? They can't ever take that."

Sybil heard Hetty's footsteps in the hall outside her room, and the rattle of Hetty's key at the door. She let the serinette die down, with a high-pitched drone.

Hetty tugged the snow-flaked woollen bonnet from her head, shrugging free from her Navy cloak. She was another of Mrs.

Winterhalter's girls, a big-boned, raucous brunette from Devon, who drank too much, but was sweet in her way, and always kind to Toby.

Sybil folded away the china-handled crank and lowered the cheap instrument's scratched lid. "I was practicing. Mrs. Winterhalter wants me to sing next Thursday."

"Bother the old drab," Hetty said. "Thought this was your night out with Mr. C. Or is it Mr. K.?" Hetty stamped warmth into her feet before the narrow little hearth, then noticed, in the lamplight, the scattering of shoes and hat-boxes from Aaron & Son. "My word," she said, and smiled, her broad mouth pinched a bit with envy. "New beau, is it? You're so lucky, Sybil Jones!"

"Perhaps." Sybil sipped hot lemon-cordial, tilting her head back to relax her throat.

Hetty winked. "Winterhalter doesn't know about this one, eh?"

Sybil shook her head and smiled. Hetty would not tell. "D'ye know anything about Texas, Hetty?"

"A country in America," Hetty said readily. "French own it, don't they?"

"That's Mexico. Would you like to go to a kinotrope show, Hetty? The former President of Texas is lecturing. I've tickets, free for the taking."

"When?"

"Saturday."

"I'm dancing then," Hetty said. "Perhaps Mandy would go." She blew warmth into her fingers. "Friend of mine comes by late tonight, wouldn't trouble you, would it?"

"No," Sybil said. Mrs. Winterhalter had a strict rule against any girl keeping company with men in her room. It was a rule Hetty often ignored, as if daring the landlord to peach on her. Since Mrs. Winterhalter chose to pay the rent directly to the landlord, Mr. Cairns, Sybil seldom had call to speak to him, and less with his sullen wife, a thick-ankled woman with a taste for dreadful hats. Cairns and his wife had never informed against Hetty, though Sybil was not sure why, for Hetty's room was next to theirs, and Hetty made a shameless racket when she brought men home—foreign diplomats, mostly, men with odd accents and, to judge by the noise, beastly habits.

"You can carry on singing if you like," Hetty said, and knelt before the ash-covered fire. "You've a fine voice. Mustn't let your gifts go to waste." She began to feed individual coals to the hearth, shivering. A dire chill seemed to enter the room then, through the cracked casement of one of the nailed-up windows, and for a strange passing moment Sybil felt a distinct presence in the air. A definite sense of observation, of eyes fixed upon her from another realm. She thought of her dead father. *Learn the voice, Sybil. Learn to speak. It's all we have that can fight them*, he had told her. This in the last few days before his arrest, when it was clear that the Rads had won again—clear to everyone, perhaps, save Walter Gerard. She had seen then, with heart-crushing clarity, the utter magnitude of her father's defeat. His ideals would be lost—not just misplaced but utterly expunged from history, to be crushed again and again and again, like the carcass of a mongrel dog under the racketing wheels of an express train. *Learn to speak, Sybil. It's all we have . . . .*

"Read to me?" Hetty asked. "I'll make tea."

"Very well." In her spotty, scattered life with Hetty, reading aloud was one of the little rituals they had that passed for domesticity. Sybil took up the day's *Illustrated London News* from the deal table, settled her crinoline about her in the creaking, damp-smelling armchair, and squinted at a front-page article. It concerned itself with dinosaurs.

The Rads were mad for these dinosaurs, it seemed. Here was an engraving of a party of seven, led by Lord Darwin, all peering intently at some indeterminate object embedded in a coal-face in Thuringia. Sybil read the caption aloud, showed the picture to Hetty. A bone. The thing in the coal was a monstrous bone, as long as a man was tall. She shuddered. Turning the page, she encountered an artist's view of the creature as it might have looked in life, a monstrosity with twin rows of angry triangular saw-teeth along its humped spine. It seemed the size of an elephant at least, though its evil little head was scarcely larger than a hound's.

Hetty poured the tea. " 'Reptiles held sway across the whole of the earth,' eh?" she quoted, and threaded her needle. "I don't believe a bloody word of it."

"Why not?"

"They're the bones of bloody giants, out of Genesis. That's what the clergy say, ain't it?"

Sybil said nothing. Neither supposition struck her as the more fantastic. She turned to a second article, this one in praise of Her Majesty's Artillery in the Crimea. She found an engraving of two handsome subalterns admiring the operation of a long-range gun. The gun itself, its barrel stout as a foundry stack, looked fit to make short work of all Lord Darwin's dinosaurs. Sybil's attention, however, was held by an inset view of the gunnery Engine. The intricate nest of interlocking gearwork possessed a queer beauty, like some kind of baroquely fabulous wallpaper.

"Have you anything that needs darning?" Hetty asked.

"No, thank you."

"Read some adverts, then," Hetty advised. "I do hate that war humbug."

There was HAVILAND CHINA, from Limoges, France; VIN MAR-IANI, the French tonic, with a testimonial from Alexandre Dumas and Descriptive Book, Portraits, and Autographs of Celebrities, upon application to the premises in Oxford Street; SILVER ELEC-TRO SILICON POLISH, it never scratches, never wears, it is unlike others; the "NEW DEPARTURE" BICYCLE BELL, it has a tone all its own; DR. BAYLEY'S LITHIA WATER, cures Bright's disease and the gouty diathesis; GURNEY'S "REGENT" POCKET STEAM-ENGINE, in-tended for use with domestic sewing machines. This last held Sybil's attention, but not through its promise to operate a machine at double the old speed at a cost of one halfpenny per hour.

Here was an engraving of the tastefully ornamented little boiler, to be heated by gas or paraffin. Charles Egremont had purchased one of these for his wife. It came equipped with a rubber tube intended to vent the waste steam when jammed under a convenient sash-window, but Sybil had been delighted to hear that it had turned Madame's drawing-room into a Turkish bath.

When the paper was finished, Sybil went to bed. She was woken around midnight by the savage rhythmic crunching of Hetty's bed-springs.

It was dim in the Garrick Theatre, dusty and cold, with the pit and the balcony and the racks of shabby seats; but it was pitch-dark below the stage, where Mick Radley was, and it smelled of damp and lime.

Mick's voice echoed up from under her feet. "Ever seen the innards of a kinotrope, Sybil?"

"I saw one once, backstage," she said. "At a music-hall, in Bethnal Green. I knew the fellow what worked it, a clacker cove."

"A sweetheart?" Mick asked. His echoing voice was sharp.

"No," Sybil told him quickly, "I was singing a bit. . . . But it scarcely paid."

She heard the sharp click of his repeating match. It caught on the third attempt and he lit a stub of candle. "Come down," he commanded. "Don't stand there like a goose, showing off your ankles." Sybil lifted her crinoline with both hands and picked her way uneasily down the steep damp stairs.

Mick reached up to grope behind a tall stage-mirror, a great gleaming sheet of silvered glass, with a wheeled pedestal and oily gears and worn wooden cranks. He retrieved a cheap black port-manteau of proofed canvas, placed it carefully on the floor before him, and squatted to undo the flimsy tin clasps. He removed a stack of perforated cards bound with a ribbon of red paper. There were other bundles in the bag as well, Sybil saw, and something else, a gleam of polished wood.

He handled the cards gently, like a Bible.

"Safe as houses," he said. "You just disguise 'em, you see—write something stupid on the wrapper, like 'Temperance Lecture—Parts One Two Three.' Then coves never think to steal 'em, or even load them up and look." Hefting the thick block, he riffled its edge with his thumb, so that it made a sharp crisp sound, like a gambler's new deck. "I put a deal of capital in these," he said. "Weeks of work from the best kino hands in Manchester. Exclusively to my design, I might point out. 'Tis a lovely thing, girl. Quite artistic, in its way. You'll soon see."

Closing the portmanteau, he stood. He carefully slid the bundle of cards into his coat-pocket, then bent over a crate and tugged out a thick glass tube. He blew dust from the tube, then gripped one end of it with a special pair of pincers. The glass cracked open with an airtight pop—there was a fresh block of lime in the tube. Mick slid it loose, humming to himself. He tamped the lime gently into the socket of a limelight burner, a great dish-shaped thing of sooty iron and gleaming tin. Then he turned a hose-tap, sniffed a bit, nodded, turned a second tap, and set the candle to it.

Sybil yelped as a vicious flash sheeted into her eyes. Mick chuckled at her over the hiss of blazing gas, dots of hot blue dazzle drifting before her. "Better," he remarked. He aimed the blazing limelight carefully into the stage-mirror, then began to adjust its cranks.

Sybil looked around, blinking. It was dank and ratty and cramped under the Garrick stage, the sort of place a dog or a pauper might die in, with torn and yellowed bills underfoot, for naughty farces like *That Rascal Jack* and *Scamps of London*. A pair of ladies' unmentionables were wadded in a corner. From her brief unhappy days as a stage-singer, she had some idea how they might have gotten there.

She let her gaze follow steam-pipes and taut wires to the gleam of the Babbage Engine, a small one, a kinotrope model, no taller than Sybil herself. Unlike everything else in the Garrick, the Engine looked in very good repair, mounted on four mahogany blocks. The floor and ceiling above and beneath it had been carefully scoured and whitewashed. Steam-calculators were delicate things, temperamental, so she'd heard; better not to own one than not cherish it. In the stray glare from Mick's limelight, dozens of knobbed brass columns gleamed, set top and bottom into solid sockets bored through polished plates, with shining levers, ratchets, a thousand steel gears cut bright and fine. It smelled of linseed oil.

Looking at it, this close, this long, made Sybil feel quite odd. Hungry almost, or greedy in a queer way, the way she might feel about . . . a fine lovely horse, say. She wanted—not to own it exactly, but possess it somehow. . . .

Mick took her elbow suddenly, from behind. She started. "Lovely thing, isn't it?"

"Yes, it's . . . lovely."

Mick still held her arm. Slowly, he put his other gloved hand against her cheek, inside her bonnet. Then he lifted her chin with his thumb, staring into her face. "It makes you feel something, doesn't it?"

His rapt voice frightened her, his eyes underlit with glare. "Yes, Mick," she said obediently, quickly. "I do feel it . . . something."

He tugged her bonnet loose, to hang at her neck. "You're not frightened of it, Sybil, are you? Not with Dandy Mick here, holding you. You feel a little special *frisson*. You'll learn to like that feeling. We'll make a clacker of you."

"Can I do that, truly? Can a girl do that?"

Mick laughed. "Have you never heard of Lady Ada Byron, then? The Prime Minister's daughter, and the very Queen of Engines!" He let her go, and swung both his arms wide, coat swinging open, a showman's gesture. "Ada Byron, true friend and disciple of Babbage himself! Lord Charles Babbage, father of the Difference Engine and the Newton of our modern age!"

She gaped at him. "But Ada Byron is a ladyship!"

"You'd be surprised who our Lady Ada knows," Mick declared, plucking a block of cards from his pocket and peeling off its paper jacket. "Oh, not to drink tea with, among the diamond squad at her garden-parties, but Ada's what you'd call fast, in her own mathematical way. . . ." He paused. "That's not to say that Ada is the best, you know. I know clacking coves in the Steam Intellect Society that make even Lady Ada look a bit tardy. But

Ada possesses genius. D'ye know what that means, Sybil? To possess genius?"

"What?" Sybil said, hating the giddy surety in his voice.

"D'ye know how analytical geometry was born? Fellow named Descartes, watching a fly on the ceiling. A million fellows before him had watched flies on the ceiling, but it took René Descartes to make a science of it. Now engineers use what he discovered every day, but if it weren't for him we'd still be blind to it."

"What do flies matter to anyone?" Sybil demanded.

"Ada had an insight once that ranked with Descartes' discovery. No one has found a use for it as yet. It's what they call pure mathematics." Mick laughed. " 'Pure.' You know what that means, Sybil? It means they can't get it to run." He rubbed his hands together, grinning. "No one can get it to run."

Mick's glee was wearing at her nerves. "I thought you hated lordships!"

"I do hate lordly privilege, what's not earned fair and square and level," he said. "But Lady Ada lives and swears by the power of gray matter, and not her blue blood." He slotted the cards into a silvered tray by the side of the machine, then spun and caught her wrist. "Your father's dead, girl! 'Tis not that I mean to hurt you, saying it, but the Luddites are dead as cold ashes. Oh, we marched and ranted, for the rights of labor and such—fine talk, girl! But Lord Charles Babbage made blueprints while we made pamphlets. And his blueprints built this world."

Mick shook his head. "The Byron men, the Babbage men, the Industrial Radicals, they own Great Britain! They own us, girl— the very globe is at their feet, Europe, America, everywhere. The House of Lords is packed top to bottom with Rads. Queen Victoria won't stir a finger without a nod from the savants and capitalists." He pointed at her. "And it's no use fighting that anymore, and you know why? 'Cause the Rads do play fair, or fair enough to manage—and you can become one of 'em, if you're clever! You can't get clever men to fight such a system, as it makes too much sense to 'em."

Mick thumbed his chest. "But that don't mean that you and I

are out in the cold and lonely. It only means we have to think faster, with our eyes peeled and our ears open. . . ." Mick struck a prize-fighter's pose: elbows bent, fists poised, knuckles up before his face. Then he flung his hair back, and grinned at her.

"That's all very well for you," Sybil protested. "You can do as you like. You were one of my father's followers—well, there were many such, and some are in Parliament now. But fallen women get ruined, d'ye see? Ruined, and stay that way."

Mick straightened, frowning at her. "Now that's exactly what I mean. You're running with the flash mob, now, but thinking like a trollop! There's no one knows who you are, in Paris! The cops and bosses have your number here, true enough! But numbers are only that, and your file's no more than a simple stack of cards. For them as know, there's ways to change a number." He sneered, to see her surprise. "It ain't done easy, here in London, I grant you. But affairs run differently, in the Paris of Louis Napoleon! Affairs run fast and loose in flash Paree, especially for an adventuress with a blarney tongue and a pretty ankle."

Sybil bit her knuckle. Her eyes burned suddenly. It was acrid smoke from the limelight, and fear. A new number in the Government's machines—that would mean a new life. A life without a past. The unexpected thought of such freedom terrified her. Not so much for what it meant in itself, though that was strange and dazzling enough. But for what Mick Radley might demand for such a thing, in fair exchange. "Truly, you could change my number?"

"I can buy you a new one in Paris. Pass you off for French or an Argie or an American refugee girl." Mick folded his elegant arms. "I promise nothing, mind you. You'll have to earn it."

"You wouldn't gull me, Mick?" she said slowly. "Because . . . because I could be really and specially sweet to a fellow who could do me such a great service."

Mick jammed his hands in his pockets, rocking back on his heels, looking at her. "Could you now," he said softly. Her trembling words had fanned something inside him, she could see it in his eyes. An eager, lustful kindling, something she dimly knew was there, a need he had, to . . . slip his fish-hooks deeper into her.

"I could, if you treated me fair and level, as your 'prentice adventuress, and not some cakey dollymop, to gull and cast aside." Sybil felt tears coming, harder this time. She blinked, and looked up boldly, and let them flow, thinking perhaps they might do some good. "You wouldn't raise my hopes and dash them, would you? That would be low and cruel! If you did that I'd—I'd jump off Tower Bridge!"

He looked her in the eye. "Bar that sniffling, girl, and listen close to me. Understand this. You're not just Mick's pretty bit o' muslin—I may have a taste for that same as any man, but I can get that where I like, and don't need you just for that. I need the blarney skill and the daring pluck that was Mr. Walter Gerard's. You're to be my 'prentice, Sybil, and I your master, and let that be how things stand with us. You'll be loyal, obedient, truthful to me, no subterfuge and no impertinence, and in return, I'll teach you craft, and keep you well—and you'll find me as kind and generous as you are loyal and true. Do I make myself clear?"

"Yes, Mick."

"We have a pact, then?"

"Yes, Mick." She smiled at him.

"Well and good," he said. "Then kneel, here, and put your hands together, so"—he joined his hands in prayer—"and make this oath. That you, Sybil Gerard, do swear by saints and angels, by powers, dominions, and thrones, by seraphim and cherubim and the all-seeing eye, to obey Michael Radley, and serve him faithfully, so help you God! Do you so swear?"

She stared at him in dismay. "Must I really?"

"Yes."

"But isn't it a great sin, to make such an oath, to a man who . . . I mean to say . . . we're not in holy wedlock. . . ."

"That's a marriage vow," he said impatiently, "and this a 'prentice oath!"

She saw no alternative. Tugging her skirts back, she knelt before him on cold gritty stone.

"Do you so swear?"

"I do, so help me God."

"Don't look so glum," he said, helping her to her feet, "that's a mild and womanly oath you swore, compared to some." He pulled her to her feet. "Let it brace you, should you have doubts or disloyal thoughts. Now take this"—he handed her the guttering candle—"and hunt up that gin-soak of a stage-manager, and tell him I want the boilers fired."

They dined that evening in the Argyll Rooms, a Haymarket resort not far from Laurent's Dancing Academy. The Argyll had private supper-rooms in which the indiscreet might spend an entire night.

Sybil was mystified by the choice of a private room. Mick was certainly not ashamed to be seen with her in public. Midway through the lamb, however, the waiter admitted a stout little gentleman with pomaded red hair and a gold chain across a taut velvet waistcoat. He was round and plush as a child's doll.

"Hullo, Corny," Mick said, without bothering to put down his knife and fork.

"Evening, Mick," the man said, with the curiously unplaceable accent of an actor, or a provincial long in service to city gentry. "I was told you'd need of me."

"And told correctly, Corny." Mick neither offered to introduce Sybil nor asked the man to sit. She began to feel quite uncomfortable. " 'Tis a brief part, so you should have little trouble remembering your lines." Mick produced a plain envelope from his coat and handed it to the man. "Your lines, your cue, and your retainer. The Garrick, Saturday night."

The man smiled mirthlessly as he accepted the envelope. "Quite some time since I played the Garrick, Mick." He winked at Sybil and took his leave with no more formality than that.

"Who's that, Mick?" Sybil asked. Mick had returned to his lamb and was spooning mint sauce from a pewter serving-pot.

"An actor of parts," Mick said. "He'll play opposite you in the Garrick, during Houston's speech."

Sybil was baffled. "Play? Opposite me?"

"You're a 'prentice adventuress, don't forget. You can expect to be called on to play many roles, Sybil. A political speech can always benefit from a bit of sweetening."

"Sweetening?"

"Never mind." He seemed to lose interest in his lamb, and pushed his plate aside. "Plenty of time for rehearsal tomorrow. I've something to show you now." He rose from the table, crossed to the door, and bolted it securely. Returning, he lifted the proofed canvas portmanteau from the carpet beside his chair and placed it before her on the Argyll's clean but much mended linen.

She'd been curious about the portmanteau. Not curious that he'd carried it with him, from the Garrick's pit, first to the printers, to examine the handbills for Houston's lecture, then on to the Argyll Rooms, but because it was of such cheap stuff, nothing at all like the gear he so obviously prided himself on. Why should Dandy Mick choose to carry about a bag of that sort, when he could afford some flash confection from Aaron's, nickel clasps and silk woven in Ada checkers? And she knew that the black bag no longer contained the kino cards for the lecture, because he'd wrapped those carefully in sheets of *The Times* and hidden them again behind the stage-mirror.

Mick undid the wretched tin clasps, opened the bag, and lifted out a long narrow case of polished rosewood, its corners trimmed with bright brass. Sybil wondered if it mightn't contain a telescope, for she'd seen boxes of this sort in the window of a firm of Oxford Street instrument-makers. Mick handled it with a caution that was very nearly comical, like some Papist called upon to move the dust of a dead Pope. Caught up in a sudden mood of child-like anticipation, she forgot the man called Corny and Mick's worrying talk about playing opposite him at the Garrick. There was something of the magician about Mick now, as he placed the gleaming rosewood case on the tablecloth. She almost expected him to furl back his cuffs: nothing here, you see, nothing here.

His thumbs swung tiny brass hooks from a pair of miniature eyelets. He paused for effect.

Sybil found that she was holding her breath. Had he brought a gift for her? Some token of her new status? Something to secretly mark her as his 'prentice adventuress?

Mick lifted the rosewood lid, with its sharp brass corners.

It was filled with playing cards. Stuffed end to end with them, a score of decks at the least. Sybil's heart fell.

"You've seen nothing like this before," he said. "I can assure you of that."

Mick pinched out the card nearest his right hand and displayed it for her. No, not a playing card, though near enough in size. It was made of some strange milky substance that was neither paper nor glass, very thin and glossy. Mick flexed it lightly between thumb and forefinger. It bent easily, but sprang rigid again as he released it.

It was perforated with perhaps three dozen tightly spaced rows of circular holes, holes no larger than those in a good pearl button. Three of its corners were slightly rounded, while the fourth was trimmed off at an angle. Near the trimmed corner, someone had written "#1" in faint mauve ink.

"Camphorated cellulose," Mick declared, "the devil's own stuff, should it touch fire, but naught else will serve the finer functions of the Napoleon."

Napoleon? Sybil was lost. "Is it a sort of kino card, Mick?"

He beamed at her, delighted. She seemed to have said the right thing.

"Have you never heard of the Great Napoleon *ordinateur*, the mightiest Engine of the French Academy? The London police Engines are mere toys beside it."

Sybil pretended to study the contents of the box, knowing it would please Mick. But it was merely a wooden box, quite handsomely made, lined with the green baize that covered billiard tables. It contained a very large quantity of the slick milky cards, perhaps several hundred.

"Tell me what this is about, Mick."

He laughed, quite happily it seemed, and bent suddenly to kiss her mouth.

"In time, in time." He straightened, reinserted the card, lowered the lid, clicked the brass hooks into place. "Every brotherhood has its mysteries. Dandy Mick's best guess is that nobody knows quite what it would mean to run this little stack. It would demonstrate a certain matter, prove a certain nested series of mathematical hypotheses. . . . All matters quite arcane. And, by the by, it would make the name of Michael Radley shine like the very heavens in the clacking confraternity." He winked. "The French clackers have their own brotherhoods, you know. Les Fils de Vaucanson, they call themselves. The Jacquardine Society. We'll be showing those onion-eaters a thing or two."

He seemed drunk to her, now, though she knew he'd only had those two bottled ales. No, he was intoxicated by the idea of the cards in the box, whatever they might be.

"This box and its contents are quite extraordinarily dear, Sybil." He seated himself again and rummaged in the cheap black bag. It yielded a folded sheet of stout brown paper, an ordinary pair of stationery-shears, a roll of strong green twine. As Mick spoke, he unfolded the paper and began to wrap the box in it. "Very dear. Traveling with the General exposes a man to certain dangers. We're off to Paris after the lecture, but tomorrow morning you'll be taking this round to the Post Office in Great Portland Street." Done with wrapping, he wound twine about the paper. "Nip this for me with the shears." She did as he asked. "Now put your finger here." He executed a perfect knot. "You'll be posting our parcel to Paris. *Poste restante.* Do you know what that means?"

"It means the parcel is held for the addressee."

Mick nodded, took a stick of scarlet sealing-wax from one trouser-pocket, his repeating match from the other. The match struck on the first try. "Yes, held there in Paris for us, safe as houses." The wax darkened and slid in the oily flame. Scarlet droplets spattered the green knot, the brown paper. He tossed the shears and the roll of twine back into the portmanteau, pocketed the wax and the match, withdrew his reservoir-pen, and began to address the parcel.

"But what *is* it, Mick? How can you know its value if you've no idea what it does?"

"Now I didn't say that, did I? I've my ideas, don't I? Dandy Mick always has his ideas. I'd enough of an idea to take the original up to Manchester with me, on the General's business. I'd enough of an idea to pump the canniest clackers for their latest compression techniques, and enough of the General's capital to commission the result on Napoleon-gauge cellulose!"

It might have been Greek, for all it meant to her.

A knock came. An evil-looking servant boy, cropheaded and snuffling, wheeled in a trolley and cleared the plates. He made a botch of it, lingering as if expecting a gratuity, but Mick ignored him, and stared coolly into space, now and then grinning to himself like a cat.

The boy left with a sneer. At length there came the rap of a cane against the door. A second of Mick's friends had arrived.

This was a heavyset man of quite astonishing ugliness, pop-eyed and blue-jowled, his squat sloping forehead fringed in an oiled parody of the elegant spit-curls the Prime Minister favored. The stranger wore new and well-cut evening dress, with cloak, cane, and top-hat, a fancy pearl in his cravat and a gold Masonic ring on one finger. His face and neck were deeply sunburnt.

Mick rose at once from his chair, shook the ringed hand, offered a seat.

"You keep late hours, Mr. Radley," the stranger said.

"We do what we can to accommodate your special needs, Professor Rudwick."

The ugly gentleman settled in his chair with a sharp wooden squeak. His bulging eyes shot Sybil a speculative look then, and for one heart-leaping moment she feared the worst, that it had all been a gull and she was about to become part of some dreadful transaction between them.

But Rudwick looked away, to Mick. "I won't conceal from you, sir, my eagerness to resume my activities in Texas." He pursed his lips. He had small, grayish, pebble-like teeth in a great slash of a mouth. "This business of playing the London social lion is a deuced bore."

"President Houston will grant you an audience tomorrow at two, if that's agreeable."

Rudwick grunted. "Perfectly."

Mick nodded. "The fame of your Texian discovery seems to grow by the day, sir. I understand that Lord Babbage himself has taken an interest."

"We have worked together at the Institute at Cambridge," Rudwick admitted, unable to hide a smirk of satisfaction. "The theory of pneumo-dynamics . . ."

"As it happens," Mick remarked, "I find myself in possession of a clacking sequence that may amuse His Lordship."

Rudwick seemed nettled by this news. "*Amuse* him, sir? Lord Babbage is a most . . . *irascible* man."

"Lady Ada was kind enough to favor me in my initial efforts . . ."

"*Favor* you?" said Rudwick, with a sudden ugly laugh. "Is it some gambling-system, then? It had best be, if you hope to catch *her* eye."

"Not at all," Mick said shortly.

"Her Ladyship chooses odd friends," Rudwick opined, with a long sullen look at Mick. "Do you know a man named Collins, a so-called oddsmaker?"

"Haven't had the pleasure," Mick said.

"The fellow's on her like a louse in a bitch's ear," Rudwick said, his sunburnt face flushing. "Fellow made me the most astounding proposition . . ."

"And?" Mick said delicately.

Rudwick frowned. "I did fancy you might know him, he seems the sort that might well run in your circles. . . ."

"No, sir."

Rudwick leaned forward. "And what of another certain gent,

Mr. Radley, very long of limb and cold of eye, who I fancy has been dogging my movements of late? Would he, perhaps, be an agent of your President Houston? Seemed to have a Texian air about him."

"My President is fortunate in the quality of his agents."

Rudwick stood, his face dark. "You'll be so kind, I'm sure, as to request the bastard to cease and desist."

Mick rose as well, smiling sweetly. "I'll certainly convey your sentiments to my employer, Professor. But I fear I keep you from your night's amusements. . . ." He walked to the door, opened it, shut it on Rudwick's broad, well-tailored back.

Mick turned, winked at Sybil. "He's off to the ratting-pits! A very low-sporting gentleman, our learned Professor Rudwick. Speaks his bloody mind, though, don't he?" He paused. "The General will like him."

Hours later, she woke in Grand's, in bed beside him, to the click of his match and the sweet reek of his cigar. He'd had her twice on the chaise behind their table in the Argyll Rooms, and once again in Grand's. She'd not known him to be so ardent before. She'd found it encouraging, though the third go had made her sore, down there.

The room was dark, save for the spill of gaslight past the curtains.

She moved a bit closer to him.

"Where would you like to go, Sybil, after France?"

She'd never considered the question. "With you, Mick. . . ."

He chuckled, and slid his hand beneath the bedclothes, his fingers closing around the mound of her womanhood.

"Where shall we go then, Mick?"

"Go with me and you'll go first to Mexico. Then north, for the liberation of Texas, with a Franco-Mexican army under the command of General Houston."

"But . . . but isn't Texas a frightfully queer place?"

"Quit thinking like a Whitechapel drab. All the world's queer, seen from Piccadilly. Sam Houston had himself a bloody palace, in Texas. Before the Texians threw him into exile, he was Britain's greatest ally in the American west. You and I, why, we could live like grandees in Texas, build a manor by some river. . . ."

"Would they truly let us do that, Mick?"

"Her Majesty's Government, you mean? Perfidious Albion?" Mick chuckled. "Well, that largely depends on British public opinion toward General Houston! We're doing all we can to sweeten his reputation here in Britain. That's why he's on this lecture tour, isn't it?"

"I see," Sybil said. "You're very clever, Mick."

"Deep matters, Sybil! Balance of power. It worked for Britain in Europe for five hundred years, and it works even better in America. Union, Confederacy, Republics of Texas and California—they all take a turn in British favor, until they get too bold, a bit too independent, and then they're taken down a peg. Divide and rule, dear." The coal-end of Mick's cigar glowed in the darkness. "If it weren't for British diplomacy, British power, America might be all one huge nation."

"What about your friend the General? Will he truly help us?"

"That's the beauty of it!" Mick declared. "The diplomats thought Sam Houston was a bit stiff-necked, didn't care for some of his actions and policies, didn't back him as strongly as they should have. But the Texian junta that replaced him is far worse. They're openly hostile to British interests! Their days are numbered. The General has had to cool his heels a bit in exile here in England, but now he's on his way back to Texas, for what's his by right." He shrugged. "Should have happened years ago. Our trouble is that Her Majesty's Government don't know their own mind! There's factions among 'em. Some don't trust Sam Houston—but the French will help us anyhow! Their Mexican clients have a border war with the Texians. They need the General!"

"You're going to war, then, Mick?" She found it difficult to imagine Dandy Mick leading a cavalry charge.

"Coup d'état, more like," he assured her. "We won't see much bloodshed. I'm Houston's political man, you see, and his man I'll stay, for I'm the one's arranged this London speaking-tour, and on to France, and I'm the one's made certain approaches as resulted in him being granted his audience with the French Emperor. . . ." But could that be true, really? "And I'm the one as runs Manchester's newest and best through the kino for him, sweetens the press and British public opinion, hires the bill-stickers. . . ." He drew on his cigar, his fingers kneading her there, and she heard him puff out a great satisfied cloud of cherry smoke.

But he mustn't have felt like doing it again, not then, because she was soon asleep and dreaming, dreaming of Texas, a Texas of rolling downs, contented sheep, the windows of gray manors glinting in late-afternoon sunlight.

Sybil sat in an aisle seat, third row back in the Garrick, thinking unhappily that General Sam Houston, late of Texas, was not drawing much of a crowd. People were filtering in as the five-man orchestra squeaked and sawed and honked. A family party was settling in the row before her, two boys, in blue jackets and trousers, with laid-down shirt-collars, a little girl in a shawl and a braided frock, then two more little girls, ushered in by their governess, a thin-looking sort with a hooked nose and watery eyes, sniffling into her handkerchief. Then the oldest boy, sauntering in, a sneer on his face. Then papa with dress-coat and cane and whiskers, and fat mama with long ringlets and a big nasty hat and three gold rings on her plump soft fingers. Finally all were seated, amid a shuffling of coats and shawls and a munching of candied orange-peel, quite patently well-behaved and expecting improvement. Clean and soaped and prosperous, in their snug machine-made clothes.

A clerky fellow with spectacles took the next seat to Sybil's, an inch-wide blue strip showing at his hairline, where he'd shaved his forehead to suggest intellect. He was reading Mick's program and sucking an acidulated lemon-drop. And past him a trio of officers, on furlough from the Crimea, looking very pleased with themselves, come to hear about an old-fashioned war in Texas, fought the old-fashioned way. There were other soldiers speckled through the crowd, bright in their red coats, the respectable sort, who didn't go for drabs and gin, but would take the Queen's pay, and learn gunnery arithmetic, and come back to work in the railroads and shipyards, and better themselves.

The place was full of bettering-blokes, really: shopkeepers and store-clerks and druggists, with their tidy wives and broods. In her father's day, such people, Whitechapel people, had been angry and lean and shabby, with sticks in their hands, and dirks in their belts. But times had changed under the Rads, and now even Whitechapel had its tight-laced scrubfaced women and its cakey clock-watching men, who read the *Dictionary of Useful Knowledge* and the *Journal of Moral Improvement*, and looked to get ahead.

Then the gas-lights guttered in their copper rings, and the orchestra swung into a flat rendition of "Come to the Bower." With a huff, the limelight flared, the curtain drew back before the kinotrope screen, the music covering the clicking of kino-bits spinning themselves into place. Broken frills and furbelows grew like black frost on the edges of the screen. They framed tall letters, in a fancy alphabet of sharp-edged Engine-Gothic, black against white:

Editions

Panoptique

Presents

And below the kinotrope, Houston entered stage-left, a bulky, shabby figure, limping toward the podium at the center of the stage. He was drowned in dimness for the moment, below the raw and focused glare of Mick's limelight.

Sybil watched him closely, curious about him, wary—her first glimpse of Mick's employer. She'd seen enough American refugees in London to have ideas about them. The Unionists dressed much like normal Britons, if they had the money for it, while Confederates tended to dress rather gaudy and flash, but peculiar, not quite proper; to judge by Houston, the Texians were an even queerer and madder lot. He was a big man, red-faced and beefy, over six feet tall in his heavy boots, his broad shoulders draped in a long coarse-woven blanket rather like a mantelet, but barbarically striped. Red and black and umber, it swept the Garrick's stage like a tragedian's toga. He had a thick mahogany cane in his right hand, and he swung it lightly now, as if he didn't need it, but his legs shook, Sybil saw, and the gold fringe trembled on the fancy seams of his trousers.

Now he mounted to the darkened podium, wiped his nose, sipped at a glass of something that plainly wasn't water. Above his head the kinotrope shuffled into a colored image, the lion of Great Britain and a sort of long-horned bull. The animals fraternized beneath small crossed banners, the Union Jack and the single-starred flag of Texas, both bright in red and white and blue. Houston was adjusting something behind his podium; a small stage-mirror, Sybil guessed, so he could check the kinotrope behind him as he spoke, and not lose his place.

The kinotrope went to black and white again, the screen's bits flickering, row by row, like falling dominoes. A portrait-bust appeared in shaded jagged lines: high balding forehead, heavy brows, thick nose bracketed by bristling cheek-whiskers that hid the ears. The thin mouth was set firmly, the cleft chin upraised. Then, below the bust, the words GENERAL SAM HOUSTON.

A second limelight flared, catching Houston at the podium, flinging him into sudden bright relief before the audience. Sybil clapped hard. She was the last to finish.

"Thank you very kindly, ladies and gentlemen of London," Houston said. He had the deep booming voice of a practiced orator, marred by a foreign drawl. "You do a stranger great honor." Houston looked across the seats of the Garrick. "I see we have many gentlemen of Her Majesty's military in the audience tonight." He shrugged the blanket back a bit and limelight glittered harshly from the medals clinging to his coat. "Your professional interest is very gratifying, sirs."

In the row before Sybil, the children were fidgeting. A little girl squealed in pain as one of her brothers punched her. "And I see we have a future British fighter here, as well!" There was a ripple of surprised laughter. Houston checked his mirror quickly, then leaned over his podium, his heavy brows knitting in grand-fatherly charm. "What's your name, son?"

The wicked boy sat bolt upright. "Billy, sir," he squeaked. "Billy . . . William Greenacre, sir."

Houston nodded gravely. "Tell me, Master Greenacre, would you like to run away from home, and live with red Indians?"

"Oh, yes, sir," the boy blurted, and then "Oh, no, sir!" The audience laughed again.

"When I was about your age, young William, I was a lad of spirit, like yourself. And that was the very course of action I pursued." The kino shuffled behind the General's head, and a colored map appeared, outlines of the various states of America, oddly shaped provinces with confusing names. Houston checked his mirror and spoke rapidly. "I was born in the American state of Tennessee. My family was of the Scottish gentry, though times were hard for us, on our little frontier farm. And though I was born an American, I felt little allegiance to the Yankee govern-ment in far Washington." The kinotrope displayed the portrait of an American savage, a mad-eyed staring creature hung with feathers, cheeks streaked with kino-blocks of warpaint. "Just across the river," Houston said, "lived the mighty nation of the Cherokee, a simple folk of natural nobility. I found this suited me far better than a life with my American neighbors. Alas, for their souls were pinched by the greed for dollars."

Houston shook his head a bit before his British audience, pained at his own allusion to an American national failing. He had their sympathy, Sybil thought. "The Cherokees won my heart," Houston continued, "and I ran from home to join them, with nothing, ladies and gentlemen, but the buckskin coat on my back, and Homer's noble tale of the Iliad in my pocket." The kinotrope shuffled itself bottom-to-top, producing an image from a Grecian urn, a warrior with a crested helmet, his spear upraised. He bore a round shield with the emblem of a raven, wings outspread. There was a light pattering of impressed applause, which Houston accepted, nodding modestly, as if it were meant for him.

"As a child of the American frontier," he said, "I can't claim to have had much fine schooling, although in later life I passed the bar and led a nation. As a youth, however, I sought my education in an ancient school. I committed every line of the blind bard's book to memory." He lifted the medal-strewn lapel of his coat, left-handed. "The heart within this scarred breast," he said, and thumped it, "still stirs to that noblest of stories, with its tales of a valor to challenge the very gods, and of unstained martial honor that endures . . . till death!" He waited for applause. At length it came, though not as warmly as he seemed to expect.

"I saw no contradiction in the lives of Homer's heroes and those of my beloved Cherokees," Houston persisted. Behind him, the Greek's javelin sprouted the dangling feathers of a hunting-spear, and war-paint daubed his face.

Houston peered at his notes. "Together we hunted bear and deer and boar, fished the limpid stream and raised the yellow corn. Around the campfire, under open skies, I told my savage brothers of the moral lessons that my youthful heart had gleaned from Homer's words. Because of this, they gave me the red-man's name of Raven, after the feathered spirit that they deem the wisest of birds."

The Greek dissolved, giving way to a grander raven, its wings spread stiffly across the screen, its chest covered by a striped shield. Sybil recognized it. It was the American eagle, symbol of the sundered Union, but the white-headed Yankee bird had become Houston's black crow. It was clever, she decided, perhaps more clever than it was worth, for two of the kinotrope bits in the screen's upper-left-corner had jammed on their spindles, showing dots of left-over blue; a tiny fault but annoying all out of proportion, like a bit of dust in one's eye. Mick's fancy clacking was working the Garrick's kino very hard.

Distracted, Sybil had lost the thread of Houston's speech. ". . . the brazen cry of the battle-trumpet, in the camp of the

Tennessee volunteers." Another kino-portrait appeared: a man who looked rather like Houston, but with a tall shock of hair in front, and hollow cheeks, identified by caption as GEN. ANDREW JACKSON.

There was a hiss of breath here and there, led by the soldiers perhaps, and the crowd stirred. Some Britons still remembered "Hickory" Jackson, without fondness. To hear Houston tell it, Jackson had also bravely fought against Indians, and even been President of America for a time; but all that meant little here. Houston praised Jackson as his patron and mentor, "an honest soldier of the people, who valued a man's true inner worth above the tinsel of wealth or show," but the applause for this sentiment was grudging at best.

Now another scene appeared, some kind of rude frontier fort. Houston narrated a tale of siege, from his early military career, when he'd fought a campaign under Jackson against the Indians called Creek. But he seemed to have lost his natural audience, the soldiers, for the three Crimea veterans in Sybil's row were still muttering angrily about Hickory Jackson. "The damned war was over before New Orleans. . . ."

Suddenly the limelight flashed blood-red. Mick was busy beneath the stage: a tinted glass filter, the sudden booming of a kettle-drum, as little kino cannons cracked gunpowder-white around the fort, and single-bit flickers of red cannon-shell arched rapidly across the screen. "Night after night we heard the Creek fanatics howling their eerie death-songs," Houston shouted, a pillar of glare beneath the screen. "The situation demanded a direct assault, with cold steel! It was said to be certain death to charge that gate. . . . But I was not a Tennessee Volunteer for nothing. . . ."

A tiny figure dashed toward the fort, no more than a few black squares, a wriggling block of bits, and the entire stage went black. There was surprised applause in the sudden darkness. The penny-boys up in the Garrick's gallery whistled shrilly. Then limelight framed Houston again. He began to boast about his wounds; two bullets in the arm, a knife-stab in the leg, an arrow into his belly—Houston didn't say the vulgar word, but he did rub that area lingeringly, as if he were dyspeptic. He'd lain all night on the battlefield, he claimed, and then been hauled for days through wilderness, on a supply cart, bleeding, raving, sick with swamp-fever. . . .

The clerky cove next to Sybil took another lemon-drop, and looked at his pocket-watch. Now a five-pointed star appeared slowly amidst the funereal black of the screen, as Houston narrated his lingering escape from the grave. One of the jammed kino-bits had popped loose again, but another had jammed in the meantime, on the lower right.

Sybil stifled a yawn.

The star brightened slowly as Houston spoke about his entry into American politics, presenting as his motive the desire to help his persecuted pet Cherokees. This was exotic enough, Sybil thought, but at its heart lay the same snicky humbugging politicians always talked, and the audience was growing restive. They would have liked more fighting, or perhaps more poetic talk about life with the Cherokees. Instead, Houston had settled into a litany of his election to some rude equivalent of Parliament, various obscure posts in provincial government, and all the while the star grew slowly, its edges branching elaborately, becoming the emblem of the government of Tennessee.

Sybil's eyelids grew heavy, fluttered, while the General blustered on.

Quite suddenly, Houston's tone changed, becoming lingering, sentimental, a honeyed lilt creeping into his drawl. He was talking about a woman.

Sybil sat up straighter, listening.

Houston had been elected Governor, it seemed, and had gotten himself some tin, and been cheery about it. And he'd found himself a sweetheart, some Tennessee gentry-girl, and married her.

But on the kino's screen, fingers of darkness crept in snake-like from the edges. They menaced the State Seal.

Governor and Mrs. Houston had scarcely settled in when wifey kicked over the traces, and fled back to her family. She'd left him a letter, Houston said, a letter that contained an awful secret. A secret he had never revealed, and had sworn to carry to his grave. "A private matter, of which a gentleman of honor cannot and should not speak. Black disaster struck me...." The newspapers—apparently they did have newspapers, in Tennessee—had attacked him. "The tattling mouths of libel poured their venom on me," Houston lamented, as the Greek shield with the raven appeared, and black kino-blobs—mud, Sybil supposed—began to spatter it.

Houston's revelations grew shocking. He'd actually gone through with it, had divorced his wife, of all the unlikely, awful things. Of course he'd lost his position in Government; outraged society had hounded him from office, and Sybil wondered why Houston had dared to mention such an ugly scandal. It was as if he expected his London audience to morally approve of a divorced man. Still, she noticed, the ladies seemed intrigued, and not entirely without sympathy perhaps. Even the fat mama fluttered at her double-chins with a fan.

General Houston was a foreigner, after all, half a savage by his own account; but when he spoke of his wife it was tenderly, as of a true love, a love slain by some cruel mysterious truth. His bellowing voice broke with unashamed emotion; he mopped at his forehead a bit, with a fancy handkerchief from his leopard-skin vest.

In truth, he wasn't a bad-looking cove, over sixty but that sort could be kinder to a girl. His confession seemed bold and manly, for he himself had brought the matter up: the divorce scandal and the secret letter from Mrs. Houston. He wouldn't stop talking about it, but neither would he tell them the secret; he'd pricked the curiosity of his audience—and Sybil herself was simply dying to know.

She chided herself, for being so cakey, for it was likely something stupid and simple, not half so deep and mysterious as he feigned. Likely his gentry-girl wasn't half so angelic as she'd looked. Likely she'd had her maiden virtue stolen from her by some good-looking Tennessee beau-trap, long before Raven

Houston came along. Men had hard rules for their brides, if never for themselves.

Likely Houston had brought it all on himself. Perhaps he had beastly vile ideas about married life, come from living with savages. Or perhaps he'd milled his wife about with his fists—for Sybil fancied he'd be a right bully-rock, in his cups.

The kino came alive with harpies, meant to symbolize Houston's slanderers, those who'd smeared his precious honor with the ink of a gutter press. Nasty crooky-back things, crowding the screen in devilish black and red. As the screen whirred steadily, they twitched their cloven hooves. Never had she seen the like, some Manchester punch-card artist having gotten the gin-horrors sure. . . . Now Houston was ranting about challenges and honor, by which he meant dueling, Americans being most famous duelists, who loved guns and shot each other at the drop of a hat. . . . He'd have killed some of those newspaper rascals, Houston insisted loudly, if he hadn't been Governor, and on his dignity. So instead he'd thrown in his cards, and gone back to live with his precious Cherokees. . . . He had a real head of steam up, now; he'd stoked himself so, it was almost frightening to watch. The audience was entertained, their reserve broken by his bulging eyes and veiny Texian neck, but none too far from disgust.

Maybe it had been something really dreadful that he'd done, Sybil thought, rubbing her hands together inside her rabbit-skin muff. Maybe it was lady's-fever, that he'd given his own wife a case of the glue. Some types of glue were horrible, and could make you mad, or blind, or crippled. Maybe that was the secret. Mick might know. Very likely Mick knew all about it.

Houston explained that he had left the United States in disgust, and gone to Texas, and at the word a map appeared, a sprawl of land in the middle of the continent. Houston claimed he'd gone there seeking land for his poor suffering Cherokee Indians, but it was all a bit confusing.

Sybil asked the clerky fellow next to her for the time. Only an hour had passed. The speech was a third gone. Her moment was coming.

"You must envision a nation many times the size of your home islands," said Houston, "with no roads greater than the grassy tracks of Indians. Without, at that time, a single mile of British railroad, and lacking the telegraph, or, indeed, Engine resources of any kind. As commander-in-chief of the Texian national forces, my orders had no courier more swift or more reliable than the mounted scout, his way menaced by the Comanche and Karankawa, by Mexican raiding-parties, and by the thousand nameless hazards of the wilderness. Small wonder then that Colonel Travis should receive my orders too late; and place his confidence, tragically, in the reinforcing-party led by Colonel Fannin. Surrounded by an enemy force fifty times his own, Colonel Travis declared his objective to be Victory or Death—knowing full well that the latter was a surely fated outcome. The defenders of the Alamo perished to a man. The noble Travis, the fearless Colonel Bowie, and David Crockett, a very legend among frontiersmen"—Messrs. Travis, Bowie, and Crockett each had a third of the kino screen, their faces gone strangely square with the cramped scale of their depiction—"bought precious time for my Fabian strategy."

More soldier talk. Now he stepped back from the podium and pointed up at the kino with his heavy polished cane. "The forces of López de Santa Anna were arrayed as you see them here, with the woods upon his left flank and the San Jacinto river-marshes at his back. His siege engineers had dug in around the baggage-train, with emplacements of sharpened timber, represented thusly. By a forced march through Burnham's Ford, however, my army of six hundred had seized the wooded banks of Buffalo Bayou, unbeknown to enemy intelligence. The assault began with a brisk cannon-fire from the Texian center. . . . Now we can witness the movement of the Texian light-cavalry. . . . The shock of the foot-charge sent the enemy reeling in confusion, throwing his artillery, which was not yet limbered, into utter disarray." The kinotrope's blue squares and lozenges slowly chased the buckling red Mexican regiments through the checkered greens and whites of woods and swamps. Sybil shifted in her seat, trying to ease the chafing of her hoop-skirt. Houston's bloodthirsty boasting was finally reaching a climax.

"The final count of the fallen numbered two Texian dead, six hundred and thirty of the invader. The massacres of Alamo and Goliad were avenged in Santanista blood! Two Mexican armies utterly defeated, with the capture of fourteen officers and twenty cannon."

Fourteen officers, twenty cannon—yes, that was her cue. Her moment had come. "Avenge us, General Houston!" Sybil shrieked, her throat constricted with stage-fright. She tried again, pulling herself to her feet, waving one arm, "Avenge *us*, General Houston!"

Houston halted, taken aback. Sybil shouted at him, shrilly. "Avenge *our* honor, sir! Avenge *Britain's* honor!" A babble of alarm rose—Sybil felt the eyes of the theatre crowd in upon her, shocked looks that people might give a lunatic. "My *brother*," she shouted, but fear had seized her, bad nerves. She hadn't expected it to be so frightening. This was worse than singing on stage, far worse.

Houston lifted both his arms, the striped blanket spreading behind him like a cloak. Somehow he calmed the crowd by the gesture, asserted command. Above his head, the kinotrope wound slowly down, its flickering domino-tricks whirring to a stop, leaving San Jacinto frozen in mid-victory. Houston fixed Sybil with a look of mingled sternness and resignation. "What is it, my dear young lady? What troubles you? Tell me."

Sybil gripped the back of the seat before her, closed her eyes tight, and sang it out. "Sir, my brother is in a Texian prison! We are British, but the Texians imprisoned him, sir! They seized his farm, and his cattle! They even stole the very railroad that he worked on, a British railroad, built for Texas. . . ." Her voice was faltering, despite herself. Mick wouldn't like that, he would scold her performance. . . . The thought put a jolt of vitality into her. She opened her eyes. "That regime, sir, the thieving Texian regime, they stole that British railroad! They robbed the workers in Texas, and the stockholders here in Britain, and paid us not a penny!"

With the loss of the kinotrope's bright play of images, the theatre's atmosphere had changed. Everything was quite different suddenly, oddly intimate and strange. It was as if she and the General were somehow framed together, two figures on a silvered daguerreotype. A young London woman, in her bonnet and elegant shawl, reaches up with eloquent distress to the old foreign hero; both part-players now, with the surprised eyes of the public silently fixed on them.

"You suffered because of the junta?" Houston said.

"Yes, sir!" Sybil cried, a practiced quaver stealing into her voice. Don't frighten them, Mick had said, but make them pity you. "Yes, the junta did it. They have flung my brother into their vile prison, for no crime, sir, but simply because my dear brother is a Houston man! He voted for you when you became President of Texas, sir! And he would vote for you today, although I fear very much they will kill him!"

"What is your brother's name, my dear lady?" Houston asked.

"Jones, sir," Sybil quickly cried, "Edwin Jones of Nacogdoches, who worked for Hedgecoxe's Railway Company."

"I believe I know young Edward!" Houston declared, his surprise evident in his tone. He clutched his cane angrily and his heavy brows knotted.

"Listen to her, Sam!" came a sudden deep voice. Sybil, alarmed, turned to look. It was the man from the Argyll Rooms—the fat actor, with his red hair and brushed velvet waistcoat. "Those junta rascals appropriated the Hedgecoxe Railway! A pretty business, that, from a supposed British ally! Is this the gratitude they show, for years of British guidance and protection?" He sat back down.

"They're nothing but thieves and villains!" Sybil shouted alertly. She groped quickly in memory, picking up the thread. "General Houston! I'm a defenseless woman, but you're a man of destiny, a man of greatness! Can't there be justice for Texas, sir? Some redress for these affronts? Must my poor brother die there in misery, while cheats and tyrants steal our British property?"

But Mick's fine rhetoric was drowned; there were shouts from the audience, here and there, over a muttered undertone of surprise and approval. Loud boyish hooting came from the penny-gallery.

A bit of London fun, all told. Perhaps, Sybil thought, she had made some of them believe her story, and pity her. Most simply howled and joked a bit, pleased to see some unexpected liveliness.

"Sam Houston was always a true friend of Britain!" Sybil shrieked, into the crowd's upturned faces. The words half-lost, useless, she raised the back of her wrist to her damp forehead. Mick had given her no more lines, so she let the strength seep from her legs and fell back, eyes fluttering, half-sinking into her seat.

"Give Miss Jones air!" Houston commanded, an excited bellow. "The lady is overcome!" Sybil watched through half-closed lids as blurred figures haltingly gathered round her. Dark evening-jackets, a rustle of crinoline, gardenia perfume, and a masculine smell of tobacco—a man seized her wrist, and felt for a pulse there with pinching fingers. A woman fanned Sybil's face, clucking to herself. Oh heaven, Sybil thought, shrinking, the fat mama from the row before her, with that intolerable oily look of a good woman doing her moral duty. A little thrill of shame and disgust shot through her. For a moment she felt genuinely weak, sinking with a buttery ease into the warmth of their concern, a half-dozen busybodies muttering around her in a shared pretense of competence, while Houston thundered on above them, hoarse with indignation.

Sybil allowed them to get her to her feet. Houston hesitated, seeing it, and there was a light gallant scatter of applause for her. She felt pale, unworthy; she smiled wanly, and shook her head, and wished she were invisible. She leaned her head on the padded shoulder of the man who had taken her pulse. "Sir, if I could go, please," she whispered.

Her rescuer nodded alertly, a little fellow with clever blue eyes.

His long greying hair was parted in the middle. "I shall see the lady home," he piped at the others. He shrugged into an opera cape, perched a tall beaver hat on his head, and lent her his arm. They walked together up the aisle, Sybil leaning on him heavily, unwilling to meet anyone's eyes. The crowd was roused, now. For the first time, perhaps, they were listening to Houston as a man, rather than as some sort of queer American exhibit.

Her little gentleman held dingy velvet aside for her as they emerged into the Garrick's chilly foyer, with its flaking gilt cupids and damp-marked faux-marble walls. " 'Tis very kind of you, sir, to help me so," Sybil offered, noting that her escort looked as though he might have money. "Are you a medical man?"

"I was a student once," he said, with a shrug. His cheeks were flushed, twin hot points of red.

"It gives a man a certain air of distinction," Sybil said, not for any particular purpose, but just to fill the silence. "Schooling of that sort, I mean."

"Hardly, madame. I wasted all my time versifying. I must say that you seem fit enough now. Very sorry to hear about that unfortunate brother of yours."

"Thank you, sir." Sybil looked at him sidelong. "I'm afraid it was very forward of me, but General Houston's eloquence carried me away."

He shot her an opaque glance, the look of a man who suspects that a woman is gulling him. "In all honesty," he said, "I do not entirely share your enthusiasm." He coughed explosively into a wadded handkerchief and wiped his mouth. "This London air will be the death of me."

"Nonetheless, I do thank you, sir, though I regret we've not been introduced. . . ."

"Keats," he said, "Mr. Keats." He drew a ticking silver chronometer from his waistcoat, a many-dialed thing the size of a small potato, and consulted it. "I'm not familiar with the district," he said distantly. "I'd thought to hail you a cabriolet, but at this hour . . ."

"Oh, no, Mr. Keats, thank you, but I shall go by the underground."

His bright eyes widened. No respectable woman rode the underground unescorted.

"But you haven't told me your profession, Mr. Keats," she said, hoping to distract him.

"Kinotropy," Keats said. "The techniques employed here tonight are of some special interest! While the screen's resolution is quite modest, and the refresh-rate positively slow, remarkable effects have been secured, one presumes through algorithmic compression—but I fear that is all a bit technical." He put away his chronometer. "Are you entirely certain you wouldn't rather I attempted to hail a cab? Do you know London well, Miss Jones? I might escort you to the local omnibus stand—'tis a railless carriage, you see. . . ."

"No, sir, thank you. You've been exceptionally kind."

"You're quite welcome," he said, his relief evident as he opened and held one of the half-glass doors to the street. Just then a skinny boy sidled rapidly up behind them, brushed past, and out of the theatre without a word. He was draped in a long dirty coat of canvas, something a fisherman might wear. A singular thing to wear to a lecture, Sybil thought, though one saw queerer garments on the poor; the sleeves flapped emptily, as though the boy were hugging himself, against a chill perhaps. His gait was odd, bent-backed, as if he were drunk or ill.

"I say there! Young man!" Mr. Keats had produced a coin, and Sybil understood that he wished the boy to hail a cab for her, but now the wet eyes gleamed at them with alarm, the pale face hollowed by gaslight. Suddenly he bolted, something dark tumbling from beneath his coat, where it rolled into the gutter. The boy halted and looked warily back at them.

He'd dropped a hat, a top-hat.

He came trotting back, eyes still on them, snatched it up, stuffed it under his coat, and off again, into the shadows, though this time not nearly so rapidly.

" 'Pon my word," Mr. Keats said in disgust, "that fellow's a thief! That water-proof is stuffed with the hats of the audience!"

Sybil could think of nothing to say.

"I imagine the rascal took cruel advantage of that commotion you caused," Keats told her, his tone lightly etched with suspicion. "Pity! One never knows who to trust these days."

"Sir, I do believe I hear the Engine getting up steam for the kinotrope. . . ."

And that was enough for him.

The installation of exhaust-fans, said the *Daily Telegraph*, had wrought a perceptible improvement in the atmosphere of the Metropolitan, though Lord Babbage himself held that a truly modern underground railway would operate on pneumatic principles exclusively, involving no combustion whatever, rather in the way mail was conveyed throughout Paris.

Seated in a second-class carriage, breathing as shallowly as possible, Sybil knew it all for humbug, or in any case the improvement part, for who knew what marvels the Rads mightn't bring forth? But hadn't the Rad papers also published the testimony of medicals, in the pay of the railroad, that sulphurous fumes were therapeutic for asthma? And it wasn't only the fumes from the Engines, but vile sewer-seepings as well, and gassy leakings from collapsible India-rubber bags, that lit the carriage-jets in their wire-netted glass shades.

It was a queer business, the underground, when you thought about it, racketing along at such speeds, through the darkness under London, where the navvies had come upon lead water-pipes of the Romans, and coins, mosaics, and archways, elephant's teeth a thousand years old . . .

And the digging went on, this and every night, for she'd heard their great machine huffing, as she'd stood by Mick on the White-chapel pavement; they worked unceasingly, the excavators, boring newer, deeper lines now, down below the tangle of sewers and gas-pipes and bricked-over rivers. The new lines were shored with steel, and soon Lord Babbage's smokeless trains would slide through them silent as eels, though she found the thought of it somehow unclean.

The lamps flared all at once, the flow of gas disturbed by a particularly sharp jolt, the faces of the other passengers seeming to leap out at her: the sallow gent with something of the successful publican about him, the round-cheeked old Quaker cleric, the drunken dandy with his coat open, his canary waistcoat all dotted down the front with claret . . .

There were no other women in the carriage.

Farewell to you, sirs, she imagined herself crying, *farewell to your London,* for she was a 'prentice adventuress now, sworn and true, bound for Paris, though the first leg of the voyage consisted necessarily of the tuppenny trip back to Whitechapel. . . .

But the clergyman had noticed her, his contempt quite open, there for anyone to see.

It was really quite horribly cold, making her way from the station to her room in Flower-and-Dean Street; she regretted her vanity, for having chosen her fine new shawl rather than her mantelet. Her teeth were chattering. Sharp frost shone in pools of gas-light on the street's new macadam.

The cobbles of London were vanishing month by month, paved over with black stuff that poured stinking hot from the maws of great wagons, for navvies to spread and smooth with rakes, before the advance of the steam-roller.

A daring fellow whisked past her, taking full advantage of the gritty new surface. Nearly recumbent within the creaking frame of a four-wheeled velocipede, his shoes were strapped to whirling cranks and his breath puffed explosively into the cold. He was bare-headed and goggled, in a thick striped jersey, a long knit scarf flapping out behind him as he sped away. Sybil supposed him an inventor.

London was rife with inventors, the poorer and madder of them congregating in the public squares to display their blueprints and models, and harangue the strolling crowds. In a week's time she'd encountered a wicked-looking device meant to crimp hair by electricity, a child's mechanical top that played Beethoven, and a scheme for electro-plating the dead.

Leaving the thoroughfare for the unimproved cobbles of Renton Passage, she made out the sign of the Hart and heard the jangle of a pianola. It was Mrs. Winterhalter who'd arranged for her to room above the Hart. The public house itself was a steady sort of place, admitting no women. It catered to junior clerks and shopmen, and offered as its raciest pleasure a pull at a coin-fed wagering-machine.

The rooms above were reached by way of steep dark stairs, that climbed below a sooty skylight to an alcove presenting a pair of identical doors. Mr. Cairns, the landlord, had rooms behind the door on the left.

Sybil climbed the stairs, fumbled a penny box of lucifers from her muff, and struck one. Cairns had chained a bicycle to the iron railing overlooking the stairwell; the bright brass padlock gleamed in the flare of the match. She shook the lucifer out, hoping that Hetty hadn't double-latched the door. Hetty hadn't, and Sybil's key turned smoothly in the lock.

Toby was there to greet her, padding silently across the bare boards to twine himself around and about her ankles, purring like sixty.

Hetty had left an oil-lamp turned down low on the deal table that stood in the hallway; it was smoking now, the wick in need of trimming. A foolish thing to have left it burning, where Toby might've sent it crashing, but Sybil felt grateful not to have found the place in darkness. She took Toby up in her arms. He smelled of herring. "Has Hetty fed you, then, dear?" He yowled softly, and batted at the ribbons of her bonnet.

The pattern of the wallpaper danced as she lifted the lamp. The hallway had seen no sunlight in all the years the Hart had stood, yet the printed flowers were gone a shade like dust.

Sybil's room had two windows, though they opened on a blank wall of grimed yellow brick, so near she could've touched it, if someone hadn't driven nails into the casements. Still, on a bright day, with the sun directly overhead, a bit of light did filter in. And Hetty's room, though larger, had only one window. If Hetty was here, now, she must be alone and asleep, as no light was visible from the crack at the bottom of her closed door.

It was good to have one's own room, one's privacy, however modest. Sybil put Toby down, though he protested, and carried the lamp to her own door, which stood slightly ajar. Inside, all was as she'd left it, though she saw that Hetty had left the latest number of the *Illustrated London News* on her pillow, with an engraving from Crimea on the front, a scene of a city all aflame. She set the lamp down on the cracked marble lid of the commode, Toby prowling about her ankles as though he expected to discover more herring, and considered what she should do.

The ticking of the fat tin alarm-clock, which she sometimes found unbearable, was reassuring now; at least it was running, and she imagined that the time it showed, quarter past eleven, was correct. She gave the winder a few turns, just for luck. Mick would come for her at midnight, and there were decisions to be made, as he'd advised her to travel very light.

She took a wick-trimmer from the commode's drawer, raised the lamp's chimney, and scissored away the blackened bit. The light somewhat improved. She threw on her mantelet against the cold, opened the lid of a japanned tin chest, and began to make an inventory of her better things. But after setting aside two changes of undergarments, it came to her that the less she took, the more Dandy Mick would have to buy for her in Paris. And if that wasn't thinking like a 'prentice adventuress, she didn't know what was.

Still, she did have some things she was 'specially fond of, and these went, along with the undergarments, into her brocade portmanteau with the split seam she'd meant to mend. There was a lovely bottle of rose-scented Portland water, half-full, a green paste brooch from Mr. Kingsley, a set of hair-brushes with imitation ebony backs, a miniature flower-press with a souvenir view of Kensington Palace, and a patent German curling-iron she'd nicked from a hair-dresser's. She added a bone-handled tooth-brush and a tin of camphorated dentifrice.

Now she took a tiny silver propelling-pencil and settled herself on the edge of her bed to write a note to Hetty. The pencil was a gift from Mr. Chadwick, with THE METROPOLITAN RAILWAY COR-PORATION engraved along its shaft; the plate was starting to flake away from the brass beneath. For paper, she found she had only the back of a handbill advertising instantaneous chocolate.

My dear Harriet, she began, *I am Off to Paris*, but then she paused, removed the pencil's cap, and used the rubber to erase those last three words, substituting *run Away with a Gentleman. Do not be alarmed. I am Well. You are welcome to any Cloathes I leave behind, and please do take Care of dear Toby and give him Herring. Yrs. sincerely, Sybil.*

It made her feel queer, to write it, and when she looked down at Toby she felt sad, and false, to leave him.

With this thought came thoughts of Radley. She was struck by a sudden and utter conviction of his falsehood.

"He *will* come," she whispered fiercely. She put the lamp and the folded note on the narrow mantel.

On the mantel lay a flat tin, brightly lithographed with the name of a Strand tobacconist. She knew that it contained Turkish cigarettes. One of Hetty's younger gentlemen, a medical student, had once urged her to take up the habit. Sybil generally avoided medical students. They prided themselves on studied beastliness. But now, in the grip of a powerful nervous impulse, she opened the tin, drew out one of the crisp paper cylinders, and inhaled its fierce perfume.

A Mr. Stanley, a barrister, well-known among the flash mob, had smoked cigarettes incessantly. Stanley, during his acquain-tanceship with Sybil, had frequently remarked that a cigarette was the thing to steel a gambler's nerve.

Fetching the lucifers, Sybil placed the cigarette between her lips, as she'd seen Stanley do, struck a lucifer, and remembered to let the bulk of the sulphur burn away before applying the flame to the cigarette's tip. She drew hesitantly on the lit cigarette and was rewarded with an acrid portion of vile smoke that set her wracking like a consumptive. Eyes watering, she nearly flung the thing away.

She stood before the grate and forced herself to continue, drawing periodically on the cigarette and flicking pale delicate ash onto the coals with the gesture Stanley had used. It was barely tolerable, she decided, and where was the desired effect? She felt abruptly ill, her stomach churning with nausea, her hands gone cold as ice. Coughing explosively, she dropped the cigarette into the coals, where it burst into flame and was swiftly consumed.

She became painfully aware of the ticking of the clock.

Big Ben began to sound midnight.

Where was Mick?

She woke in darkness, filled with a fear she couldn't name. Then she remembered Mick. The lamp had gone out. The coals were dead. Scrambling to her feet, she fetched the box of lucifers, then felt her way into her room, where the tinny ticking of the clock guided her to the commode.

When she struck a match, the face of the clock seemed to swim in the sulphur glare.

It was half past one.

Had he come when she was sleeping, knocked, had no answer, and gone away without her? No, not Mick. He'd have found a way in, if he wanted her. Had he gulled her, then, for the cakey girl she surely was, to trust his promises?

A queer sort of calm swept over her, a cruel clarity. She remembered the departure date on the steamship ticket. He wouldn't sail from Dover till late tomorrow, and it seemed unlikely that he and General Houston would be departing London, after an important lecture, in the dead of night. She'd go to Grand's, then, and find Mick, confront him, and plead, threaten blackmail, exposure, whatever proved necessary.

What tin she had was in her muff. There was a cab-stand in

Minories, by Goodman's Yard. She would go there now, and rouse a cabman to take her to Piccadilly.

Toby cried once, piteously, as she closed the door behind her. She scraped her shin cruelly in the dark, on Cairns' chained bicycle.

She was half the way down Minories to Goodman's Yard when she remembered her portmanteau, but there was no turning back.

Grand's night doorman was heavy-set, cold-eyed, chin-whiskered, stiff in one leg, and very certainly wouldn't allow Sybil into his hotel, not if he could help it. She'd twigged him from a block away, climbing down from her cabriolet—a big gold-braided bugaboo, lurking on the hotel's marble steps under great dolphin-wreathed lamps. She knew her doormen well enough; they played a major role in her life.

It was one thing to enter Grand's on Dandy Mick's arm, by daylight. But to walk in boldly from the midnight streets, as an unescorted woman, was another matter. Only whores did that, and the doorman would not let whores in. But she might think of a likely story to gull him, perhaps, if she thought of a very good lie, and if he were stupid, or careless, or weary. Or she might try to bribe him, though she had little enough of tin left, after the cab. And she was dressed proper, not in the flash clothes of a dollymop. She might, at a pinch, distract him. Smash a window with a cobblestone, and run past him when he came to look. It was hard to run in a crinoline, but he was lame, and slow. Or find a street-boy to throw a stone for her. . . .

Sybil stood in darkness, by the wooden hoardings of a construction site. Broadside posters loomed over her, bigger than bed-sheets, with great tattered shouting print: DAILY NEWS *World-Wide Circulation,* LLOYD'S NEWS *Only One Penny,* SOUTH-EASTERN RAILWAY *Ramsgate & Margate* 7/6. Sybil pulled one hand from her muff and gnawed feverishly at her fingernail, which smelled of Turkish tobacco. She was dully surprised to notice that her hand was blue-white with the cold, and trembling badly.

Pure luck, it seemed, rescued her then, or the nod of a sorrow-
ing angel, for a shining gurney brougham came to a chugging
halt in front of Grand's, its blue-coated fireman jumping down to
lower the hinged step. Out came a rollicking mob of drunken
Frenchmen in scarlet-lined capes, with brocade waistcoats and
tasseled evening-canes, and two of them had women with them.

Sybil grabbed up her skirt on the instant and scurried forward,
head down. Crossing the street, she was hidden from the doorman by the barricade of the gurney's gleaming coachwork. Then
she simply walked around it, past the great wood-spoked wheels
with their treads of rubber, and boldly joined the group. The
Frenchies were parley-vousing at each other, mustache-stroking
and giggling, and did not seem to notice her, nor care. She smiled
piously at no one in particular, and stood very close to a tall one,
who seemed drunkest. They staggered up the marble stairs, and
the tall Frenchman slapped a pound-note at the doorman's hand,
with the careless ease of a man who didn't know what real money
was. The doorman blinked at it and touched his braided hat.

And Sybil was safely inside. She walked with the jabbering
Frenchies across a wilderness of polished marble to the hotel-
desk, where they collected their keys from the night-clerk and
staggered up the curving stairway, yawning and grinning, leaving
Sybil behind at the counter.

The night-clerk, who spoke French, was chuckling over something he'd overheard. He sidled down the length of linteled
mahogany, with a smile for Sybil. "How may I be of service,
madame?"

The words came hard, almost stammering at first. "Could you
tell me please, has a Mr. Michael . . . or, rather . . . is General Sam
Houston still registered here?"

"Yes, madame. I did see General Houston, earlier this evening.
However, he's in our smoking-room now. . . . Perhaps you could
leave a message?"

"Smoking-room?"

"Yes—over there, behind the acanthus." The clerk nodded
toward a massive door at the corner of the lobby. "Our smoking-

room is not for the ladies, of course. . . . Forgive me, madame, but you seem a bit distressed. If the matter's vital, perhaps I should send a page."

"Yes," Sybil said, "that would be wonderful." The night-clerk obligingly produced a sheet of cream-laid hotel stationery and proffered his gold-nibbed reservoir-pen.

She wrote hastily, folded the note, scrawled MR. MICHAEL RADLEY on the back. The night-clerk crisply rang a bell, bowed in response to her thanks, and went about his business.

Shortly, a yawning and sour-faced little page appeared and placed her note on a cork-topped salver.

Sybil trailed anxiously behind as he trudged to the smoking-room. "It is for the General's personal secretary," she said.

" 'Tis awright, miss, I know 'im." He heaved one-handed at the smoking-room door. As it opened, and the page passed through, Sybil peered in. As the door slowly closed, she had a long glimpse of Houston, bare-headed, shiny-faced, and sweaty-drunk, with one booted foot propped on the table, beside a cut-glass decanter. He had a wicked-looking jack-knife in his hand, and was puffing smoke and jabbing at something—*whittling*, that was it, for the floor around his leather chair was littered with wood-shavings.

A tall bearded Englishman murmured something to Houston. The stranger had his left arm caught in a white silk sling, and looked sad-eyed and dignified and important. Mick stood at his side, bending at the waist to light the man's cheroot. Sybil saw him rasping at a steel sparker, on the end of a dangling rubber gas-tube, and then the door shut.

Sybil sat on a chaise-longue in the echoing marble lobby, warmth stealing through her damp, grimy shoes; her toes began to ache. Then the page emerged with Mick on his heels, Mick smiling back into the smoking-room and sketching out a cheery half-salute. Sybil rose from her seat. Seeing her there, his narrow face went bleak.

He came to her quickly, took her elbow. "Bloody Christ," he muttered, "what kind of silly note was that? Can't you make sense, girl?"

"What is it?" she pleaded. "Why didn't you come for me?"

"Bit of a contretemps, I'm afraid. Case of the fox biting his own arse. Might be funny if it weren't so bleeding difficult. But having you here now may change matters. . . ."

"What's gone wrong? Who's that gentry cove with the gammy arm?"

"Bloody British diplomat as doesn't care for the General's plan to raise an army in Mexico. Never you mind him. Tomorrow we'll be in France, and he'll be here in London, annoyin' someone else. At least I hope so. . . . The General's queered things for us, though. Drunk as a lord and he's pulled one of his funny little tricks. . . . He's a nasty bastard when he drinks, truth to tell. Starts to forget his friends."

"He's gulled you somehow," Sybil realized. "He wants to cut you loose, is that it?"

"He's nicked my kino-cards," Mick said.

"But I mailed them to Paris, *poste restante*," Sybil said. "Just as you told me to do."

"Not those, you goose—the kino-cards from the speech!"

"Your theatre cards? He stole 'em?"

"He knew I had to pack my cards, take 'em along with me, don't you see? So he kept a watch on me somehow, and now he's nicked 'em from my baggage. Says he won't need me in France after all, so long as he's got my information. He'll hire some onion-eater can run a kino on the cheap. Or so he says."

"But that's theft!"

" 'Borrowing,' according to him. Says he'll give me back my cards, as soon as he's had 'em *copied*. That way I don't lose nothin', you see?"

Sybil felt dazed. Was he teasing her? "But isn't that *stealing*, somehow?"

"Try arguing that with Samuel bloody Houston! He stole a whole damn country once, stole it clean and picked it to the bone!"

"But you're his man! You can't let him steal from you."

Mick cut her off. "When it comes to that—you might well ask how I had that fancy French program made. You might say I borrowed the General's money for it, so to speak." He showed his teeth in a grin. "Not the first time we've tried such a stunt on one another. It's a bit of a test, don't you see? Fellow has to be a right out-and-outer, to travel with General Houston. . . ."

"Oh Lord," Sybil said, collapsing into her crinoline on the chaise. "Mick, if you but knew what I've been thinking. . . ."

"Brace up, then!" He hauled her to her feet. "I need those cards and they're in his room. You're going to find them for me, and nick 'em back. And I'm going back in there and brass it out, cool as ice." He laughed. "The old bastard mightn't have tried this, if not for my tricks at his lecture. You an' Corny Simms made him feel he was right and fly, pulling strings! But we'll make a pigeon of him yet, you and I, together. . . ."

"I'm afraid, Mick," Sybil said. "I don't know how to steal things!"

"You little goose, of course you do," Mick said.

"Well, will you come with me and help, then?"

"Of course not! He'd know then, wouldn't he? I told him you were a newspaper friend of mine. If I stay too long talking, he'll smell a rat sure." He glared at her.

"All right," Sybil said, defeated. "Give me the key to his room."

Mick grunted. "Key? I haven't any bloody key."

A wash of relief went through her. "Well, then, I'm not a cracksman, you know!"

"Keep your voice down, else you'll tell everyone in Grand's . . ." His eyes glinted furiously. He was drunk, Sybil realized. She'd never seen Mick really drunk before, and now he was lushed, lightning-struck. It didn't show in his voice or his walk, but he was crazy and bold with it. "I'll get you a key. Go to that counter-man, blarney him. Keep him busy. And don't look at me." He gave her half a shove. "Go!"

Terrified, she returned to the counter. The Grand's telegraph stood at the far end, a ticking brass machine on a low marble pedestal decorated with leafy gilt vines. Within a sort of bell-glass, a gilded needle swung to and fro, pointing out letters in a concentric alphabet. With every twitch of the needle, something in the marble base clunked methodically, causing another quarter-inch of neatly perforated yellow paper tape to emerge from the marble base. The night-clerk, who was punching binder-holes in a bundle of fan-fold paper, set his work aside, clipped on a pince-nez, and came toward her.

"Yes, madame?"

"I need to send a telegram. It is rather urgent."

The clerk deftly assembled a small box of punch-cards, a hinged brass perforator, a neatly ruled form. He took out the reservoir-pen Sybil had used earlier. "Yes, madame. Citizen-number?"

"Oh . . . Would that be my number, or his?"

"That would depend, madame. Are you planning to pay by national credit?"

"May I charge it to my room?" Sybil hedged.

"Certainly, madame. Room number?"

Sybil hesitated for as long as she dared. "I suppose I'll pay cash, actually."

"Very well. Now, the addressee's citizen-number?"

"I'm afraid I don't know it, actually." She blinked at the clerk and began to chew on one knuckle.

He was very patient. "You *do* have a name and address, though?"

"Oh yes," Sybil said hastily. "Mr. Charles Egremont, M.P., 'The Beeches,' Belgravia, London."

The clerk wrote this down. "It is rather more costly to send a wire with only an address, madame. It's more efficient to route it direct through the Central Statistics Bureau." Sybil had not been looking for Mick. She had been afraid to look. Now, from the corner of her eye, she saw a dark form scuttle across the lobby floor. Mick was bent almost double, with his shoes off, the laces knotted around his neck. He charged headlong at the waist-high mahogany counter, grabbed the forward edge two-handed, vaulted over it in a split-second, and vanished.

He had made no sound at all.

"Something to do with the way an Engine handles messages," the clerk was explaining.

"Indeed," Sybil said. "But I haven't his citizen-number. I shall have to pay the extra, then, shan't I? This is very important."

"Yes, madame. I'm sure it is. Pray go on, and I shall take dictation."

"I don't suppose I should begin with my address and the date? I mean, a telegram's not a letter, really, is it?"

"No, madame."

"Or his address, either?"

"Brevity is the essence of telegraphy, madame."

Mick would be creeping to the hotel's mahogany peg-board, which hung clustered with room-keys. She couldn't see him, but now she imagined she could hear him moving, almost smell him, and the clerk needed only to glance to his right to discover a sneak-thief creeping toward him, crazy-eyed and crouching like an ape.

"Please take this down," Sybil quavered. "Dear Charles." The clerk began scribbling. "Nine years ago you put me to the worst dishonor that a woman can know."

The clerk stared in horror at his pen, a hot flush creeping up past his collar.

"Charles, you promised me that you would save my poor father. Instead you corrupted me, body and soul. Today I am leaving London, in the company of powerful friends. They know very well what a traitor you were to Walter Gerard, and to me. Do not attempt to find me, Charles. It would be useless. I do hope that you and Mrs. Egremont will sleep soundly tonight." Sybil shuddered. "Sign that 'Sybil Gerard,' if you please."

"Yes, madame," the clerk muttered, eyes downcast as Mick sprang silently back over the counter in his stocking feet. Mick crouched low, hidden by the counter's bulk, then crept off quickly on his haunches, waddling across the marble floor, like a monstrous duck. In a moment he had rolled behind a pair of overstuffed chairs.

"What do I owe?" Sybil asked the clerk politely.

"Two and six," the clerk stammered, quite unable to meet her eyes.

She counted it out from the little clasp-purse she took from her muff, and left the red-faced clerk at his station, punching telegram-cards from his box.

Mick came strolling like a gentleman across the lobby. He paused beside a reading-rack hung with neatly ironed newspapers. He bent down, coolly re-tying his shoes, straightened, and she saw the glint of metal in his hand. Not bothering even to catch her eye, he tucked the key behind a cut-velvet cushion on the chaise-longue. Then he stood briskly, straightened his tie, brushed at his sleeves, and strode straight off into the smoking-room.

Sybil sat for a moment on the chaise, pretending to read a gold-spined monthly, *Transactions of the Royal Society*. Carefully, with the fingertips of her right hand, she fished behind her for the key. Here it was, with the number "24" engraved on the oval brass. She yawned, in what she hoped was a ladylike fashion, and stood, to retire upstairs, entirely as if she had a room there.

Her feet ached.

As she trudged along the silent gas-lit hall, toward Houston's suite, she felt a sudden amazement at having struck out at Charles Egremont. Needing some dramatic message to distract the clerk, she'd blurted out threats and rage. It had come boiling out of her, almost without her will. It puzzled her, and even frightened her, after having imagined that she'd almost forgotten the man.

She could imagine the fear on Egremont's face when he read her telegram. She remembered his face well enough, fatuous and successful, which always looked as though it meant well, always apologized, always preached at her, and whined, and begged, and wept, and sinned. He was a fool.

But now she'd let Mick Radley set her to thieving. If she were clever, she should walk out of the Grand Hotel, vanish into the depths of London, and never see Radley again. She should not let the 'prentice oath hold her. To break an oath was frightening, but no more vile than her other sins. Yet somehow here she was; she had let him do with her as he would.

She stopped before the door, looked up and down the deserted corridor, fingered the stolen key. Why was she doing this? Because Mick was strong, and she was weak? Because he knew secrets that she didn't? For the first time, it occurred to her that she might be in love with him. Perhaps she did love him, in some strange way, and if that were true, it might explain matters to her, in a way which was almost soothing. If she were in love, she had a right to burn her bridges, to walk on air, to live by impulse. And if she loved Radley, it was finally something she knew, which he didn't. Her secret alone.

Sybil unlocked the door nervously, rapidly. She slipped through, shut it behind her, set her back against it. She stood in darkness.

There was a lamp in the room somewhere. She could smell its burnt wick. In the wall opposite, the outline emerged of a square curtained window to the street, between the curtains a faint knife-slice of upwashed gas-light. She faltered her way into the room, hands outstretched, until she felt the solid polished bulk of a bureau, and made out the dim sheen of a lamp-chimney there. She lifted the lamp, shook it. It had oil. Now she needed a lucifer.

She felt for drawers in the bureau. For some reason they were already open. She rustled through them. Stationery. Useless, and someone had spilled ink in one of the drawers; she could smell it.

Her fingers brushed a box of lucifers, which she recognized less by touch than by the dry familiar rattle. Her fingers, really, didn't seem to be working properly. The first lucifer popped and fizzled out, refusing to light, filling the room with a vile smell of sulphur. The second showed her the lamp. Her hands were trembling badly as she raised the chimney and applied flame to the wick.

She saw her own lamp-lit reflection staring wild-eyed from tilted cheval-glass, then doubled in beveled mirrors set into the twin doors of a wardrobe. She noticed clothing scattered on the bed, on the floor. . . .

A man was sitting on the arm of a chair, crouched there like a great shadowed crow, an enormous knife in his hand.

He stood then, but slowly, with a creak of leather, like some huge wooden puppet that had lain years in the dust. He was wrapped in a long and shapeless grey coat. His nose and jaw were draped with a dark kerchief.

"Best be quiet now, missy," he said, holding up the massive blade—dark, cleaver-like steel. "Sam comin'?"

Sybil found her voice. "Please don't kill me!"

"Old goat still whorin', is he?" The slow Texian voice slid forth like treacle; Sybil could barely make out his words. "You his fancy-gal?"

"No!" Sybil said, her voice strangled. "No, I'm not, I swear it! I . . . I came here to steal from him, and that's the truth!"

There was a ghastly silence.

"Take a look 'round you."

Sybil did so, trembling. The room had been ransacked.

"Nothin' here to steal," the man said. "Where is he, gal?"

"He's downstairs," Sybil said. "He's drunk! But I don't know him, I swear! My man sent me here, that's all! I didn't want to do this! He made me do it!"

"Quiet, now," he said. "I wouldn't hurt a white woman, 'less I had to. Put out that lamp."

"Let me go," she pleaded. "I'll go straight away! I meant no harm!"

"Harm?" The slow voice was heavy with gallows certainty. "What harm there is, it's for Houston, and that's justice."

"I didn't steal the cards! I didn't touch them!"

" 'Cards'?" He laughed, a dry sound at the back of his throat.

"The cards don't belong to Houston. He stole them!"

"Houston stole plenty," the man said, but clearly he was puzzled. He was thinking about her, and was not happy about it. "What they call you?"

"Sybil Jones." She took a breath. "I'm a British subject!"

"My," the man said. He clicked his tongue.

His masked face was unreadable. Sweat shone on a strip of pale smooth skin across the top of his forehead. A hat-brim had rested there, Sybil realized, to shield him from the Texian sun. He came forward now and took the lamp from her, turning down the wick. His fingers, when they brushed her hand, were dry and hard as wood.

In the darkness, there was only the pounding of her heart and the Texian's terrible presence.

"You must be lonely here in London," Sybil blurted, desperate to avoid another silence.

"Maybe Houston's lonesome. I got a better conscience." The Texian's voice was sharp. "You ever ask if he's lonesome?"

"I don't know him," she insisted.

"You're here. A woman come alone to his rooms."

"I came for the kino-cards. Paper cards, with holes in them. That's all, I swear!" No answer. "Do you know what a kino-trope is?"

" 'Nother damn machine," the Texian said wearily.

Another silence.

"Don't lie to me," he said at last. "You're a whore, that's all. You ain't the first whore I ever seen."

She heard him cough behind his kerchief, and snort wetly. "You ain't bad-lookin', though," he said. "In Texas, you could marry. Start all over."

"I'm sure that would be wonderful," Sybil said.

"Never enough white women in the country. Get you a decent man, 'stead o' some pimp." He lifted his kerchief, and spat on the floor.

"Hate pimps," he announced tonelessly. "Hate 'em like I hate Injuns. Or Mexicans. Mexican Injuns . . . French Mexican Injuns with guns, three, four hundred strong. On horseback, got them wind-up rifles, closest thing to devils on earth."

"But the Texians are heroes," Sybil said, desperately trying to remember a name from Houston's speech. "I heard about . . . about Alamo."

"Goliad," the voice gone to a dry whisper, "I was at Goliad."

"I heard about that, too," Sybil said quickly. "That must have been glorious."

The Texian hawked, spat again. "Fought 'em two days. No water. Colonel Fannin surrendered. They took us prisoner, all the niceties, polite as you please. Next day they marched us out of town. Shot us down in cold blood. Just lined us up. Massacred us."

Sybil said nothing.

"Massacred the Alamo. Burned all the bodies. . . . Massacred the Meir Expedition. Made 'em *pick beans.* Little clay lottery pot, pull out a black bean and they kill you. That's Mexicans for you."

"Mexicans," she repeated.

"Comanches are worse."

From somewhere off in the night came the scream of a great friction-brake, and then a dull distant pounding.

Black beans. Goliad. Her head was a Babel. Beans and massacre and this man whose skin was like leather. He stank like a navvy, of horses and sweat. Down Neal Street she'd once paid tuppence to view a diorama of some vast waste in America, a nightmare of twisted stone. The Texian looked born from such a place, and it came to her then that all the wildernesses of Houston's speech, all the places with such queer improbable names, were truly real, inhabited by creatures such as this. And Mick had said that Houston had stolen a country once, and now this one had followed, avenging angel. She fought down an insane desire to laugh.

She remembered the old woman then, the vendor of rock-oil in Whitechapel, and the queer look she'd given Mick when he'd questioned her. Did others work in concert with the angel of Goliad? How had so strange a figure managed to enter Grand's tonight, to enter a locked room? Where could such a man hide, even in London, even amid the tattered hordes of American refugees?

"Say he's drunk?" the Texian said.

Sybil started horribly. "What?"

"Houston."

"Oh. Yes. In the smoking-room. Very drunk."

"Be his last, then. He alone?"

"He . . ." Mick. "He's with a tall man. I don't know him."

"Beard on 'im? Arm broke?"

"I . . . Yes."

He made a sucking sound between his teeth; then leather creaked as he shrugged.

Something rattled, to Sybil's left. In the faint glow from the curtained window she glimpsed the gleaming facets of the cut-glass door-knob as it began to twist. The Texian leapt from his chair.

With the palm of one hand pressed tight against her mouth, he held the great dirk before her, a hideous thing like an elongated cleaver, tapering to a point. A length of brass ran along its spine; with the blade inches from her eyes she saw notches and nicks along the brass. And then the door was opening, Mick ducking through, his head and shoulders stenciled out by the light in the corridor.

She must have struck her head against the wall when the Texian flung her aside, but then she was kneeling, the crinoline bunched beneath her, watching the man hoist Mick against the wall, a single great hand about his throat, the heels of Mick's shoes beating a frantic tattoo against the wainscoting—until the long blade struck, twisted, struck again, filling the room with the hot reek of Butcher Row.

And all that happened after, in that room, was a dream to Sybil, or a play she watched, or some kino-show wrought with balsa-bits so numerous, so tiny, and so cleverly worked, as to blur reality. For the Texian, lowering Mick quietly to the floor, closed and re-locked the door, his movements unhurried and methodical.

She swayed where she knelt, then sagged against the wall behind the bureau. Mick was dragged away, heels scraping, into the deeper darkness beside the wardrobe. The Texian knelt over him—there was a rustle of clothing, the slap of the card-case flung aside, a jingle of change and the sound of a single coin, falling, rolling, spinning on the hardwood floor. . . .

And there came from the door a scratching, the rattle of metal on metal—the sound of a drunken man trying a keyhole.

Houston, throwing the door wide, lurched forward on his heavy stick. He belched thunderously and rubbed the site of his old wound. "Sons of bitches," he said, hoarse with drink, listing violently, the stick coming down with a sharp crack at each step. "Radley? Come out, you little whelp." He'd neared the bureau now, and Sybil snatched her fingers back silently, afraid of the weight of his boots.

The Texian closed the door.

"Radley!"

"Evenin', Sam."

Her room above the Hart seemed distant as childhood's first memories, here in the smell of slaughter, in this dark where giants moved—Houston reeled suddenly to slash at the curtains with his cane, tore them open, gas-light catching the patterns of frost on the glass of each mullioned pane, illuminating the Texian's kerchief and the grim eyes above it, eyes distant and merciless as winter stars. Houston staggered at the sight, the striped blanket sliding from his shoulders. His medals gleamed, quivered.

"Rangers sent me, Sam." Mick's little pepperbox pistol looked a toy in the Texian's hand, the clustered barrels winking as he took aim.

"Who are you, son?" Houston asked, all trace of drunkenness abruptly gone from his deep voice. "You Wallace? Take off that neckcloth. Face me man-to-man. . . ."

"You ain't giving no more orders, General. Shouldn't ought to have took what you did. You robbed us, Sam. Where is it? Where's that treasury money?"

"Ranger," Houston said, his voice a rich syrup of patience and sincerity, "you've been misled. I know who sent you, and I know their lies and slanders against me. But I swear to you that I stole nothing—those funds are mine by right, the sacred trust of the Texas government-in-exile."

"You sold Texas out for British gold," the Ranger said. "We need that money, for guns and food. We're starvin', and they're killin' us." A pause. "And you mean to help 'em do it."

"The Republic of Texas can't defy the world's great powers, Ranger. I know it's bad in Texas, and my heart aches for my country, but there can't be peace till I'm back in command."

"You got no money left, do you?" the Ranger said. "I looked, and it ain't here. You sold your fancy estate in the countryside. . . . You threw it all away, Sam, on whores and drink and fancy theatre shows for foreigners. And now you want to come back with a Mexican army. You're a thief, and a drunk, and a traitor."

"God damn you," Houston roared, and flung open his coat with both hands, "you're a cowardly assassin, you filthy-mouthed son of a bitch. If you think you have the guts to kill the father of your country, then shoot for the heart." He thumped his chest.

"For Texas." The pepperbox spat a flare of orange flame, edged with blue, hurling Houston back against the wall. Houston crashed to the floor as the avenger pounced, crouching to thrust the muzzles of the little pistol against the gaudy leopard waistcoat. There was a gun-blast into Houston's chest, then another, then a loud snap as the delicate trigger broke in the Ranger's fist.

The Ranger flung Mick's gun aside. Houston sprawled, unmoving, red sparks crawling through the fur of the leopard waistcoat.

There were sleepy shouts of alarm from another room. The Texian seized Houston's cane and began to batter the window; glass shattered, crashing to the pavement below; mullions gave way, and then he was scrambling out, across the sill. He froze there, for an instant, icy wind tugging at his long coat, and Sybil, in her trance, was reminded of her first sight of him: a vast dark crow, poised now for flight.

He jumped from sight, Houston's destroyer, the angel of Goliad, and was gone, leaving her in silence and rising terror, as if his vanishing had broken a spell. She began to crawl forward, quite without aim and cruelly hampered by her crinoline, yet it was as if her limbs moved of their own accord. The heavy cane lay on the floor, but its head, a gilt brass raven, had snapped free of the shaft.

Houston moaned.

"Please be quiet," she said. "You're dead."

"Who are you?" he said, and coughed.

The floor was littered with shards of glass, sharp under her palms. No. Bright. Like pebbles. The cane, she saw, was hollow, and had spilled its tight nesting of cotton-wool, where more of the pebbles nested. Bright, bright diamonds. Her hands scooped them together, wadding the cotton-wool, to thrust the lot into her bodice, between her breasts.

She turned to Houston then. He still lay on his back, and she watched in fascination as a bloodstain spread along his ribs. "Help me," Houston grunted. "I can't breathe." He tugged at his waistcoat's buttons and it came open, showing neat inner pockets of black silk, stuffed tight with dense packs of paper: thick punch-card packs in glued brown wrappers, their intricate perforations surely ruined now by the hot impact of bullets. . . . And blood, for at least one slug had struck him true.

Sybil rose, and walked, giddily, toward the door. Her foot squelched moistly in the red-splashed shadows by the wardrobe, and she looked down, to see an open card-case in red morocco, with a pair of tickets in a heavy nickel-plate clip. She stooped, picked it up.

"Get me to my feet," Houston demanded, his voice stronger now, tinged with urgency and irritation. "Where's my walking-stick? Where's Radley?"

The room seemed to rock beneath her, like a ship at sea, but she crossed to the door, opened it, stepped out, closed it behind her, and continued, like any gentry-girl, along the gas-lit and utterly respectable corridors of Grand's Hotel.

*   *   *

The South-Eastern Railway Company's London Bridge Terminus was a vast drafty hall of iron and soot-blown glass. Quakers moved among the avenues of benches, offering pamphlets to the seated travelers. Red-coated Irish soldiers, red-eyed from the night's gin, glowered at the close-shaven missionaries as they passed. The French passengers all seemed to be returning home with pineapples, sweet exotic bounty from the docks of London. Even the plump little actress who sat opposite Sybil had her pineapple, its green spikes protruding from a covered basket at her feet.

The train flew through Bermondsey and out into little streets of new brick, red tile. Dust-heaps, market-gardens, waste-ground. A tunnel.

The darkness about her stank of burnt gunpowder.

Sybil closed her eyes.

When she opened them, she saw crows flapping above a barren down, and the wires of the electric telegraph all alive, blurring, moving up and down in the intervals between poles, dancing in the wind of her passage toward France.

This image, surreptitiously daguerreotyped by a member of the Public Morals Section of the Sûreté Générale, January 30, 1855, presents a young woman seated at a table on the terrace of the Café Madeleine, No. 4 Boulevard Malesherbes. The woman, seated alone, has a china teapot and cup before her. Justification of the image reveals certain details of costume: ribbons, frills, her cashmere shawl, her gloves, her earrings, her elaborate bonnet. The woman's clothing is of French origin, and new, and of high quality. Her face, slightly blurred by long camera exposure, seems pensive, lost in thought.

Justification of background detail reveals No. 3 Boulevard Malesherbes, the offices of the Compagnie Sud Atlantique Transport Maritimes. The office window contains a large model steamboat with three funnels, a French-designed craft for the trans-Atlantic colonial trade. A faceless elderly man, evidently an accidental subject, seems lost in contemplation of the ship; his lone figure emerges therefore from the swiftly moving blurs of the Parisian street-crowd. His head is bare, his shoulders slump, and he leans heavily on a cane, apparently of cheap rattan. He is as unaware of the young woman's proximity as she is of his.

She is Sybil Gerard.

He is Samuel Houston.

Their paths diverge forever.

SECOND ITERATION

Derby Day

H E IS FROZEN in mid-stride as he edges diagonally into the depths of the holiday crowd. The angle of aperture has captured a fraction of his face: high cheekbone, thick dark beard trimmed close, right ear, stray lock of hair visible between corduroy coat-collar and striped cap. The cuffs of his dark trousers, buttoned tight in leather spats above hobnailed walking-boots, are speckled to the shins with the chalky mud of Surrey. The left epaulet of his worn, water-proof coat buttons sturdily over the strap of a military-issue binocular case; the lapels flap open in the heat, showing stout gleaming toggles of brass. His hands are jammed deep in the long coat's pockets.

His name is Edward Mallory.

He tramped through a lacquered gleam of carriages, blindered horses cropping noisily at the turf, amid childhood smells of harness, sweat, and grassy dung. His hands inventoried the contents of his various pockets. Keys, cigar-case, billfold, card-case. The thick staghorn handle of his multi-bladed Sheffield knife. Field notebook—most precious item of all. A handkerchief, a pencil-stub, a few loose shillings. A practical man, Dr. Mallory knew that every sporting-crowd has its thieves, none of them dressed to match their station. Anyone here might be a thief. It is a fact; it is a risk.

A woman blundered into Mallory's path, and his hobnails tore the flounce of her skirt. Turning, wincing, she tugged herself loose with a squeak of crinoline as Mallory touched his cap, and marched quickly on. Some farmer's wife, a clumsy, great red-cheeked creature, civilized and English as a dairy-cow. Mallory's eye was still accustomed to a wilder breed, the small brown wolf-women of the Cheyenne, with their greased black braids and beaded leather leggings. The hoop-skirts in the crowd around him seemed some aberrant stunt of evolution; the daughters of Albion had got a regular scaffolding under there now, all steel and whalebone.

Bison; that was it. American bison, just that very hoop-skirt silhouette, when the big rifle took them down; they had a way of falling, in the tall grass, suddenly legless, a furry hillock of meat. The great Wyoming herds would stand quite still for death, merely twitching their ears in puzzlement at the distant report of the rifle.

Now Mallory threaded his way among this other herd, aston-ished that mere fashion could carry its mysterious impetus so far. The men, among their ladies, seemed a different species, noth-ing so extreme—save, perhaps, their shiny toppers, though his inner eye refused to find any hat exotic. He knew too much about hats, knew too many of the utterly mundane secrets of their manufacture. He could see at a glance that most of the hats around him were dead cheap, Engine-made, pre-cut in a factory, though looking very nearly as fine as a craftsman-hatter's work, and at half the price or less. He had helped his father in the little haberdashery in Lewes: punching, stitching, blocking, sewing. His father, dipping felt in the mercury bath, had seemed not to mind the stench. . . .

Mallory was not sentimental about the eventual death of his father's trade. He put it from his mind, seeing that drink was being sold from a striped canvas tent, men crowding the counter, wiping foam from their mouths. A thirst struck him at the sight of it. Veering around a trio of sporting-gents, crops under their arms, who argued the day's odds, he reached the counter and tapped it with a shilling.

"Pleasure, sar?" asked the barman.

"A huckle-buff."

"Sussex man, sar?"

"I am. Why?"

"Can't make you a proper huckle-buff, sar, as I haven't barley-water," the fellow explained, looking briskly sad. "Not much call for it outside Sussex."

"Very nearly two years since I've tasted huckle-buff," Mallory said.

"Mix you a lovely bumbo, sar. Much like a huckle-buff. No? A good cigar, then. Only tuppence! Fine Virginia weed." The barman presented a crooked cheroot from a wooden box.

Mallory shook his head. "When I've the taste for something, I'm a stubborn man. A huckle-buff or nothing."

The barman smiled. "Won't be drove? A Sussex man, sure! I'm a county-man meself. Take this fine cigar gratis, sir, with my complimums."

"Very decent of you," Mallory said, surprised. He strolled off, shaking a lucifer from his cigar-case. Firing the match on his boot, he puffed the cheroot into life and tucked his thumbs jauntily in the arm-holes of his waistcoat.

The cigar tasted like damp gunpowder. He yanked it from his mouth. A cheap paper band girdled the foul, greenish-black leaf, a little foreign flag with stars and bars and the motto VICTORY BRAND. Yankee war-rubbish; he flung it away, so that it bounced sparking from the side of a gypsy-wagon, where a dark-headed child in rags snatched it quickly up.

To Mallory's left, a spanking new steam-gurney chugged into the crowd, the driver erect at his station. As the man drew his brake-lever, a bronze bell clanged in the gurney's maroon prow, people scattering sulkily before the vehicle's advance. Above them, passengers lounged in velvet coach-seats, the folding spark-shield accordioned back to admit the sun. A grinning old swell in kid gloves sipped champagne with a pair of young misses, either daughters or mistresses. The gurney's door gleamed with a coat-of-arms, cog-wheel azure and crossed hammers argent. Some Rad's emblem unknown to Mallory, who knew the arms of every savant Lord—though he was weak on the capitalists.

The machine was headed east, toward the Derby garages; he fell in behind it, letting it clear his path, easily keeping pace and smiling as draymen struggled with frightened horses. Pulling his notebook from his pocket, stumbling a little in the gouged turf-tracks of the brougham's thick wheels, he thumbed through the colorful pages of his spotter's guide. It was last year's edition; he could not find the coat-of-arms. Pity, but it meant little, when new Lords were ennobled weekly. As a class, the Lordships dearly loved their steam-chariots.

The machine set its course for the gouts of greyish vapor rising behind the pillared grandstands of Epsom. It humped slowly up the curb of a paved access-road. Mallory could see the garages now, a long rambling structure in the modern style, girdered in skeletal iron and roofed with bolted sheets of tin-plate, its hard lines broken here and there by bright pennants and tin-capped ventilators.

He followed the huffing land-craft until it eased into a stall. The driver popped valves with a steaming gush. Stable-monkeys set to work with greasing-gear as the passengers decamped down a folding gangway, the Lord and his two women passing Mallory on their way toward the grandstand. Britain's self-made elite, they trusted he was watching and ignored him serenely. The driver lugged a massive hamper in their wake. Mallory touched his own striped cap, identical with the driver's, and winked, but the man made no response.

Strolling the length of the garages, spotting steamers from his guidebook, Mallory marked each new sighting with his pencil-stub and a small thrill of satisfaction. Here was Faraday, great

savant-physicist of the Royal Society, there Colgate the soap magnate, and here a catch indeed, the visionary builder Brunel. A
very few machines bore old family arms; landowners, whose
fathers had been dukes and earls, when such titles had existed.
Some of the fallen old nobility could afford steam; some had
more initiative than others, and did what they could to keep up.

Arriving at the southern wing, Mallory found it surrounded by
a barricade of clean new saw-horses, smelling of pitch. This
section, reserved for the racing-steamers, was patroled by a squad
of uniformed foot-police. One of them carried a spring-wind
Cutts-Maudslay of a model familiar to Mallory, the Wyoming
expedition having been provided with six of them. Though the
Cheyenne had regarded the stubby Birmingham-made machine-
carbine with a useful awe, Mallory knew that it was temperamental to the point of unreliability. Inaccurate to the point of
uselessness as well, unless one were popping off the entire thirty
rounds into a pack of pursuers—something Mallory himself had
once done from the aft firing-position of the expedition's steam-
fortress.

Mallory doubted that the fresh-faced young copper had any
notion what a Cutts-Maudslay might do if fired into an English
crowd. He shook off the dark thought with an effort.

Beyond the barricade, each separate stall was carefully
shielded from spies and odds-makers by tall baffles of tarpaulin,
tautly braced by criss-crossed cables threaded through flagpoles.
Mallory worked his way through an eager crowd of gawkers and
steam-hobbyists. Two coppers stopped him brusquely at the gate.
He displayed his citizen's number-card and his engraved invitation from the Brotherhood of Vapor Mechanics. Making careful
note of his number, the policemen checked it against a thick
notebook crammed with fan-fold. At length they pointed out the
location of his hosts, cautioning him not to wander.

As a further precaution, the Brotherhood had appointed their
own look-out. The man squatted on a folding-stool outside the
tarpaulin, squinting villainously and clutching a long iron span-
ner. Mallory proffered his invitation. The guard stuck his head

past a narrow flap in the tarpaulin, shouted, "Your brother's here, Tom," and ushered Mallory through.

Daylight vanished in the stink of grease, metal-shavings, and coal-dust. Four Vapor Mechanics, in striped hats and leather aprons, were checking a blueprint by the harsh glare of a carbide lamp; beyond them, a queer shape threw off highlights from curves of enameled tin.

He took the thing for a boat, in the first instant of his surprise, its scarlet hull absurdly suspended between a pair of great wheels. Driving-wheels, he saw, stepping closer; the burnished piston-brasses vanished into smoothly flared openings in the insubstantial-looking shell or hull. Not a boat; it resembled a teardrop, rather, or a great tadpole. A third wheel, quite small and vaguely comical, was swivel-mounted at end of the long tapered tail.

He made out the name painted in black and gilt across the bulbous prow, beneath a curved expanse of delicately leaded glass: *Zephyr.*

"Come, Ned, join us!" his brother sang out, beckoning. "Don't be shy!" The others chuckled at Tom's sauciness as Mallory strode forward, his hobnails scraping the floor. His little brother Tom, nineteen years old, had grown his first mustache; it looked as though a cat could lick it off. Mallory offered his hand to his friend, Tom's master. "Mr. Michael Godwin, sir!" he said.

"Dr. Mallory, sir!" said Godwin, a fair-haired engineer of forty years, with mutton-chop whiskers over cheeks pitted by small-pox. Small and stout, with shrewd, hooded eyes, Godwin began a bow, thought better of it, clapped Mallory gently across the back, and introduced his fellows. They were Elijah Douglas, a journey-man, and Henry Chesterton, a master of the second degree.

"A privilege, sirs," Mallory declared. "I expected fine things from you, but this is a revelation."

"What do you think of her, Dr. Mallory?"

"A far cry from our steam-fortress, I should say!"

"She was never made for your Wyoming," Godwin said, "and

that accounts for a certain lack of guns and armor. Form emerges from function, as you so often told us."

"Small for a racing-gurney, isn't she?" Mallory ventured, somewhat at a loss. "Peculiarly shaped."

"Built upon principles, sir, newly discovered principles indeed. And a fine tale behind her invention, having to do with a colleague of yours. You recall the late Professor Rudwick, I'm sure."

"Ah, yes, Rudwick," Mallory muttered, then hesitated. "Hardly your new-principle man, Rudwick . . ."

Douglas and Chesterton were watching him with open curiosity.

"We were both paleontologists," Mallory said, suddenly uncomfortable, "but the fellow fancied himself gentry of a sort. Put on fine airs and entertained outmoded theories. Rather muddy in his thinking, in my opinion."

The two mechanics looked doubtful.

"I'm not one to speak ill of the dead," Mallory assured them. "Rudwick had his friends, I've mine, and there's an end to it."

"You do remember," Godwin persisted, "Professor Rudwick's great flying reptile?"

"*Quetzalcoatlus,*" Mallory said. "Indeed, that was a coup; one can't deny it."

"They've studied its remains in Cambridge," Godwin said, "at the Institute of Engine Analytics."

"I plan to do a bit of work there myself, on the Brontosaurus," Mallory said, unhappy with the direction the conversation seemed to be taking.

"You see," Godwin continued, "the cleverest mathematicians in Britain were snug there, spinning their great brass, while you and I froze in the mud of Wyoming. Pecking holes in their cards to puzzle out how a creature of such a size could fly."

"I know about the project," Mallory said. "Rudwick published on the topic. But 'pneumo-dynamics' isn't my field. Frankly, I'm not sure there's much to it, scientifically. It seems a bit . . . well . . . *airy,* if you follow me." He smiled.

"Great practical applications, possibly," Godwin said. "Lord Babbage himself took a hand in the analysis."

Mallory thought about it. "I'll concede there's likely something to pneumatics, then, if it's caught the eye of the great Babbage! To improve the art of ballooning, perhaps? Balloon-flight, that's a military field. There's always ample funding for the sciences of war."

"No, sir; I mean in the practical design of machinery."

"A flying machine, you mean?" Mallory paused. "You're not trying to tell me this vehicle of yours can *fly*, are you?"

The mechanics laughed politely. "No," Godwin said, "and I can't say that all that airy Engine-spinning has come to much, directly. But we now understand certain matters having to do with the behavior of air in motion, the principles of atmospheric resistance. New principles, little-known as yet."

"But we mechanics," said Mr. Chesterton proudly, " 'ave put 'em to practical use, sir, in the shaping of our *Zephyr*."

" 'Line-streaming,' we call it," Tom said.

"So you've 'line-streamed' this gurney of yours, eh? That's why it looks so much like, er . . ."

"Like a fish," Tom said.

"Exactly," said Godwin. "A fish! It's all to do with the action of fluids, you see. Water. Air. Chaos and turbulence! It's all in the calculations."

"Remarkable," Mallory said. "So I take it that these principles of turbulence—"

A sudden blistering racket erupted from a neighboring stall. The walls shook and a fine sifting of soot fell from the ceiling.

"That'll be the Italians," Godwin shouted. "They've brought in a monster this year!"

"Makes a mortal hogo of a stink!" Tom complained.

Godwin cocked his head. "Hear them try-rods clacking on the down-stroke? Bad tolerances. Slovenly foreign work!" He doffed his cap and dusted soot against his knee.

Mallory's head was ringing. "Let me buy you a drink!" he shouted.

Godwin cupped his ear blankly. "What?"

Mallory pantomimed; lifted a fist to his mouth, with his thumb cocked. Godwin grinned. He had a quick, bellowed word with Chesterton, over the blueprints. Then Godwin and Mallory ducked out into the sunshine.

"Bad try-rods," the guard outside said smugly. Godwin nodded, and handed the man his leather apron. He took a plain black coat, instead, and traded his engineer's cap for a straw wide-awake.

They left the racing-enclosure. "I can only spare a few minutes," Godwin apologized. " 'The Master's eye melts the metal,' as they say." He hooked a pair of smoked spectacles over his ears. "Some of these hobbyists know me, and might try to follow us. . . . But never mind that. It's good to see you again, Ned. Welcome back to England."

"I won't keep you long," Mallory said. "I wanted a private word or two. About the boy, and such."

"Oh, Tom's a fine lad," said Godwin. "He's learning. He means well."

"I hope he'll prosper."

"We do our best," Godwin said. "I was sorry to hear from Tom about your father. Him taking so ill, and all."

" 'Ould Mallory, he won't a-go till he's guv away his last bride,' " Mallory quoted, in his broadest Sussex drawl. "That's what Father always tells us. He wants to see all his girls married. He's a game sort, my poor old dad."

"He must take great comfort in a son like yourself," Godwin said. "So, how does London suit you? Did you take the holiday train?"

"I've not been in London. I've been in Lewes, with the family. Rode the morning train from there to Leatherhead; then I tramped it."

"You walked to the Derby from Leatherhead? That's ten miles or more!"

Mallory smiled. "You've seen me tramp twenty, cross-country in the badlands of Wyoming, hunting fossils. I'd a taste to see good English countryside again. I'm only just back from Toronto, with all our crates of plastered bones, while you've been here for months, getting your fill of this." He waved his arm.

Godwin nodded. "What do you make of the place, then—now you're home again?"

"London Basin anticline," Mallory said. "Tertiary and Eocene chalk-beds, bit of modern flinty clay."

Godwin laughed. "We're all of us modern flinty clay. . . . Here we go, then; these lads sell a decent brew."

They walked down a gentle slope to a crowded dray laden with ale-kegs. The proprietors had no huckle-buff. Mallory bought a pair of pints.

"It was good of you to accept our invitation," Godwin said. "I know that you're a busy man, sir, what with your famous geologic controversies and such."

"No busier than yourself," Mallory said. "Solid engineering work. Directly practical and useful. I envy that, truly."

"No, no," said Godwin. "That brother of yours, he thinks the world of you. So do we all! You're the coming man, Ned. Your star is rising."

"We had excellent luck in Wyoming, certainly," Mallory said. "We made a great discovery. But without you and your steam-fortress, those red-skins would have made short work of us."

"They weren't so bad, once they cozied up and had a taste of whiskey."

"Your savage respects British steel," Mallory said. "Theories of old bones don't much impress him."

"Well," Godwin said, "I'm a good Party man, and I'm with Lord Babbage. 'Theory and practice must be as bone and sinew.' "

"That worthy sentiment calls for another pint," said Mallory. Godwin wanted to pay. "Pray allow me," Mallory said. "I'm still spending my bonus, from the expedition."

Godwin, pint in hand, led Mallory out of ear-shot of the other drinkers. He gazed about carefully, then doffed his specs and looked Mallory in the eye. "Do you trust in your good fortune, Ned?"

Mallory stroked his beard. "Say on."

"The touts are quoting odds of ten-to-one against our *Zephyr*."

Mallory chuckled. "I'm no gambler, Mr. Godwin! Give me solid facts and evidence, and there I'll take my stand. But I'm no flash fool, to hope for unearned riches."

"You took the risk of Wyoming. You risked your very life."

"But that depended on my own abilities, and those of my colleagues."

"Exactly!" Godwin said. "That's my own position, to the very letter! Listen a moment. Let me tell you about our Brotherhood of Vapor Mechanics."

Godwin lowered his voice. "The head of our trades-union, Lord Scowcroft . . . He was simple Jim Scowcroft in the bad old days, one of your popular agitators, but he made his peace with the Rads. Now he's rich, and been to Parliament and such; a very clever man. When I went to Lord Scowcroft with my plans for the *Zephyr*, he spoke to me just as you did now: facts and evidence. 'Master first-degree Godwin,' he says, 'I can't fund you with the hard-earned dues of our Brothers unless you can show me, in black and white, how it shall profit us.'

"So I told him: 'Your Lordship, the construction of steam-gurneys is one of the nicest luxury trades in the country. When we go to Epsom Downs, and this machine of ours leaves the competitors eating her dust, the gentry will stand in queues for the famous work of the Vapor Mechanics.' And that's how it will be, Ned."

"If you win the race," Mallory said.

Godwin nodded somberly. "I make no cast-iron promises. I'm an engineer; I know full well how iron can bend, and break, and rust, and burst. You surely know it too, Ned, for you saw me work repair on that blasted steam-fortress till I thought I should go mad. . . . But I know my facts and figures. I know pressure differentials, and engine duty, and crank-shaft torque, and wheel diameters. With disaster barred, our little *Zephyr* will breeze past her rivals as if they were stock-still."

"It sounds splendid. I'm glad for you." Mallory sipped his ale. "Now tell me what should happen if disaster strikes?"

Godwin smiled. "Then I lose, and am left penniless. Lord Scowcroft was liberal, by his own lights, but there are always extra costs in such a project. I've put everything in my machine: my expedition bonus from the Royal Society, even a small bequest I had of a maiden aunt, God rest her."

Mallory was shocked. "Everything?"

Godwin chuckled drily. "Well, they can't take what I *know*, can they? I shall still have my skills; mayhap I'd undertake another Royal Society expedition. They pay well enough. But I'm risking all I have in England. It's fame or famine, Ned, and naught between."

Mallory stroked his beard. "You startle me, Mr. Godwin. You always seemed such a practical man."

"Dr. Mallory, my audience today is the very cream of Britain. The Prime Minister is here today. The Prince Consort is in attendance. Lady Ada Byron is here, and betting lavishly, if rumor's true. When will I have another such chance?"

"I do follow your logic," Mallory said, "though I can't say I approve. But then, your station in life allows such a risk. You're not a married man, are you?"

Godwin sipped his ale. "Neither are you, Ned."

"No, but I have eight younger brothers and sisters, my old dad mortal ill, my mother eaten-up with the rheumatics. I can't gamble my family's livelihood."

"The odds are ten-to-one, Ned. Fool's odds! They should be five-to-three in *Zephyr*'s favor."

Mallory said nothing. Godwin sighed. "It's a pity. I dearly wanted to see some good friend win that bet. A big win, a flash win! And I myself can't do it, you see? I wanted to, but I've spent my last pound on *Zephyr*."

"Perhaps a modest wager," Mallory ventured. "For friendship's sake."

"Bet ten pounds for me," Godwin said suddenly. "Ten pounds, as a loan. If you lose, I'll pay you back somehow, in days to come. If you win, we'll split a hundred pounds tonight, half-and-half. What do you say? Will you do that for me?"

"Ten pounds! A heavy sum . . ."

"I'm good for it."

"I trust that you are. . . ." Mallory now saw no easy way to refuse. The man had given Tom a place in life, and Mallory felt the debt. "Very well, Mr. Godwin. To please you."

"You shan't regret it," Godwin said. He brushed ruefully at the frayed sleeves of his frock-coat. "Fifty pounds. I can use it. A triumphant inventor, on the rise in life and such, shouldn't have to dress like a parson."

"I shouldn't think you'd waste good money on vanities."

"It's not vanity to dress as befits one's station." Godwin looked him over, sharp-eyed. "That's your old Wyoming tramping-coat, isn't it?"

"A practical garment," Mallory said.

"Not for London. Not for giving fancy lectures to fine London ladies with a modish taste in natural-history."

"I'm not ashamed of what I am," Mallory said stoutly.

"Simple Ned Mallory," Godwin nodded, "come to Epsom in an engineer's cap, so the lads won't feel anxious at meeting a famous savant. I know why you did that, Ned, and I admire it. But mark my word, you'll be Lord Mallory some day, as surely as we stand here drinking. You'll have a fine silk coat, and a ribbon on your pocket, and stars and medals from all the learned schools. For you're the man dug up the great Land Leviathan, and made wondrous sense from a tangle of rocky bones. That's what you are now, Ned, and you might as well face up to it."

"It's not so simple as you think," Mallory protested. "You don't know the politics of the Royal Society. I'm a Catastrophist. The Uniformitarians hold sway, when it comes to the granting of tenures and honors. Men like Lyell, and that damned fool Rudwick."

"Charles Darwin's a Lordship. Gideon Mantell's a Lordship, and his Iguanodon's a shrimp, ranked next to your Brontosaur."

"Don't you speak ill of Gideon Mantell! He's the finest man of science Sussex ever had, and he was very kind to me."

Godwin looked down into his empty mug. "I beg your pardon," he said. "I spoke a bit too frankly, I can see that. We're far from wild Wyoming, where we sat about a campfire as simple brother Englishmen, scratching wherever it itched."

He put his smoked spectacles on. "But I remember those theory-talks you'd give us, explaining what those bones were all about. 'Form follows function.' 'The fittest survive.' New forms lead the way. They may look queer at first, but Nature tests them fair and square against the old, and if they're sound in principle, then the world is theirs." Godwin looked up. "If you can't see that your theory is bone to my sinew, then you're not the man I take you for."

Mallory removed his cap. "It's I who should beg your pardon, sir. Forgive my foolish temper. I hope you'll always speak to me frankly, Mr. Godwin, ribbons on my chest or no. May I never be so unscientific as to close my eyes to honest truth." He offered his hand.

Godwin shook it.

A fanfare rang from across the course, the crowd responding with a rustle and a roar. All around them, people began to move, migrating toward the stands like a vast herd of ruminants.

"I'm off to make that wager we discussed," Mallory said.

"I must get back to my lads. Join us after the run? To split the winnings?"

"Certainly," Mallory said.

"Let me take that empty pint," Godwin offered. Mallory gave it to him, and walked away.

Having taken leave of his friend, Mallory instantly regretted his promise. Ten pounds was a stiff sum indeed; he himself had survived on little more per annum, during his student days.

And yet, he considered, strolling in the general direction of the book-makers' canopied stalls, Godwin was a most exacting technician and a scrupulously honest man. He had no reason whatever to doubt Godwin's estimates of the race's outcome, and a man who wagered handsomely on *Zephyr* might leave Epsom that evening with a sum equivalent to several years' income. If one were to bet thirty pounds, or forty . . .

Mallory had very nearly fifty pounds on deposit in a City bank, the better part of his expedition bonus. He wore an additional twelve in the stained canvas money-belt firmly cinched beneath his waistcoat.

He thought of his poor father gone feeble with hatter's madness, poisoned by mercury, twitching and muttering in his chair by the hearth in Surrey. A portion of Mallory's money was already allocated for the coal that fed that hearth.

Still, one might come away with *four hundred pounds*. . . . But no, he would be sensible, and wager only the ten, fulfilling his agreement with Godwin. Ten pounds would be a sharp loss, but one he could bear. He worked the fingers of his right hand between the buttons of his waistcoat, feeling for the buttoned flap of the canvas belt.

He chose to place his bet with the thoroughly modern firm of Dwyer and Company, rather than the venerable and perhaps marginally more reputable Tattersall's. He had frequently passed Dwyer's brightly lit establishment in St. Martin's Lane, hearing the deep brassy whirring of the three Engines they employed. He did not care to lay such a wager with any of the dozens of individual book-makers elevated above the throng on their high stools, though they were nearly as reliable as the larger firms. The crowd kept them so; Mallory himself had witnessed the near lynching of a defaulting betting-man at Chester. He still recalled the grisly shout of "Welsher!" pitched like a cry of "Fire!" going up inside the railed enclosure, and the rush against a man in a black cap, who was hurled down and savagely booted. Beneath the surface of the good-natured racing-throng lay an ancient ferocity. He'd discussed the incident with Lord Darwin, who'd likened the action to the mobbing of crows. . . .

His thoughts turned to Darwin as he queued for the steam-racing wicket. Mallory had been an early and passionate supporter of the man, whom he regarded as one of the great minds of the age; but he'd come to suspect that the reclusive Lord, though clearly appreciating Mallory's support, considered him rather brash. When it came to matters of professional advancement, Darwin was of little use. Thomas Henry Huxley was the man for that, a great social theorist as well as an accomplished scientist and orator. . . .

In the queue to Mallory's immediate right lounged a swell in subdued City finery, that day's number of *Sporting Life* tucked beneath an immaculate elbow. As Mallory watched, the man stepped to the wicket and placed a wager of one hundred pounds on a horse called Alexandra's Pride.

"Ten pounds on the *Zephyr*, to win," Mallory told the betting-clerk at the steam-wicket, presenting a five-pound note and five singles. As the clerk methodically punched out the wager, Mallory studied the odds arrayed in kino-bits above and behind the glossy faux-marble of the papier-mâché counter. The French were heavily favored, he saw, with the *Vulcan* of the Compagnie Géné-rale de Traction, the driver one M. Raynal. He noted that the Italian entry was in little better position than Godwin's *Zephyr*. Word of the try-rods?

The clerk passed Mallory a flimsy blue copy of the card he'd punched. "Very good, sir, thank you." He was already looking past Mallory to the next customer.

Mallory spoke up. "Will you accept a check drawn on a City bank?"

"Certainly, sir," the clerk replied, raising one eyebrow as if noticing Mallory's cap and coat for the first time, "provided they are imprinted with your citizen-number."

"In that case," Mallory said, to his own amazement, "I shall wager an additional forty pounds on the *Zephyr*."

"To win, sir?"

"To win."

Mallory fancied himself a rather keen observer of his fellow man. He possessed, Gideon Mantell had long ago assured him, the naturalist's requisite eye. Indeed, he owed his current position in the scientific hierarchy to having used that eye along a monotonous stretch of rock-strewn Wyoming river-bank, distinguishing form amid apparent chaos.

Now, however, appalled by the recklessness of his wager, by the enormity of the result in the event of his losing, Mallory found no comfort in the presence and variety of the Derby crowd. The eager roaring of massed and passionate greed, as the horses ran their course, was more than he could bear.

He left the stands, almost fleeing, hoping to shake the nervous energy from his legs. A dense mass of vehicles and people had congregated on the rails of the run-in, shrieking their enthusiasm as the horses passed in a cloud of dust. The poorer folk, these, mostly those unwilling to put down a shilling fee for admission to the stands, mixed with those who entertained or preyed upon the crowd: thimble-riggers, gypsies, pick-pockets. He began shoving his way through toward the outskirts of the crowd, where he might catch his breath.

It occurred to Mallory suddenly that he might have lost one of his betting-slips. The thought almost paralyzed him. He stopped dead, his hands diving into his pockets.

No—the blue flimsies were still there, his tickets to disaster. . . .

He was almost trampled by a jostling pair of horses. Shocked and angered, Mallory grabbed at the harness of the nearer horse, caught his balance, shouted a warning.

A whip cracked near his head. The driver was trying to fight his way free of the entangling crowd, standing on the box of an open brougham. The fellow was a race-track dandy, gotten up in a suit of the most artificial blue, with a great paste ruby glinting in a cravat of lurid silk. Beneath the pallor of a swelling forehead, accentuated by dark disheveled locks, his bright gaunt eyes moved constantly, so that he seemed to be looking everywhere at once—except at the race-course, which still compelled the attention of everyone, save himself and Mallory. A queer fellow, and part of a queerer trio, for the passengers within the brougham were a pair of women.

One, veiled, wore a dark, almost masculine dress; and as the brougham halted she rose unsteadily and groped for its door. She tried to step free, with a drunken wobble, her hands encumbered by a long wooden box, something like an instrument-case. But the second woman made a violent grab for her veiled companion, yanking the gentlewoman back into her seat.

Mallory, still holding the leather harness, stared in astonishment. The second woman was a red-haired tart, in the flash garments appropriate to a gin-palace or worse. Her painted, pretty features were marked with a look of grim and utter determination.

Mallory saw the red-haired tart strike the veiled gentlewoman. It was a blow both calculated and covert, jabbing her doubled knuckles into the woman's short ribs with a practiced viciousness. The veiled woman doubled over and collapsed back into her seat.

Mallory was stung into immediate action. He dashed to the side of the brougham and yanked open the lacquered door. "What is the meaning of this?" he shouted.

"Go away," the tart suggested.

"I saw you strike this lady. How dare you?"

The brougham lurched back into motion, almost knocking Mallory from his feet. Mallory recovered swiftly, dashed forward, seized the gentlewoman's arm. "Stop at once!"

The gentlewoman rose again to her feet. Beneath the black veil her rounded, gentle face was slack and dreamy. She tried to step free again, seeming unaware that the carriage was in motion. She could not get her balance. With a quite natural, ladylike gesture, she handed Mallory the long wooden box.

Mallory stumbled, clutching the ungainly case with both hands. Shouts arose from the milling crowd, for the tout's careless driving had infuriated them. The carriage rattled to a halt again, the horses snorting and beginning to plunge.

The driver, shaking with rage, tossed his whip aside and leapt free. He marched on Mallory, shoving by-standers aside. He whipped a pair of squarish, rose-tinted spectacles from his pocket, and slipped them over the pomaded hair at his ears.

Halting before Mallory, he squared his sloping shoulders and extended one canary-gloved hand with a peremptory gesture.

"Return that property at once," he commanded.

"What is this about?" Mallory countered.

"I'll have that box now, or it will be the worse for you."

Mallory stared down at the little man, quite astonished at this bold threat. He almost laughed aloud, and would have done so, save that the fellow's darting eyes behind the square spectacles had a maddened gleam, like a laudanum fiend's.

Mallory set the case deliberately between his muddied boots. "Madame," he called, "step free, if you will. These people have no right to compel you—"

The tout reached swiftly within his gaudy blue coat and lunged forward like a jack-in-the-box. Mallory fended him off with an open-handed push, and felt a stinging jolt tear at his left leg.

The tout half-stumbled, caught himself, leapt forward again with a snarl. There was a narrow gleam of steel in his hand.

Mallory was a practicing disciple of Mr. Shillingford's system of scientific boxing. In London, he sparred weekly in one of the private gymnasia maintained by the Royal Society, and his months in the wilds of North America had served as an introduction to the roughest sort of scrapping.

Mallory parried the man's knife-arm with the edge of his own left arm and drove his right fist against the fellow's mouth.

He had a brief glimpse of the stiletto, fallen on the trampled turf: a viciously narrow double-edged blade, the handle of black gutta-percha. Then the man was upon him, bleeding from the mouth. There was no method whatever to the attack. Mallory assumed Shillingford's First Stance and had at the villain's head.

Now the crowd, which had drawn back from the initial exchange and the flash of steel, closed around the two, the innermost ring consisting of working-men and the race-course types who preyed on them. They were a burly, hooting lot, delighted to see a bit of claret spilt in unexpected circumstances. When Mallory took his man fair upon the chin with one of his best, they cheered, caught the fellow as he fell in their midst, and hurled him back, square into the next blow. The dandy went down, the salmon silk of his cravat dashed with blood.

"I'll destroy you!" he said from the ground. One of his teeth—the eye-tooth by the look of it—had been bloodily shattered.

"Look out!" someone shouted. Mallory turned at the cry. The red-haired woman stood behind him, her eyes demonic, something glinting in her hand—it seemed to be a glass vial, odd as that was. Her eyes darted downward—but Mallory stepped prudently between her and the long wooden box. There followed a moment's tense stand-off, while the tart seemed to weigh her alternatives—then she rushed to the side of the stricken tout.

"I'll destroy you utterly!" the tout repeated through bloodied lips. The woman helped him to his feet. The crowd jeered at him for a coward and empty braggart.

"Try it," Mallory suggested, shaking his fist.

The tout's eyes met his in reptilian fury, as the man leaned heavily on his woman; then the two of them were gone, stumbling into the throng. Mallory snatched up the box triumphantly, turned and shoved his way through the laughing ring of men. One of them clapped him heartily on the back. He made for the abandoned brougham.

He pulled himself up and inside, into worn velvet and leather. The noise of the crowd was dying down; the race was over; someone had won.

The gentlewoman sat slumped in the shabby seat, her breath stirring the veil. Mallory looked quickly about for possible attackers, but saw only the crowd; saw it all in a most curious way, as if the instant were frozen, daguerreotyped by some fabulous process that captured every least shade of the spectrum.

"Where is my chaperone?" the woman asked, in a quiet, distracted voice.

"And who might your chaperone be, madame?" Mallory said, a

bit dizzily. "I don't think your friends were any proper sort of escort for a lady. . . ."

Mallory was bleeding from the wound in his left thigh; it was seeping through his trouser-leg. He sat heavily in the worn plush of the seat, pressed his palm against his wounded leg, and peered into the woman's veil. Elaborate ringlets, pale and seeming shot with grey, showed the sustained attentions of a gifted lady's-maid. But the face seemed to possess a strange familiarity.

"Do I know you, madame?" Mallory asked.

There was no answer.

"May I escort you?" he suggested. "Do you have any *proper* friends at the Derby, madame? Someone to look after you?"

"The Royal Enclosure," she murmured.

"You desire to go to the Royal Enclosure?" The idea of troubling the Royal Family with this dazed mad-woman was rather more than Mallory was willing to countenance. Then it struck him that it would be a very simple matter to find police there; and this was a police business of some kind, without a doubt.

Humoring the unhappy woman would be his simplest course of action. "Very well, ma'am," he said. He tucked the wooden box under one arm and offered her his other elbow. "We shall proceed at once to the Royal Enclosure. If you would come with me, please."

Mallory led her toward the stands, through a torrent of people, limping a bit. As they walked, she seemed to recover herself somewhat. Her gloved hand rested on his forearm as lightly as a cobweb.

Mallory waited for a break in the hubbub. He found one at last beneath the whited pillars of the stands. "May I introduce myself, ma'am? My name is Edward Mallory. I am a Fellow of the Royal Society; a paleontologist."

"The Royal Society," the woman muttered absently, her veiled head nodding like a flower on a stalk. She seemed to murmur something further.

"I beg your pardon?"

"The Royal Society! We have sucked the life-blood from the mysteries of the universe. . . ."

Mallory stared.

"The fundamental relations in the science of harmony," the woman continued, in a voice of deep gentility, great weariness, and profound calm, "are susceptible to mechanical expression, allowing the composition of elaborate and scientific pieces of music, of any degree of complexity or extent."

"To be sure," Mallory soothed.

"I think, gentlemen," the woman whispered, "that when you see certain productions of mine, you will not despair of me! In their own way, my marshaled regiments shall ably serve the rulers of the earth. And of what materials shall my regiments consist? . . . Vast *numbers*."

She had seized Mallory's arm with feverish intensity.

"We shall march in irresistible power to the sound of *music*." She turned her veiled face to him, with a queer sprightly earnestness. "Is not this very mysterious? Certainly *my* troops must consist of *numbers* or they can have no existence at all. But then, what *are* these numbers? There is a riddle. . . ."

"Is this your box, ma'am?" Mallory said, offering it to her, hoping to spark some return to sense.

She looked at the box, without apparent recognition. It was a handsome thing of polished rosewood, its corners bound in brass; it might have been a lady's glove-box, but it was too stark, and lacked elegance. The long lid was latched shut by a pair of tiny brass hooks. She reached out to stroke it with a gloved forefinger, as if assuring herself of its physical existence. Something about it seemed to sting her into a dawning recognition of her own distress. "Will you hold it for me, sir?" she asked Mallory at last, her quiet voice trembling with a strange, piteous appeal. "Will you hold it for me in safe-keeping?"

"Of course!" Mallory said, touched despite himself. "Of course I will hold it for you; as long as you like, madame."

They worked their way slowly up the stands to the carpeted stairs that led to the Royal Enclosure. Mallory's leg smarted sharply, and his trouser was sticky with blood. He was dizzier than he felt he should have been from such a minor wound; something about the woman's queer speech and odder demeanor had turned his head. Or perhaps—the dark thought occurred to him—there had been some sort of venom coating the tout's stiletto. He was sorry now that he had not snatched up the stiletto for a later analysis. Perhaps the mad-woman too had been somehow narcotized; likely he had foiled some dark plot of abduction. . . .

Below them, the track had been cleared for the coming gurney-race. Five massive gurneys—and the tiny, bauble-like *Zephyr*—were taking their places. Mallory paused a moment, torn, contemplating the frail craft upon which his fortunes now so absurdly hinged. The woman took that moment to release his arm and hasten toward the white-washed walls of the Royal Box.

Mallory, surprised, hurried after her, limping. She paused for a moment beside a pair of guards at the door—plain-clothes policemen, it seemed, very tall and fit. The woman brushed aside her veil, with a swift gesture of habit, and Mallory caught his first proper glimpse of her face.

She was Ada Byron, the daughter of the Prime Minister. Lady Ada Byron, the Queen of Engines.

She slipped through the door, beyond the guards, without so much as a glance behind her, or a single word of thanks. Mallory, lugging the rosewood box, hurried after her at once. "Wait!" he cried. "Your Ladyship!"

"Just a moment, sir!" the larger policeman said, quite politely. He held up a beefy hand, looked Mallory up and down, noting the wooden case, the dampened trouser-leg. His mustached mouth quirked. "Are you a guest in the Royal Enclosure, sir?"

"No," Mallory said. "But you must have seen Lady Ada step through here a moment ago. Something quite dreadful has happened to her; I'm afraid she's in some distress. I was able to be of some assistance—"

"Your name, sir?" barked the second policeman.

"Edward . . . Miller," Mallory blurted, a sudden chill of protective suspicion striking him at the last instant.

"May I see your citizen-card, Mr. Miller?" said the first policeman. "What's in that box you carry? May I look inside it,
please?"

Mallory swung the box away, took a step back. The policeman
stared at him with a volatile mix of disdain and suspicion.

There was a loud report from the track below. Steam whistled
from a ruptured seam in the Italian gurney, fogging out across
the stands like a geyser. There was some small panic in the stands.
Mallory seized this opportunity to hobble off; the policemen,
worried perhaps about the safety of their post, did not choose to
pursue him.

He hurried, limping, down the stands, losing himself as soon
as possible amid the crowd. Some notion of self-preservation
caused him to snatch his striped engineer's cap from his head
and shove it in the pocket of his coat.

He found a place in the stands, many yards from the Royal
Enclosure. He balanced the brass-bound box across his knees.
There was a trifling rip in his trouser-leg, but the wound beneath
it was still oozing. Mallory grimaced in confusion as he sat, and
pressed the palm of his hand against the aching wound.

"Damme," said a man on the bench behind him, his voice thick
with self-assurance and drink. "This false start will take the pressure down. Simple matter of specific heat. It means the biggest
boiler wins surely."

"Which one's that, then?" said the man's companion, perhaps
his son.

The man ruffled through a racing tip-sheet. "That'll be the
Goliath. Lord Hansell's racer. Her sister-craft won last year. . . ."

Mallory looked down upon the hoof-beaten track. The driver
of the Italian racer was being carried off on a stretcher, having
been extricated with some difficulty from the cramped confines
of his pilot's station. A column of dirty steam still rose from the
rent in the Italian boiler. Racing-attendants hitched a team of
horses to the disabled hulk.

Tall white gouts rose briskly from the stacks of the other racers.

The crenellations of polished brass crowning the stack of the *Goliath* were especially impressive. It utterly dwarfed the slender, peculiarly delicate stack of Godwin's *Zephyr,* braced with guy-wires, which repeated in cross-section the teardrop formula of line-streaming.

"A terrible business!" opined the younger man. "I do believe the burst took that poor foreigner's head clean off, quite."

"Not a bit of it," said the older man. "Fellow had a fancy helmet."

"He's not moving, sir."

"If the Italians can't compete properly in the technical arena, they've no business here," the older man said sternly.

A roar of appreciation came from the crowd as the disabled steamer was hauled free by the laboring horses. "We'll see some proper sport now!" said the older man.

Mallory, waiting tensely, found himself opening the rosewood box, his thumbs moving on the little brass catches as if by their own volition. The interior, lined with green baize, held a long stack of milky-white cards. He plucked one free from the middle of the stack. It was an Engine punch-card, cut to a French specialty-gauge, and made of some bafflingly smooth artificial material. One corner bore the handwritten annotation "#154," in faint mauve ink.

Mallory tucked the card carefully back into place and shut the box.

A flag was waved and the gurneys were off.

The *Goliath* and the French *Vulcan* lurched at once into the lead. The unaccustomed delay—the fatal delay, Mallory thought, his heart crushed within him—had cooled the tiny boiler of the *Zephyr,* leading no doubt to a vital loss of impetus. The *Zephyr* rolled in the wake of the greater machines, bumping half-comically in their deep-gouged tracks. It could not seem to get a proper traction.

Mallory did not find himself surprised. He was full of fatal resignation.

Vulcan and *Goliath* began to jostle for position at the first turn. The three other gurneys fell into file behind them. The *Zephyr,* quite absurdly, took the widest possible turn, far outside the tracks of the other craft. Master second-degree Henry Chesterton, at the wheel of the tiny craft, seemed to have gone quite mad. Mallory watched with the numb calm of a ruined man.

The *Zephyr* lurched into an impossible burst of speed. It slipped past the other gurneys with absurd, buttery ease, like a slimy pumpkin-seed squeezed between thumb and forefinger. At the half-mile turn, its velocity quite astonishing, it teetered visibly onto two wheels; at the final lap, it struck a slight rise, the entire vehicle becoming visibly airborne. The great driving-wheels rebounded from earth with a gout of dust and a metallic screech; it was only at that moment that Mallory realized that the great crowd in the stands had fallen into deathly silence.

Not a peep rose from them as the *Zephyr* whizzed across the finish-line. It slithered to a halt then, bumping violently across the gouged tracks left by the competition.

A full four seconds passed before the stunned track-man managed to wave his flag. The other gurneys were still rounding a distant bend a full hundred yards behind.

The crowd suddenly burst into astonished outcry—not joy so much as utter disbelief, and even a queer sort of anger.

Henry Chesterton stepped from the *Zephyr.* He tossed back a neck-scarf, leaned at his ease against the shining hull of his craft, and watched with cool insolence as the other gurneys labored painfully across the finish line. By the time they arrived, they seemed to have aged centuries. They were, Mallory realized, relics.

Mallory reached into his pocket. The blue slips of betting-paper were utterly safe. Their material nature had not changed in the slightest, but now these little blue slips infallibly signified the winning of four hundred pounds. No, *five hundred* pounds in all—fifty of that to be given to the utterly victorious Mr. Michael Godwin.

Mallory heard a voice ring in his ears, amid the growing tumult of the crowd. "I'm rich," the voice remarked calmly. It was his own voice.

He was rich.

This image is a formal daguerreotype of the sort distributed by the British aristocracy among narrow circles of friendship and acquaintance. The photographer may have been Albert, the Prince Consort, a man whose much-publicized interest in scientific matters had made him an apparently genuine intimate of Britain's Radical elite. The dimensions of the room, and the rich drapery of its back-drop, strongly suggest the photographing salon that Prince Albert maintained at Windsor Palace.

The women depicted are Lady Ada Byron and her companion and soi-disant chaperone, Lady Mary Somerville. Lady Somerville, the authoress of *On the Connection of the Physical Sciences* and the translator of Laplace's *Celestial Mechanics,* has the resigned look of a woman accustomed to the vagaries of her younger companion. Both women wear gilded sandals, and white draperies, somewhat akin to a Greek toga, but strongly influenced by French neo-classicism. They are, in fact, the garments of female adepts of the Society of Light, the secret inner body and international propaganda arm of the Industrial Radical Party. The elderly Mrs. Somerville also wears a fillet of bronze marked with astronomical symbols, a covert symbol of the high post this *femme savante* occupies in the councils of European science.

Lady Ada, her arms bare save for a signet-ring on her right forefinger, places a laurel wreath about the brow of a marble bust of Isaac Newton. Despite the careful placement of the camera, the strange garb does not flatter Lady Ada, and her face shows stress. Lady Ada was forty-one years old in late June 1855, when this daguerreotype was taken. She had recently lost a large sum of money at the Derby, though her gambling-losses, common knowledge among her intimates, seem to have covered the loss of even larger sums, most likely extorted from her.

She is the Queen of Engines, the Enchantress of Number. Lord

Babbage called her "Little Da." She has no formal role in government, and the brief flowering of her mathematical genius is far
behind her. But she is, perhaps, the foremost link between her
father, the Great Orator of the Industrial Radical Party, and
Charles Babbage, the Party's grey eminence and foremost social
theorist.

Ada is the mother.

Her thoughts are closed.

THIRD ITERATION
Dark-Lanterns

Picture Edward Mallory ascending the splendid central staircase in the Palace of Paleontology, its massive ebony railing supported by a black-enameled iron-work depicting ancient ferns, cycads, and ginkgoes.

Say that he is followed by a red-faced bellman burdened with a dozen glossy parcels, fruit of a long afternoon's careful, methodical shopping. As Mallory climbs, he sees that Lord Owen is heaving his massive way down the stairs, a peevish look in his rheumy eyes. The eyes of the distinguished reptile anatomist resemble shelled oysters, Mallory thinks, peeled and prepped for dissection. Mallory doffs his hat. Owen mutters something that might be a greeting.

At the turn of the first broad landing, Mallory glimpses a group of students seated by the open windows, quietly debating, while twilight settles over the crouching plaster behemoths of the Palace's rock-gardens.

A breeze disturbs the long linen curtains.

*　　　　　*　　　　　*

Mallory turned, right-face, left-face, before the wardrobe mirror. Unbuttoning the coat, he thrust his hands into the trouser-pockets, the better to display the waistcoat, which was woven in a dizzy mosaic of tiny blue-and-white squares. Ada Checkers, the tailors called them, the Lady having created the pattern by programming a Jacquard loom to weave pure algebra. The waistcoat carried off the whole business, he thought, though still it needed something, perhaps a cane. Flicking the hinge of his cigar-case, he offered a prime Havana to the gent in the mirror. A fine gesture but one couldn't carry a silver cigar-case about like a lady's muff; that was a faggot-above-a-load, surely.

A sharp metallic tapping issued from the speaking-tube set into the wall beside the door. Crossing the room, he flicked open the rubber-lined brass lid. "Mallory here!" he bellowed, bending. The desk-clerk's voice rose up, a distant hollow-throated ghostliness. "Visitor for you, Dr. Mallory! Shall I send up his card?"

"Yes, please!" Mallory, unaccustomed to closing the pneumatic grate, fumbled at the gilt-tin clasp. A cylinder of black gutta-percha shot from the tube as if fired from a gun, impacting solidly against the wall opposite. Hastening to fetch it, Mallory noted without surprise that the papered plaster wall there was already peppered with dents. He unscrewed the lid of the cylinder and shook out its contents. *Mr. Laurence Oliphant*, on lavish cream-laid card-stock, *Author and Journalist*. A Piccadilly address and a telegram-number. A journalist of some pretensions, to judge by his card. Vaguely familiar name. Hadn't he read something by an Oliphant in *Blackwood's*? Turning the card over, he examined the Engine-stippled portrait of a pale-haired gentleman gone balding in front. Large brown spaniel eyes, a quizzical half-smile, a draggle of beard beneath the chin. With the beard and the baldness, Mr. Oliphant's narrow skull looked as long as an Iguanodon's.

Mallory tucked the card into his notebook and glanced about his room. His bed was littered with the truck of his shopping: charge-slips, tissue-paper, glove-boxes, shoe-lasts.

"Please tell Mr. Oliphant I'll meet him in the lobby!"

Quickly filling the pockets of his new trousers, he let himself out, locking the door, and strode down the hall, past white walls of pocked and dotted fossil limestone framed by sweating columns of square dark marble, his new shoes squeaking with his every step.

Mr. Oliphant, unexpectedly long of limb, and most neatly but sumptuously dressed, reclined against the front desk, his back to the clerk. With elbows resting against the marble counter-top, and feet crossed at the ankles, the journalist's ramshackle pose conveyed the gentleman sportsman's easy indolence. Mallory, having met more than his share of gin-and-water reporters, hacks pursuing wide-eyed articles on the great Leviathan, registered a faint twinge of anxiety; this fellow evinced the smooth self-possession of the extremely well-advantaged.

Mallory introduced himself, discovering a sinewy strength in the journalist's long-fingered hand.

"I'm on the business of the Geographical Society," Oliphant announced, loudly enough to be overheard by a nearby group of loitering savants. "Exploration Committee, you see. Wondered if I mightn't consult you on a certain matter, Dr. Mallory."

"Of course," Mallory said. The Royal Geographical Society was lavishly funded; its powerful Exploration Committee decided upon the recipients of the Geographical's grants.

"May I suggest we speak in private, sir?"

"Surely," Mallory agreed, and followed the journalist into the Palace's saloon, where Oliphant found a quiet corner half-shadowed by a lacquered Chinese screen. Mallory threw back his coat-tails and took a chair. Oliphant perched at the far end of a red silk couch, his back to the wall. He gazed limpidly down the length of the saloon, and Mallory saw that he was checking for eavesdroppers.

"You seem to know the Palace well," Mallory ventured. "Are you often here, on your Committee's work?"

"Not frequently, no, though I once met a colleague of yours here, a Professor Francis Rudwick."

"Ah, Rudwick, yes; poor chap." Mallory was nettled a bit, but not surprised, to meet a professional connection of Rudwick's. Rudwick had rarely missed a chance to scruffle grant-money, from whatever source.

Oliphant nodded soberly. "I'm no savant, Dr. Mallory. I'm a writer of travel-books, actually. Trifles, really, though some have met with a degree of public favor."

"I see," Mallory said, convinced he'd the fellow's number now: wealthy idler, dilettante. Very likely he'd family connections. Most such eager dabblers were quite worthless to Science.

"Within the Geographical, Dr. Mallory," Oliphant began, "there presently exists intense debate as to our proper subject-matter. You are, perhaps, aware of the controversy?"

"I've been overseas," Mallory said, "and have missed a deal of news."

"No doubt you've been fully occupied with your own scientific controversy." Oliphant's smile was disarming. "Catastrophe versus Uniformity. Rudwick spoke of the matter often. Quite fiercely, I must say."

"A difficult business," Mallory muttered, "rather abstruse . . ."

"I personally found Rudwick's argument weak," Oliphant said offhandedly, to Mallory's pleasant surprise. The journalist leaned forward, with flattering attention. "Permit me to further explain the purpose of my visit, Dr. Mallory. Within the Geo-graphical, some consider that the Society might be better ad-vised, rather than plunging into Africa to discover the sources of the Nile, to investigate the sources of our own society. Why confine exploration to physical geography, when there are so many problems of political, and indeed moral, geography, prob-lems as yet unsolved?"

"Interesting," Mallory said, quite at a loss as to what his visitor might be getting at.

"As a prominent explorer," Oliphant said, "what might you say to a proposition of the following sort?" The man's gaze, curiously, seemed fixed now on the middle distance. "Suppose, sir, that one were to explore not the vastness of Wyoming but a specific corner of our own London. . . ."

Mallory nodded meaninglessly, and briefly entertained the possibility that Oliphant was mad.

"Mightn't we then, sir," the man continued, with a slight shiver, as of suppressed enthusiasm, "make utterly objective, entirely statistical investigations? Mightn't we examine society, sir, with a wholly novel precision and intensity? Divining, thereby, new principles—from the myriad clusterings of population over time, sir; from the most obscure travels of currency from hand to hand; from the turbulent flows of traffic. . . . Topics we now vaguely call police matters, health matters, public services—but perceived, sir, as by an all-searching, an all-pervasive, a scientific eye!"

There was far too much of the enthusiast's gleam in Oliphant's gaze, a sudden fierce kindling that showed his air of languor as a sham.

"In theory," Mallory hedged, "the prospect seems promising. As a practical matter, I doubt that the scientific societies could provide the Engine-resources necessary to such a broad and ambitious project. I myself have had to struggle to arrange a simple stress-analysis of the bones I've discovered. Engine-work is in constant demand. In any case, why should the Geographical Society tackle this matter? Why take funding from necessary foreign exploration-work? I should think perhaps a direct Parliamentary inquiry. . . ."

"But Government lack the vision necessary, the sense of intellectual adventure, the objectivity. Suppose it were the Engines of the police, though, instead of those of, say, the Cambridge Institute. What would you say then?"

"The Engines of the police?" Mallory said. The idea was quite extraordinary. "How should the police agree to a loan of their Engines?"

"The Engines are frequently idle at night," Oliphant said.

"Are they, really?" Mallory said. "My word, that *is* interesting. . . . But if those Engines were put to the use of Science, Mr.

Oliphant, I imagine other, more urgent projects would quickly consume the idle spinning-time. A proposal like yours would need powerful backing to make its way to the front of the queue."

"But, in theory, you do agree?" Oliphant persisted. "If the resources were available, you'd find the basic tenet worthy?"

"I would have to see a detailed proposal before I could actively support such a project, and I frankly doubt my voice would carry much weight in your Geographical Society. I'm not a Fellow there, you know."

"You underestimate your growing fame," Oliphant protested. "The nomination of Edward Mallory—discoverer of the Land Leviathan—would carry the Geographical with great ease."

Mallory was speechless.

"Rudwick became a Fellow," Oliphant said smoothly. "After the pterodactyl business."

Mallory cleared his throat. "I'm sure it's a worthy—"

"I shall consider it an honor if you will let me see to the matter personally," Oliphant said. "There will be no difficulty, I can promise you."

Oliphant's air of assurance brooked no doubt. Mallory recognized the fait accompli. He had been neatly maneuvered. There was no graceful way to refuse the favor, and a Fellowship in the wealthy and powerful Geographical was certainly not to be scorned. It would be a professional boon. He could see the Fellowship in his mind's eye, tacked to his name: Mallory, F.R.S., F.R.G.S. "The honor is all mine, sir," Mallory said, "though I fear you too much trouble yourself on my account."

"I take a profound interest in paleontology, sir."

"I'm surprised that a writer of travel-books would take such an interest."

Oliphant steepled his elegant fingers and brought them to his long, bare upper-lip. "I have found, Dr. Mallory, that 'journalist' is a usefully vague term, allowing one to make any number of odd inquiries. By nature, I am a man of broad but woefully shallow curiosity." Oliphant spread his hands. "I do what I can to be useful to true scholars, though I doubt I fully deserve my present unsought role in the inner circle of the august Geographical. Overnight fame has peculiar repercussions, you see."

"I must confess I'm not familiar with your books," Mallory said. "I've been overseas, and far behind in my reading. I take it you hit the public mark, then, and had a great success?"

"Not the *books*," Oliphant said, with surprised amusement. "I was involved in the Tokyo Legation affair. In Japan. Late last year."

"An outrage against our embassy in Japan, am I correct? A diplomat was injured? I was in America . . ."

Oliphant hesitated, then bent his left arm, tugging back coat-sleeve and immaculate cuff to reveal a puckered red scar at the outer joint of his left wrist. A knife-slash. No, worse than that: a saber-blow, into the tendons. Mallory noticed for the first time that two of the fingers on Oliphant's left hand were permanently bent.

"You, then! Laurence Oliphant, the hero of the Tokyo Legation! Now I remember the name." Mallory stroked his beard. "You should have put *that* upon your card, sir, and I would have recalled you instantly."

Oliphant worked his sleeve back, looking mildly embarrassed. "A Japanese sword-wound makes so odd a *carte d'identité*. . . ."

"Your interests are varied indeed, sir."

"Sometimes one can't avoid certain entanglements, Dr. Mallory. In the interests of the nation, as it were. I think you yourself know that situation very well."

"I'm afraid I don't follow you. . . ."

"Professor Rudwick, the *late* Professor Rudwick, certainly knew of such entanglements."

Mallory now grasped the nature of Oliphant's allusion. He spoke up roughly. "Your card, sir, declares you a journalist. These are not matters one discusses with a journalist."

"Your secret, I fear, is far from hermetic," said Oliphant, with polite disdain. "Every member of your Wyoming expedition knows the truth. Fifteen men, some less discreet than one might hope. Rudwick's men knew of his covert activities as well. Those who arranged the business, who asked you to carry out their scheme, know as well."

"And how, sir, do *you* know?"

"I've investigated Rudwick's murder."

"You think Rudwick's death was linked to his . . . American activities?"

"I know that to be the case."

"Before we go any further, I must be sure where we stand, Mr. Oliphant. When you say 'activities,' what exactly do you mean? Speak plain, sir. Define your terms."

"Very well." Oliphant looked pained. "I refer to the official body that persuaded you to smuggle repeating rifles to the American savages."

"And the name of this body?"

"The Royal Society's Commission on Free Trade," Oliphant said patiently. "They exist—officially—to study international trade-relations. Tariffs, investments, and so forth. Their ambition, I fear, over-reaches that authority."

"The Commission on Free Trade is a legitimate branch of Government."

"In the realm of diplomacy, Dr. Mallory, your actions might be construed as clandestinely arming the enemies of nations with whom Britain is not officially at war."

"And shall I conclude," Mallory began angrily, "that you take a very dim view of—"

"Gun-running. Though it has its place in the world, make no mistake." Oliphant was watching for eavesdroppers again. "But it must never be undertaken by self-appointed zealots with an over-weening notion of their role in foreign policy."

"You don't care for amateurs in the game, then?"

Oliphant met Mallory's eye, but said nothing.

"You want professionals, then, Mr. Oliphant? Men like yourself?"

Oliphant leaned forward, elbows on his knees. "A *professional* agency," he said precisely, "would not abandon its men to be eviscerated by foreign agents in the very heart of London, Dr. Mallory. And that, sir, I must inform you, is very near the position you find yourself in today. The Commission on Free Trade will help you no longer, however thoroughly you've done their work. They have not even informed you of the threat to your life. Am I wrong, sir?"

"Francis Rudwick died in a brawl in a ratting-den. And that was months ago."

"It was last January—five months only. Rudwick had returned from Texas, where he had been secretly arming the Comanche tribe with rifles supplied by your Commission. On the night of Rudwick's murder, someone attempted to take the life of the former President of Texas. President Houston very narrowly escaped. His secretary, a British citizen, was brutally knifed to death. The murderer is still very much at large."

"You think a Texian killed Rudwick, then?"

"I think it almost certain. Rudwick's activities may be poorly known here in London, but they're quite obvious to the unhappy Texians, who regularly extract British bullets from the corpses of their fellows."

"I dislike the way you paint the business," Mallory said, with a slow prickle of anger. "If we hadn't given them guns, they wouldn't have helped us. We might have dug for years, if it weren't for Cheyenne help. . . ."

"I doubt one could make that case to a Texas Ranger," Oliphant said. "For that matter, I doubt one could make it to the popular press. . . ."

"I've no intention of speaking to the press. I regret having spoken with you. Clearly you're no friend of the Commission."

"I already know far more about the Commission than I should have cared to discover. I came here to convey a warning, Dr. Mallory, not to request information. It is I who have spoken too openly—have been forced to do so, since the Commission's blundering has very obviously endangered your life, sir."

There was force in the argument. "A point well taken," Mallory admitted. "You have warned me, sir, and I thank you for that." He thought for a moment. "But what of the Geographical Society, Mr. Oliphant? What is their place in this?"

"An alert and observant traveler may serve his nation's interests with no prejudice to Science," Oliphant said. "The Geographical has long been a vital source of intelligence. Map-making, naval routes . . ."

Mallory pounced. "You don't call them 'amateurs', then, Mr. Oliphant? Though they too muck about with dark-lanterns, where they oughtn't?"

A silence stretched. "They're *our* amateurs," Oliphant said drily.

"But what, precisely, is the difference?"

"The *precise* difference, Dr. Mallory, is that the Commission's amateurs are being murdered."

Mallory grunted. He leaned back in the chair. Perhaps there was real substance to Oliphant's dark theory. The sudden death of Rudwick, his rival, his most formidable enemy, had always seemed too convenient a stroke of fortune. "What does he look like, then, this Texian assassin of yours?"

"He is described as tall, dark-haired, and powerfully built. He wears a broad-brimmed hat and a long pale greatcoat."

"He wouldn't be a ratty little race-track swell with a protruding forehead"—Mallory touched his temple—"and a stiletto in his pocket?"

Oliphant's eyes widened. "Dear heaven," he said softly.

Suddenly Mallory found he was enjoying himself. Discomfiting the suave spy had touched some deep vein of satisfaction. "Had a nick at me, this feller," Mallory said, in his broadest Sussex drawl. "Derby Day, at the races. Uncommon nasty little rascal. . . ."

"What happened?"

"I knocked the scoundrel down," Mallory said.

Oliphant stared at him, then burst into laughter. "You're a man of unexpected resources, Dr. Mallory."

"I might say the same of you, sir." Mallory paused. "I have to tell you, though, I don't believe the man was after me. He'd a girl with him, a track-dolly, the two of them bullying a lady—"

"Do go on," Oliphant urged, "this is uncommonly interesting."

"I'm afraid I can't," Mallory said. "The lady in question was a *personage*."

"Your discretion, sir," Oliphant said evenly, "does you credit as a gentleman. A knife-attack, however, is a serious crime. Have you not informed the police?"

"No," Mallory said, savoring Oliphant's contained agitation, "the lady again, you see. I feared to compromise her."

"Perhaps," Oliphant suggested, "it was all a charade, calculated to involve you in a supposed gambling-brawl. Something similar was worked on Rudwick—who died, you well recall, in a ratting-den."

"Sir," Mallory said, "the lady was none other than Ada Byron."

Oliphant stiffened. "The Prime Minister's daughter?"

"There is no other."

"Indubitably," Oliphant said, a sudden brittle lightness in his tone. "It does strike me, though, that there are any number of women who resemble Lady Ada, our Queen of Engines being a queen of fashion as well. Thousands of women follow her mode."

"I've never been introduced, Mr. Oliphant, but I've seen her in Royal Society sessions. I've heard her lecture on Engine mathematics. I am not mistaken."

Oliphant took a leather notebook from his jacket, propped it against one knee, and uncapped a reservoir-pen. "Tell me, please, about this incident."

"In strictest confidence?"

"You have my word."

Mallory presented a discreet version of the facts. He described Ada's tormentors, and the circumstances, to the best of his ability, but he made no mention of the wooden case with its French Engine-cards of camphorated cellulose. Mallory considered this a private matter between the Lady and himself; she had burdened him with the guardianship of this strange object of hers, and he regarded this as a sacred obligation. The wooden case of cards, carefully wrapped in white specimen-linen, lay hidden among the plastered fossils in one of Mallory's private lockers at the Museum of Practical Geology, awaiting his further attention.

Oliphant closed his notebook, put away his pen, and signaled the waiter for drinks. The waiter, recognizing Mallory, brought him a huckle-buff. Oliphant had a pink gin.

"I would like you to meet some friends of mine," Oliphant said. "The Central Statistics Bureau maintain extensive files on the criminal classes—anthropometric measurements, Engine-portraits, and so forth. I should like you to try to identify your assailant and his female accomplice."

"Very well," Mallory said.

"You shall be assigned police protection, as well."

"Protection?"

"Not a common policeman, of course. Someone from the Special Bureau. They are very discreet."

"I can't have some copper tagging always at my heels," Mallory said. "What would people say?"

"I worry rather more what they'll say if you were to be found gutted in some passage. Two prominent dinosaur-savants, the both of them mysteriously murdered? The press would run quite wild."

"I need no guard. I'm not frightened of the little pimp."

"He may well be unimportant. We shall at least know that, if you are able to identify him." Oliphant sighed delicately. "No doubt it's all a very trumpery affair, according to the standards of Empire. But I should reckon it as including the command of money; the services, when needed, of that shady sort of Englishman, who lives in the byways of foreign life in London; and lastly, the secret sympathy of American refugees, fled here from the wars that convulse that continent."

"And you imagine that Lady Ada has fallen somehow into this dire business?"

"No, sir, none of it. You may rest assured that that cannot possibly be the case. The woman you saw cannot have been Ada Byron."

"Then I regard the matter as settled," Mallory said. "If you were to tell me Lady Ada's interests were at hazard, I might agree to almost any measure. As things stand, I shall take my own chances."

"The decision is entirely yours, of course," Oliphant said coolly. "And perhaps it is still early in the game to take such stern measures. You have my card? Let me know how matters develop."

"I will."

Oliphant stood. "And remember, should anyone ask, that today we have discussed nothing more than the affairs of the Geographical Society."

"You've yet to tell me the name of your own employers, Mr. Oliphant. Your true employers."

Oliphant somberly shook his long head. "Such knowledge never profits, sir; there is nothing but grief in such questions. If you're wise, Dr. Mallory, you'll have nothing more to do with dark-lanterns. With luck, the whole affair will simply come to nothing, in the end, and will fade away, without trace, as a nightmare does. I shall certainly put your name forward for the Geographical, as I have promised, and I do hope that you will seriously consider my proposal regarding possible uses of the Bow Street Engines."

Mallory watched as this extraordinary personage rose, turned, and strode away, across the Palace's rich carpet, his long legs flashing like scissors.

Clutching his new valise with one hand, the overhead straps with another, Mallory inched his way along the crowded aisle of the omnibus to the rattling exit-platform. When the driver slowed for a filthy tarmac-wagon, Mallory jumped for the curb.

Despite his best efforts, Mallory had boarded the wrong 'bus. Or perhaps he had ridden too far on the correct vehicle, well past his destination, while engrossed in the latest number of the *Westminster Review*. He'd purchased the magazine because it carried an article of Oliphant's, a witty post-mortem on the conduct of the Crimean War. Oliphant, it developed, was something of an expert on the Crimean region, having published his *The Russian Shores of the Black Sea* a full year prior to the outbreak of hostilities. The book detailed a jolly but quite extensive Crimean holiday which Oliphant had undertaken. To Mallory's newly alerted eye, Oliphant's latest article bristled with sly insinuation.

A street-arab whipped with a broom of twigs at the pavement before Mallory's feet. The boy glanced up, puzzled. "Pardon, guv?" Mallory realized with an unhappy start that he had been talking to himself, standing there in rapt abstraction, muttering aloud over Oliphant's deviousness. The boy, grasping at Mallory's attention, did a back-somersault. Mallory tossed him tuppence, turned at random, and walked away, shortly discovering himself in Leicester Square, its gravel walks and formal gardens an excellent place to be robbed or ambushed. Especially at night, for the streets about featured theatres, pantos, and magic-lantern houses.

Crossing Whitcomb, then Oxenden, he found himself in Haymarket, strange in the broad summer daylight, its raucous whores absent now and sleeping. He walked the length of it, for curiosity's sake. It looked very different by day, shabby and tired of itself. At length, noting Mallory's pace, a pimp approached him, offering a packet of French-letters, sure armor against the lady's-fever.

Mallory bought them, dropping the packet into his valise.

Turning left, he marched into the chuffing racket of busy Pall Mall, the wide macadam lined by the black iron palings of exclusive clubs, their marbled fronts set well back from the street-jostle. Off Pall Mall, at the far end of Waterloo Place, stood the Duke of York's memorial. The Grand Old Duke of York, Who Had Ten Thousand Men, was a distant soot-blackened effigy now, his rotund column dwarfed by the steel-spired headquarters of the Royal Society.

Mallory had his bearings now. He tramped the elevated pedestrian-bridge, over Pall Mall, while below him sweating kerchief-headed navvies ripped at the intersection with a banging steel-armed excavator. They were preparing the foundation of a new monument, he saw, doubtless to the glory of the Crimean victory. He strode up Regent Street to the Circus, where the crowd poured endlessly forth from the underground's sooty marble exits. He allowed himself to be swept into swift currents of humanity.

There was a potent stench here, a cloacal reek, like burning vinegar, and for a moment Mallory imagined that this miasma emanated from the crowd itself, from the flapping crannies of their coats and shoes. It had a subterranean intensity, some fierce deep-buried chemistry of hot cinders and septic drippings, and now he realized that it must be pistoned out somehow, forced from the hot bowels of London by the charging trains below. Then he was being jostled up Jermyn Street, and in a moment he was smelling the heady wares of Paxton and Whitfield's cheese emporium. Hurrying across Duke Street, the stench forgotten, he paused below the wrought-iron lamps of the Cavendish Hotel, secured the fastenings of his valise, then crossed to his destination, the Museum of Practical Geology.

It was an imposing, sturdy, fortress-like edifice; Mallory thought it much like the mind of its Curator. He trotted up the steps into a welcome stony chill. Signing the leather-bound visitor's book with a flourish, he strode on, into the vast central hall, its walls lined with shining glass-fronted cabinets of rich mahogany. Light poured down from the great cupola of steel and glass, where a lone cleaner dangled now in his shackled harness, polishing one pane after another in what Mallory supposed would amount to an unending rota.

On the Museum's ground floor were displayed the Vertebrata, along with various pertinent illustrations of the marvels of stratigraphical geology. Above, in a railed and pillared gallery, were a series of smaller cabinets containing the Invertebrata. The day's crowd was of gratifying size, with surprising numbers of women and children, including an entire uniformed class of scruffy, working-class school-boys from some Government academy. They studied the cabinets with grave attention, aided by red-jacketed guides.

Mallory ducked through a tall, unmarked door and down a hall flanked by locked storerooms. At the hall's end, a single magisterial voice was audible through the closed door of the Curator's office. Mallory knocked, then listened, smiling, as the voice completed a particularly orotund rhetorical period. "Enter," rang the voice of the Curator. Mallory stepped inside as Thomas Henry Huxley rose to greet him. They shook hands. Huxley had been dictating to his secretary, a bespectacled young man with the look of an ambitious graduate student. "That will be all for now, Harris," Huxley said. "Send in Mr. Reeks, please, with his sketches of the Brontosaurus."

The secretary tucked his penciled notes into a leather folio and left, with a bow to Mallory.

"How've you been, Ned?" Huxley looked Mallory up and down, with the narrow-set, pitilessly observant eyes that had discovered "Huxley's Layer" in the root of the human hair. "You look very well indeed. One might even say splendid."

"Had a bit of luck," Mallory said gruffly.

To Mallory's surprise, he saw a small, fair-haired boy, neatly dressed in a flat-collared suit and knee-breeches, emerge from behind Huxley's heaped desk. "And who is *this*?" Mallory said.

"Futurity," Huxley quipped, bending to pick up the child. "My son, Noel, come to help his father today. Say how-do-you-do to Dr. Mallory, son."

"How do you do, Mr. Mellowy?" the boy piped.

"*Doctor Mallory*," Huxley corrected gently.

Noel's eyes widened. "Are you a *medical* doctor, Mr. Mellowy?" The thought clearly alarmed him.

"Why, you could scarcely walk when last we met, Master Noel," Mallory boomed heartily. "And here you are today, quite the little gentleman." He knew that Huxley doted on the child. "How's your baby brother, then?"

"He has a sister now as well," Huxley announced, setting the boy down. "Since you were in Wyoming."

"You must be happy at that, Master Noel!"

The little boy smiled briefly, with guarded politeness. He

hopped up into his father's chair. Mallory set his valise atop a bookcase, which contained a morocco-bound set of the works of Cuvier in the original. "I have an item that may interest you, Thomas," he said, opening his valise. "A gift for you from the Cheyenne." Remembering to tuck the French-letters beneath the *Westminster Review,* he brought out a string-tied paper bundle and carried it to Huxley.

"I hope this isn't one of those ethnographical curios," Huxley said, smiling, as he parted the string neatly with a paper-knife. "I can't abide those wretched beads and whatnot. . . ."

The paper held six shriveled brown wafers, the size of half-crowns.

"A helpful bequest to you from a Cheyenne medicine man, Thomas."

"Rather like our Anglican bishops, are they?" Huxley smiled, holding one of the leathery objects to the light. "Dried vegetable matter. A cactus?"

"I would think so."

"Joseph Hooker of Kew could tell us."

"This witch-doctor chap had a fair grasp of the purpose of our expedition. He fancied that we meant to re-vivify the dead monster, here in England. He said that these wafers would enable you to journey far, Thomas, and fetch back the creature's soul."

"And what do I do, Ned, string them on a rosary?"

"No, Thomas, you eat them. You eat them, chant, beat drums, and dance like a dervish, until you fall down in a fit. That's the standard methodology, I take it." Mallory chuckled.

"Certain vegetable toxins have the quality of producing visions," Huxley remarked, putting the wafers carefully away in a desk-drawer. "Thank you, Ned. I'll see they're properly catalogued, later. I fear the pressure of business has confounded our Mr. Reeks. He is usually more prompt."

"It's a good crowd out there, today," Mallory offered, to fill the silence. Huxley's boy had pulled a toffee from his pocket and was unwrapping it with surgical precision.

"Yes," Huxley said, "Britain's museums, our fortresses of intellect, as the P.M. puts it in his eloquent way. Still, no use denying that education, mass education, is the single great work at hand. Though there are days when I would throw it all over, Ned, to be a field-man like yourself again."

"You're needed here, Thomas."

"So they tell me," Huxley said. "I do try to get out, once a year. Wales, mostly . . . tramp the hills. It restores the soul." He paused. "Did you know I am up for a Lordship?"

"No!" Mallory cried, delighted. "Tom Huxley, a Lord! 'Struth! What splendid news."

Huxley looked unexpectedly morose. "I saw Lord Forbes at the Royal Society. 'Well,' Forbes said, 'I am glad to tell you that you are all right for the House of Lords; the selection was made on Friday night, and I hear that you were one of those selected.' " Huxley, without apparent effort, had Forbes' gestures, his phrasing, even his tone of voice. He glanced up. "I haven't seen the List, but the authority of Forbes is such that I feel somewhat assured."

"Of course!" Mallory exulted. "A stout fellow, Forbes!"

"I shan't feel entirely certain until I receive official confirmation," Huxley said. "I confess, Ned, to some anxiety about it, the health of the Prime Minister being what it is."

"Yes, a pity he's ill," Mallory said. "But why should that concern you so? Your accomplishments speak for themselves!"

Huxley shook his head. "The timing seems no accident. I suspect this is some ploy of Babbage and his elite cronies, a last attempt to pack the Lords with scientific savants while Byron still holds sway."

"That's a dark suspicion," Mallory said. "You were Evolution's greatest advocate in debate! Why question your good fortune? It seems to me a matter of simple justice!"

Huxley grasped his own lapels, two-handed, a gesture of deep sincerity. "Whether I have the Lordship or not, I can say one thing: I have left my case to stand on its own strength. I have never asked for special favor. If the title is mine, it is not through any intrigue of my own."

"Intrigue does not enter into it!" Mallory said.

"Of course it does!" Huxley snapped. "Though you'll not hear me say it publicly." He lowered his voice. "But you and I have known each other many years now. I count you as an ally, Ned, and a friend of truth."

Huxley began to pace the Turkish carpet before his desk. "It is no use, our having any false modesty about a matter so important. We have certain vital duties to perform; to ourselves, to the outside world, and to Science. We swallow praise, which is no great pleasure, and endure multitudinous difficulties, involving a good deal of unquestionable pain, pain and even danger."

Mallory was unsettled, taken aback both by the speed of the news and the sudden weight of Huxley's sincerity. Yet Huxley had always been like this, he thought; even as a young student, there had been a shock and an impetus to the man's company. For the first time since Canada, Mallory felt himself back in his true world, in the cleaner, higher plane that Huxley's mind inhabited. "Danger of what kind?" he asked belatedly.

"Moral danger. Physical danger as well. There is always hazard in the struggle for worldly power. A Lordship is a political post. Party and Government, Ned. Money and law. Temptation, perhaps ignoble compromise . . . The nation's resources are finite; competition is sharp. The niche of Science and Education must be defended; nay, expanded!" Huxley smiled grimly. "Somehow we must grasp the nettle. The alternative would be to lie still and let the devil have his way with the world to come. And I for one should rather burst to pieces, than see Science prostituted!"

Startled by Huxley's bluntness, Mallory glanced at the little boy, who was sucking his toffee and kicking his bright shiny shoes against the chair-legs.

"You're the man for the task, Thomas," Mallory said. "You know that you may have whatever help I can offer, if the cause ever needs me."

"It cheers me to hear that, Ned. I do trust in your strength of heart, your stubborn fixity of purpose. Proved true as steel, two years' hard labor in the Wyoming wilderness! Why, there are men I see every week, who claim great devotion to Science, yet dream of nothing but gold medals and professors' caps."

Huxley was pacing faster. "An abominable blur of cant, of humbug and self-seeking, surrounds everything in England to-day." Huxley stopped dead. "That is to say, Ned, that I sometimes suppose that I myself am tainted, the possibility of which I hold in morbid dread."

"Never," Mallory assured him.

"It's good to have you back among us," Huxley said, resuming his pacing. "And famous, better yet! We must capitalize on that advantage. You must write a travel-book, a thorough account of your exploits."

"Odd that you should mention that," Mallory said. "I have just such a book here in my bag. *The Mission to China and Japan*, by Laurence Oliphant. A very clever chap, it seems."

"Oliphant of the Geographical? Man's a hopeless case; too clever by half, and lies like a politician. No, I propose a popular rendition, something a mechanic can understand, the sort of chap who furnishes his sitting-room with a Pembroke table and a crockery shepherd and shepherdess! I tell you, Ned, that it's vital to the great work. Good money in it as well."

Mallory was taken aback. "I talk well enough when I've a head of steam up, but to write a whole book in cold blood . . ."

"We'll find you a Grub Street hack to varnish the rougher bits," Huxley said, "a common enough stratagem, believe me. This fellow Disraeli, whose father founded *Disraeli's Quarterly,* you know. Bit of a madcap. Writes sensation-novels. Trash. But he's steady enough when he's sober."

"Benjamin Disraeli? My sister Agatha dotes on his romances."

Something in Huxley's nod was meant to tell Mallory that a female of the Huxley clan would not be caught dead with a popular novel. "We must talk about your Royal Society Symposium, Ned, your forthcoming address on the Brontosaurus. It will be quite the event, a very useful public podium. Do you have a good picture, for publicity?"

"Why, no," Mallory said.

"Maull and Polyblank are your men, then, daguerreotypists to the gentry."

"I'll make a note of that."

Huxley crossed to the mahogany-framed blackboard behind his desk, taking up a sterling chalk-holder. *Maull & Polyblank,* he wrote, in quick, flowing cursive.

He turned. "You'll need a kinotropist as well, and I've just the fellow. He does a good deal of Royal Society work. Tends to somewhat excessively fancy work, so he'll steal your show with his clacking, given half a chance. Loading every rift with ore, as he puts it. But he's a clever little chap."

John Keats, he wrote.

"This is invaluable, Thomas!"

Huxley paused. "There's another matter, Ned. I hesitate to mention it."

"What is that?"

"I don't wish to wound your personal feelings."

Mallory smiled falsely. "I do know I'm not much of a speaker, but I have held my own in the past."

Huxley paused, then lifted his hand abruptly. "What do you call this?"

"I call it a piece of chalk," Mallory said, humoring him.

"Chaark?"

"Chalk!" Mallory repeated.

"We must do something about those broad Sussex vowels, Ned. There's a fellow I know, an elocutionist. Very discreet little man. French, actually, but he speaks the finest English you've ever heard. A week's lessons with him would do wonders."

Mallory scowled. "You're not saying I *need* wonders, I should hope?"

"Not at all! It's a simple matter of educating one's ear. You'd be surprised to know how many rising public speakers have patronized this gentleman." *Jules D'Alembert,* Huxley wrote. "His lessons are a bit dear, but—"

Mallory took the name down.

A knock came at the door. Huxley swiped at the board with the dusty felt of an ebony-handled eraser. "Enter!" A stocky man in a plaster-spotted apron appeared. "You'll remember Mr. Trenham Reeks, our Assistant Curator."

Reeks tucked a tall folio-binder under his arm and shook Mallory's hand. Reeks had lost some hair and put on weight since Mallory had last seen him. "Sorry for the delay, sir," Reeks said. "We're having a time of it in the studio, casting those vertebrae. Astonishing structure. The sheer scale presents terrific problems."

Huxley cleared a space on his desk. Noel tugged his father's sleeve, and whispered something. "Oh, very well," Huxley said. "Pardon us a moment, gentlemen." He led Noel from the office.

"Congratulations on your promotion, Mr. Reeks," Mallory said.

"Thank you, sir," Reeks said. He opened the binder, then set a ribboned pince-nez on his nose. "And thank you for this great discovery. Though I must say, it challenges the very scale of our institution!" He tapped at a sheet of graphed foolscap. "As you may see."

Mallory studied the sketch, a floor-plan of the Museum's central hall, with the skeleton of the Leviathan superimposed. "Where's its skull?" he said.

"The neck extends completely into the entrance-hall," Reeks said proudly. "We shall have to move several cabinets. . . ."

"Do you have a side-view?"

Reeks plucked it from the sheaf of sketches. Mallory examined it, scowling. "What is your authority for this anatomical arrangement?"

"There are very few published papers on the creature, to date," Reeks said, hurt. "The longest and most thorough is by Dr. Foulke, in last month's *Transactions*." He offered the magazine from within the folder.

Mallory brushed it aside. "Foulke has completely distorted the nature of the specimen."

Reeks blinked. "Dr. Foulke's reputation—"

"Foulke is a Uniformitarian! He was Rudwick's cabinet-man,

one of his closest allies. Foulke's paper is a tissue of absurdities. He claims that the beast was cold-blooded and semi-aquatic! That it ate soft water-plants and moved sluggishly."

"But a creature of this vast size, Dr. Mallory, this enormous weight! It would seem that a life in water, to support the mass alone . . ."

"I see," Mallory broke in. He struggled to regain his temper. It was no use annoying poor Reeks; the man was a functionary, who knew no better, and meant well. "This explains why you have its neck stretched out limply, almost at floor-level . . . and it also accounts for the lizard-like—no, the *amphibian*—jointing of its legs."

"Yes, sir," Reeks said. "One envisions it harvesting water-plants with that long neck, you see, seldom needing to move its great body very far, or very swiftly. Except perhaps to wade away from predators, if there were anything hungry enough to tackle such a monster."

"Mr. Reeks, this creature was not some great soft-bodied salamander. You have been made the victim of a grave misconception. This creature was like a modern elephant, like a giraffe, but on a far greater scale. It was evolved to rip out and devour the tops of trees."

Mallory took a pencil from the desk and began to sketch rapidly and expertly. "It spent much of its time on its hind legs, propped on its tail, with its head far above the ground. Make a note of this thickening in the caudal vertebrae. A sure sign of enormous pressure, from a bipedal stance." He tapped the blueprint, and went on. "A herd of these creatures could have demolished an entire forest in short order. They migrated, Mr. Reeks, as elephants do, over vast distances, and quickly, changing the very landscape with their devastating appetites. The Brontosaur had an erect, narrow-chested stance, its legs quite columnar and vertical, for the swift, stiff-kneed stride of an elephant. None of this frog-like business."

"I modeled the stance on the crocodile," Reeks protested.

"The Cambridge Institute of Engine Analytics has completed

my stress-analysis," Mallory said. He stepped to his valise, pulled out a bound sheaf of fan-fold paper, and slapped it down. "The creature could not have stood a moment on dry land, with its legs in that absurd position."

"Yes, sir," Reeks said quietly. "That accounts for the aquatic hypothesis."

"Look at its toes!" Mallory said. "They're thick as foundation-stones; not the webbed feet of a swimmer. And look at the flanges of its spinal vertebrae. This creature levered itself up at the hip-joint, to reach great heights. Like a construction-crane!"

Reeks removed his pince-nez. He began to polish it with a linen kerchief from his trouser-pocket. "This is not going to please Dr. Foulke," he said. "Or his colleagues either, I daresay."

"I've not yet begun with that lot," Mallory said.

Huxley re-entered the office, leading his son by the hand. He looked from Reeks to Mallory. "Oh dear," he said. "Already deep into it, I see."

"It's this nonsense of Foulke's," Mallory said. "He seems determined to prove that dinosaurs were unfit to live! He's portrayed my Leviathan as a buoyed slug, sucking up pond-weed."

"You must agree it hadn't much of a brain," Huxley said.

"It doesn't follow, Thomas, that it was torpid. Everyone admits that Rudwick's dinosaur could fly. These creatures were swift and active."

"Actually, now that Rudwick's no longer with us, there's some revisionary thought on that topic," Huxley said. "Some say his flying reptile could only glide."

Mallory bit back a curse, for the sake of the child in the room. "Well, it all comes back to basic theory, doesn't it," he said. "The Uniformitarian faction wish these creatures to seem dull and sluggish! Dinosaurs will then fit their slope of gradual development, a slow progression to the present day. Whereas, if you grant the role of Catastrophe, you admit a far greater state of Darwinian fitness for these magnificent creatures, wounding as that may seem to the vanities of tiny modern-day mammals on the order of Foulke and his cronies."

Huxley sat down. He propped one hand against his whiskered cheek. "You disagree with the arrangement of the specimen?"

"It seems Dr. Mallory prefers it standing," Reeks said. "Prepared to dine upon a tree-top."

"Could we manage that position, Mr. Reeks?"

Reeks looked startled. He tucked his pince-nez in a pocket behind his apron. Then he scratched his head. "I think perhaps we might, sir. If we mounted it under the skylight, and braced it from the ceiling-girders. Might have to bend its neck a bit. . . . We could aim its head at the audience! It *would* be quite dramatic."

"A sop to the Cerberus of popularity," Huxley said. "Though I question the consequences to the fluttered nerves of paleontology. I confess I'm not at all at ease with this argument. I've not yet read Foulke's paper, and you, Mallory, have yet to publish on the topic. And I shouldn't care to add to the heat of the Catastrophist debate. 'Natura non facit saltum.' "

"But Nature *does* leap," Mallory said. "The Engine simulations prove it. Complex systems can make sudden transformations."

"Never mind the theory. What can you make of the evidence directly at hand?"

"I can make a good case. I will, at my public lecture. Not a perfect case, but better than the opposition's."

"Would you stake your reputation as a scholar on it? Have you considered every question, every objection?"

"I could be wrong," Mallory said. "But not so entirely wrong as they are."

Huxley tapped his desk with a reservoir-pen. "What if I ask— as an elementary matter—how this creature could have eaten woody foliage? Its head is scarcely larger than a horse's, and its teeth are remarkably poor."

"It didn't chew with its teeth," Mallory said. "It had a gizzard, lined with grinding stones. Judging by the size of the ribcage, this organ must have been a yard long and weighed perhaps a hundred pounds. A hundred-weight of gizzard has more muscular power than the jaws of four bull elephants."

"Why would a reptile need that quantity of nourishment?"

"It wasn't warm-blooded per se, but it had a high metabolism. It's a simple matter of surface-to-volume ratios. A bodily mass of that size retains its heat even in cold weather." Mallory smiled. "The equations are simply calculated, requiring no more than an hour on one of the Society's smaller Engines."

"Dire trouble will come of this," Huxley murmured.

"Are we to let politics stand in the way of truth?"

"*Touché.* He has us, Mr. Reeks. . . . I'm afraid you must alter your painstaking plans."

"The lads in the studio love a challenge, sir," Reeks said loyally. "And if I may say so, Dr. Huxley, a controversy does wonders for our attendance."

"One more minor matter," Mallory said quickly. "The condition of the skull. Alas, the specimen's skull is quite fragmentary, and will require close study, and a certain amount of conjecture. I should like to join you in the studio on the matter of the skull, Mr. Reeks."

"Certainly, sir. I'll see that you're given a key."

"Lord Gideon Mantell taught me everything I knew about the modeling of plaster," Mallory declared, with a show of nostalgia. "It's been too long since I last came to grips with that worthy craft. It will be a great pleasure to observe the latest advances in technique, in such exemplary surroundings."

Huxley smiled, with a hint of dubiousness. "I do hope we can satisfy you, Ned."

Mopping the back of his neck with a kerchief, Mallory unhappily contemplated the headquarters of the Central Statistics Bureau.

Ancient Egypt had been dead for twenty-five centuries, but Mallory had come to know it well enough to dislike it. The French excavation of the Suez Canal had been an heroic business, so that all things Egyptian had become the Parisian mode. The rage had seized Britain as well, leaving the nation awash with scarab neck-pins, hawk-winged teapots, lurid stereographs of toppled ob-elisks, and faux-marble miniatures of the noseless Sphinx.

Manufacturers had Engine-embroidered that whole beast-headed rabble of pagan godlets on curtains and carpets and carriage-robes, much to Mallory's distaste, and he had come to take an especial dislike to silly maunderings about the Pyramids, ruins which inspired exactly the sort of chuckle-headed wonderment that most revolted his sensibilities.

He had, of course, read admiringly of the engineering feats of Suez. Lacking coal, the French had fueled their giant excavators with bitumen-soaked mummies, stacked like cordwood and sold by the ton. Still, he resented the space usurped by Egyptology in the geographical journals.

The Central Statistics Bureau, vaguely pyramidal in form and excessively Egyptianate in its ornamental detail, squatted solidly in the governmental heart of Westminster, its uppermost stories slanting to a limestone apex. For the sake of increased space, the building's lower section was swollen out-of-true, like some great stone turnip. Its walls, pierced by towering smokestacks, supported a scattered forest of spinning ventilators, their vanes annoyingly hawk-winged. The whole vast pile was riddled top to bottom with thick black telegraph-lines, as though individual streams of the Empire's information had bored through solid stone. A dense growth of wiring swooped down, from conduits and brackets, to telegraph-poles crowded thick as the rigging in a busy harbor.

Mallory crossed the hot sticky tarmac of Horseferry Road, wary of the droppings of the pigeons clustered in the web-work of cable overhead.

The Bureau's fortress-doors, framed by lotus-topped columns and Briticized bronze sphinxes, loomed some twenty feet in height. Smaller, work-a-day doors were set into their corners. Mallory, scowling, strode into cool dimness and the faint but pervasive odors of lye and linseed oil. The simmering London stew was behind him now, but the damned place had no windows. Egyptianate jets lit the darkness, their flames breezily guttering in fan-shaped reflectors of polished tin.

He showed his citizen-card at the visitors' desk. The clerk—or perhaps he was some sort of policeman, for he wore a new-fangled Bureau uniform with an oddly military look—made careful note of Mallory's destination. He took an Engine-printed floor-plan of the building from beneath his counter, and marked out Mallory's twisting route in red ink.

Mallory, still smarting from the morning's meeting with the Nominations Committee of the Geographical, thanked the man rather too brusquely. Somehow—he didn't know which devious strings had been pulled back-stage, but the plot was clear enough—Foulke had maneuvered his way onto the Geographical's Nominations Committee. Foulke, whose aquatic theory of Brontosaurus had been spurned by Huxley's museum, had taken Mallory's arborivore hypothesis as a personal attack, with the result that an ordinarily pleasant formality had become yet another public trial for radical Catastrophism. Mallory had won his Fellowship, in the end, Oliphant having laid the ground too well for Foulke's last-minute ambush to succeed, but the business still rankled. He sensed damage to his reputation. Dr. Edward Mallory—"Leviathan Mallory," as the penny-papers insisted on having it—had been made to seem fanatical, even petty. And this in front of dignified geographers of the first rank, men like Burton of Mecca and Elliot of the Congo.

Mallory followed his map, muttering to himself. The fortunes of scholarly warfare, Mallory thought, had never seemed to favor him as they did Thomas Huxley. Huxley's feuds with the powers-that-be had only distinguished him as a wizard of debate, while Mallory was reduced to trudging this gas-lit mausoleum, where he hoped to identify a despicable race-track pimp.

Taking his first turn, he discovered a marble bas-relief depicting the Mosaic Plague of Frogs, which he had always numbered among his favorite Biblical tales. Pausing in admiration, he was very nearly run down by a steel push-cart, stacked to the gunwales with decks of punch-cards.

"Gangway!" yelped the carter, in brass-buttoned serge and a messenger's billed cap. Mallory saw with astonishment that the man wore wheeled boots, stout lace-ups fitted with miniature axles and spokeless rounds of rubber. The fellow shot headlong down the hall, expertly steering the heavy cart, and vanished around a corner.

Mallory passed a hall, blocked off with striped saw-horses, where two apparent lunatics, in gas-lit gloom, crept slowly about on all fours. Mallory stared. The creepers were plump, middle-aged women, dressed throat-to-foot in spotless white, their hair confined by snug elastic turbans. From a distance their clothing had the eerie look of winding-sheets. As he watched, one of the pair lurched heavily to her feet and began to tenderly wipe the ceiling with a sponge-mop on a telescoping pole.

They were charwomen.

Following his map to a lift, he was ushered in by a uniformed attendant and carried to another level. The air, here, was dry and static, the corridors busier. There were more of the odd-looking policemen, admixed with serious-looking gentlemen of the capital: barristers perhaps, or attorneys, or the legislative agents of great capitalists, men whose business it was to acquire and retail knowledge of the attitudes and influence of the public. Political men, in short, who dealt entirely in the intangible. And though they presumably had their wives, their children, their brownstone homes, here they struck Mallory as vaguely ghost-like or ecclesiastical.

Some yards on, Mallory was forced to abruptly dodge a second wheeled messenger. He caught himself against a decorative cast-iron column. The metal scorched his hands. Despite its lavish ornamentation—lotus blossoms—the column was a smokestack. He could hear it emitting the muffled roar and mutter of a badly adjusted flue.

Consulting his map again, he entered a corridor lined left and right with offices. White-coated clerks ducked from door to door, dodging young messenger-boys rolling about with card-laden wheelbarrows. The gas-lights were brighter here, but they fluttered in a steady draft of wind. Mallory glanced over his shoulder.

At the end of the hall stood a giant steel-framed ventilator-fan. It squealed faintly, on an oiled chain-drive, propelled by an unseen motor in the bowels of the pyramid.

Mallory began to feel rather dazed. Likely this had all been a grave mistake. Surely there were better ways to pursue the mystery of Derby Day, than hunting pimps with some bureaucratic crony of Oliphant's. The very air of the place oppressed him, scorched and soapy and lifeless, the floors and walls polished and gleaming. . . . He'd never before seen a place so utterly free of common dirt. . . . These halls reminded him of something, another labyrinthine journey. . . .

Lord Darwin.

Mallory and the great savant had been walking the leaf-shadowed hedgy lanes of Kent, Darwin poking at the moist black soil with his walking-stick. Darwin talking, on and on, in his endless, methodical, crushingly detailed way, of earthworms. Earthworms, always invisibly busy underfoot, so that even great sarsen-stones slowly sank into the loam. Darwin had measured the process, at Stonehenge, in an attempt to date the ancient monument.

Mallory tugged hard at his beard, his map forgotten in his hand. A vision came to him of earthworms churning in catastrophic frenzy, till the soil roiled and bubbled like a witches' brew. In years, mere months perhaps, all the monuments of slower eons would sink shipwrecked to primeval bedrock. . . .

"Sir? May I be of service?"

Mallory came to himself with a start. A white-coated clerk was confronting him, staring into his face with bespectacled suspicion. Mallory glared back, confused. For a divine moment he had poised on the brink of revelation, and now it was gone, as miserably inglorious as a failed sneeze.

Worse yet, Mallory now realized he had been muttering aloud again. About earthworms, presumably. Gruffly, he proffered his map. "Looking for Level 5, QC-50."

"That would be Quantitative Criminology, sir. This is Deterrence Research." The clerk pointed at a shingle hung above a nearby office door. Mallory nodded numbly.

"QC is just past Nonlinear Analysis, around the corner to your right," the clerk said. Mallory moved on. He could feel the clerk's skeptical eyes on his back.

The QC section was a honeycomb of tiny partitions, the neck-high walls riddled with asbestos-lined cubbyholes. Gloved and aproned clerks sat neatly at their slanted desks, examining and manipulating punch-cards with a variety of specialized clacker's devices: shufflers, pin-mounts, isinglass color-coders, jeweler's loupes, oiled tissues, and delicate rubber-tipped forceps. Mallory watched the familiar work with a happy lurch of reassurance.

QC-50 was the office of the Bureau's Undersecretary for Quantitative Criminology, whose name, Oliphant had said, was Wakefield.

Mr. Wakefield possessed no desk, or rather his desk had encompassed and devoured the entirety of his office, and Wakefield worked from within it. Writing-tables sprang from wall-slots on an ingenious system of hinges, then vanished again into an arcane system of specialized cabinetry. There were newspaper-racks, letter-clamps, vast embedded card-files, catalogues, code-books, clackers'-guides, an elaborate multi-dialed clock, three telegraph-dials whose gilded needles ticked out the alphabet, and printers busily punching tape.

Wakefield himself was a pallid Scot with sandy, receding hair. His glance, if not positively evasive, was extremely mobile. A pronounced overbite dented his lower-lip.

He struck Mallory as very young for a man of his position, perhaps only forty. No doubt, like most accomplished clackers, Wakefield had grown up with the Engine trade. Babbage's very first Engine, now an honored relic, was still less than thirty years old, but the swift progression of Enginery had swept a whole generation in its wake, like some mighty locomotive of the mind.

Mallory introduced himself. "I regret my tardiness, sir," Mallory said. "I found myself a bit lost in your halls."

This was no news to Wakefield. "May I offer you tea? We have a very fine sponge cake."

Mallory shook his head, then opened his cigar-case with a flourish. "Smoke?"

Wakefield went pale. "No! No thank you. A fire hazard, strictly against regulations."

Mallory put his case away, chagrined. "I see. . . . But I don't see any real harm in a fine cigar, do you?"

"Ashes!" Wakefield said firmly. "And pneumatic particles! They float through air, soil the cog-oil, defile the gearing. And to clean the Bureau's Engines—well, I needn't tell you that's a Sisyphean task, Dr. Mallory."

"Surely," Mallory mumbled. He tried to change the subject. "As you must know, I am a paleontologist, but I have some small expertise in clacking. How many gear-yards do you spin here?"

"Yards? We measure our gearage in *miles* here, Dr. Mallory."

" 'Struth! That much power?"

"That much trouble, you might as easily say," Wakefield said, with a modest flick of his white-gloved hand. "Heat builds up from spinning-friction, which expands the brass, which nicks the cog-teeth. Damp weather curdles the gear-oil—and in dry weather, a spinning Engine can even create a small Leyden-charge, which attracts all manner of dirt! Gears gum and jam, punch-cards adhere in the loaders. . . ." Wakefield sighed. "We've found it pays well to take every precaution in cleanliness, heat, and humidity. Even our tea-cake is baked specially for the Bureau, to reduce the risk of crumbs!"

Something about the phrase "the risk of crumbs" struck Mallory as comic, but Wakefield had such a sober look that it was clear no jest was intended. "Have you tried Colgate's Vinegar-Cleanser?" Mallory asked. "They swear by it at Cambridge."

"Ah yes," Wakefield drawled, "the dear old Institute of Engine Analytics. I wish *we* had the leisurely pace of the academics! They pamper their brass at Cambridge, but here in public service, we must run and re-run the most grueling routines till we warp the decimal-levers."

Mallory, having been recently to the Institute, was up-to-date and determined to show it. "Have you heard of the new Cambridge compilers? They distribute gear-wear much more evenly—"

Wakefield ignored him. "For Parliament and the police, the Bureau is simply a resource, you see. Always on demand, but kept on a tight lead for all of that. Funding, you see. They cannot fathom our requirements, sir! The old sad story, as I'm sure you know. Man of science yourself. I don't mean to be disrespectful, but the House of Commons can't tell true clacking from a wind-up cooking-jack."

Mallory tugged his beard. "It does seem a pity. *Miles* of gearing! When I imagine what might be accomplished with that, the prospect is breathtaking."

"Oh, I'm sure you'd catch your breath soon enough, Dr. Mallory," Wakefield said. "In clacking, demand always expands to overmatch the capacity. It's as if it were a law of Nature!"

"Perhaps it is a law," Mallory said, "in some realm of Nature we've yet to comprehend. . . ."

Wakefield smiled politely and shot a glance at his clock. "A shame, when one's higher aspirations are overwhelmed by daily practicalities. I don't often have the chance to discuss Engine philosophy. Except with my soi-disant colleague, Mr. Oliphant, of course. Has he, perhaps, told you of his visionary schemes for our Engines?"

"Only quite briefly," Mallory said. "It seemed to me his plans for, er, social studies, would demand more Engine-power than we have in Great Britain. To monitor every transaction in Piccadilly, and so forth. Struck me as a Utopian fancy, frankly."

"In theory, sir," Wakefield responded, "it is *entirely* possible. We naturally keep a brotherly eye on the telegram-traffic, credit-records, and such. The human element is our only true bottle-neck, you see, for only a trained analyst can turn raw Engine-data into workable knowledge. And the ambitious scale of that effort, when compared with the modest scale of the Bureau's current funding for personnel—"

"I'm sure I wouldn't care to add to the pressing burden of your duty," Mallory broke in, "but Mr. Oliphant did indicate that you might help me to identify a criminal at large and his female accomplice. Having completed two of your request-forms in triplicate, I dispatched them in by special messenger. . . ."

"Last week, yes." Wakefield nodded. "And we've done our best for you. We're always happy to oblige gentlemen as peculiarly distinguished as Mr. Oliphant and yourself. An assault, and a threat of death against a prominent savant, is a serious matter, of course." Wakefield plucked up a needle-sharp pencil and a gridded pad of paper. "But a rather commonplace business, to attract Mr. Oliphant's specialized interests, isn't it?"

Mallory said nothing.

Wakefield looked grave. "You needn't fear to speak frankly, sir. This isn't the first time that Mr. Oliphant, or his superiors, have called on our resources. And, of course, as a sworn officer of the Crown, I can guarantee you the strictest confidentiality. Nothing you say will leave these walls." He leaned forward. "So. What can you tell me, sir?"

Mallory thought hard and quickly. Whatever blunder Lady Ada had committed—whatever act of desperation or recklessness had led her into the clutches of the tout and his whore—he could not imagine it helped by the name "Ada Byron" going onto that gridded pad. And Oliphant, of course, would not approve.

So Mallory feigned a reluctant confession. "You have me at a disadvantage, Mr. Wakefield, for I don't believe there's much to the matter—nothing to truly earn me the privilege of your attention! As I said in my note to you, I encountered a drunken gambler at the Derby, and the rascal made a bit of a show with a knife. I thought little enough of it—but Mr. Oliphant suggested that I might be in genuine danger. He reminded me that one of my colleagues was murdered recently, in odd circumstances. And the case is still unresolved."

"Professor Fenwick, the dinosaur savant?"

"Rudwick," Mallory said. "You know the case?"

"Stabbed to death. In a ratting-den." Wakefield tapped his

teeth with the pencil's rubber. "Made all the papers, threw quite a bad light on the savantry. One feels that Rudwick rather let the side down."

Mallory nodded. "My sentiments exactly. But Mr. Oliphant seemed to feel that the incidents might be connected."

"Gamblers, stalking and killing savants?" Wakefield said. "I see no motive, frankly. Unless perhaps, and do forgive the suggestion, a large gambling debt is involved. Were you and Rudwick close friends? Wagering companions, perhaps?"

"Not at all. I scarcely knew the man. And I owe no such debts, I assure you."

"Mr. Oliphant does not believe in accident," Wakefield said. He seemed to have been convinced by Mallory's evasion, for he was clearly losing interest. "Of course, it is only prudent of you to identify the rascal. If that's all you need of us, I'm sure we can be of service. I'll have a staffer take you to the library, and the Engines. Once we've this assailant's number, we'll be on firmer ground."

Wakefield flipped up a hinged rubber stopper and shouted into a speaking-tube. A young Cockney clerk appeared, in gloves and apron. "This is our Mr. Tobias," Wakefield said. "He's at your disposal." The interview was over—Wakefield's eyes were already glazing with the press of other business. He gave a mechanical bow. "Pleasure-to-have-met-you, sir. Please let me know if-we-can-be-of-any-further-service."

"You're most kind," Mallory said.

The boy had shaven an inch of scalp at his hairline, elevating his forehead for a modishly intellectual look, but time had passed since the clerk's last barbering, for he now had a prickly ridge of stubble across the front of his noggin. Mallory followed him out of the maze of cubicles into a hallway, noting his odd, rolling gait. The clerk's shoe-heels were worn so badly that the nails showed, and his cheap cotton stockings had bagged at the ankles.

"Where are we going, Mr. Tobias?"

"Engines, sir. Downstairs."

They paused at the lift, where an ingenious indicator showed that it was on another floor. Mallory reached into his trouser-pocket, past the jack-knife and the keys. He pulled out a golden guinea. "Here."

"What's this then?" Tobias asked, taking it.

"It is what we call a tip, my boy," Mallory said, with forced joviality. " 'To Insure Promptness,' you know."

Tobias examined the coin as if he had never seen the profile of Albert before. He gave Mallory a sharp and sullen look from behind his spectacles.

The lift's door opened. Tobias hid the coin in his apron. He and Mallory stepped aboard amid a small crowd, and the attendant ratcheted the cage down into the Bureau's bowels.

Mallory followed Tobias out of the lift, past a rack of pneumatic mail-chutes, and through a pair of swinging doors, their edges lined with thick felt. They were alone again. Tobias stopped short. "You should know better than to offer gratuities to a public servant."

"You look as if you could use it," Mallory said.

"Ten days' wage? Expect I could. Providin' I find you right and fly."

"I mean no harm," Mallory said mildly. "This place is strange territory. In such circumstances, I've found it wise to have a native guide."

"What's wrong with the boss, then?"

"I was hoping you'd tell *me* that, Mr. Tobias."

More than the coin, the remark itself seemed to win Tobias over. He shrugged. "Wakey's not so bad. If I were him, I wouldn't act any different. But he ran *your* number today, guv'nor, and pulled a stack on you nine inches high. You've some talkative friends, you do, Mr. Mallory."

"Did he now?" Mallory said, forcing a smile. "That file must make interesting reading. I'd surely like a look at it."

"I do suppose that intelligence might find its way to improper hands," the boy allowed. "Of course, 'twould be worth a fellow's job, if he were caught at it."

"Do you like your work, Mr. Tobias?"

"Pay's not much. Gas-light ruins your eyes. But it has advantages." He shrugged again, and pushed his way through another door, into a clattering anteroom, three of its walls lined with shelves and card-files, the fourth with fretted glass.

Behind the glass loomed a vast hall of towering Engines—so many that at first Mallory thought the walls must surely be lined with mirrors, like a fancy ballroom. It was like some carnival deception, meant to trick the eye—the giant identical Engines, clock-like constructions of intricately interlocking brass, big as rail-cars set on end, each on its foot-thick padded blocks. The white-washed ceiling, thirty feet overhead, was alive with spinning pulley-belts, the lesser gears drawing power from tremendous spoked flywheels on socketed iron columns. White-coated clackers, dwarfed by their machines, paced the spotless aisles. Their hair was swaddled in wrinkled white berets, their mouths and noses hidden behind squares of white gauze.

Tobias glanced at these majestic racks of gearage with absolute indifference. "All day starin' at little holes. No mistakes, either! Hit a key-punch wrong and it's all the difference between a clergyman and an arsonist. Many's the poor innocent bastard ruined like that. . . ."

The tick and sizzle of the monster clockwork muffled his words.

Two men, well-dressed and quiet, were engrossed in their work in the library. They bent together over a large square album of color-plates. "Pray have a seat," Tobias said.

Mallory seated himself at a library table, in a maple swivel-chair mounted on rubber wheels, while Tobias selected a card-file. He sat opposite Mallory and leafed through the cards, pausing to dab a gloved finger in a small container of beeswax. He retrieved a pair of cards. "Were these your requests, sir?"

"I filled out paper questionnaires. But you've put all that in Engine-form, eh?"

"Well, QC took the requests," Tobias said, squinting. "But we had to route it to Criminal Anthropometry. This card's seen use—they've done a deal of the sorting-work already." He rose suddenly and fetched a loose-leaf notebook—a clacker's guide. He compared one of Mallory's cards to some ideal within the book, with a look of distracted disdain. "Did you fill the forms out *completely*, sir?"

"I think so," Mallory hedged.

"Height of suspect," the boy mumbled, "reach. . . . Length and width of left ear, left foot, left forearm, left forefinger."

"I supplied my best estimates," Mallory said. "Why just the left side, if I may ask?"

"Less affected by physical work," Tobias said absently. "Age, coloration of skin, hair, eyes. Scars, birthmarks . . . ah, now then. Deformities."

"The man had a bump on the side of his forehead," Mallory said.

"Frontal plagiocephaly," the boy said, checking his book. "Rare, and that's why it struck me. But that should be useful. They're spoony on skulls, in Criminal Anthropometry." Tobias plucked up the cards, dropped them through a slot, and pulled a bell-rope. There was a sharp clanging. In a moment a clacker arrived for the cards.

"Now what?" Mallory said.

"We wait for it to spin through," the boy said.

"How long?"

"It always takes twice as long as you think," the boy said, settling back in his chair. "Even if you double your estimate. Something of a natural law."

Mallory nodded. The delay could not be helped, and might be useful. "Have you worked here long, Mr. Tobias?"

"Not long enough to go mad."

Mallory chuckled.

"You think I'm joking," Tobias said darkly.

"Why do you work here, if you hate it so?"

"Everyone hates it, who has a spark of sense," Tobias said. "Of course, it's fine work here, if you work the top floors, and are one of the big'uns." He jabbed his gloved thumb, discreetly, at the ceiling. "Which I ain't, of course. But mostly, the work needs little folk. They need us by the scores and dozens and hundreds. We come and go. Two years of this work, maybe three, makes your eyes and your nerves go. You can go quite mad from staring at little holes. Mad as a dancing dormouse." Tobias slid his hands into his apron-pockets. "I'll wager you think, sir, from looking at us low clerks dressed like so many white pigeons, that we're all the same inside! But we ain't, sir, not at all. You see, there's only so many people in Britain who can read and write, and spell and add, as neat as they need here. Most coves who can do that, they'll get far better work, if they've a mind to look. So the Bureau gets your . . . well . . . unsettled sorts." Tobias smiled thinly. "They've even hired *women* sometimes. Seamstresses, what lost their jobs to knitting-jennies. Government hire 'em to read and punch cards. Very good at detail-work, your former seamstresses."

"It seems an odd policy," Mallory said.

"Pressure of circumstance," Tobias said. "Nature of the business. You ever work for Her Majesty's Government, Mr. Mallory?"

"In a way," Mallory said. He'd worked for the Royal Society's Commission on Free Trade. He'd believed their patriotic talk, their promises of back-stage influence—and they'd cut him loose to fend for himself, when they were through with him. A private audience with the Commission's Lord Galton, a warm handshake, an expression of "deep regret" that there could be "no open recognition of his gallant service. . . ." And that was all. Not so much as a signed scrap of paper.

"What kind of Government work?" Tobias said.

"Ever seen the so-called Land Leviathan?"

"In the museum," Tobias said. "Brontosaurus they call it, a reptile elephant. Had its teeth in the end of its trunk. The beast ate trees."

"Clever chap, Tobias."

"You're Leviathan Mallory," Tobias said, "the famous savant!" He flushed bright red.

A bell rang. Tobias leapt to his feet. He took a pamphlet of accordioned paper from a tray in the wall.

"In luck, sir. Male suspect is done. I told you the skull business would help." Tobias spread the paper on the table, before Mallory.

It was a collection of stipple-printed Engine-portraits. Dark-haired Englishmen with hangdog looks. The little square picture-bits of the Engine-prints were just big enough to distort their faces slightly, so that the men all seemed to have black drool in their mouths and dirt in the corners of their eyes. They all looked like brothers, some strange human sub-species of the devious and disenchanted. The portraits were nameless; they had citizen-numbers beneath them. "I hadn't expected dozens of them," Mallory said.

"We could have narrowed the choice, with better parameters on the anthropometry," Tobias said. "But just take your time, sir, and look closely. If we have him, he's here."

Mallory stared at the glowering ranks of numbered scape-graces, many of them with disquietingly misshapen heads. He remembered the tout's face with great clarity. He remembered it twisted with homicidal rage, bloody spittle in the cracked teeth. The sight was etched forever in his mind's eye, as vivid as the knuckle-shapes of the beast's spine, when first he'd seen his great prize jutting from the Wyoming shale. In one long dawning moment, then, Mallory had seen through those drab stone lumps and perceived the immanent glow of his own great glory, his coming fame. In just such a manner, he had seen, in the tout's face, a lethal challenge that could transform his life.

But none of these dazed and sullen portraits matched the memory. "Is there any reason why you *wouldn't* have this man?"

"Perhaps your man has no criminal record," Tobias said. "We could run the card again, to check against the general population. But that would take us weeks of Engine-spinning, and require a special clearance from the people upstairs."

"Why so long, pray?"

"Dr. Mallory, we have everyone in Britain in our records. Everyone who's ever applied for work, or paid taxes, or been arrested." Tobias was apologetic, painfully eager to help. "Is he a foreigner perhaps?"

"I'm certain he was British, and a blackguard. He was armed and dangerous. But I simply don't see him here."

"Perhaps it is a bad likeness, sir. Your criminal classes, they like to puff out their cheeks for criminal photography. Wads of cotton up their noses, and suchlike tricks. I'm sure he's there, sir."

"I don't believe it. Is there another possibility?"

Tobias sat down, defeated. "That's all we have, sir. Unless you want to change your description."

"Might someone have *removed* his portrait?"

Tobias looked shocked. "That would be tampering with official files, sir. A felony transportation-offense. I'm sure none of the clerks would have done such a thing." There was a heavy pause.

"However?" Mallory urged.

"Well, the files are sacrosanct, sir. It is what we're all about here, as you know. But there *are* certain highly placed officials, from outside the Bureau—men who serve the confidential safety of the realm. If you know the gents I mean."

"I don't believe I do," Mallory said.

"A very few gentlemen, in positions of great trust and discretion," Tobias said. He glanced at the other men in the room, and lowered his voice. "Perhaps you've heard of what they call 'the Special Cabinet'? Or the Special Bureau of the Bow Street police . . . ?"

"Anyone else?" Mallory said.

"Well, the Royal Family, of course. We are servants of the Crown here, after all. If Albert himself were to command our Minister of Statistics . . ."

"What about the Prime Minister? Lord Byron?"

Tobias made no reply. His face had soured.

"An idle question," Mallory said. "Forget I asked it. It's a scholar's habit, you see—when a topic interests me, I explore its specifics, even to the point of pedantry. But it has no relevance here." Mallory peered at the pictures again, with a show of close attention. "No doubt it is my own fault—the light here is not all it might be."

"Let me turn up the gas," the boy said, half-rising.

"No," Mallory said. "Let me save my attention for the woman. Perhaps we'll have better luck there."

Tobias sank back in his seat. As they awaited the Engine-spin, Mallory feigned a relaxed indifference. "Slow work, eh, Mr. Tobias? A lad of your intelligence must long for a greater challenge."

"I do love Engines," Tobias said. "Not these great lummox monsters, but the cleverer, aesthetic ones. I wanted to learn clacking."

"Why aren't you in school, then?"

"Can't afford it, sir. The family doesn't approve."

"Did you try the National Merit Exams?"

"No scholarship for me—I failed the calculus." Tobias looked sullen. "I'm no scientist, anyway. It's art that I live for. Kinotropy!"

"Theatre work, eh? They say it's in the blood."

"I spend every spare shilling on spinning-time," the boy said. "We have a little club of enthusiasts. The Palladium rents its kinotrope to us, during the wee hours. You see quite amazing things, sometimes, along with a deal of amateur drivel."

"Fascinating," Mallory said. "I hear that, er . . ." He had to struggle to recall the man's name. "I hear that John Keats is quite good."

"He's old," the boy said, with a ruthless shrug. "You should see Sandys. Or Hughes. Or Etty! And there's a clacker from Manchester whose work is quite splendid—Michael Radley. I saw a show of his here in London, last winter. A lecture tour, with an American."

"Kinotrope lectures can be very improving."

"Oh, the speaker was a crooked Yankee politician. If I had my way, they'd throw the speaker out entirely, and run silent pictures."

Mallory let the conversation lapse. Tobias squirmed a bit, wanting to speak again and not quite daring to take that liberty, and then the bell rang. The boy was up like a shot, with a scratchy skid of his worthless shoes, and back with another set of fan-fold paper.

"Red-heads," he said, and smiled sheepishly.

Mallory grunted. He studied the women with close attention. They were fallen women, ruined women, with the sodden look of fall and ruin marked indelibly in the little black picture-bits of their printed femininity. Unlike the men, the female faces somehow leapt to life for Mallory. Here a round-faced Cockney creature, with a look more savage than a Cheyenne squaw. There a sweet-eyed Irish girl whose lantern jaw had surely embittered her life. There a street-walker with rat's-nest hair and the blear of gin. There, defiance; here, tight-lipped insolence; there, a frozen cajoling look from an Englishwoman with her nape pinched for too long in the daguerreotype's neck-brace.

The eyes, with their calculated plea of injured innocence, held him with a shock of recognition. Mallory tapped the paper, looking up. "Here she is!"

Tobias started. "That's rum, sir! Let me take that number." He punched the citizen-number into a fresh card with a small mahogany switch-press, then fed the card through the wall-tray again. He carefully emptied the bits of punched-out paper into a hinge-topped basket.

"This will tell me all about her, will it?" Mallory said. He reached inside his jacket for his notebook.

"Mostly, sir. A printed summary."

"And may I take these documents away with me for study?"

"No, sir, strictly speaking, as you're not an officer of the law. . . ." Tobias lowered his voice. "Truth to tell, sir, you could pay a common magistrate, or even his clerk, and have this intelligence for a few shillings, under the rose. Once you've someone's number, the rest is simple enough. It's a common clacker trick, to read the Engine-files on someone of the criminal class—they call it 'pulling his string,' or being 'up on a cake.'"

Mallory found this news of remarkable interest. "Suppose I asked for my own file?" he said.

"Well, sir, you're a gentleman, not a criminal. You're not in the common police-files. Your magistrates, and court-clerks and such, would have to fill out forms, and show good cause for the search. Which we don't grant easily."

"Legal protocols, eh?" Mallory said.

"No, sir, it's no law that stops us, but the simple trouble of it. Such a search consumes Engine-time and money, and we're always over budget in both. But if an M.P. made that request, or a Lordship . . ."

"Suppose I had a good friend here in the Bureau," Mallory said. "Someone who admired me for my generous ways."

Tobias looked reluctant, and a bit coy. "It ain't a simple matter, sir. Every spinning-run is registered, and each request must have a sponsor. What we did today is done in Mr. Wakefield's name, so there'll be no trouble in that. But your friend would have to forge some sponsor's name, and run the risk of that imposture. It is fraud, sir. An Engine-fraud, like credit-theft or stock-fraud, and punished just the same, when it's found out."

"Very enlightening," Mallory said. "I've found that one always profits by talking to a technical man who truly knows his business. Let me give you my card."

Mallory extracted one of his Maull & Polyblank cartes-de-visite from his pocket-book. Folding a five-pound note, he pinched it against the back of his card and passed it over. It was a handsome sum. A deliberate investment.

Tobias dug about beneath his apron, found a greasy leather wallet, stuffed in Mallory's card and money, and extracted a dog-eared bit of shiny pasteboard. J. J. TOBIAS, ESQ., the card said, in grotesquely elaborate Engine-Gothic. KINOTROPY, AND THEATRE COLLECTIBLES. There was a Whitechapel address. "Never mind that telegraph number at the bottom," Tobias told him. "I had to stop renting it."

"Have you any interest in French kinotropy, Mr. Tobias?" Mallory said.

"Oh, yes, sir," nodded Tobias. "Some lovely material is coming out of Montmartre these days."

"I understand the best French *ordinateurs* employ a special gauge of card."

"The Napoleon gauge," Tobias said readily. "Smaller cards of an artificial substance, which move very swiftly in the compilers. That speed is quite handy in kino-work."

"Do you know where a fellow might rent one of these French compilers, here in London?"

"To translate data from French cards, sir?"

"Yes," Mallory said, feigning an only casual interest. "I expect to receive some data from a French colleague, involving a scientific controversy—rather abstruse, but still a matter of some scholarly confidentiality. I prefer to examine it privately, at my own convenience."

"Yes, sir," Tobias said. "That is to say, I do know a fellow with a French compiler, and he'd let you do whatever you like with it, if the pay were right. Last year, there was quite a mode in London clacking-circles for the French standard. But sentiment has turned quite against it, what with the troubles of the Grand Napoleon."

"Really," Mallory said.

Tobias nodded, delighted to show his authority. "I believe it's felt now, sir, that the French were far ahead of themselves with their vast Napoleon project, and made something of a technical misstep!"

Mallory stroked his beard. "That wouldn't be British professional envy talking, I hope."

"Not at all, sir! It's common knowledge that the Grand Napoleon suffered some dire mishap early this year," Tobias assured him, "and the great Engine has never spun quite properly since." He lowered his voice. "Some claim sabotage! Do you know that French term, *sabotage*? Comes from '*sabots*,' the wooden shoes worn by French workers. They can kick an Engine half off its blocks!" Tobias grinned at this prospect, with a glee that rather disquieted Mallory. "The French have Luddite troubles of a sort, you see, sir, much as we once did, years ago!"

Two short notes were sounded on a steam-whistle, reverberat-

ing through the white-washed ceiling. The two studious gentlemen, who had been joined by an equally studious third, now
closed their albums and left.

The bell rang once more, summoning Tobias to the wall-tray.
The boy rose slowly, straightened a chair, wandered down the
length of the table, examined the albums for non-existent dust,
and shelved them. "I think that's our answer waiting," Mallory
said.

Tobias nodded shortly, his back to Mallory. "Very likely, sir, but
I'm on overtime, see. Those two blasts on the horn . . ."

Mallory rose impatiently and strode to the tray.

"No, no," Tobias yelped, "not without gloves! Pray let me do it!"

"Gloves, indeed! Who's to know?"

"Criminal Anthropometry, that's who! This is their room, and
nothing they hate worse than the smudges from bare fingers!"
Tobias turned with a sheaf of documents. "Well, sir, our suspect is
one Florence Bartlett, née Russell, late of Liverpool. . . ."

"Thank you, Tobias," Mallory said, creasing the sheaf of fan-
fold so as to slip it more easily into his Ada-Checkered waistcoat.
"I do appreciate your help."

One arctic Wyoming morning, the frost thick on the brown and
beaten prairie-grass, Mallory had crouched beside the tepid
boiler of the expedition's steam-fortress, prodding at its meager
buffalo-dung fire, trying to thaw an iron-hard strip of the jerked
beef that the men ate for breakfast, lunch, and dinner. At that
moment of utter misery, his beard rimed with frozen breath and
his shovel-blistered fingers frost-bitten, Mallory had sworn a solemn oath that he would never again curse the summer heat.

But never had he expected so vile a swelter in London.

The night had passed without a breath of wind, and his bed had
seemed a fetid stew. He'd slept atop the sheets, a drenched Turkish
towel spread across his nakedness, and had risen every hour to
dampen the towel again. Now the mattress was soaked and the
whole room seemed as hot and close as a greenhouse. It stank of

stale tobacco as well, for Mallory had smoked half-a-dozen of his fine Havanas over the criminal record of Florence Russell Bartlett, which dealt primarily with the murder of her husband, a prominent Liverpool cotton-merchant, in the spring of 1853.

The modus operandi had been poisoning by arsenic, which Mrs. Bartlett had extracted from fly-paper and administered over a period of weeks in a patent medicine, Dr. Gove's Hydropathic Strengthener. Mallory, from his nights down Haymarket, knew that Dr. Gove's was in fact a patent aphrodisiac, but the file made no mention of this fact. The fatal illness in 1852 of Bartlett's mother, and of her husband's brother in 1851, were also recorded, their respective certificates of death citing perforated ulcer and cholera morbus. These purported illnesses featured symptoms very like those of arsenic poisoning. Never formally accused of these other deaths, Mrs. Bartlett had escaped custody, overpowering her jailer with a concealed derringer.

The Central Statistics Bureau suspected her of having fled to France, Mallory assumed, because someone had appended translations of French police-reports of 1854 dealing with a *crime passionel* trial in the Paris assizes. One "Florence Murphy," abortionist, purportedly an American refugee, was arrested and tried for the crime of *vitriolage*, the flinging of sulphuric acid with intent to disfigure or maim. The victim, Marie Lemoine, wife of a prominent Lyons silk-merchant, was an apparent rival.

But "Mrs. Murphy" had vanished from custody, and from all subsequent French police-records, during the first week of her trial as a *vitrioleuse*.

Mallory sponged his face, neck, and armpits in tap-water, thinking bleakly of vitriol.

He was perspiring freely again as he laced his shoes. Leaving his room, he discovered that the city's queer summer had overwhelmed the Palace. Sullen humidity simmered over the marble floors like an invisible swamp. The very palms at the foot of the stairs seemed Jurassic. He trudged to the Palace's dining-room, where four cold hard-boiled eggs, iced coffee, a kippered herring, some broiled tomato, a bit of ham, and a chilled melon somewhat restored him. The food here was rather good, though the kipper had smelled a bit off—small wonder, in heat like this. Mallory signed the chit, and left to fetch his mail.

He had been unjust to the kipper. Outside the dining room, the Palace itself stank: bad fish, or something much like it. There was a soapy perfume in the front lobby, left from the morning's mopping, but the air was heavy with the humid distant reek of something dreadful, and apparently long-dead. Mallory knew he had smelled that reek before—it was sharp, like acid, mixed with the greasy stench of a slaughterhouse—but he could not place the memory. In a moment the stink was gone again. He stepped to the desk for his mail. The wilted clerk greeted him with a show of courtesy; Mallory had won the staff's loyalty with generous tips. "Nothing in my box?" said Mallory, surprised.

"Too *small*, Dr. Mallory." The clerk bent to lift a large woven-wire basket, crammed to the brim with envelopes, magazines, and packages.

" 'Struth!" Mallory said. "It gets worse every day!"

The clerk nodded knowingly. "The price of fame, sir."

Mallory was overwhelmed. "I suppose I shall have to read through all of this. . . ."

"If I may be so bold, sir, I think you might do well to engage a private secretary."

Mallory grunted. He had a loathing of secretaries, valets, butlers, chambermaids, the whole squalid business of service. His own mother had been in service once, with a wealthy family in Sussex, in the old days before the Rads. The fact rankled.

He carried the heavy basket into a quiet corner of the library and began to sort through it. Magazines first: the gold-spined *Transactions of the Royal Society, Herpetology of All Nations, Journal of Dynamickal Systematics, Annales Scientifiques de l'Ecole des Ordinateurs*, with what seemed to be an interesting article on the mechanical miseries of the Grand Napoleon. . . . This business of the scholarly subscriptions had been a faggot-above-a-load, though he supposed it kept the editors happy, happy editors being half the key to placing one's own articles.

Then the letters. Swiftly, Mallory divided them into piles. Begging-letters first. He had made the mistake of answering a few, that had seemed especially tearful and sincere, and now the scheming rascals had swarmed upon him like lice.

A second pile of business-letters. Invitations to speak, requests for interviews, bills from shopmen, Catastrophist bone-men and rock-hounds offering co-authorship of learned papers.

Then the letters in feminine hand. The broody-hens of natural history—"flower-snippers," Huxley called them. They wrote in their scores and dozens, most merely to request his autograph, and, if he so pleased, a signed carte-de-visite. Others would send him coy sketches of common lizards, requesting his expertise in reptile taxonomy. Others would express a delicate admiration, perhaps accompanied with verses, and invite him to tea if he was ever in Sheffield, or Nottingham, or Brighton. And some few, often marked by spiky handwriting, *triple underlining!!!*, and ribboned locks of hair, would express a warm womanly admiration, and this in terms so bold as to be quite disconcerting. There had been a remarkable flurry of these after his fancy portrait had appeared in *The Englishwoman's Domestic Weekly*.

Mallory stopped suddenly. He had almost flung aside a letter from his sister Ruth. Dear little Ruthie—but of course the baby of the family was a good seventeen years old now. He opened the letter at once.

DEAR NED,

I write to you at Mother's dictation as her hands are quite bad today. Father thanks you very much for the splendid lap-rug from London. The French liniment has helped my hands (Mother's) very nicely thow more in the knees than the hands. We all miss you much in Lewes thow we know you are busy on yr great affairs of the Royal Society! We read aloud each of yr American adventures as they are written by Mr. Disraeli in *Family Museum*. Agatha asks will you please please get her Mr. Disraeli's autograph as her favorite novel is his "Tancred"! But our great news is that our dear Brian is back from Bombay, safely with us this very day June 17! And he has brought with him our dear brother-to-be Lt. Jerry Rawlings, also of the Sussex Artillery, who asked our Madeline to wait for him and of course she did. Now they are to be married, and Mother wants you to know particularly that it will NOT be in a Church but a civil seremony with the J.P. Mr. Witherspoon in Lewes City Hall. Will you attend June 29 as Father gives away almost his last bride—I did not want to write that but Mother made me.

All our Love,

RUTH MALLORY (*Miss*)

So—Little Madeline, with her man at last. Poor creature, four years was a long engagement, more worrisome still when betrothed to a soldier in a tropical pest-hole like India. She had taken his ring at eighteen, and was now all of twenty-two. A long engagement was a cruel thing to ask of a young and lively girl, and Mallory had seen, in his last visit, that the ordeal had sharpened Madeline's tongue and temper, and made her almost a trial to the household. Soon there would be no one left at home to look after the old folks but little Ruthie. And when Ruth married— well, he would consider that matter in due time. Mallory rubbed his sweating beard. Madeline had had life harder than Ernestina, or Agatha, or Dorothy. She should have something fine for herself, Mallory resolved. A wedding-gift that would prove that she had put an end to her unhappy time.

Mallory took the letter-basket to his room, piled the mail on the floor beside his overflowing bureau, and left the Palace, dropping the basket at the desk on his way out.

A group of Quakers, men and women, stood on the pavement outside the Palace. They were droning another of their intolerable sermonizing ditties, something about a "railway to Heaven," by the sound of it. The song did not seem to have much to do with Evolution, or blasphemy, or fossils; but perhaps the sheer monotony of their bootless protests had exhausted even the Quakers.

He hurried past them, ignoring their proffered pamphlets. It was hot, uncommon hot, beastly hot. There was not a ray of sun, but the air was mortally still and the high cloudy sky had a leaden, glowering look, as if it wanted to rain but had forgotten the trick of it.

Mallory walked down Gloucester Road to the corner of Cromwell. There was a fine new equestrian statue of Cromwell at the intersection; Cromwell was a great favorite of the Rads. And there were 'buses too, six an hour, but they were all crammed to the gunwales. No one wanted to walk in weather like this.

Mallory tried the Gloucester Road underground, by the corner of Ashburn Mews. As he prepared to descend the stairs a thin crowd came up at a half-run, fleeing a reek of such virulence that it stopped him in his tracks.

Londoners were used to odd smells from their undergrounds, but this stench was clearly of another order entirely. Compared to the sullen heat of the streets, the air was chill, but it had a deathly scent, like something gone rotten in a sealed glass jar. Mallory went to the ticket-office; it was closed, with a sign up saying WE APOLOGIZE FOR THE INCONVENIENCE. No mention of the actual nature of the problem.

Mallory turned. There were horse-drawn cabs at Bailey's Hotel, across Courtfield Road. He prepared to cross the street, but then noticed a cab waiting quite near him at the curb, apparently idle. Signaling the driver, he went to the door. There was a passenger still inside the cab. Mallory waited politely for the man to debark. Instead, the stranger, seeming to resent Mallory's gaze, pressed a kerchief to his face and half-sunk below the level of the window. He began coughing. Perhaps the man was ill, or had just come up from the underground and not yet caught his breath.

Annoyed, Mallory crossed the street and engaged a cab at Bailey's. "Piccadilly," he ordered. The driver clicked to his sweating nag and they rolled east up Cromwell Road. Once under-way, with a faint breeze at the window, the heat became less oppressive and Mallory's spirits rose. Cromwell Road, Thurloe Place,

Brompton Road—in their vast rebuilding schemes, the Government had reserved these sections of Kensington and Brompton to a vast concourse of Museums and Royal Society Palaces. One by one they passed his window in their sober majesty of cupolas and colonnades: Physics, Economics, Chemistry. . . . One might complain of some Radical innovations, Mallory mused, but there was no denying the sense and justice of fine headquarters for scholars engaged in the noblest work of mankind. Surely, in their aid to Science, the Palaces had repaid the lavish cost of their construction at least a dozen times.

Up Knightsbridge and past Hyde Park Corner to the Napoleon Arch, a gift from Louis Napoleon to commemorate the Anglo-French Entente. The great iron arch, with its lavish skeleton of struts and bolting, supported a large population of winged cupids and draperied ladies with torches. A handsome monument, Mallory thought, and in the latest taste. Its elegant solidity seemed to deny that there had ever been a trace of discord between Great Britain and her staunchest ally, Imperial France. Perhaps, thought Mallory wryly, the "misunderstandings" of the Napoleonic Wars could be blamed on the tyrant Wellington.

Though London possessed no monuments to the Duke of Wellington, it sometimes seemed to Mallory that unspoken memories of the man still haunted the city, an unlaid ghost. Once, the great victor of Waterloo had been exalted here, as the very saviour of the British nation; Wellington had been ennobled, and had held the highest office in the land. But in modern England he was vilified as a swaggering brute, a second King John, the butcher of his own restless people. The Rads had never forgotten their hatred for their early and formidable enemy. A full generation had passed since Wellington's death, but Prime Minister Byron still often spattered the Duke's memory with the acid of his formidable eloquence.

Mallory, though a loyal Radical Party man, was unconvinced by mere rhetorical abuse. He privately entertained his own opinion of the long-dead tyrant. On his first trip to London at the age of six, Mallory had once seen the Duke of Wellington—passing in his gilded carriage in the street, with a clopping, jingling escort of armed cavalry. And the boy Mallory had been vastly impressed—not simply by that famous hook-nosed face, high-collared and whiskered, groomed and stern and silent—but by his own father's awestruck mix of fear and pleasure at the Duke's passage.

Some faint tang of that childhood visit to London—in 1831, the first year of the Time of Troubles, the last of England's old regime—still clung to Mallory whenever he saw the capital. Some few months later, in Lewes, his father had cheered wildly when news came of Wellington's death in a bomb atrocity. But Mallory had secretly wept, stirred to bitter sorrow for a reason he could not now recall.

His seasoned judgment saw the Duke of Wellington as the outmoded, ignorant victim of an upheaval beyond his comprehension; more Charles the First than King John. Wellington had foolishly championed the interests of declining and decadent Tory blue-bloods, a class destined to be swept from power by the rising middle-class and the savant meritocrats. But Wellington himself had been no blue-blood; he had once been plain Arthur Wellesley, of rather modest Irish origin.

Further, it seemed to Mallory that as a soldier, Wellington had displayed a very praiseworthy mastery of his craft. It was only as a civil politician, and a reactionary Prime Minister, that Wellington had so thoroughly misjudged the revolutionary tenor of the coming age of industry and science. He had paid for that lack of vision with his honor, his power, and his very life.

And the England that Wellington had known and misruled, the England of Mallory's childhood, had slid through strikes, manifestos, and demonstrations, to riots, martial law, massacres, open class-warfare, and near-total anarchy. Only the Industrial Radical Party, with their boldly rational vision of a comprehensive new order, had saved England from the abyss.

But even so, Mallory thought. Even so, there should be a monument somewhere. . . .

The cabriolet rolled up Piccadilly, passing Down Street, Whitehorse Street, Half-Moon Street. Mallory thumbed through his address-book, and found Laurence Oliphant's carte-de-visite. Oliphant lived on Half-Moon Street. Mallory had half a mind to stop the cab and see if Oliphant were at home. If, unlike most posh courtiers, Oliphant perhaps rose before ten, he might have something like a bucket of ice in his household and perhaps a drop of something to open the pores. The thought of boldly interrupting Oliphant's day, and perhaps surprising him at some covert intrigue, was a pleasant one to Mallory.

But first things first. Perhaps he would try Oliphant when his errand was done.

Mallory stopped the cab at the entrance to the Burlington Arcade. The gigantic iron-framed ziggurat of Fortnum & Mason lurked across the street, amid an array of jewelers and exclusive shops. The cabbie severely overcharged him, but Mallory took no notice, being in an expansive mood. It seemed the cabbies were imposing on everyone. Some small distance down Piccadilly, another man had leapt from his cab and was arguing, in a vulgar fashion, with his driver.

Mallory had found nothing to equal shopping in its gratifying demonstration of the power of his new-found wealth. He had won his money through an act of half-mad bravado, but the secret of its origin was safe with him. London's credit-machines clicked for the vaporous profits of gambling as readily as they did for the widow's mite.

So what was it to be? This giant iron vase, with octagonal base, with eight open-work screens hanging before its fluted pedestal, giving a singular lightness and elegance to the entire object? This carved box-wood bracket with sculpted canopy, the intended mounting of a Venetian-glass thermometer? This ebony salt-cellar enriched with columns and elaborate sunken panels, accompanied by a silver salt-spoon rich with trefoils, oak-leaves, a spiral-girded stem, and the monogram of one's choice?

Within J. Walker & Co., a small but marvelously tasteful establishment amid the bay-windowed shops of the famed Arcade, Mallory discovered a gift that seemed to him perfectly apt. It was an eight-day clock which struck the quarters and hours on fine cathedral-tone bells. The timepiece, which also displayed the date, the day of the week, and the phases of the moon, was an outstanding piece of British precision craftsmanship, though naturally the elegant clock-stand would claim more admiration from the mechanically undiscerning. The stand, of the finest lacquered papier-mâché inlaid with turquoise-blue glass, was surmounted by a group of large gilt figures. These represented a young and decidedly attractive Britannia, very lightly robed, admiring the progress made by Time and Science in the civilization and happiness of the people of Britain. This laudable theme was additionally illustrated by a series of seven graven scenes, revolving weekly on hidden gear-work within the clock's base.

The price was nothing less than fourteen guineas. It seemed that an item of this artistic rarity could not be denominated in simple pounds-shillings-and-pence. The crass pragmatic thought struck Mallory that the happy couple might be better served with a jingling handful of fourteen guineas. But the money would soon go, as money always did when one was young. A fine clock like this one might adorn one's home for generations.

Mallory bought the clock with cash, refusing the offer of credit, with a year to pay. The clerk, a supercilious elderly man, sweating into a starched Regency collar, demonstrated the system of cork chocks that secured the gear-work from the exigencies of travel. The clock was provided with a latched and handled case, lined with form-fitting cork under burgundy velvet.

Mallory knew he could never wedge his prize into a crowded steam-bus. He would have to hire another cabriolet, and lash the clock-case to its roof. A bothersome proposition, London being haunted by the young thieves known as "dragsmen," monkey-like rascals who leapt with saw-tooth dirks onto the roofs of passing carriages, to cut the leather straps securing luggage. By the time the cab pulled to a stop, the thieves would have scampered scot-free into the depths of some evil rookery, passing their swag from hand to hand until the private contents of the victim's valise ended up in a dozen rag-and-bone shops.

Mallory lugged his purchase through the far gate of the Burlington Arcade, where the constable on guard gave him a cheery salute. Outside, in Burlington Gardens, a young man in a dented hat and shabby, greasy coat, who had been sitting apparently much at his ease on the rim of a cement planter, rose suddenly to his feet.

The shabby young man limped toward Mallory, his shoulders slumped in theatrical despair. He touched the brim of his hat, essayed a pathetic smile, and began to speak to Mallory, all in one breath. "I ask your pardon sir but if you would excuse the liberty of being so addressed in the public street by one who is almost reduced to rags though it has not always been so and by no fault of my own but through ill health in my family and many unmerited sufferings it would be a great obligation sir to know the time."

The time? Could this man somehow know that Mallory had just purchased a large clock? But the shabby man paid no attention to Mallory's sudden confusion, for he continued on eagerly, in the same insinuating monotone.

"Sir it is not begging that is my intention for I was brought up by the best of mothers and begging is not my trade I should not know how to follow such a trade if such were my shameful wish for I would sooner die of deprivation but sir I implore you in the name of charity to allow me the honor of acting as your porter to carry that case that burdens you for whatever price that your humanity may put upon my services—"

The shabby man broke off short. He looked, wide-eyed, over Mallory's shoulder, his mouth assuming a sudden tight-clamped, pinchy look, like a seamstress biting off a thread. The shabby man took three careful steps backward, slowly, keeping Mallory between himself and whatever it was that he saw. And then he turned directly on his flapping, newspaper-stuffed heels and walked swiftly away, without any limp, into the crowded sidewalks of Cork Street.

Mallory turned at once and looked behind him. There was a tall, long-shanked, slender man behind him, with a button-nose and long side-whiskers, in a short Albert coat and plain trousers. Even as Mallory's gaze caught him, the man raised a handkerchief to his face. He coughed, in a gentlemanly way, then he dabbed at his eyes a bit. Then he seemed, with a sudden theatrical start, to have recalled something he had forgotten. He turned away, and began to wander back toward the Burlington Arcade. He had not once looked straight at Mallory.

Mallory himself took a sudden pretended interest in the clasps of his clock-case. He set his case down, bent, and looked at the bits of shiny brass with his mind racing and a chill in his spine. The rascal's handkerchief trick had given him away. Mallory recognized him now as the man he had seen by the underground station in Kensington; the coughing gent, who would not give up his cab. What's more, thought Mallory, his mind hot with insight, the coughing gent was also the rude man who'd argued with the cabbie about his fare, in Piccadilly. He had followed Mallory the whole distance from Kensington. He was trailing him.

Mallory seized his clock-case in a fierce grip and began to walk quietly down Burlington Gardens. He turned right on Old Bond Street. His nerves were tingling now, with a stalker's instinct. He had been a fool to turn and stare at first. Perhaps he had given himself away to his pursuer. Mallory did not turn and look again, but ambled along with his best pretense at leisure. He paused before a jeweler's velvet racks of cameos and bracelets and evening tiaras for Her Ladyship, and watched the street behind him, in the iron-barred shining glass.

He saw the Coughing Gent reappear almost at once. The man hung well back for the moment, careful to keep groups of London shoppers between himself and Mallory. The Coughing Gent was perhaps thirty-five, with a bit of grey in his side-whiskers, and a dark machine-stitched Albert coat that did not look like anything remarkable. His face was that of anyone in London, perhaps a little heavier, a little colder in the eyes, with a grimmer mouth beneath the button-nose.

Mallory took another turn, left up Bruton Street, his clock-case growing more awkward by the step. The shops here lacked conveniently angled glass. He doffed his hat to a pretty woman, and pretended to glance back at her ankles. The Coughing Gent was still with him.

Perhaps the Coughing Gent was a confederate of the tout and his woman. A hired ruffian; a murderer, with a derringer in the pocket of that Albert coat. Or a vial of vitriol. The hair rose at the base of Mallory's skull, anticipating the sudden impact of the assassin's bullet, the wet burning splash of corrosion.

Mallory began to walk more quickly, the case banging painfully against his leg. Into Berkeley Square, where a small steam-crane, chugging gamely between a pair of splintered plane-trees, swung a great cast-iron ball into a crumbling Georgian facade. A crowd of spectators was enjoying the sight. He joined them behind the saw-horse barricade, amid the acrid smell of ancient plaster, and sensed a moment's safety. He spied out the Coughing Gent with a sidelong glance. The fellow looked sinister enough, and anxious, having lost Mallory in the crowd for the time being. But he did not seem mad with hatred, or nerved to kill; he was glancing about among the legs of the spectators, hunting for Mallory's clock-case.

Here was a chance to lose the rascal. Mallory made a swift break down the length of the Square, taking advantage of the cover of the trees. At the Square's far end he turned down Charles Street, lined right and left with enormous eighteenth-century houses. Lordly homes, their ornate iron-work hung with modern coats-of-arms. Behind him a sumptuous gurney emerged from its carriage-house, giving Mallory the chance to stop, and turn, and study the street.

His gambit had failed. The Coughing Gent was mere yards behind, a bit winded perhaps and red-faced in the sullen heat, but not deceived. He was waiting for Mallory to move again, careful not to look at him. Instead, he gazed with apparent longing at the entrance of a public-house named I Am the Only Running Footman. It occurred to Mallory to double back and enter the Running Footman, where he might lose the Coughing Gent in the crowd. Or perhaps he could leap, at the last moment, onto a departing omnibus—if he could cram his precious case aboard.

But Mallory saw little real hope in these expedients. This fellow had the firm advantage of the terrain and all the sneaking tricks of the London criminal. Mallory felt like a lumbering Wyoming bison. He trudged ahead with the heavy clock. His hand ached; he was becoming weary. . . .

At the foot of Queens Way, a dragline and two excavators were wreaking progressive havoc in the ruins of Shepherd Market. A hoarding surrounded the site, the boards cracked and knotholed by eager spectators. Kerchief-headed women and chaw-spitting costermongers, displaced from their customary sites, had set up a last-ditch rag-shop just outside the fence. Mallory walked down the line of ill-smelling oysters and limp vegetables. At the end of the hoarding, some accident of planning had left a narrow alleyway; dusty planks to one side, crumbled brick to the other. Rank weeds sprouted between piss-damp ancient cobbles. Mallory peered in as a bonneted crone arose from a squat, adjusting her skirts. She walked past him without a word. Mallory touched his hat.

Heaving the case above his head, he set it gently atop the wall of mossy brick. He shored it up securely with a chunk of decayed mortar, then placed his hat beside it.

He flattened his back against the wall of planks.

The Coughing Gent appeared. Mallory lunged for the man, and punched him in the pit of the belly with all his strength. The man doubled over with a spit and a wheeze, and Mallory clouted him with a short left to the side of the jaw. The man's hat flew off, and he tumbled to his knees.

Mallory grabbed the back of the villain's Albert coat and flung him hard against the bricks. The man rebounded, sprawled headlong, and lay gasping, his whiskered face smeared with filth. Mallory snatched him up two-handed, by the throat and lapel. "Who are you!"

"Help," the man croaked feebly, "murder!"

Mallory dragged the man three yards down the alley. "Don't

play the fool with me, you blackguard! Why are you following me? Who paid you? What's your name?"

The man clawed desperately at Mallory's wrist. "Let me go. . . ." His coat had flown open. Mallory glimpsed the brown leather of a shoulder-holster and reached at once for the weapon in it.

It was not a gun. It came out in his hand like a long oiled snake. A truncheon, with a braided leather handle and a thick black shaft of India-rubber, flattened at the end to a swollen tip like a shoehorn's. It had a spring-steel whippiness, as if it were built around a coil of iron.

Mallory brandished the ugly device, which felt as if it could easily break bones. The Coughing Gent cowered before him. "Answer my questions!"

A bolt of wet lightning blasted the back of Mallory's head. His senses almost left him; he felt himself fall, but caught himself against the filthy cobblestones with arms as numb and heavy as legs of mutton. A second blow fell, but glancingly, across his shoulder. He rolled back and snarled—a thick, barking sound, a cry he had never heard from his own throat. He kicked out at his attacker, somehow caught the man's shin. The man hopped back, cursing.

Mallory had lost the truncheon. He lurched up, scrambling, into a giddy crouch. The second man was portly and small. He wore a round derby hat, mashed down almost to his eyebrows. He stood over the outstretched legs of the Coughing Gent and made a menacing slash at Mallory with a sausage-like leather cosh.

Blood coursed down Mallory's neck as a wave of nauseated dizziness struck. He felt he might faint at any moment, and animal instinct told him that if he fell now, he would surely be beaten to death.

He turned and fled the alley on wobbling legs. His head seemed to rattle and squeak, as if the sutures of his skull had ruptured. Red mist swirled like oil before his eyes.

He tottered a short way down the street, and rounded a corner, gasping. He propped himself against a wall, hands braced on his knees. A respectable man and woman passed him, and stared in vague distaste. With his nose running, his mouth clogged with nausea, he glared back at them, feebly defiant. He sensed somehow that if the bastards smelled his blood they would surely tear him down.

Time passed. More Londoners strolled past him, with looks of indifference, curiosity, faint disapproval, thinking him drunk or sick. Mallory peered through his tears at the building across the street, at the neatly enameled cast-iron sign on its corner.

Half-Moon Street. Half-Moon Street, where Oliphant lived.

Mallory felt in his pocket for his field-book. It was still there, the familiar touch of its sturdy leather binding like a blessing to him. With trembling fingers, he found Oliphant's card.

Once he had reached the address, at the far end of Half-Moon Street, he was no longer weaving on his feet. The ugly giddiness in his skull had changed to a painful throbbing.

Oliphant lived in a Georgian mansion, divided for modern renters. The ground floor had an elaborate iron railing and a curtained bay-window commanding the peaceful vista of Green Park. It was altogether a pleasantly civilized place, entirely unsuitable for a man who was aching, stunned, and dripping blood. Mallory pounded fiercely with the elephant-headed knocker.

A man-servant opened the door. He looked Mallory up and down. "May I help you . . . ? Oh, my word." He turned, raised his voice to a shout. "Mr. Oliphant!"

Mallory tottered into the entrance hall, all elegant tile and waxed wainscoting. Oliphant appeared almost at once. In spite of the hour, he was formally dressed, with the smallest of bow-ties and a chrysanthemum boutonniere.

Oliphant seemed to grasp the situation with a single keen-eyed glance. "Bligh! Go at once to the kitchen; fetch brandy from cook. A basin of water. And some clean towels."

Bligh, the man-servant, vanished. Oliphant stepped to the open door, glanced warily up and down the street, then shut and locked the door securely. Taking Mallory's arm, he guided him into the parlor, where Mallory lowered himself wearily on a piano-bench.

"So you've been attacked," Oliphant said. "Set upon from behind. A cowardly ambush, by the look of it."

"How bad is it? I can't see."

"A blow from a blunt instrument. The skin is broken and you have a considerable bruise. It's bled rather freely, but is clotting now."

"Is it serious?"

"I've seen worse." Oliphant's tone was ironically cheerful. "But it's quite spoilt that handsome jacket of yours, I'm afraid."

"They stalked me all through Piccadilly," Mallory said. "I didn't see the second one, until it was too late." He sat up suddenly. "Damn! My clock! A clock, a wedding gift. I left it in an alleyway by Shepherd Market. Those rascals will have stolen it!"

Bligh reappeared, with towels and basin. He was shorter and older than his master, clean-shaven and thick-necked, with bulging brown eyes. His hairy wrists were thick as a collier's. He and Oliphant shared an air of easy respect, as though the man were a trusted family retainer. Oliphant dabbed a towel in the basin and stepped behind Mallory. "Be quite still, please."

"My clock," Mallory repeated.

Oliphant sighed. "Bligh, do you think you could see to this gentleman's mislaid property? There's a degree of danger, of course."

"Yes, sir," Bligh said stolidly. "And the guests, sir?"

Oliphant seemed to think it over, dabbing wetly at the back of Mallory's skull. "Why don't you take the guests with you, Bligh? I'm sure they'd enjoy the outing. Take them out the back way. Try not to create too much of a public spectacle."

"What shall I tell them, sir?"

"Tell them the truth, of course! Tell them that a friend of the household has been assaulted by foreign agents. But tell them they mustn't kill anyone. And if they don't find this clock of Dr. Mallory's, they mustn't think it a reflection on their abilities. Make a joke of it if you must, but don't allow them to feel they've lost prestige."

"I understand, sir," Bligh said, and left.

"Sorry to impose," Mallory muttered.

"Nonsense. It's what we're here for." Oliphant offered Mallory two fingers of very good brandy, in a crystal tumbler.

With the brandy, the dry-throated shock oozed out of Mallory, leaving him in pain, but far less numb and harried. "You were right and I was wrong," he declared. "They were stalking me like an animal! They were no common ruffians; they meant me harm, I'm sure of it."

"Texians?"

"Londoners. A tall cove with side-whiskers, and a little fat one in a derby hat."

"Hirelings." Oliphant dabbled a towel in the basin. "You could do with a stitch or two, I think. Shall I summon a doctor? Or do you trust me to do it? I've done a bit of surgeon's work, in rough country."

"So have I," Mallory said. "Pray go ahead if you think it necessary."

He had another gulp of Oliphant's brandy while the man fetched needle and thread. Then Mallory doffed his coat, clenched his jaw, and stared at the blue floral wallpaper while Oliphant deftly pierced the torn skin and sutured it. "Not a bad job," Oliphant said, pleased. "Stay out of unwholesome effluvia and you'll likely escape without a fever."

"All London's an effluvium today. This beastly weather . . . I don't trust doctors, do you? They don't know what they're talking about."

"Unlike diplomats, or Catastrophists?" Oliphant's charming smile made it impossible for Mallory to take offense. Mallory picked his jacket from the piano-bench. Bloodstains matted its collar. "Now what? Shall I go to the police?"

"That's your privilege, of course," Oliphant said, "though I would trust to your patriotic discretion to leave certain matters unmentioned."

"Certain matters such as Lady Ada Byron?"

Oliphant frowned. "To speculate wildly about the Prime Minister's daughter would, I'm afraid, be a very *severe* indiscretion."

"I see. And what about my gun-running for the Royal Society's Commission on Free Trade, then? I make the unfounded assumption that the Commission's scandals differ from Lady Ada's."

"Well," said Oliphant. "Gratifying as it would be to me personally to see your Commission's blunders publicly exposed, I fear that entire business must remain sub-rosa—in the interests of the British nation."

"I see. What exactly is left to me to say to the police, then?"

Oliphant smiled thinly. "That you were struck on the head by an unnamed ruffian for unknown reasons."

"This is ridiculous," Mallory snapped. "Aren't you Government mandarins good for anything? This isn't some game of parlor charades, you know! I identified that female fiend who helped hold Lady Ada captive! Her name is—"

"Florence Bartlett," Oliphant said. "And pray keep your voice down."

"How did you—?" Mallory stopped. "Your friend Mr. Wakefield, is it? I suppose he watched all my business at the Statistics Bureau, and dashed off at once to tell you everything."

"It's Wakefield's business, however tedious, to watch the business of his own blessed Engines," Oliphant said calmly. "I was expecting *you* to tell me, actually—now that you know that you were enticed by an authentic *femme fatale*. But you don't seem eager to share your information, sir."

Mallory grunted.

"This is no matter for the common police," Oliphant said. "I told you earlier that you should have special protection. Now, I'm afraid I must insist."

"Bloody hell," Mallory muttered.

"I've the very man for this assignment. Inspector Ebenezer Fraser, of the Bow Street Special Branch. The *very* Special Branch, so you mustn't say that too loudly; but you'll find Inspec-

tor Fraser—or *Mister* Fraser, as he prefers to be called in public—
to be most capable, most understanding, and very discreet. I
know you'll be safe in Fraser's hands—and I cannot tell you what
a relief that will be to me."

A door shut in the back of the house. There were footsteps,
scrapings and clinkings, strange voices. Then Bligh reappeared.

"My clock!" Mallory cried. "Thank heaven!"

"We found it atop a wall, with a bit of brick propping it up,
rather hidden away," Bligh said, setting down the case. "Scarcely
a scratch on it. I surmise the ruffians cached it there, for later
looting, sir."

Oliphant nodded, with an arched eyebrow at Mallory. "Fine
work, Bligh."

"And then there was this, sir." Bligh produced a trampled
topper.

"It's that rascal's," Mallory declared. The Coughing Gent's
crushed hat had been liberally soaked in a puddle of stale piss,
though no one saw fit to mention this unspeakable fact.

"Sorry to miss your own hat, sir," Bligh said. "Likely stolen by
some street-arab."

Oliphant, with the faintest wince of involuntary distaste, examined the ruined topper, turning it over and inverting the lining.
"No maker's mark."

Mallory glanced at it. "Engine-made. From Moses & Son, I
should say. About two years old."

"Well." Oliphant blinked. "I presume that evidence rules out
any foreigner. A London veteran, surely. A user of cheap ma-
cassar oil, but a man of enough cranial capacity to have a certain
cunning. Put it in the rubbish, Bligh."

"Yes, sir." Bligh left.

Mallory patted the clock-case with deep satisfaction. "Your
man Bligh has done me a great service. Do you think he would
object to a gratuity?"

"Most decidedly," Oliphant said.

Mallory felt the gaffe. He gritted his teeth. "What about these
guests of yours? Might I be permitted to thank them?"

Oliphant smiled with abandon. "Why not!"

He led Mallory into the dining room. The mahogany legs had been detached from Oliphant's dining-table, and the great polished surface now sat on its corners of carven gingerbread, mere inches above the floor. Five Asian men sat about it, in cross-legged alien dignity: five sober men in their stocking feet, wearing tailored evening-suits from Savile Row. All the men sported tall silk toppers, tugged low over their clippered heads. Their hair was very short and very dark.

And a woman was with them as well, kneeling at the table's foot. She had a look of mask-like composure and a silky black wealth of hair. She was wrapped in some voluminous native garb, bright with swallows and maple-leaves.

"Doctor Edward Mallory *san o goshokai shimasu*," Oliphant said. The men rose with peculiar grace; rocking back a bit, sliding one foot beneath them, and coming up quite suddenly to a supple-legged stance, as if they were ballet dancers.

"These gentlemen are in the service of His Imperial Majesty the Mikado of Japan," Oliphant said. "This is Mr. Matsuki Koan, Mr. Mori Arinori, Mr. Fusukawa Yukichi, Mr. Kanaye Nagasawa, Mr. Hisanobu Sameshima." The men bowed from the hips, each in turn.

Oliphant had made no attempt to introduce the woman; she sat with expressionless rigidity, as if secretly resenting the gaze of an Englishman. Mallory thought it wise not to mention the matter, or pay her much attention. Instead, he turned to Oliphant. "Japanese, are they? You speak the lingo, do you?"

"A diplomatic smattering."

"Would you please thank them for so gallantly fetching my clock, then?"

"We understand you, Dr. Marori," said one of the Japanese. Mallory had immediately forgotten their impossible names, but thought that this one might be called Yukichi. "It is honor to us to assist British friend of Mr. Laurence Oliphant, to whom our sovereign has expressed obligation." Mr. Yukichi bowed again.

Mallory was utterly at sea. "Thank you for that courteous

speech, sir. You're a very well-spoken gentleman, I must say. I'm not a diplomat myself, but I do thank you sincerely. Very kind of all of you. . . ."

The Japanese conferred among themselves. "We hope you are not badly hurt by barbaric assault on your British person by foreigners," said Mr. Yukichi.

"No," Mallory said.

"We did not see your enemy, nor any rude or violent person." Mr. Yukichi's tone was mild, but his glinting eyes left Mallory little doubt as to what Yukichi and his friends would have done had they met such a ruffian. As a group, the five Japanese had a refined, scholarly air; two were wearing rimless spectacles, and one had a ribboned monocle and dandyish yellow gloves. But they were all young and deft and sturdy, and their toppers were perched on their heads like Viking helmets.

Oliphant's long legs buckled suddenly beneath him, and he sat at the head of the table with a smile. Mallory sat too, his knee-caps popping loudly. The Japanese followed Oliphant's lead, quickly tucking themselves into the same positions of arid dignity. The woman had not moved so much as an inch.

"Under the circumstances," Oliphant mused, "dreadful hot day, a tiring foray after enemies of the realm—a small libation is in order." He lifted a brass bell from the table and rang it. "So, let's get friendly, eh? *Nani o onomi ni narimasu ka?*"

The Japanese conferred, their eyes widening, with happy nods and sharp grunts of approval. "Uisuki . . ."

"Whiskey, an excellent choice," said Oliphant.

Bligh arrived momentarily, with a trolley of liquor bottles. "We're low on ice, sir."

"What's that, Bligh?"

"Iceman wouldn't sell cook but a bit. Price has trebled since last week!"

"Well, ice wouldn't fit into the doll's bottle, anyway," said Oliphant lightly, just as if that remark made sense. "Now, Dr. Mallory, pay close heed. Mr. Matsuki Koan, who happens to hail from the very advanced province of Satsuma, was just demonstrating to us one of the marvels of Japanese craft—who was the craftsman again, Mr. Matsuki?"

"She is made by sons of Hosokawa family," said Mr. Matsuki, bowing in place. "Our lord—*Satsuma daimyo*—is patron."

"I believe Mr. Matsuki will do the honors, Bligh," said Oliphant. Bligh handed Mr. Matsuki a whiskey bottle; Mr. Matsuki began to decant it into an elegant ceramic jug, at the right hand of the Japanese woman. She made no response. Mallory began to wonder if she were ill, or paralyzed. Then Mr. Matsuki fitted the little jug into her right hand with a sharp wooden click. He rose, and fetched a gilded crank-handle. He stuck the device into the small of her back and began to twist it, his face expressionless. A high-pitched coiling sound emerged from the woman's innards.

"She's a dummy!" Mallory blurted.

"More a marionette, actually," Oliphant said. "The proper term is 'automaton,' I believe."

Mallory drew a breath. "I see! Like one of those Jacquot-Droz toys, or Vaucanson's famous duck, eh?" He laughed. It was now obvious at a glance that the mask-like face, half-shrouded by the elegant black hair, was in fact carved and painted wood. "That blow must have addled my brains. Heaven, what a marvel."

"Every hair in her wig put in by hand," Oliphant said. "She's a royal gift, for Her Britannic Majesty. Though I imagine the Prince Consort, and especially young Alfred, might take quite a fancy to her as well."

The automaton began pouring drinks. There was a hinge within her robed elbow, and a second in her wrist; she poured whiskey with a gentle slither of cables and a muted wooden clicking. "She moves much like an Engine-guided Maudsley lathe," Mallory noted. "Is that where they got the plans?"

"No, she's entirely native," said Oliphant. Mr. Matsuki was passing little ceramic cups of whiskey down the table. "Not a bit of metal in her—all bamboo, and braided horsehair, and whalebone springs. The Japanese have known how to make such dolls for many years—*karakuri*, they call them."

Mallory sipped his whiskey. Scotch single-malt. He was already a bit squiffed from Oliphant's brandy—now the sight of the doll made him feel as if he had blundered into a Christmas pantomine. "Does she walk?" he asked. "Play the flute perhaps? Or any of that business?"

"No, she simply pours," said Oliphant. "With either hand, though."

Mallory felt the eyes of the Japanese fixed on him. It was clear that the doll was no particular marvel to them. They wanted to know what he, a Briton, thought of her. They wanted to know if he was impressed.

"She is *very* impressive," he blurted. "Especially so, given the primitive nature of Asia!"

"Japan is the Britain of Asia," Oliphant said.

"We know she is not much," said Mr. Yukichi, his eyes glinting.

"No, she's a marvel, truly," Mallory insisted. "Why, you could charge admission."

"We know she is not much, compared to your great British machines. It is as Mr. Oliphant says—we are your younger brothers in this world."

"We will learn," said another Japanese, speaking for the first time. He was likely the one called Arinori. "We have great obligation to Britain! Britain opened our ports with the iron fleet. We have awaked, and learnt great lesson you have teached us. We have destroyed our Shogun and his backward *bakufu*. Mikado will lead us now, in great new progress age."

"We will be allies with you," said Mr. Yukichi, nobly. "The Britain of Asia will bring civilization and enlightenment to all Asian peoples."

"That's very laudable of you," said Mallory. "It's a bit of a hard slog, though, civilization, building an empire. Takes several centuries, you know. . . ."

"We learn everything from you now," said Mr. Arinori. His face was flushed; the whiskey and heat seemed to have kindled a fire in him. "We build great schools and navies, like you. In Choshu, we have an Engine! We will buy more Engines. We will build our own Engines!"

Mallory chuckled. The queer little foreigners seemed so young, so idealistic—intelligent, and above all sincere. He felt quite sorry for them. "Well! It's a fine dream, young sir, and does you credit! But it's no simple matter. You see, we in Britain have devoted great effort to those Engines—you might well call that the central aim of our nation! Our savants have worked on Enginery for decades now. For you, in a few short years, to achieve what we have done . . ."

"We will make whatever sacrifice is necessary," said Mr. Yukichi, calmly.

"There are other ways to improve the homeland of your race," Mallory said. "But what you propose is simply impossible!"

"We will make whatever sacrifice is necessary."

Mallory glanced at Oliphant, who sat with a fixed smile, watching the wind-up girl filling china cups. Perhaps the faint chill in the air was only Mallory's imagination. Yet he felt he had blundered somehow.

There was silence, broken only by the ticking automaton. Mallory got to his feet, his head pounding. "I appreciate your kindness, Mr. Oliphant. And the help of your guests, of course. But I can't stay, you know. Very pleasant here, but press of business . . ."

"You're quite sure?" Oliphant asked cordially.

"Yes."

Oliphant lifted his voice. "Bligh! Send cook's boy to fetch Dr. Mallory a cab."

Mallory's night passed in sodden fatigue. He woke from a confused dream, in which he argued Catastrophism with the Coughing Gent, to hear repeated knocking at his door.

"A moment!" He flung his bare legs from bed, yawned groggily, and tenderly cradled the back of his skull. His bruise had bled a bit in the night, leaving a pinkish stain on the pillow-slip, but the swelling was down and he did not feel feverish. Likely it was the therapeutic work of Oliphant's excellent liquor.

Pulling a nightshirt over his perspiring nudity, he wrapped himself in a dressing-gown and opened the door. The Palace concierge, an Irishman named Kelly, stood in the hall with a pair of glum-faced chars. They were equipped with mops, galvanized buckets, black rubber funnels, and a push-cart crowded with stoppered jeroboams.

"What is the time, Kelly?"

"Nine of the clock, sir." Kelly entered, sucking his yellow teeth. The women trundled in after him with their cart. Gaudy paper labels declared each ceramic bottle to contain "Condy's Patent Oxygenating Deodorizer, One Imp. Gallon."

"What's all this?"

"Manganate of soda, sir, to see to the Palace plumbing. We plan to flush every closet. Clear the Palace pipes out, straight down to the main drains."

Mallory adjusted his robe. It embarrassed him to appear with his feet and ankles bared before the charwomen. "Kelly, it won't do a dashed bit of good if you flush your pipes straight to Hell. This is metropolitan London, in a wretched hot summer. Even the Thames stinks."

"Have to do something, sir," Kelly said. "Our guests are complaining, most vigorously. I can't say as I blame them, sir."

The women funneled a jug of the decoction, which was bright purple, into the bowl of Mallory's water-closet. The deodorizer emitted a piercing ammoniacal reek, far more vile in its own way than the lingering taint in his rooms. They scrubbed wearily at the porcelain, sneezing, until Kelly pulled the cistern-chain with a magisterial gesture.

Then they left, and Mallory dressed. He checked his notebook. The afternoon's schedule was crowded, but the morning had only a single appointment. Mallory had already learned that Disraeli's tardiness made it best to allot him half the day. With luck, he might find time to take his jacket in for French cleaning, or have a barber trim the clots from his hair.

When he went down to the dining-room, two other late breakfasters were chatting over tea. One was a cabinet-man named

Belshaw, the other a museum underling whose name might be Sydenham. Mallory couldn't quite recall.

Belshaw looked up as Mallory entered the room. Mallory nodded civilly. Belshaw gazed back at him with barely concealed astonishment. Mallory walked past the two men, taking his customary seat beneath the gilt gas chandelier. Belshaw and Sydenham began to talk in low, urgent tones.

Mallory was nonplussed. He had never been formally introduced to Belshaw, but could the man possibly resent a simple nod? Now Sydenham, his pudgy face gone pale, was casting sidelong glances at Mallory. Mallory wondered if his fly was open. It was not. But the men's eyes goggled with apparently genuine alarm. Had his wound opened, was his hair dripping blood down his neck? It did not seem so. . . .

Mallory gave his breakfast order to a waiter; the servant's face, too, was wooden, as if the choice of kippers and eggs were a grave indiscretion.

Mallory, growing steadily more confused, had a mind to confront Belshaw on the matter, and began to rehearse a little speech. But Belshaw and Sydenham rose suddenly, quitting their tea, and left the dining-room. Mallory ate his breakfast with grim deliberation, determined not to let the incident upset him.

He went to the front desk to fetch his basket of mail. The usual desk-clerk was not on duty; taken down with a catarrh of the lungs, his replacement said. Mallory retired with his basket to his customary seat in the library. There were five of his Palace colleagues present, gathered in a corner of the room, where they were anxiously conversing. As Mallory glanced up, he thought he caught them staring at him—but this was nonsense.

Mallory sorted through his correspondence with desultory interest, his head aching slightly and his mind already drifting. There was a tedious burden of necessary professional correspondence, and the usual tiresome freight of admiring missives and begging-letters. Perhaps the engagement of a personal secretary might in fact be unavoidable.

Struck by an odd inspiration, Mallory wondered if young

Mr. Tobias of the Central Statistics Bureau might not be just the man for this post. Perhaps an offer of alternate employment would increase the fellow's daring in the office, for there was much at the Bureau that Mallory longed to peruse. The file on Lady Ada, for instance, should such a fabulous item exist. Or the slippery Mr. Oliphant, with his ready smiles and vague assurances. Or Lord Charles Lyell, the medal-heavy savant chief of the Uniformitarian faction.

These three worthies were likely well above his reach, Mallory thought. But he might well ferret out a bit of data on Peter Foulke: a sinister rascal whose web of underhanded intrigue was ever more manifest.

He would have it all out somehow; Mallory felt quite sure of that, as he shuffled through his mail-basket. The whole occulted business would slowly emerge, like bones chipped from their bed of shale. He had glimpsed the closeted skeletons of the Rad elite. Now, given time and a chance to work, he would wrench the mystery whole from its stony matrix.

His attention was caught by a most unusual packet. It was of non-standard dimensions, rather blocky and square, and it bore a colorful set of French express-stamps. The ivory-yellow envelope, astonishingly slick and stiff, was of a most unusual water-proof substance, something like isinglass. Mallory took out his Sheffield knife, selected the smallest of several blades, and worried the thing open.

The interior bore a single French Engine-card, of the Napoleon gauge. Mallory, with growing alarm, shook the card free, onto the table-top. He did this with some difficulty, for the slick interior of the envelope was queerly damp. It was dewy with a chemical moisture, giving off an increasingly virulent stench as it was exposed to air.

The card, a blank without holes, bore a neat block of tiny black print, all in capitals.

TO DR. EDWARD MALLORY, PALACE OF PALEONTOLOGY, LONDON:
YOU ARE IN GUILTY POSSESSION OF A PROPERTY STOLEN AT EPSOM.

YOU WILL RETURN THIS PROPERTY TO US, WHOLE AND COMPLETE, FOLLOWING THE ORDERS GIVEN YOU IN THE PERSONAL NOTICES COL- UMNS OF THE LONDON DAILY EXPRESS. UNTIL WE RECEIVE THIS PROP- ERTY, YOU WILL SUFFER A VARIETY OF DELIBERATE PUNISHMENTS, CULMINATING, IF NECESSARY, IN YOUR ENTIRE AND UTTER DESTRUC- TION. EDWARD MALLORY: WE KNOW YOUR NUMBER, YOUR IDENTITY, YOUR HISTORY, AND YOUR AMBITIONS; WE ARE FULLY COGNIZANT OF YOUR EVERY WEAKNESS. RESISTANCE IS USELESS; SWIFT AND COMPLETE SUBMISSION IS YOUR ONLY HOPE. CAPTAIN SWING

Mallory sat in astonishment, memory rushing vividly upon him. Wyoming again, a morning when he'd risen from his camp-bed to find a rattlesnake dozing in his body-heat. He had felt the serpent squirming below his back in the depths of his sleep, but had drowsily ignored it. Here now was the sudden scaly proof.

He snatched the card up, examining it minutely. Camphorated cellulose, damp with something pungent—and the tiny black letters were beginning to fade. The flexible card had grown hot in his fingers. He dropped it at once, choking back a yelp of surprise. The card lay warping on the table-top, then began flaking into layers thinner than the finest onion-skin, while browning nastily at the edges. A feather of yellowish smoke began to rise, and Mallory realized that the thing was about to burst into flame.

He snatched hastily within the basket, came up with the latest thick grey issue of the *Quart. Jrl. Geol. Soc.*, and swiftly swatted the card. After two sharp blows, it came apart into a thready curling mess, half-mixed with the blistered finish of the table-top.

Mallory slit open a begging-letter, tossed the contents out un-read, and swept the ash into the envelope, with the sharp-edged spine of the geological journal. The table did not seem too badly damaged. . . .

"Dr. Mallory?"

Mallory looked up, with a guilt-stricken start, into the face of a stranger. The man, a tall and cleanshaven Londoner, very plainly dressed, with a gaunt, unsmiling look, stood across the library table from Mallory, papers and a notebook in one hand.

"A very poor specimen," Mallory said, in a sudden ecstasy of impromptu deception. "Pickled in camphor! A dreadful technique!" He folded the envelope and slid it in his pocket.

The stranger silently offered a carte-de-visite.

Ebenezer Fraser's card bore his name, a telegram-number, and a small embossed Seal of State. Nothing else. The other side offered a stippled portrait with the look of stone-faced gravity that seemed the man's natural expression.

Mallory rose to offer his hand, then realized that his fingers were tainted with acid. He bowed instead, sat at once, and wiped his hand furtively on the back of his trouser-leg. The skin of thumb and forefinger felt dessicated, as if dipped in formaldehyde.

"I hope I find you well, sir," Fraser murmured, seating himself across the table. "Recovered from yesterday's attack?"

Mallory glanced down the length of the library. The other patrons were still clumped together at the far side of the room, and seemed very curious indeed about his antics and Fraser's sudden appearance.

"A trifle," Mallory hedged. "Might happen to anyone, in London."

Fraser lifted one dark eyebrow, by a fraction.

"Sorry my mishap should cause you to take trouble, Mr. Fraser."

"No trouble, sir." Fraser opened a leather-bound notebook and produced a reservoir-pen from within his plain, Quakerish jacket. "Some questions?"

"Truth to tell, I'm rather pressed for time at the moment—"

Fraser silenced him with an impassive look. "Been here three hours, sir, awaiting your convenience."

Mallory began a fumbling apology.

Fraser ignored him. "I witnessed something quite curious outside, at six o'clock this morning, sir. A young news-boy, crying to the world that Leviathan Mallory was arrested for murder."

"Me? Edward Mallory?"

Fraser nodded.

"I don't understand. Why should any news-boy cry any such damnable lie?"

"Sold a deal of his papers," Fraser said drily. "Bought one meself."

"What on earth did this paper have to say about me?"

"Not a word of news about any Mallory," Fraser said. "You may see for yourself." He dropped a folded newspaper on the table-top: a London *Daily Express*.

Mallory set the newspaper carefully atop his basket. "Some wicked prank," he suggested, his throat dry. "The street-arabs here are nerved for anything. . . ."

"When I stepped out again, the little rascal had hooked it," Fraser said. "But a deal of your colleagues heard that news-boy crying his tale. Been the talk of the place all morning."

"I see," Mallory said. "That accounts for a certain . . . well!" He cleared his throat.

Fraser watched him impassively. "You'd best see this now, sir." He took a folded document from his notebook, opened it, and slid it across the polished mahogany.

An Engine-printed daguerreotype. A dead man, full length on a slab, a bit of linen tucked about his loins. The picture had been taken in a morgue. The corpse had been knifed open from belly to sternum with a single tremendous ripping thrust. The skin of chest and legs and bulging belly was marble pale, in eerie contrast to the deeply sunburnt hands, the florid face.

It was Francis Rudwick.

There was a caption at the bottom of the picture. *A Scientific Autopsy*, it read. *The "batrachian" subject is pithed and opened in a catastrophic dissection. First in a Series.*

"God in Heaven!" Mallory said.

"Official police morgue record," Fraser said. "Seems it fell into the hands of a mischief-maker."

Mallory stared at it in horror-struck amazement. "What can it mean?"

Fraser readied his pen. "What is 'batrachian,' sir?"

"From the Greek," Mallory blurted. "*Batrachos*, amphibian.

Frogs and toads, mostly." He struggled for words. "Once—years ago, in a debate—I said that his theories . . . Rudwick's geological theories, you know . . ."

"I heard the story this morning, sir. It seems well-known among your colleagues." Fraser flipped pages in his notebook. "You said to Mr. Rudwick: 'The course of Evolution does not conform to the batrachian sluggishness of your intellect.' " He paused. "Fellow did look a bit froggy, didn't he, sir?"

"It was in public debate at Cambridge," Mallory said slowly. "Our blood was up. . . ."

"Rudwick claimed you were 'mad as a hatter,' " Fraser mused. "Seems you took that remark very ill."

Mallory flushed. "He had no right to say that, with his gentry airs—"

"You were enemies."

"Yes, but—" Mallory wiped his forehead. "You can't believe *I* had anything to do with *this*!"

"Not by your own intention, I am sure," Fraser said. "But I believe you're a Sussex man, sir? Town called Lewes?"

"Yes?"

"Seems that some scores of these pictures have been mailed from the Lewes postal office."

Mallory was stunned. "*Scores* of them?"

"Mailed far and wide to your Royal Society colleagues, sir. Anonymously."

"Christ in Heaven," Mallory said, "they mean to destroy me!"

Fraser said nothing.

Mallory stared at the morgue picture. Suddenly the simple human pity of the sight struck him, with terrible force. "Poor damned Rudwick! Look what they've done to him!"

Fraser watched him politely.

"He was one of us!" Mallory blurted, stung into angry sincerity. "He was no theorist, but a damned fine bone-digger. My God, think of his poor family!"

Fraser made a note. "Family—must inquire into that. Very likely they've been told you murdered him."

"But I was in Wyoming when Rudwick was killed. Everyone knows that!"

"A wealthy man might hire the business done."

"I'm not a wealthy man."

Fraser said nothing.

"I wasn't," Mallory said, "not then . . ."

Fraser leafed deliberately through his notebook.

"I won the money gambling."

Fraser showed mild interest.

"My colleagues have noticed how I spend it," Mallory concluded, with a chill sensation. "And wondered whence the money came. And they talk about me behind my back, eh?"

"Envy does set tongues wagging, sir."

Mallory felt a sudden giddy dread. Menace filled the air like a cloud of wasps. After a moment, in Fraser's tactful silence, Mallory rallied himself. He shook his head slowly, set his jaw. He would not be mazed or driven. There was work to do. There was evidence at hand. Mallory bent forward with a scowl, and studied the picture fiercely. " 'First of a series,' this says. This is a threat, Mr. Fraser. It implies similar murders to follow. 'A catastrophic dissection.' This refers to our scientific quarrel—as if he'd died because of that!"

"Savants take their quarrels very seriously," Fraser said.

"Can you mean to say that my colleagues believe *I* sent this? That I hire assassins like a Machiavel; that I am a dangerous maniac who boasts of murdering his rivals?"

Fraser said nothing.

"My God," Mallory said. "What am I to do?"

"My superiors have set this case within my purview," Fraser said formally. "I must ask you to trust in my discretion, Dr. Mallory."

"But what am I to do about the damage to my reputation? Am I to go to every man in this building, and beg his pardon, and tell him . . . tell him I am not some hellish ghoul?"

"Government will not allow a prominent savant to be harassed in this manner," Fraser assured him quietly. "Tomorrow, in Bow

Street, the Commissioner of Police will issue a statement to the Royal Society, declaring you a victim of malicious slander, and innocent of all suspicion in the Rudwick affair."

Mallory rubbed his beard. "Will that help, you think?"

"If necessary, we will issue a public statement to the daily newspapers, as well."

"But might not such publicity arouse more suspicion against me?"

Fraser shifted a bit in his library chair. "Dr. Mallory, my Bureau exists to destroy conspiracies. We are not without experience. We are not without our resources. We will not be trumped by some shabby clique of dark-lanternists. We mean to have the lot of these plotters, branch and root, and we will do it sooner, sir, if you are frank with me, and tell me all you know."

Mallory sat back in his chair. "It is in my nature to be frank, Mr. Fraser. But it is a dark and scandalous story."

"You need not fear for my sensibilities."

Mallory looked about at the mahogany shelves, the bound journals, the leather-bound texts and outsized atlases. Suspicion hung in the air like a burning taint. After yesterday's street-assault, the Palace had seemed a welcome fortress to him, but now it felt like a badger's bolthole. "This ain't the place to tell it," Mallory muttered.

"No, sir," Fraser agreed. "But you should go about your scientific business, same as always. Put a bold face on matters, and likely your enemies will think their stratagems failed."

The advice seemed sound to Mallory. At the least, it was action. He rose at once to his feet. "Go about my daily business, eh? Yes, I should think so. Quite proper."

Fraser rose as well. "I will accompany you, sir, with your permission. I trust we will put a sharp end to your troubles."

"You might not think so, if you knew the whole damned business," Mallory grumbled.

"Mr. Oliphant has informed me on the matter."

"I doubt it," Mallory grunted. "He has closed his eyes to the worst of it."

"I'm no bloody politician," Fraser remarked, in his same mild tone. "Shall we be on our way, sir?"

Outside the Palace, the London sky was a canopy of yellow haze.

It hung above the city in gloomy grandeur, like some storm-fleshed jellied man-o'-war. Its tentacles, the uprising filth of the city's smokestacks, twisted and fluted like candle-smoke in utter stillness, to splash against a lidded ceiling of glowering cloud. The invisible sun cast a drowned and watery light.

Mallory studied the street around him, a London summer morning made strange by the eerie richness of the sooty amber light.

"Mr. Fraser, you're a London man born and bred, I take it."

"Yes, sir."

"Have you *ever* seen weather like this?"

Fraser considered, squinting at the sky. "Not since I were a lad, sir, when the coal-fogs were bad. But the Rads built taller stacks. Nowadays it blows off into the counties." He paused. "Mostly."

Mallory considered the flat clouds, fascinated. He wished he'd spent more time on the doctrines of pneumo-dynamics. This pot-lid of static cloud displayed an unhealthy lack of natural turbulence, as though the dynamical systematics of the atmosphere had stagnated somehow. The stinking underground, the droughty, sewage-thickened Thames, and now this. "Doesn't seem as hot as yesterday," he muttered.

"The gloom, sir."

The streets were such a crush as only London could produce. The omnibuses and cabriolets were all taken, every intersection jammed with rattle-traps and dogcarts, with cursing drivers and panting, black-nostriled horses. Steam-gurneys chugged slug-gishly by, many towing rubber-tired freight-cars loaded with provisions. It seemed the gentry's summer exodus from London was becoming a rout. Mallory could see the sense in it.

It was a long walk to Fleet Street, and his appointment with Disraeli. It seemed best to try the train and endure the Stink.

But the British Brotherhood of Sappers and Miners stood on strike at the entrance to Gloucester Road Station. They had set up pickets and banners across the walk, and were heaping sandbags, like an army of occupation. A large crowd looked on, keeping good order; they did not seem annoyed by the strikers' boldness, but seemed curious, or cowed. Perhaps they were glad to see the underground shut; more likely they were simply afraid of the sand-hogs. The helmeted strikers had boiled up from their underground workings like so many muscular kobolds.

"I don't like the look of this, Mr. Fraser."

"No, sir."

"Let's have a word with these fellows." Mallory crossed the street. He accosted a squat, veiny-nosed sand-hog, who was bawling at the crowd and forcing leaflets upon them. "What's the trouble here, brother sapper?"

The sand-hog looked Mallory up and down, and grinned around an ivory toothpick. There was a large gold-plated hoop in his ear—or perhaps real gold, as the Brotherhood was a wealthy union, owning many ingenious patents. "I'll give ye the long and short of it, mister, since ye ask so civil-like. 'Tis the goddamn' bloody hare-brained pneumatic trains! We told Lord Babbage, in petition, that the bleedin' tunnels never would air proper. But some spunking bastard savant give us some fookin' nonsense lecture, and now the bastard things've gone sour as rotten piss."

"That's a serious matter, sir."

"Yer fookin' right it is, cove."

"Do you know the name of the consulting savant?"

The sand-hog talked the question over with a pair of his helmeted friends. "Lordship name of Jefferies."

"I know Jefferies!" Mallory said, surprised. "He claimed that Rudwick's pterodactyl couldn't fly. Claimed he'd proven it a 'torpid gliding reptile' that couldn't flap its own wings. The rascal's an incompetent! He should be censured for fraud!"

"Savant yerself, are ye, mister?"

"Not one of his sort," Mallory said.

"What about yer pal the fookin' copper here?" The sand-hog

tugged agitatedly at the ring in his ear. "Wouldn't be taking all this down in yer bleeding notebooks, would ye?"

"Not at all," Mallory said with dignity. "Simply wanted to know the full truth of the matter."

"Ye want to know the bloody truth, yer savantship, you'll crawl down there and scrape yerself a bucketful of that moldy shite off the bricks. Sewermen o' twenty years' standing are tossing their guts from the Stink."

The sand-hog moved to confront a woman in banded crinoline. "Ye can't go down there, darlin', ain't a single train rolling in London—"

Mallory moved on. "We haven't heard the last of this!" he muttered aloud, vaguely in Fraser's direction. "When a savant takes on industrial consultation, he needs to be sure of his facts!"

"It's the weather," Fraser said.

"Not at all! It's a matter of savantry ethics! I got such a call myself—fellow in Yorkshire, wants to build a glass conservatory on the pattern of Brontosaurus spine and ribs. The vault-work is fine and efficient, I told him, but the glass seals will surely leak. So, no job, and no consulting-fee—but my reputation as a scholar is upheld!" Mallory snorted on the oily air, cleared his throat, and spat into the gutter. "I can't believe that damned fool Jefferies would give Lord Babbage such poor advice."

"Never saw any savant talk straight to a sand-hog. . . ."

"Then you don't know Ned Mallory! I honor any honest man who truly knows his business."

Fraser considered this. He seemed a bit dubious, if one could judge by his leaden expression. "Dangerous working-class rioters, your sand-hogs."

"A fine Radical union. They stood stoutly by the Party in the early days. And still do."

"Killed a deal of police, in the Time of Troubles."

"But those were Wellington's police," Mallory said.

Fraser nodded somberly.

There seemed little help for it but to walk all the way to Disraeli's. Fraser, whose long-legged, loping stride matched Mallory's with ease, was nothing loath. Retracing their steps, they entered Hyde Park, Mallory hoping for a breath of fresher air. But here the summer foliage seemed half-wilted in the oily stillness, and the greenish light beneath the boughs was extraordinary in its glum malignity.

The sky had become a bowl of smoke, roiling and thickening. The untoward sight seemed to panic the London starlings, for a great flock of the little birds had risen over the park. Mallory watched in admiration as he walked. Flocking activity was a very elegant lesson in dynamical physics. Quite extraordinary how the systematic interaction of so many little birds could form vast elegant shapes in the air: a trapezoid, then a lopped-off pyramid, becoming a flattened crescent, then bowing up in the center like the movement of a tidal surge. There was likely a good paper in the phenomenon.

Mallory stumbled on a tree-root. Fraser caught his arm. "Sir."

"Yes, Mr. Fraser?"

"Keep an eye peeled, if you would. We might perhaps be followed."

Mallory glanced about him. It was not much use; the park was crowded and he could see no sign of the Coughing Gent or his derbied henchman.

On Rotten Row, a small detachment of amazon cavalry— "pretty horse-breakers" they were called in the papers, this being a euphemism for well-to-do courtesans—had gathered about one of their number, thrown from her side-saddle by her chestnut gelding. Mallory and Fraser, as they came closer, saw that the beast had collapsed, and lay frothily panting in the damp grass by the side of the trail. The rider was muddied but unhurt. She was cursing London, and the filthy air, and the women who had urged her to gallop, and the man who had bought her the horse.

Fraser politely ignored the unseemly spectacle. "Sir, in my line of work we learn to cultivate the open air. There are no doors ajar or keyholes about us at the moment. Will you inform me of your troubles, in your own plain words, as you yourself have witnessed the events?"

Mallory tramped on silently for some moments, juggling the matter in his mind. He was tempted to trust Fraser; of all those men in authority whose aid he might have sought in his troubles, this sturdy policeman alone seemed primed to boldly grapple problems at their root. Yet there was much hazard in that trust, and the risk was not to himself alone.

"Mr. Fraser, the reputation of a very great lady is involved in this affair. Before I speak, I must have your word as a gentleman that you will not damage the lady's interests."

Fraser walked on with a meditative air, hands clasped behind his back. "Ada Byron?" he asked at length.

"Why, yes! Oliphant told you the truth, did he?"

Fraser slowly shook his head. "Mr. Oliphant is very discreet. But we of Bow Street are often called upon to put the muzzle on the Byrons' family difficulties. One might almost say that we specialize in the effort."

"But you seemed to know almost at once, Mr. Fraser! How could that be?"

"Sad experience, sir. I know those words of yours, I know that worshipful tone—'the interests of a very great lady.'" Fraser gazed about the gloomy park, taking in the curved benches of teak and iron, crowded with open-collared men, flush-faced women fanning themselves, wilted hordes of city children gone red-eyed and peevish in the stinking heat. "Your duchesses, your countesses, they all had their fancy mansions burnt down in the Time of Troubles. Your Rad Ladyships may put on airs, but no one calls them 'great ladies' in quite that old-fashioned way, unless referring to the Queen herself, or our so-called Queen of Engines."

He stepped carefully over the small feathered corpse of a starling, lying quite dead in the graveled path, with its wings spread and its small wrinkled claws in the air. A few yards on, the two slowed to pick their way through a score of them. "Perhaps you'd best begin at the beginning, sir. Start with the late Mr. Rudwick, and that business."

"Very well." Mallory wiped sweat from his face. His kerchief came away dotted with specks of soot. "I am a Doctor of Paleontology. It follows that I'm a good Party man. My family is somewhat humble, but thanks to the Rads I took a doctorate, with honors. I loyally support my Government."

"Go on," Fraser said.

"I had two years in South America, bone-digging with Lord Loudon, but I was not a leading savant on my own account. When I was offered the chance to lead my own expedition, generously financed, I took it. And so, I later learned, did poor Francis Rudwick, for similar reasons."

"You both took the money of the Royal Society's Commission on Free Trade."

"Not merely their financing, but their orders, Mr. Fraser. I took fifteen men across the American frontier. We dug bones, of course, and we made a great discovery. But we also smuggled guns to the red-skins, to help them keep the Yankees at bay. We mapped routes down from Canada, taking the lay of the land in detail. If there's war between Britain and America some day . . ." Mallory paused. "Well, there's an almighty war in America already, is there not? We are with the southern Confederates, in all but name."

"You had no idea that Rudwick might be in danger from these secret activities?"

"Danger? Of course there was danger. But not at home in England. . . . I was in Wyoming when Rudwick was killed here; I knew nothing of it, till I read of it in Canada. It was a shock to me. . . . I fought bitterly with Rudwick over theory, and I knew he had gone to dig in Mexico, but I didn't know that he and I had the same secret. I didn't know that Rudwick was a Commission dark-lantern man; I only knew that he excelled at our profession." Mallory sighed on the foul air. His own words surprised him; he had never fully admitted these matters even to himself. "I rather envied Rudwick, I suppose. He was somewhat my elder, and he was a pupil of Buckland's."

"Buckland?"

"One of the greatest men of our field. He's gone now as well.

But truth to tell, I didn't know Rudwick well. He was an unpleasant man, haughty and cold in his relations. He was at
his best exploring overseas, at a good distance from decent society." Mallory wiped the back of his neck. "When I read of his
death in a low brawl, I wasn't entirely surprised at the manner
of it."

"Do you know if Rudwick ever knew Ada Byron?"

"No," Mallory said, surprised. "I don't know. He and I were not
that highly placed in savant circles—not at Lady Ada's level,
certainly! Perhaps they were introduced, but I think I should
have known it had she favored him."

"He was brilliant, you said."

"But not *galante*."

Fraser changed the subject. "Oliphant seems to believe that
Rudwick was killed by the Texians."

"I don't know about any Texians," Mallory said angrily. "Who
knows anything about Texas? A damned wilderness, seas and
continents away! If the Texians killed poor Rudwick, I suppose
the Royal Navy should shell their ports in reprisal, or something
of the sort." He shook his head. The whole foul business, which
had once seemed so daring and clever to him, now seemed
something inglorious and vile, little more than a low cheat. "We
were fools to get involved in that Commission's work, Rudwick
and I. A few rich lords, scheming in camera to harass the Yankees. The Yankee republics are already tearing at each other's
throats, over slavery or provincial rights or some other damned
foolishness! Rudwick died because of that, when he might be
alive now, and digging up marvels. It makes me ashamed!"

"Some might say it was your patriotic duty. That you did it for
the interests of England."

"I suppose so," Mallory said, shaking himself, "but it's a great
relief to speak out on the matter, after so long a silence."

Fraser did not seem much impressed by the story. Mallory
surmised it was an old and tiresome tale to Inspector Fraser of
the Special Branch, or perhaps a mere fragment of larger and

more shadowy misdoings. But Fraser did not pursue the matter of politics; he confined himself to the facts of crime. "Tell me about the first attack on your own person."

"That came at the Derby. I saw a veiled lady within a hired cab, treated dreadfully by a man and woman, whom I took to be criminals—the woman being one Florence Russell Bartlett, as I presume you know?"

"Yes. We are searching most vigorously for Mrs. Bartlett."

"I could not identify her male companion. But I may have overheard his name: 'Swing.' Or 'Captain Swing.' "

Fraser seemed a touch surprised. "Did you tell that fact to Mr. Oliphant?"

"No." Mallory, feeling himself on thin ice, said nothing more.

"Perhaps that's just as well," Fraser said, after a thoughtful pause. "Mr. Oliphant's a bit fanciful at times, and 'Captain Swing' is quite a famous name in conspiracy; a mythical personage, much like 'Ned Ludd,' or 'General Ludd.' The Swing bands were Luddites of the countryside, years ago. Arsonists mostly, rick-burners. But in the Time of Troubles, they grew savage, and killed a deal of the landed gentry, and burned down their fine mansions."

"Ah," said Mallory. "Do you think this fellow is a Luddite, then?"

"There are no more Luddites," Fraser said calmly. "They're as dead as your dinosaurs. I rather suspect some mischievous antiquary. We have this fellow's description, we have our methods—when we take him, we'll quiz him on his taste in false identities."

"Well, this fellow's certainly no rural laborer—he's some sort of Frenchified race-track dandy. When I defended the lady, he went for me with a stiletto! Nicked me in the leg. I suppose I'm lucky that the blade was not venomed."

"Perhaps it was," Fraser said. "Most poisons are far less potent than the public supposes. . . ."

"Well, I knocked the rascal down, and drove them off from their victim. The tout swore twice that he would kill me. 'Destroy' me, was the word he used. . . . Then I realized that the lady could be only Lady Ada Byron. She began to talk in a very strange manner—as if drugged, or frightened witless. . . . She begged me to escort her to the Royal Enclosure, but as we approached the Royal Box, she escaped me by a trick—without so much as a word of thanks for my pains."

Mallory paused, fingering the contents of his pockets. "I suppose that's the gist of the matter, sir. Shortly after, I won a good deal of money, wagered on a steam-gurney built by a friend of mine. He gave me very useful information, and it changed me in a moment from a modest scholar to a man of means." Mallory tugged his beard. "Great as that change has been, it seemed much the lesser wonder at the time."

"I see." Fraser walked on silently. They approached Hyde Park Corner, where men stood on soap-boxes, haranguing the crowd and coughing. Fraser and Mallory fell silent as they walked among the clumped and skeptical listeners.

They crossed the frantic crackling bustle of Knightsbridge, Mallory waiting for Fraser to speak, but the policeman said nothing. At the tall iron gates of Green Park, Fraser turned and watched the street behind them for a long moment. "We can cut short through Whitehall," he said at last. "I know a back way."

Mallory nodded. He followed Fraser's lead.

At Buckingham Palace, the guard was changing. The Royal Family, as was their habit, were summering in Scotland, but the elite Brigade of Guards carried out the daily ritual in the Queen's absence. The Palace troops proudly marched in the very latest and most efficient British military gear, dun-colored Crimean battle-garb, scientifically spattered to deceive the enemy eye. The clever fabric had utterly confused the Russians, by all accounts. Behind the marchers, a team of artillery horses towed a large military calliope, its merry piping and rousing drones sounding strangely forlorn and eerie in the still, foul air.

Mallory had been waiting for Fraser to reach a conclusion. At last he could wait no longer. "Do you believe I met Ada Byron, Mr. Fraser?"

Fraser cleared his throat, and spat discreetly. "Yes, sir, I do. I don't much like the matter, but I don't see much to marvel at in it."

"You don't?"

"No, sir. I believe I see the root of it, clear enough. It is gambling-trouble. Lady Ada has a Modus."

"A Modus—what is that?"

"It is a legend in sporting circles, Dr. Mallory. A Modus is a gambling-system, a secret trick of mathematical Enginery, to defeat the odds-makers. Every thieving clacker wants a Modus, sir. It is their philosopher's stone, a way to conjure gold from empty air!"

"Can that be done? Is such an analysis possible?"

"If it is possible, sir, perhaps Lady Ada Byron could do it."

"The friend of Babbage," Mallory said. "Yes—I can believe it. Indeed I can!"

"Well, perhaps she has a Modus, perhaps she only thinks she does," Fraser said. "I'm no mathematician, but I know there's never been any betting-system that worked worth a damn. In any case, she's blundered into something nasty again." Fraser grunted in disgust. "She's pursued that clackers' phantom for years now, and rubbed shoulders with very ugly company— sharpers, low clackers, loan-makers, and worse. She's amassed gambling-debts, to the point of open scandal!"

Absently, Mallory hooked his thumbs within his money-belt. "Well! If Ada's truly found a Modus, she won't have debts much longer!"

Fraser offered Mallory a look of pity for such naïveté. "A true Modus would destroy the institutions of the Turf! It would wreck the livelihood of all your sporting-gents. . . . Ever seen a track-crowd mill-up about a welsher? That's the sort of stir a Modus would bring. Your Ada may be a great blue-stocking, but she hasn't any more common sense than a housefly!"

"She is a great savant, Mr. Fraser! A great genius. I have read her papers, and the superb mathematics . . ."

" 'Lady Ada Byron, Queen of Engines,' " Fraser said, in an

utterly leaden tone that had more weariness than contempt. "A strong-minded woman! Much like her mother, eh? Wears green spectacles and writes learned books. . . . She wants to upset the universe, and play at dice with the hemispheres. Women *never* know when to stop. . . ."

Mallory smiled. "Are you a married man, Mr. Fraser?"

"Not I," Fraser said.

"Nor I, not yet. And Lady Ada never married. She was a bride of Science."

"Every woman needs a man to hold her reins," Fraser said. "It's God's plan for the relations of men and women."

Mallory scowled.

Fraser saw his look, and thought the matter over again. "It's Evolution's adaptation for the human species," he amended.

Mallory nodded slowly.

Fraser seemed markedly reluctant to meet Benjamin Disraeli, making some brief excuse about watching the streets for spies, but Mallory thought it far more likely that Fraser knew Disraeli's reputation, and did not trust the journalist's discretion. And small wonder.

Mallory had met many men-of-affairs in London, but "Dizzy" Disraeli was the Londoner's Londoner. Mallory did not much respect Disraeli, but he did find him amusing company. Disraeli knew, or pretended to know, all the back-stage intrigues in the Commons, all the rows of publishers and learned societies, all the soirées and literary Tuesdays at Lady So-and-So's and Lady This-and-That's. He had a sly way of alluding to this knowledge that was almost magical.

Mallory happened to know that Disraeli had in fact been black-balled at three or four gentlemen's clubs, perhaps because, although a professed and respectable agnostic, Disraeli was of Jewish descent. But the man's modes and manners somehow left the invincible impression that any Londoner who did not know "Dizzy" was an imbecile, or moribund. It was like a mystic aura, a miasma that surrounded the fellow, and there were times when Mallory himself could not help but believe it.

A female servant in mobcap and apron showed Mallory in. Disraeli was awake and eating his breakfast, strong black coffee and a stinking platter of mackerel fried in gin. He wore slippers, a Turkish robe, and a tasseled velvet fez. "Morning, Mallory. Dreadful morning. Beastly."

"It is, rather."

Disraeli crammed the last of his mackerel into his mouth and began to stuff the first pipe of the day. "Actually, you're just the fellow I need to see today, Mallory. Bit of a clacker, technical expert?"

"Oh?"

"New damned thing, I bought it just last Wednesday. The shopman swore it would make life easier." Disraeli led the way into his office, a room reminiscent of Mr. Wakefield's office in the Central Statistics Bureau, though far less ambitious in scale, and littered with pipe-dottles, lurid magazines, and half-eaten sandwiches. The floor was crowded with carved blocks of cork and heaps of shredded excelsior.

Mallory saw that Disraeli had bought himself a Colt & Maxwell Typing Engine, and had managed to haul the thing out of its packing-crate and set it upright on its curved iron legs. It squatted on the stained oak boards before a patent office-chair.

"Looks all right," Mallory said. "What is the problem?"

"Well, I can pump the treadle, and I can manage the handles well enough," Disraeli said. "I can get the little needle to move to the letters I want. But nothing comes out."

Mallory opened the side of the casing, deftly threaded the perforated tape through its gearing-spools, then checked the loading-chute for the fan-fold paper. Disraeli had failed to engage the sprockets properly. Mallory sat in the office-chair, foot-pumped the typer up to speed, and grasped the crank-handles. "What shall I write? Dictate something."

" 'Knowledge is power,' " Disraeli said readily.

Mallory cranked the needle back and forth through its glass-dialed alphabet. Perforated tape inched out, winding neatly onto its spring-loaded spool, and the rotating printing-wheel made a reassuring popping racket. Mallory let the flywheel die down and ratcheted the first sheet of paper out of its slot. KNOWLEDGEE IS PPOWER, it said.

"Takes a dab hand," Mallory said, handing the page to the journalist. "But you'll get used to it."

"I can scribble faster than this!" Disraeli complained. "And in a better hand, by far!"

"Yes," Mallory said patiently, "but you can't reload the tape; bit of scissors and glue, you can loop your punch-tape through and the machine spits out page after page, so long as you push the treadle. As many copies as you like."

"Charming," Disraeli said.

"And of course you can revise what you've written. Simple matter of clipping and pasting the tape."

"Professionals *never* revise," Disraeli said sourly. "And suppose I want to write something elegant and long-winded. Something such as . . ." Disraeli waved his smoldering pipe. " 'There are tumults of the mind, when, like the great convulsions of Nature, all seems anarchy and returning chaos; yet often, in those moments of vast disturbance, as in the strife of Nature itself, some new principle of order, or some new impulse of conduct, develops itself, and controls, and regulates, and brings to an harmonious consequence, passions and elements which seem only to threaten despair and subversion.' "

"That's rather good," Mallory said.

"Like it? From your new chapter. But how am I to concentrate on eloquence while I'm pushing and cranking like a washer-woman?"

"Well, if you make some mistake, you can always reprint a new page fresh from the tape."

"They claimed this device would *save* me paper!"

"You might hire a skilled secretary, and dictate."

"They said it would save me *money*, as well!" Disraeli puffed at the amber tip of his long-stemmed meerschaum. "I suppose it can't be helped. The publishers will force the innovation on us. Already the *Evening Telegraph* is setting up entirely with Engines. Quite a to-do about it in Government. The typesetting brotherhoods, you know. But enough shop-talk, Mallory. To work, eh? I'm afraid we must hasten. I should like to take notes for at least two chapters today."

"Why?"

"I'm leaving London for the Continent, with a group of friends," Disraeli said. "Switzerland, we think. Some little cantonment high in the Alps where a few jolly scribes can draw a breath of fresh air."

"It is rather bad outside," Mallory said. "Very ominous weather."

"It's the talk of every salon," Disraeli told him, seating himself at his desk. He began to hunt through cubbyholes for his sheaf of notes. "London always stinks in summer, but they're calling this 'The Great Stink.' All the gentry have their travels planned, or are gone already! There shall scarcely be a fashionable soul left in London. They say Parliament itself will flee upstream to Hampton Court, and the Law Courts to Oxford!"

"What, truly?"

"Oh yes. Dire measures are in the works. All planned sub rosa of course, to prevent mob panic." Disraeli turned in his chair and winked. "But measures are coming, you may depend upon that."

"What sort of measures, Dizzy?"

"Rationing water, shutting off smokestacks and gas-lights, that sort of thing," Disraeli said airily. "One may say what one likes about the institution of merit-lordship. But at least it has guaranteed that the leadership of our country is not *stupid*."

Disraeli spread his notes across the desk. "The Government have highly scientific contingency plans, you know. Your invasions, your fires, your droughts and plagues..." He leafed through the notes, licking his thumb. "Some people dote on contemplating disasters."

Mallory found this gossip difficult to believe. "What exactly is contained in these 'contingency plans'?"

"All sorts of things. Evacuation plans, I suppose."

"Surely you're not implying that Government intend to evacuate London."

Disraeli smiled wickedly. "If you smelled the Thames outside Parliament, you wouldn't wonder that our solons want to bolt."

"That bad, eh?"

"The Thames is a putrid, disease-ridden tidal sewer!" Disraeli proclaimed. "Thickened with ingredients from breweries, gasworks, and chemical and mineral factories! Putrid matter hangs like vile seaweed from the pilings of Westminster Bridge, and every passing steamer churns up a feculent eddy that nearly overwhelms her crew with foetor!"

Mallory smiled. "Wrote an editorial about it, did we?"

"For the *Morning Clarion* . . ." Disraeli shrugged. "I admit my rhetoric is somewhat over-colored. But it has been a damned odd summer, and that's the truth. A few days of good soaking rain, to flush out the Thames and break these odd stifling clouds, and all will be well with us. But much more of this freak weather, and those who are elderly, or weak of lung, may suffer greatly."

"You think so, truly?"

Disraeli lowered his voice. "They say the cholera is loose again in Limehouse."

Mallory felt a dreadful chill. "*Who* says it?"

"Dame Rumour. But who will doubt her in these circumstances? In such a vile summer, it's all too likely that effluvia and foetor will spread a deadly contagion." Disraeli emptied his pipe and began re-loading it from a rubber-sealed humidor stuffed with black Turkish shag. "I dearly love this city, Mallory, but there are times when discretion must outweigh devotion. You have family in Sussex, I know. If I were you, I should leave at once, and join them."

"But I have a speech to deliver. In two days. On the Brontosaurus. With kinotrope accompaniment!"

"Cancel the speech," Disraeli said, fussing with a repeating-match. "Postpone it."

"I cannot. It is to be a great occasion, a great professional and popular event!"

"Mallory, there shan't be anyone to see it. No one who matters, anyway. You'll be wasting your breath."

"There shall be working-men," Mallory said stubbornly. "The humbler classes can't afford to leave London."

"Oh," Disraeli nodded, puffing smoke. "That will be splendid. The sort of fellows who read tuppenny dreadfuls. Be sure to commend me to your audience."

Mallory set his jaw stubbornly.

Disraeli sighed. "Let's to work. We've a lot to do." He plucked the latest issue of *Family Museum* from a shelf. "What did you think of last week's episode?"

"Fine. The best yet."

"Too much damned scientific theory in it," Disraeli said. "It needs more sentimental interest."

"What's wrong with theory, if it is good theory?"

"No one but a specialist wants to read about the hinging pressures of a reptile's jawbone, Mallory. Truth to tell, there's only one thing people really want to know about dinosaurs: why the damned things are all dead."

"I thought we agreed to save that for the end."

"Oh, yes. Makes a fine climax, that business with the great smashing comet, and the great black dust-storm wiping out all reptilian life and so forth. Very dramatic, very catastrophic. That's what the public *likes* about Catastrophism, Mallory. Catastrophe *feels* better than this Uniformity drivel about the Earth being a thousand million years old. Tedious and boring—boring on the face of it!"

"An appeal to vulgar emotion is neither here nor there!" Mallory said hotly. "The evidence supports me! Look at the Moon—absolutely covered with comet-craters!"

"Yes," Disraeli said absently, "rigorous science, so much the better."

"No one can explain how the Sun could burn for even ten

million years. No combustion could last that long—it violates elementary laws of physics!"

"Give it a rest for a moment. I'm all with your friend Huxley that we should enlighten the public ignorance, but one must throw the dog a bone every once in a while. Our readers want to know about Leviathan Mallory, the man."

Mallory grunted.

"That's why we must get back to the business of this Indian girl."

Mallory shook his head. He had been dreading this. "She wasn't a 'girl.' She was a native woman. . . ."

"We've already explained that you've never married," Disraeli said patiently. "You won't acknowledge any English sweetheart. The time has come to bring out this Indian maiden. You don't have to be indecent or blunt about matters. Just a few kind words about her, a gallantry or two, a few dropped hints. Women dote on that business, Mallory. And they read far more than men do." Disraeli picked up his reservoir-pen. "You haven't even told me her name."

Mallory sat in a chair. "The Cheyenne don't have names as we do. Especially not their women."

"She must have been called something."

"Well, sometimes she was called Widow-of-Red-Blanket, and sometimes she was called Mother-of-Spotted-Snake, or Mother-of-Lame-Horse. But I couldn't swear to any of those names, actually. We had this drunken half-breed Frenchie with us as interpreter, and he lied like a cur."

Disraeli was disappointed. "You never spoke directly to her, then?"

"I don't know. I got to where I could manage pretty well with the hand-signs. Her name was Wak-see-nee-ha-wah, or Wak-nee-see-wah-ha, something much like that."

"How would it be if I call her 'Prairie Maiden'?"

"Dizzy, she was a widow. She had two grown children. She was missing some teeth and was lean as a wolf."

Disraeli sighed. "You're not co-operating, Mallory."

"All right." Mallory tugged his beard. "She was a good seam-stress; you could say that. We won her, ah, friendship, by giving her needles. Steel needles, rather than bison-bone splinters. And glass beads, of course. They all want glass beads."

" 'Shy at first, Prairie Flower was won over by her innate love for feminine accomplishments,' " Disraeli said, scribbling.

Disraeli teased at the edges of the matter, bit by bit, as Mallory squirmed in his chair.

It was nothing like the truth. The truth could not be written on civilized paper. Mallory had put the whole squalid business suc-cessfully out of his mind. But he had not forgotten it, not really. As Disraeli sat scribbling his sentimental treacle, the truth surged back at Mallory with savage vividness.

It was snowing outside the conical tents and the Cheyenne were drunk. Whooping howling drunken pandemonium, because the wretches had no real idea what liquor was; for them it was a poison and an incubus. They pranced and staggered like bed-lamites, firing their rifles into the empty American heavens, and they fell on the frozen ground in the grip of visions, showing nothing but the whites of eyes. Once they had started, they would go on for hours.

Mallory had not wanted to go in to the widow. He had fought the temptation for many days, but the time had finally come when he realized it would do his soul less damage to simply get the business over with. So he had drunk two inches from one of the whiskey bottles, two inches of cheap Birmingham rotgut, shipped over with the rifles. He had gone inside the tent where the widow sat crouched in her blankets and leathers over the dung-fire. The two children left, their round brown faces squint-ing bleakly against the wind.

Mallory showed her a new needle, and did the business with his hands, lewd gestures. The widow nodded, with the exaggerated wobble of someone to whom a nod was a foreign language, and slid back into her nest of hides, and lay on her back with her legs spread, and stretched her arms up. Mallory climbed up over her, got under the blankets with her, pulled his taut and aching member out of his trousers, and forced it between her legs. He had thought it would be over with quickly, and perhaps without much shame, but it was too strange and upsetting to him. The rutting went on for a long time, and finally she began to look at him with a kind of querulous shyness, and plucked curiously at the hair of his beard. And at last the warmth, the sweet friction, the rank animal smell of her, thawed something in him, and he spent long and hard, spent inside her, though he had not meant to do that. The three other times he went to her, later, he withdrew, and did not risk getting the poor creature with child. He was very sorry he had done it even once. But if she was with child when they left, the odds were great that it was not his at all, but one of the other men's.

At length Disraeli moved on to other matters and things became more easy. But Mallory left Disraeli's rooms full of bitter confusion. It was not Disraeli's flowery prose that had stirred up the devil in him, but the savage power of his own memories. The vital animus had returned with a vengeance. He was stiff and restless with lust, and felt out of his own command. He had not had a woman since Canada, and the French girl in Toronto had not seemed wholly clean. He needed a woman, badly. An Englishwoman, some country girl with solid white legs and fat fair freckled arms. . . .

Mallory made his way back to Fleet Street. Out in the open air, his eyes began to smart almost at once. There was no sign of Fraser in the hustling crowds. The gloom of the day was truly extraordinary. It was scarcely noon, but the dome of St. Paul's was shrouded in filthy mist. Great rolling wads of oily fog hid the spires and the giant bannered adverts of Ludgate Hill. Fleet Street was a high-piled clattering chaos, all whip-cracking, steam-snorting, shouting. The women on the pavements crouched under soot-stained parasols and walked half-bent, and men and women alike clutched kerchiefs to their eyes and noses. Men and boys lugged family carpet-bags and rubber-handled traveling-cases, their cheery straw boaters already speckled with detritus. A crowded excursion-train chugged past on the spidery elevated track of the London, Chatham & Dover, its cloud of cindered exhaust hanging in the sullen air like a banner of filth.

Mallory studied the sky. The thready jellyfish mess of rising smoke was gone now, swallowed in a looming opaque fog. Here and there, gray flakes of something like snow were settling delicately over Fleet Street. Mallory examined one that lit on his jacket-sleeve, a strange slaggy flake of crystallized grit. At his touch it burst into the finest ash.

Fraser was shouting at him from beneath a lamp-post across the street. "Dr. Mallory!" Fraser beckoned in a manner that was, for him, remarkably animated; Mallory realized belatedly that Fraser had likely been shouting at him for some time.

Mallory fought and dodged his way across the traffic: cabs, carts, a large stumbling herd of bleating, wheezing sheep. The effort of it set him gasping.

Two strangers stood beneath the lamp-post with Fraser, both their faces tightly swathed with white kerchiefs. The taller fellow had been breathing through his kerchief for some time, for the cloth beneath his nose was stained yellow-brown. "Take 'em off, lads," Fraser commanded. Sullenly, the two strangers tugged their kerchiefs below their chins.

"The Coughing Gent!" Mallory said, stunned.

"Permit me," Fraser said wryly. "This is Mr. J. C. Tate, and this is his partner, Mr. George Velasco. They style themselves confidential agents, or something of the sort." Fraser's mouth grew thinner, became something almost like a smile. "I believe you gents have already met Dr. Edward Mallory."

"We know 'im," Tate said. There was a swollen purple bruise on the side of Tate's jaw. The kerchief had hidden it. "Bloody lunatic, he is! Violent bloody maniac, as ought to be in Bedlam."

"Mr. Tate was an officer on our metropolitan force," Fraser said, fixing Tate with a leaden stare. "Till he lost the post."

"I resigned!" Tate declared. "I quit on principle, as there's no way to get justice done in the public police in London, and you know that as well as I do, Ebenezer Fraser."

"As for Mr. Velasco, he's one of your would-be dark-lantern

men," Fraser said mildly. "Father came to London as a Spanish royalist refugee, but our young Mr. George is apt to turn his hand to anything—false passports, keyhole-peering, blackjacking prominent savants in the street. . . ."

"I am a native-born British citizen," said the swarthy little half-breed, with an ugly glare at Mallory.

"Don't put on airs, Fraser," Tate said. "You walked a beat same as me, and if you're a big brass-hat now, it's only so you can sit on dirty scandals for the Government. Clap the darbies on us, Fraser! Take us into custody! Do your worst! I've my own friends, you know."

"I won't let Dr. Mallory hit you, Tate. Stop worrying. But do tell us why you've been dogging him."

"Professional confidentiality," Tate protested. "Can't nark on a patron."

"Don't be a fool," Fraser said.

"Your gentleman here is a bloody murderer! Had his rival gutted like a fish!"

"I did no such thing," Mallory said. "I'm a Royal Society scholar, not some back-alley conspirator!"

Tate and Velasco exchanged glances of amazed skepticism. Velasco began to snicker helplessly.

"What's so amusing?" Mallory said.

"They were hired by one of your colleagues," Fraser said. "This is a Royal Society intrigue. Is that not so, Mr. Tate?"

"I told you I ain't tellin'," Tate said.

"Is it the Commission on Free Trade?" Mallory demanded. No answer. "Is it Charles Lyell?"

Tate rolled his smoke-reddened eyes and elbowed Velasco in the ribs. "He's as pure as the snow, your Dr. Mallory is, just as you say, Fraser." He wiped his face with his stained kerchief. "Things've come to a pretty pass, damn it all, with London stinking to perdition and the country in the hands of learned lunatics with too much money and hearts of stone!"

Mallory felt the strong impulse to give the insolent rascal another sharp taste of the fist, but with a swift effort of will he

throttled the useless instinct. He stroked his beard with a pro-
fessorial air, and smiled on Tate, coldly and deliberately.

"Whoever your employer may be," Mallory said, "he shan't be
very happy that Mr. Fraser and I have found you out."

Tate watched Mallory narrowly, saying nothing. Velasco put
his hands in his pockets and looked ready to sidle off at any
moment.

"We may have come to blows earlier," Mallory said, "but I pride
myself that I can rise above a natural resentment, and see our
situation objectively! Now that you've lost the cover of deceit
under which you have been stalking me, you're of no use to your
patron anymore. Is that not so?"

"What if it is?" Tate asked.

"The two of you might still be of considerable use to a certain
Ned Mallory. What is he paying you, this fancy patron fellow?"

"Have a care, Mallory," Fraser warned.

"If you've watched me at all closely, you must be aware that I'm
a generous man," Mallory insisted.

"Five shillings a day," Tate muttered.

"Each," Velasco put in. "Plus expenses."

"They're lying," Fraser said.

"I'll have five golden guineas waiting for you, in my rooms at
the Palace of Paleontology, at the end of this week," Mallory
promised. "In exchange for that sum, I want you to treat your
former patron exactly as you've treated me—simple poetic justice, as it were! Stalk him secretly, wherever he goes, and tell me
everything he does. That's what you were hired for, is it not?"

"More or less," Tate admitted. "We might think about that,
squire, if you gave us that tin on deposit."

"I might give you some part of the money," Mallory allowed.
"But then you must give me information on deposit."

Velasco and Tate looked hard at one another. "Give us a moment to confer about it." The two private detectives wandered
away through the jostle of sidewalk traffic and sought shelter in
the leeway of an iron-fenced obelisk.

"Those two aren't worth five guineas in a year," Fraser said.

"I suppose they are vicious rascals," Mallory agreed, "but it scarcely matters what they are, Fraser. I'm after what they know."

Tate returned at length, the kerchief back over his face. "Cove name of Peter Foulke," he said, his voice muffled. "I wouldn't have said that—wild horses couldn't drag it out of me—only the bugger puts on airs and orders us about like a bloody Lordship. Don't trust our integrity. Don't trust us to act in his interests. Don't seem to think we know how to do our own job."

"To hell with him," Velasco said. Stuck between kerchief and derby-brim, the spit-curls on his cheeks stuck out like greased wings. "Velasco and Tate don't cross the Specials for any Peter bloody Foulke."

Mallory offered Tate a crisp pound-note from his book. Tate looked it over, folded it between his fingers with a card-sharper's dexterity, and made it vanish. "Another of those for my friend here, to seal the deal?"

"I suspected it was Foulke all along," Mallory said.

"Then here's something you don't know, squire," Tate said. "We ain't the only ones dogging you. While you hoof along like an elephant, talking to yourself, there's this flash cove and his missus on your heels, three days in the last five."

Fraser spoke up sharply. "But not today, eh?"

Tate chuckled behind his kerchief. "Reckon they saw you and hooked it, Fraser. That vinegar phiz of yours would make 'em hedge off, sure. Jumpy as cats, those two."

"Do they know you saw them?" Fraser said.

"They ain't stupid, Fraser. They're up and flash. He's a racing-cove or I miss my guess, and she's a high-flyer. The dolly tried talking velvet to Velasco here, wanted to know who hired us." Tate paused. "We didn't say."

"What did they say about themselves?" Fraser said sharply.

"She said she was Francis Rudwick's sister," Velasco said. "Investigating her brother's murder. Said that straight out, without my asking."

"Of course we didn't believe that cakey talk," Tate said. "She don't look a bit like Rudwick. Nice-looking bit o' muslin, though. Sweet face, red hair, more likely she was Rudwick's convenient."

"She's a murderess!" Mallory said.

"Funny thing, squire, that's just what she says about you."

"Do you know where to find them?" Fraser asked.

Tate shook his head.

"We could look," Velasco offered.

"Why don't you do that while you follow Foulke," Mallory said, in a burst of inspiration. "I have a notion they might all be in league somehow."

"Foulke's away in Brighton," Tate said. "Couldn't abide the Stink—delicate sensibilities. And if we're to go to Brighton, Velasco and I could do with the railway fare—expenses, you know."

"Bill me," Mallory said. He gave Velasco a pound-note.

"Dr. Mallory wants that bill fully itemized," Fraser said. "With receipts."

"Right and fly, squire," Tate said. He touched the brim of his hat with a copper's salute. "Delighted to serve the interests of the nation."

"And keep a civil tongue in your head, Tate."

Tate ignored him, and leered at Mallory. "You'll be hearing from us, squire."

Fraser and Mallory watched them go. "I reckon you're out two pounds," Fraser said. "You'll never see those two again."

"Cheap at the price, perhaps," Mallory said.

"No it ain't, sir. There's far cheaper ways."

"At least I shan't be coshed from behind any longer."

"No, sir, not by them."

Mallory and Fraser ate gritty sandwiches of turkey and bacon from a glass-sided hot-cart. They were once again unable to hire a cabriolet. None were visible in the street. The underground stations were all closed, with angry sand-hog pickets shouting foul abuse at passers-by.

The day's second appointment, in Jermyn Street, was a severe disappointment to Mallory. He had come to the Museum to confer about his speech, but Mr. Keats, the Royal Society kinotropist, had sent a telegram declaring himself very ill, and Huxley had been dragooned into some committee of savant Lordships meeting to consider the emergency. Mallory could not even manage to cancel his speech, as Disraeli had suggested, for Mr. Trenham Reeks declared himself unable to make such a decision without Huxley's authority, and Huxley himself had left no forwarding address or telegram-number.

To add salt to the wound, the Museum of Practical Geology was almost deserted, the cheery crowds of school-children and natural-history enthusiasts depleted to a few poor sullen wretches clearly come in for the sake of cleaner air and some escape from the heat. They slouched and loitered under the towering skeleton of the Leviathan as if they longed to crack its mighty bones and suck the marrow.

There was nothing for it but to tramp back to the Palace of Paleontology and prepare for the night's dinner with the Young Men's Agnostic Association. The Y.M.A.A. were a savantry student-group. Mallory, as lion of the evening, would be expected to make a few after-dinner remarks. He'd been quite looking forward to the event, as the Y.M.A.A. were a jolly lot, not at all as pompous as their respectable name might suggest, and the all-male company would allow him to make a few unbuttoned jests suitable for young bachelors. Mallory had heard several such, from "Dizzy" Disraeli, that he thought very good indeed. But now he wondered how many of his erstwhile hosts were left in London, or how the young men might manage to gather together, if they were still so inclined, and worst yet, what the dining might be like in the upstairs room of the Black Friar pub, which was near Blackfriars Bridge and just upwind of the Thames.

The streets were visibly emptying. Shop after shop bore CLOSED signs. Mallory had hoped to find a barber to trim his hair and beard, but he'd had no such luck. London's citizenry had fled, or gone to earth behind tight-closed windows. Smoke had settled to ground-level and mixed with a foetid fog, a yellow pea-soup of it everywhere, and it was difficult to see the length of a half-block. The rare pedestrians emerged from obscurity like well-dressed ghosts. Fraser led the way, uncomplaining and uner-ring, and Mallory supposed that the veteran copper could have led them through the London streets blindfolded, with near as much ease. They wore their kerchiefs over their faces now. It seemed a sensible precaution, though it rather bothered Mallory that Fraser now seemed gagged as well as reticent.

"The kinotropes are the sticking-point," Mallory opined, as they tramped up the Brompton Road, the spires of its scientific palaces obscured by foetor. "It wasn't like this before I left En-gland. Two years ago the damned things were nowhere near so common. Now I'm not allowed to give a public speech without one." He coughed. "It gave me a turn to see that long panel back in Fleet Street, mounted in front of the *Evening Telegraph*, clack-ing away like sixty, over the heads of the crowd! 'Trains Closed As Sand-Hogs Strike,' the thing said. 'Parliament Decries State of Thames.'"

"What's wrong with that?" Fraser asked.

"It doesn't *say* anything," Mallory said. "*Who* in Parliament? *What* state of the Thames, specifically? What did Parliament say about it? Wise things or foolish things?"

Fraser grunted.

"There is a wicked pretense that one has been informed. But no such thing has truly occurred! A mere slogan, an empty litany. No arguments are heard, no evidence is weighed. It isn't news at all, only a source of amusement for idlers."

"Some might say it's better for idlers to know a bit than nothing at all."

"Some might be damned fools, then, Fraser. This kino-sloganry is like printing bank-notes with no gold to back them, or writing checks on an empty account. If that is to be the level of rational discourse for the common folk, then I must say three cheers for the authority of the House of Lords."

A fire-gurney chugged slowly past them, with weary firemen on its running-boards, their clothing and faces blackened at their work, or perhaps by the London air itself, or perhaps by the streaming stinking soot of the gurney's own smokestacks. To Mallory, it seemed a strangely ironic thing that a fire-gurney should propel itself through the agency of a heap of blazing coal. But perhaps there was sense in it after all, for in weather like this a team of horses would be hard put to gallop a block.

Mallory was anxious to soothe his raw throat with a huckle-buff, but it seemed smokier inside the Palace of Paleontology than out. There was a harsh stench, like burnt linen.

Perhaps Kelly's imperial gallons of manganate of soda had eaten through the pipes. In any case, this Stink seemed to have finally defeated the Palace guests, for there was scarcely a soul in the lobby, and not a murmur from the dining-room.

Mallory was looking for service in the saloon, amid the lacquered screens and red silk upholstery, when Kelly himself appeared, his face taut and resolute. "Dr. Mallory?"

"Yes, Kelly?"

"I've bad news for you, sir. An unhappy event here. A fire, sir."

Mallory glanced at Fraser.

"Yes, sir," the concierge said. "Sir, when you left today, did you perhaps leave clothing near the gas-jet? Or a cigar still smoldering?"

"You don't mean to say the fire was in my room!"

"I fear so, sir."

"A serious fire?"

"The guests thought it so, sir. So did the firemen." Kelly said nothing of the feelings of the Palace staff, but his face made his sentiments clear.

"I always turn out the gas!" Mallory blurted. "I don't recall exactly—but I *always* turn out the gas."

"Your door was locked, sir. Firemen had to break it in."

"We'll want a look," Fraser suggested mildly.

The door of Mallory's room had been axed in, and the warped

floor was awash with sand and water. Mallory's heaps of magazines and paper correspondence had blazed up very fiercely,
thoroughly consuming his desk and a great blackened swatch of
the carpet. There was a huge charred hole in the wall behind the
desk and the ceiling above it, with naked joists and rafters gone to
charcoal, and Mallory's wardrobe, replete with all his London
finery, burnt to cindered rags and smashed mirror-glass. Mallory
was beside himself with anger and a deep foreboding shame.

"You locked your door, sir?" Fraser asked.

"I always do. Always!"

"May I see your key?"

Mallory handed Fraser his key-chain. Fraser knelt quietly beside the splintered door-frame. He examined the keyhole closely,
then rose to his feet.

"Were there any suspicious characters reported in the hall?"
Fraser asked Kelly.

Kelly was offended. "May I ask who you are to inquire, sir?"

"Inspector Fraser, Bow Street."

"No, Inspector," Kelly said, sucking his teeth. "No suspicious
characters. Not to my personal knowledge!"

"You'll keep this matter confidential, Mr. Kelly. I assume that
like other Royal Society establishments you take only guests who
are accredited savants?"

"That is our firm policy, Inspector!"

"But your guests are allowed visitors?"

"Male visitors, sir. Properly escorted ladies—nothing scandalous, sir!"

"A well-dressed hotel cracksman," Fraser concluded. "And arsonist. Not so good an arsonist as he is a cracksman, for he was
rather clumsy in the way he heaped those papers below the desk
and the wardrobe. He'd a skeleton bar-key for this tumbler-lock.
Had to scrape about a bit, but I doubt it took him five full
minutes."

"This beggars belief," Mallory said.

Kelly looked near tears. "A savant guest burned out of his

room! I don't know what to say! I have not heard of such a wickedness since the days of Ludd! 'Tis a shame, Dr. Mallory—a foul shame!"

Mallory shook his head. "I should have warned you of this, Mr. Kelly. I have dire enemies."

Kelly swallowed. "We know, sir. There's much talk of it among the staff, sir."

Fraser was examining the remnants of the desk, poking about in the litter with the warped brass hanger-rod from the wardrobe. "Tallow," he said.

"We carry insurance, Dr. Mallory," Kelly said hopefully. "I don't know if our policy covers exactly this sort of matter, but I do hope we can make good your losses! Please accept my most sincere apologies!"

"It scotches me," Mallory said, looking about the wreckage. "But not so great a hurt as perhaps they hoped! I keep all my most important papers in the Palace safety-box. And of course I never leave money here." He paused. "I assume the Palace safe remains unrifled, Mr. Kelly."

"Yes, sir," Kelly said. "Or rather—let me see to that at once, sir." He left hastily, bowing.

"Your friend the Derby stiletto-man," Fraser said. "He did not dare dog you today, but once we'd left, he crept up here, cracked the door, and lit candles among your heaped-up papers. He was long and safely gone before the alarm was raised."

"He must know a deal about my schedule," Mallory said. "Knows all about me, I daresay. He's plundered my number. He's taken me for a cake."

"In a manner of speaking, sir." Fraser tossed the brass pole aside. "He's a trumped-up amateur. Your skilled arsonist uses liquid paraffin, which consumes itself and all it touches."

"I shan't make that dinner with the Agnostics tonight, Fraser. I've nothing to wear!"

Fraser stood quite still. "I can see you face misfortune very bravely—like a scholar and a gentleman, Dr. Mallory."

"Thank you," Mallory said. There was a silence. "Fraser, I need a drink."

Fraser nodded slowly.

"For Heaven's sake, Fraser, let us go somewhere where we can do some genuine, blackguard, poverty-stricken drinking, with no false gingerbread glitter thrown over everything! Let us away from the fashionable Palace, to a house where they don't mind letting in a man with nothing left but the coat on his back!" Mallory kicked about in the rubble of his wardrobe.

"I know what you need, sir," Fraser said soothingly. "A cheery place to let off a bit of steam—where there's drink and dance and lively ladies."

Mallory discovered the blackened brass toggles of his Wyoming military-coat. The sight of this stung him deeply. "You wouldn't be trying to nanny me, would you, Fraser? I suppose Oliphant told you to nanny me. I think that would be a mistake. I'm in a mood for trouble, Fraser."

"I don't mistake you at all, sir. The day has been very unkind. But then, you've yet to see Cremorne Gardens."

"The only thing I want to see is the stiletto-man in the sights of a buffalo-rifle!"

"I understand that sentiment perfectly, sir."

Mallory opened his silver cigar-case—at least he still had that possession—and lit his last prime Havana. He puffed it hard, until the calm of good tobacco hit his blood. "On the other hand," he said at last, "I suppose your Cremorne Gardens might well do in a pinch."

Fraser led the way, far down Cromwell Lane, past the great pile of pale brick that was the Diseased Chest Hospital: a nightmarishly dire place this evening, Mallory could not help but think.

A vague notion of medical grimness continued to prey on Mallory's mind, so much so that they stopped at the next public-house, where Mallory had four or possibly five shots of a surprisingly decent whiskey. The pub was crowded with New Brompton locals, who seemed quite cheery in a cozy, besieged sort of way, though they kept slipping tuppenny bits into a pianola that tinkled "Come to the Bower," a song Mallory loathed. There was no rest for him here. In any case, it was not Cremorne Gardens.

They came across the first sign of real trouble a few blocks down New Brompton Road, by Bennett & Harper's Patent Floor-Covering Manufactory. An unruly crowd of uniformed men milled at the gates of the sprawling factory. Industrial trouble of some sort.

It took Fraser and Mallory some time to discover that the crowd actually consisted almost entirely of policemen. Bennett & Harper's produced a gaily patterned water-proof stuff made of burlap, ground cork, and coal derivatives, suitable for trimming and gluing-down in the kitchens and baths of the middle-class. They also produced great volumes of effluent from half-a-dozen stacks, which clearly the city would temporarily be better off without. The first officials on the scene—or at least they claimed that distinction—had been a group of inspectors from the Royal Patent Office, pressed into emergency industrial duty by a Government contingency plan. But Messrs. Bennett and Harper, anxious not to lose the day's production, had challenged the patent-men's legal authority to shut down their works. They were soon confronted by two more inspectors from a Royal Society industrial committee, who claimed precedent. The local constable had been attracted by the uproar, followed by a flying-squad of Bow Street metropolitans arriving in a commandeered steambus. Most 'buses had now been seized by Government, along with the city's cab-fleet, in accordance with contingency measures intended to deal with rail strikes.

The police had immediately shut down the stacks, fine work and a credit to the Government's good intentions, but the manufactory's workers were still on the premises, idle and very restive, for no one had mentioned a holiday with pay, though the workers clearly felt they deserved one under the circumstances. It also remained to be seen who was responsible for guarding the property of Messrs. Bennett and Harper, and who would be responsible for giving the official word to start the boilers again.

Worst of all, there seemed to be dire problems with the police telegraph-service—routed, presumably, through the Westminster pyramid of the Central Statistics Bureau. There must be trouble there from the Stink, Mallory surmised. "You're Special Branch, Mr. Fraser," Mallory said. "Why don't you straighten these dullards out?"

"Very witty," Fraser said.

"I wondered why we hadn't seen officers patrolling the streets. They must be snarled up in the premises of factories all over London!"

"You seem awfully pleased about the matter," Fraser said.

"Bureaucrats!" Mallory scoffed cheerily. "They might have known this would happen, if they'd properly studied Catastrophist theory. It is a concatenation of synergistic interactions; the whole system is on the period-doubling route to Chaos!"

"What does that mean, pray?"

"Essentially," Mallory said, smiling behind his kerchief, "in layman's terms, it means that everything gets twice as bad, twice as fast, until everything falls completely apart!"

"That's savantry talk. You don't presume that has anything to do with real matters here in London, do you?"

"Very interesting question!" Mallory nodded. "Deep metaphysical roots! If I model a phenomenon accurately, does that mean I understand it? Or might it be simple coincidence, or an artifact of the technique? Of course, as an ardent simulationist, I myself put much faith in Engine-modeling. But the doctrine can be questioned, no doubt of it. Deep waters, Fraser! The sort of thing that old Hume and Bishop Berkeley used to thrive on!"

"You're not drunk, are you, sir?"

"Just a bit elevated," Mallory said. "Squiffy, you might say." They tramped on, wisely leaving the police to their squabbling.

Mallory suddenly felt the loss of his good old Wyoming togglecoat. He missed his canteen, his spyglass, the snug stiffness of a rifle over his back. The look of a cold, clean, wild horizon where life was fully lived and death was swift and honest. He wished he were out of London, on expedition again. He could cancel all his engagements. He could apply for funding to the Royal Society, or better yet, the Geographical. He would leave England!

"You needn't do that, sir," Fraser said. "Might make matters worse, actually."

"Was I talking aloud?"

"A bit, sir. Yes."

"Where could a man get a first-class game-rifle here in town, Fraser?"

They were behind Chelsea Park now, in a place called Camera Square, where the shops offered fancy optical goods: talbotypes, magic-lanterns, phenakistoscopes, telescopes for the amateur stargazer. There were toy microscopes for the boy-savant of the house, boys often taking a strong interest in the wriggling animalcules in pond-water. The minute creatures were of no practical interest, but their study might lead young minds to the doctrines of genuine Science. Stung by sentiment, Mallory paused before a window displaying such microscopes. They reminded him of kindly old Lord Mantell, who had given him his first job tidying-up about the Lewes Museum. From there he'd moved to cataloguing bones and birds'-eggs, and at last to a real Cambridge scholarship. The old Lord had been a bit eager with the birch-switch, he now recalled, but likely no more than Mallory had deserved.

There came an odd whizzing sound from up the pavement. Mallory glanced in that direction and saw a queer half-crouching ghostly figure emerge from the fog, clothing flapping about it with speed, a pair of walking-canes doubled up under its arms.

Mallory jumped back at the last possible instant as the boy shot past him with a yowling whoop. A London boy, thirteen or so, on rubber-wheeled boots. The boy turned swiftly, skidded to an expert stop, and began to pole himself back up the pavement with the walking-sticks. Presently, an entire pack of boys had surrounded Mallory and Fraser, leaping and yelping in devilish glee. None of the others had wheeled shoes, but nearly all wore the little square cloth masks that Bureau clerks donned to tend their Engines.

"Say, you lads!" Fraser barked, "where did you get those masks?"

They ignored him. "That was dead flash!" one of them shouted. "Do it again, Bill!" Another boy cocked his leg three times with an odd ritual motion, then jumped high in the air and crowed "Sugar!" Those around him laughed and cheered.

"Calm down, you," Fraser ordered.

"Vinegar phiz!" a wicked boy fleered at him. "Shocking bad hat!" The whole pack of them burst into raucous hilarity.

"Where are your parents?" Fraser demanded. "You shouldn't be running about in this weather."

"Nuts and knuckles!" sneered the boy in wheeled shoes. "Forward all, my hearty crew! Panther Bill commands!" He jabbed his walking-sticks down and off. The others followed, yelling and whooping.

"Far too well-dressed to be street-arabs," Mallory remarked.

The boys had run off a short distance and were setting up for a game of crack-the-whip. Swiftly, each boy grabbed the next by the arm, forming a chain. The boy on wheels took the tail-end.

"Don't like the look of that," Mallory muttered.

The chain of boys swung out across Camera Square, each link gathering impetus, and suddenly the wheel-footed boy shot loose from the end like a stone from a catapult. He skidded off with a scream of devilish glee, hit some small discontinuity in the pavement, and tripped headlong into a sheet of plate-glass.

Shards of glass burst from the store-front, toppling like guillotine blades.

Young Panther Bill lay upon the pavement, seemingly stunned or dead. There was an awful moment of shocked silence.

"Treasure!" shrilled one of the boys. With maddened shrieks, the pack scrambled for the broken store-front and began grabbing every display-item in sight: telescopes, tripods, chemical glassware—

"Halt!" Fraser shouted. "Police!" He reached inside his coat, yanked his kerchief down, and sounded three sharp blasts on a nickel-plate police-whistle.

The boys fled instantly. A few dropped their snatched booty, but the rest clutched their prizes fiercely and ran like Barbary apes. Fraser hoofed it after them, Mallory at his heels, reaching the store-front where Panther Bill still lay sprawled. As they approached, the boy levered himself up on his elbow and shook his bleeding head.

"You're hurt, son," Mallory said.

"I'm right and fly!" said Panther Bill sluggishly. His scalp was slashed to the bone and blood was pouring over both his ears. "Hands off me, you masked bandits!"

Belatedly, Mallory pulled his own kerchief down and tried to smile at the boy. "You're injured, son. You need help." Together with Fraser, he bent over the boy.

"Help!" the boy screeched. "Help me, my crew!"

Mallory turned to look. Perhaps one of the other boys could be sent for aid.

A glittering triangular shard of flung glass spun from the fog, catching Fraser square in the back. The policeman jerked upright with a look of wide-eyed animal shock.

Panther Bill scrambled off on his hands and knees and jumped to his skidding feet. There was a loud smash from another store-front nearby, the musical clatter of glass, and delighted screams.

The glass-shard protruded in shocking fashion from Fraser's back. It was imbedded in him. "They're going to kill us!" Mallory cried, hauling Fraser along by the arm. Behind them glass was bursting like bombs, some of it flung blindly to shatter against the walls, some cascading from its shop-front mullions.

"Bloody hell . . . ," Fraser muttered.

Panther Bill's cry rang through the fog. "Treasure, my hearties! Treasure!"

"Clench your teeth," Mallory said. Folding his kerchief to protect his hand, he plucked the shard from Fraser's back. To his great relief, it came out of a piece. Fraser shuddered.

Mallory helped him gently out of his coat. Gore had streaked Fraser's shirt to the waistline, though it seemed not as bad as it might have been. The glass-shard had stabbed the chamois-leather strap of Fraser's shoulder-holster, which held a stout little pepperbox. "Your holster stopped most of it," Mallory said. "You're cut, but it's not deep, not through the ribs. We need to staunch that bleeding. . . ."

"Police station," Fraser nodded, "Kings Road West." He had gone very pale.

A fresh cascade of smashing glass echoed distantly behind them.

They walked on swiftly, Fraser wincing with each step. "You'd better stay with me," he said. "Spend the night at the police station. This has become very bad."

"Surely," Mallory said. "Don't trouble yourself."

"I mean it, Mallory."

"To be sure."

Two hours later Mallory was in Cremorne Gardens.

The document under analysis is a holographic letter. The letterhead has been removed, and the sheet was hastily folded. There is no date, but holographic analysis establishes that it is the genuine script of Edward Mallory, written in haste, and in a condition suggesting some loss of muscular coordination.

The paper-stock, of modest quality and badly yellowed by age, is of a sort in common governmental use in the mid-1850s. Its probable origin is the Kings Road West police station.

The text, in a badly faded ink from a pen-nib worn by long use, reads as follows:

MADAME.

I have told no one. But someone must be told. I conclude that you must be my confidante, for there is no one else.

When I took your property into my safe-keeping, I did so

freely. Your request is one I honor as I would a royal command, and your enemies are, of course, my own. It is the highest privilege of my life to act as your paladin.

Pray do not be alarmed for my safety. I beg you, take no steps on my behalf that might endanger yourself. Any risk in this battle I assume gladly, but there is indeed risk. Should the worst befall me, it is likely that your property would never be recovered.

I have examined the cards. I believe I have some inkling of their use, though they are far beyond my meager skill in Enginery. If this was an impertinence, I beg your pardon.

I have bound the cards securely in wrappings of clean linen, and personally sealed them away within an airtight container of plaster. That container is the skull of the Brontosaurus specimen in the Museum of Practical Geology in Jermyn Street. Your property now reposes in perfect safety some thirty feet above the ground. No human soul knows this, excepting yourself, and

Your Ladyship's most humble servant,
EDWARD MALLORY, F.R.S., F.R.G.S.

FOURTH ITERATION
Seven Curses

THIS OBJECT IS a patriotic funerary plaque in dense white porcelain, of the sort produced to commemorate the deaths of royalty and heads of state. Beneath an originally colorless glaze, cracked and yellowed by processes of time, are visible the features of Lord Byron.

Tens of thousands of these objects were sold throughout England during the months following the Prime Minister's death. The plaques themselves were of a standard manufacture, held in readiness for the demise of any sufficiently noted personage. The image of Byron, surrounded by wreaths, ornate scroll-work, and figures representative of the early history of the Industrial Radical Party, has been Engine-stippled upon a film of transparent material, which was then transferred to the plaque, glazed, and fired.

To Byron's left, amid stippled scroll-work, a crowned British lion poses rampant above the blurred coils of a defeated serpent, most probably meant to represent the Luddite cause.

It was sometimes remarked upon, both during and after Byron's rise to leadership, that his maiden speech in the House of Lords, February, 1812, urged clemency for the Luddites. Byron himself, questioned in this regard, is widely believed to have replied, "But there were Luddites, sir, and then there were Luddites." While this remark may be apocryphal, it is wholly in keeping with what is known of the Prime Minister's personality, and would seem to refer to the extraordinary severity with which he later put down and suppressed the popular Manchester-based anti-industrial movement led by Walter Gerard. For this was a form of Luddism attacking, not the old order, but the order that the Rads themselves had established.

This object was once the property of Inspector Ebenezer Fraser, of the Bow Street Special Branch.

Mallory had stayed with Fraser, watching the police surgeon at work with dirty sponge and bandage, until he was sure that Fraser was fully distracted. To further ease Fraser's evident suspicions, Mallory had borrowed a sheet of police stationery and set to the task of composing a letter.

In the meantime, the Kings Road station had slowly filled with bellowing ruffian drunks and various species of rioter. It was very interesting as a social phenomenon, but Mallory was in no mood to spend the night on a cheerless cot in some raucous cell. His taste was most stubbornly set on something else entirely.

So he had politely asked directions of a harried and exhausted sergeant, noted them with care in his field-book, and eased out of the station. He'd had no problem finding Cremorne Gardens.

The situation there was nicely indicative of the city's crisis dynamic. It was quite calm. No one in the Gardens seemed aware of events beyond, the shock-waves of localized dissolution having not yet permeated the system.

And it did not stink so badly here. The Gardens were on the Chelsea Reach, well upstream of the worst of the Thames. There was a faint night-breeze off the river, somewhat fishy but not altogether unpleasant, and the fog was broken by the great leafy boughs of Cremorne's ancient elms. The sun had set, and a thousand cloudy gas-lights twinkled for the pleasure of the public.

Mallory could imagine the pastoral charm of the Gardens in happier times. The place had bright geranium-beds, plots of well-rolled lawn, pleasant vine-enshrouded kiosks, whimsical plaster follies, and of course the famous Crystal Circle. And the "monster platform" as well, a great roofed and wall-less ballroom, where thousands might have strolled or waltzed or polkaed on the shoe-streaked wooden deck. There were liquor-stands inside, and food, and a great horse-cranked panmelodium playing a medley of selections from favorite operas.

There were not, however, thousands present tonight. Perhaps three hundred people circulated listlessly, and no more than a hundred of these were respectable. This hundred were weary of confinement, Mallory assumed, or courting couples braving all unpleasantness to meet. Of the remainder, two-thirds were men, more or less desperate, and prostitutes, more or less brazen.

Mallory had two more whiskeys at the platform's bar. The whiskey was cheap and smelled peculiar, either tainted by the Stink or doctored with hartshorn or potash or quassia. Or perhaps indian-berry, for the stuff had the color of bad stout. The whiskey-shots sat in his stomach like a pair of hot coals.

There was only a bit of dancing going on, a few couples attempting a self-conscious waltz. Mallory was not much of a dancer at the best of times. He watched the women. A tall, finely shaped young woman danced with an older, bearded gentleman. The fellow was stout and looked gouty in his knees, but the woman stood tall as a dart and danced with as much grace as a professional, the brass heels of her dolly-boots glinting in the light. The sway of her petticoats suggested the shape and size of the haunches beneath. No padding or whalebone was there. She'd fine ankles in red stockings and her skirts were two inches higher than propriety allowed.

He could not see her face.

The panmelodium struck up another tune, but the stout gentleman seemed winded. The pair of them stopped and moved off among a group of friends: an older, modest-looking woman in a bonnet, two other young girls who looked like dollymops, and another older gentleman who looked bleak-faced and foreign, from Holland perhaps or one of the Germanies. The dancing girl was talking with the others and tossing her head as if laughing. She had fine brunette hair and a bonnet knotted round her throat and hanging down her back. A fine, solid, womanly back and slim waist.

Mallory began walking slowly toward them. The girl talked with seeming earnestness to the foreign man, but his face showed reluctance and a seeming disdain. The girl sketched out something like a half-reluctant curtsey, then turned away from him.

Mallory saw her face for the first time. She had a strange long jaw, thick eyebrows, and a broad mobile slash of a mouth, lips edged with rouge. It was not exactly an ugly face, but decidedly plain. Yet there was a sharp, reckless look in her grey eyes and a strangely voluptuous expression that caught him as he stood. And she had a splendid form. He could see it as she walked—rolled, slid almost—to the bar. Again those marvelous hips and the line of that back. She leaned across the bar to chaff with the barman and her skirt rose behind her almost to her redstockinged calf. The sight of her muscular leg thrilled him with a jolt of lewd intensity. It was as if she had kicked him with it.

Mallory moved to the bar. She was not chaffing with the barman but arguing with him, in a half-painful, nagging, womanly way. She was thirsty and had no cash and said that her friends were paying. The barman didn't believe her, but would not say so straight out.

Mallory tapped a shilling on the bar. "Barman, give the lady what she wants."

She looked at him with annoyed surprise. Then she recovered herself, and smiled, and looked at him through half-shut lashes. "You know what I like best, Nicholas," she told the barman.

He brought her a flute of champagne and relieved Mallory of

his money. "I love champagne," she told Mallory. "You can dance like a feather when you drink champagne. Do you dance?"

"Abominably," Mallory said. "May I go home with you?"

She looked him up and down, and the corner of her mouth moved, with a wry but voluptuous smirk. "I'll tell you in a moment." And she went to rejoin her friends.

Mallory did not wait, for he thought it likely a gull. He walked slowly about the monster promenade and looked at other women, but then he saw the tall plain-faced girl beckoning. He went to her.

"I think I can go with you, but you may not like it," she said.

"Why shouldn't I?" he said. "I like *you*."

She laughed. "I don't mean in that way. I don't live here in Brompton; I live in Whitechapel."

"That's a long way."

"The trains aren't running. And we can't get a cab at all. I was afraid I would sleep in the park!"

"What about your friends?" Mallory asked.

The girl tossed her head, as if to say she didn't care for them. Her fine neck showed a bit of machine-made lace at the hollow of her throat. "I want to go back to Whitechapel. Will you take me? I haven't any money, not a tuppence."

"All right," Mallory said. He offered her his arm. "It's a five-mile walk—but your legs are a marvel."

She took his elbow and smiled at him. "We can catch a river-steamer at Cremorne Pier."

"Oh," Mallory said. "Down the Thames, eh?"

"It's not very dear." They walked down the steps of the monster platform into the twinkling gas-lit darkness. "You're not from London, are you? A traveling-gent."

Mallory shook his head.

"Will you give me a sovereign if I sleep with you?"

Mallory, surprised at her bluntness, said nothing.

"You can stay all night," she said. "I've a very nice room."

"Yes, that's what I want."

He stumbled a bit on the gravel walk. She steadied him, then boldly met his eyes. "You're a bit lushed, are you? But you look good-natured. What do they call you?"

"Edward. Ned, mostly."

"That's my name, too!" she said. "Harriet Edwardes, with an 'e' on the end. My stage-name. But my friends call me Hetty."

"You have the figure of a goddess, Hetty. I'm not surprised you're on the stage."

She gave him that bold, grey-eyed look. "You like wicked girls, Ned? I hope you do, for I'm in a mood to do wicked things tonight."

"I like them fine," Mallory said. He grabbed her by her tapered waist, thrust one hand against her swelling bosom, and kissed her mouth. She gave a little surprised shriek, and then threw her arms around his neck. They kissed a long while beneath the dark bulk of an elm. He felt her tongue against his teeth.

She pulled back a bit. "We have to get home, Ned. All right?"

"All right," he said, breathing hard. "But show me your legs now. Please?"

She looked up and down the path, then lifted her petticoats to the knee and dropped them again.

"They're perfection," he said. "You could sit to painters."

"I *have* sat to painters," she said, "and it don't pay."

A steamer sounded at Cremorne Pier. They ran to it and got aboard with moments to spare. The effort sent whiskey racing through Mallory's head. He gave the girl a shilling to pay the four-pence toll, and found a canvas steamer-chair up near the bow. The little ferry got up steam, its side-wheels slapping black water. "Let's go in the saloon," she said. "There's drink."

"I like to see London."

"I don't think you'll like what you see on this trip."

"I will if you stay with me," he said.

"How you talk, Ned," she said, and laughed. "Funny, I thought you were a copper at first, you looked so stern and solemn. But coppers don't talk like that, drunk or sober."

"You don't like compliments?"

"No, they're sweet. But I like champagne, too."

"In a moment," Mallory said. He was drunker than he liked to be. He stood and walked to the bow railing and gripped it hard, squeezing sensation back into his fingertips. "Damned dark in the city," he said.

"Why, it is," she said, standing near him. She smelled of salt sweat and tea-rose and cunt. He wondered if she had much hair there and what its color was. He was dying to see it. "Why is that, Ned?"

"What?"

"Why is it so dark? Is it the fog?"

"Gas-lights," he said. "Government have a scheme to turn off the gas-lights because they smoke so."

"How clever of them."

"Now people are running about in the blackened streets, smashing everything in sight."

"How do you know that?"

He shrugged.

"You're not a copper?"

"No, Hetty."

"I don't like coppers. They're always talking as if they know things you don't know. And they won't tell you how they know it."

"I could tell you," Mallory said. "I should like to tell you. But you wouldn't understand."

"Of course I'd understand, Ned," Hetty said in a voice as bright as peeling paint. "I love to hear clever men talk."

"London is a complex system out of equilibrium. It's like—it's like a drunken man, blind drunk, in a room with whiskey bottles. The whiskey is hidden—so he's always walking about looking for it. When he finds a bottle, he takes a long drink, but puts it down and forgets it at once. Then he wanders and looks again, over and over."

"Then he runs out of liquor and has to buy more," Hetty said.

"No. He never runs out. There's a demon that tops up the bottles constantly. That's why it is an open dynamical system. He walks round and round in the room, forever, never knowing what his next step may be. All blind and unknowing, he traces circles, figure-eights, every figure that a skater might make, but he never leaves the boundaries. And then one day the lights go out, and he instantly runs headlong out of the room and into outer darkness. And anything may happen then, anything at all, for the outer darkness is Chaos. It is Chaos, Hetty."

"And you like that, eh?"

"What?"

"I don't know what that means that you just said; but I can tell you like it. You like to think about it." With a gentle, quite natural movement, she put her hand against the front of his trousers. "Isn't it stiff!" She snatched her hand back and grinned triumphantly.

Mallory looked hastily about the deck. There were other people out, a dozen or so. It seemed none of them were watching, but it was hard to tell in the foggy darkness. "You tease," he said.

"Pull it out, and you'll see how I tease."

"I'd rather wait for the proper time and place."

"Fancy a man saying that," she said, and laughed.

The steady slapping paddle-wheels suddenly changed their tenor. The black Thames gave up a vile rush of stench and the crisping sound of bubbles.

"Oh, it's horrid," cried Hetty, clapping a hand to her mouth. "Let's go in the saloon, Ned, please!"

A strange curiosity pinned Mallory in place. "Does it get worse than this? Down-river?"

"Much worse," Hetty said through her fingers. "I've seen folk swoon away."

"Why do the ferries still run, then?"

"They always run," Hetty said, half-turning away. "They're mail-boats."

"Oh," Mallory said. "Could I buy a stamp here?"

"Inside," said Hetty, "and you can buy me something, too."

Hetty lit an oil-lamp in the cramped little hallway of her upstairs lodging in Flower-and-Dean Street. Mallory, powerfully glad to be free of the fog-choked eeriness of back-street Whitechapel, edged past her into the parlor. A square, plank-topped table held a messy stack of illustrated tabloids, somehow still delivered despite the Stink. In the dimness he could make out fat Engine-printed headlines bemoaning the poor state of the Prime Minister's health. Old Byron was always feigning sickness, some gammy foot or rheumy lung or raddled liver.

Hetty entered the parlor with her glowing lamp, and faded roses bloomed in the dusty wallpaper. Mallory dropped a gold sovereign on the table-top. He hated trouble in these matters, and always paid in advance. She noted the ring of the coin, smiling. Then she kicked off her street-muddied dolly-boots, and walked, swaying, to a doorway, which she flung open. A grey cat ran out, mewing, and she fussed at it, petting it and calling it Toby. She let it out to the stairs. Mallory watched her do this, and stood flat-footed in unhappy patience.

"Well, then, come on with you," she said, tossing her plaited brown head.

The bedroom was small enough, and shabby, with a pressed-oak two-poster and a tall, tarnished cheval-glass that looked as if it had once cost some money. Hetty set the lamp on the badly delaminated veneer of a bedside commode and began to pick at the buttons of her blouse, pulling her arms from the sleeves and tossing the garment aside as if clothing were more trouble to her than she cared for. Stepping deftly out of her skirt, she began to remove her corset and a stiff crinkled petticoat.

"You wear no crinoline," Mallory noted hoarsely.

"Don't like 'em." She popped the waistband of the petticoat and laid it aside. She deftly picked the wire hooks of the corset and eased its laces open, then wriggled it over her hips and stood there, breathing in relief, in her lace chemise.

Mallory got out of his jacket and shoes. His member strained at his fly-buttons. He was anxious to get it out of his trousers, but didn't care to parade his erect prick by lamplight.

Hetty jumped into the bed in her chemise, the worn springs complaining loudly. Mallory sat on the edge of the bed, which smelled powerfully of cheap orange-water and Hetty's sweat, and got his trousers and unmentionables off, leaving himself in his shirt.

Leaning off the bed, he unbuttoned one compartment of his money-belt and removed a French-letter. "I'll do it in armor, dear," he muttered. "Is that all right?"

Hetty sat up brightly on her elbow. "Let me see it, then." Mallory showed her the rolled membrane of sheep-gut. "It isn't one of those queer ones," she noted, with apparent relief. "Do as you like, dearie."

Mallory carefully peeled the device over the taut skin of his prick. This was better, Mallory thought, happier for this act of foresight. It felt more as if he knew what he was doing here, and that he would be safe after all, and get his money's worth as well. He climbed under the dingy sheet.

Hetty wrapped her strong arms around his neck and kissed him fiercely with her great crooked mouth, as if she meant to glue it to him. Mallory, startled, felt her tongue writhing about on his teeth like a slick warm eel. The strange sensation powerfully stimulated his virility. He struggled atop her, her solid flesh feeling marvelous through the obscenely thin veil of the chemise, and fought with the garment till he had it up about her waist. Hetty made enthusiastic groaning noises as Mallory groped about in the damp fleece between her legs. Finally, seeming impatient, Hetty reached down without ceremony and jammed his prick into her cunt.

She stopped sucking his mouth as they began to rut. Soon they were breathing like steam-gurneys, the bed creaking and jouncing beneath them like a badly tuned panmelodium. "Oh, Ned, darling!" she yelped suddenly, setting eight sharp fingernails into his back. "What a fine big one it is! I'm going to spend!" And she writhed under him in near-convulsion. Jolted by the strangeness of a woman speaking English in the midst of sexual congress, he spent abruptly, as if the seed were wrenched unwilling from his flesh by the hard lewd plunging of her loins.

After a quiet, panting moment, Hetty kissed his bearded

cheek with the half-shy lash-fluttering look of a woman con-
quered by desire. "That was fine indeed, Ned. You really do know
how to do it. Now let's have something to eat, shall we? I'm bloody
starving."

"Good," Mallory said, rolling off the sweaty cradle of her hips.
He felt grateful to her, as he always did to any woman who had
favored him, and a bit ashamed of himself, and of her as well. But
very hungry, too. He had not eaten in many hours.

"We can get a nice petit-souper downstairs from the Hart. Mrs.
Cairns can fetch it up for us. She's my landlady what lives next
door."

"Fine," Mallory said.

"You'll have to pay for it and tip her, though." Hetty rolled from
bed, her chemise rucked up. She tugged it loose, but the glimpse
of her magnificent backside sent a wash of gratified amazement
through him. She knuckle-thumped the bedroom wall in quick
staccato. After a slow moment there was an answering knock.

"Your friend's up late?" Mallory said.

"She's used to this business," Hetty told him, sliding back in
bed with a chorus of squeaks. "Never you mind Mrs. Cairns. She
mills her poor husband about every Wednesday and keeps the
whole building awake."

Mallory carefully removed his French-letter, which had
stretched out of shape but not torn, and dropped it into the pot-
de-chambre. "Should we open a window? It's damned hot. . . ."

"No, don't let in the Stink, dearie!" Hetty grinned in the
lamplight, and scratched herself beneath the sheet. "Anyway, the
windows don't open."

"Why not?"

"The casements are all nailed tight. The girl who used to live
here, last winter . . . Queer little thing, with a po-face and fine
gentry airs, but awful frightened of her enemies. She nailed all
the windows shut, I think. They finally got her even so, poor
creature."

"How is that, then?" Mallory asked.

"Oh, she never brought her men here, that I ever saw, but

finally the coppers came here looking for her, Specials, if you know the kind I mean. And they gave me a sharp time of it too, the bastards, as if I knew what she did, or who her friends were. I didn't even know her real name. Sybil something. Sybil Jones."

Mallory tugged at his beard. "What *did* she do, this Sybil Jones?"

"She had a child by an M.P. when she was young," Hetty said. "Fellow name of, well, I doubt you want to know. She was a politician's tart, who used to sing a bit. Me, I'm a tart who poses. *Connaissez-vous poses plastiques?*"

"No." Mallory noted without surprise that a flea had landed on his bare knee-cap. He caught it, then cracked it bloodily between his thumbnails.

"We dress in tight leotards colored just like skin, and swan about and let gentlemen gawk at us. Mrs. Winterhalter—you saw her tonight in Cremorne, bossing us about—she's my manageress, as they say. The crowd was dreadful thin tonight, and those Swede diplomats we was with are as tight as a chicken's arse. So it was a bit of luck for me that you showed."

A rapping came at the door of the hall. Hetty rose. "Donnez-moi four shillings," she said. Mallory gave her some coins, which swiftly vanished as she left. Hetty returned with a dented and chipped japanned tray and displayed a misshapen loaf of bread, a lump of ham, mustard, four fried sausages, and a dusty split of warm champagne.

Filling two stained champagne-flutes, she began to eat her supper, quite composedly, without speaking. Mallory gazed fixedly at her dimpled arms and shoulders and the swell of her heavy, dark-nippled breasts in the thin chemise, and wondered a bit about the plainness of her face. He drank a glass of the acrid, bad champagne, and ate the greenish ham in famished mouthfuls.

Hetty finished the sausages. Then, with a crooked smile, she slid out of bed, and squatted by its side, hoisting the chemise to her waist. "That champagne runs right through you, don't it? I need the pot. Don't look unless you want to." Mallory looked aside politely and listened to the rattle of piss.

"Let's wash," she said. "I'll fetch a basin." She came back with an enameled pan of reeking London water, and sponged at herself with a loofah.

"Your form is splendid," Mallory said. Her hands and feet were small, but the columnar roundness of her calves and thighs were marvels of mammalian anatomy. Her great solid buttocks were faultless. They seemed weirdly familiar to him, like the white female buttocks he had seen in a dozen historical canvases. It occurred to him that likely they were the very same. Her neat-lipped cunt was furred with auburn hair.

She smiled at his stare. "Would you like to see me naked?"

"Very much."

"For a shilling?"

"All right."

She threw off her chemise with apparent relief, sweat standing out all over her. She sponged tenderly at her dripping armpits. "I can stand in pose, not moving at all, for full five minutes at a time," she said, slurring a bit. She had drunk nearly all of the champagne. "Have you a watch? Ten shilling an' I'll do it! Do you bet I can?"

"I'm sure you can do it," Mallory said.

Hetty bent gracefully, grasped her left ankle, and lifted it straight above her head, her leg stiff at the knee. She began spinning about, slowly, shuffling on heel and toe. "You like it?"

"Wonderful," Mallory said, stunned.

"Look, I can put both my hands quite flat on the floor," she said, bending at the waist. "Most London girls are so tight-laced they'd break in bloody half if they tried this." Then she went into a split on the floor, and gazed up at him, drunken and trium-phant.

"I never lived till I came to London," Mallory said.

"Take off your shirt, then, and let's fuck starkers." Her long-jawed face was flushed, her grey eyes bulging. Mallory took his shirt off. She advanced on him with the enamel basin. "Fucking naked's fine in beastly hot weather like this. I *always* like to fuck naked. My, you have fine firm flesh on you, an' I do like a man with some hairiness. Let's have a look at your prick." She grabbed it forthrightly, skinned it back and examined it, then dabbled it in the basin. "You're not sick, dear—there's nothing wrong with you, it's quite a fine one. Why not fuck me without that nasty sausage-skin and save yourself nine pence?"

"Nine pence isn't much," Mallory said. He put on another French-letter, then mounted her. He rutted nakedly, sweating like a blacksmith. The sweat was pouring off the both of them, with a reek of bad champagne, yet the sticky skin of her great teats felt quite cool against his naked chest. She galloped along under him, her eyes shut and her tongue showing at the corner of her crooked mouth, and put the backs of her heels sharply into his buttocks. At last he spent, groaning between clenched teeth at the burning rush through his prick. There was a roaring in his ears.

"You're a bawdy devil, my Ned, and sure." Her neck and shoulders were red with prickly heat.

"So are you," Mallory gasped.

"I am, dear, and I like to do it with a man who knows how to treat a girl. Let's have some nice bottled ale, then. More cooling than that champagne."

"All right. Fine."

"And some papirosi. Do you like papirosi?"

"What are those, exactly?"

"Turkish cigarettoes, from the Crimea. They're all the rage since the war."

"You smoke tobacco?" Mallory asked, surprised.

"I learnt it from Gabrielle," she said, climbing from bed. "Gabrielle, she lived here after Sybil left. She was a Frenchie from Marseilles. But she sailed to French Mexico last month, with one of her embassy soldiers. She married him, lucky thing." Hetty wrapped herself in a robe-de-nuit of yellow silk. In the lantern-light it looked a fine garment, despite its frayed hems. "Sweet she was, Gabrielle. Donnez-moi four shillings, dear. No, five."

"Can you change a pound-note?" Mallory said. Hetty gave him fifteen shillings, with a sour look, and vanished into the parlor.

She was absent a long time—chatting with Mrs. Landlord, it seemed. Mallory lay at ease in her bed, listening to strange distant echoes of the great metropolis: bells ringing, distant high-pitched cries, bangs that might be gunshots. He was as drunk as a Lordship, it seemed, and Lordship felt mortal fine. The weight would be back on his heart soon enough, and no doubt redoubled for the sin, but for the moment fleshly pleasure had lifted him, and he felt quite free and feather-light.

Hetty returned with a wire crate of bottles in one hand, puffing a lit cigaretto with the other.

"You took a long time," he said.

She shrugged. "A bit of trouble downstairs. Some ruffians." She set the crate down, pulled a bottle out, and flung it to him. "Feel how cool—they keep these in the cellar. Nice, ain't it?"

Mallory unloosed the complex stopper of porcelain, cork, and levered wire, and thirstily drank. NEWCASTLE ALE, the bottle said, in molded letters of raised glass. A modern brewery where they made the liquor in great steel vats near the size of a ship-of-the-line. Fine machine-made brew, free of any cheater's taint of jalap or indian-berry.

Hetty got into the bed in her robe, drained the last of a bottle, and opened another. "Take the robe off," Mallory said.

"You didn't give me my shilling."

"Here, then."

She slipped the coin under the mattress, and smiled. "You're a rum'un, Neddie. I like you." She took the robe off, flung it at the iron coat-hook on the back of the door, missed. "I'm in a rare mood tonight. Let's have another go."

"In a bit," Mallory said, and yawned. His lids felt heavy suddenly, grainy. The back of his head throbbed, where Velasco had smacked him, it seemed an age ago. It seemed an age since he had done anything but drink and rut.

Hetty gripped his limp prick and began to fondle it. "When did you last have a woman, Ned?"

"Ah . . . two months, I think. Three."

"And who was she?"

"She was . . ." She had been a whore in Canada, but Mallory suddenly stopped. "Why do you ask?"

"Tell me. I like to hear about it. I like to know what the fancy do."

"I don't know anything about that. Nor do you, I imagine."

Hetty released his prick and folded her arms. She leaned back against the headboard, then lit another papirosi, scraping her lucifer against a rough patch of plaster. She blew smoke through her oddly shaped nose—a disconcerting sight, for Mallory. "You don't think I know anything," she said. "I've heard such things as you don't imagine, I'll wager."

"No doubt," Mallory said politely. He finished his ale.

"Did you know that old Lady Byron flogs her husband naked? His prick won't stand till she beats him on the arse with a German riding-crop, and I'd that straight from a copper, who was sweet on me, who had it from an upstairs servant in the household!"

"Oh?"

"That Byron family is dead bawdy and wicked to the core. He's too old now, but in his younger days he'd fuck a sheep, Lord Byron would. He'd fuck a bush if he thought a sheep was in it! His wife's no better. She doesn't fuck other men, but she's of the flogging sisterhood."

"Remarkable," Mallory said. "What about their daughter, then?"

Hetty said nothing for a moment. He was surprised at the sudden gravity of her expression. "She's dead flash, Ada is. She's the greatest whore in all of London."

"Why do you say that?"

"Because she fucks whoever she pleases, and none dare make a peep about what she does. She's had half the House of Lords, and they all tag at her skirts like little boys. And call themselves her favorites and her paladins, and if any man breaks troth and dares breathe a word against her, then the others see to it that he comes to a very bad end. They all ring round her, and protect her, and worship her like Romish priests do their Madonna."

Mallory grunted. It was whore's talk, not a proper thing to say. He knew that Lady Ada had her gallants, but the thought that she let men have her, that there was shoving and spending, prick and cunt in the mathematical bed of the Queen of Engines . . . . Best not to think about it. His head had a whiskey-spin, somehow.

"Your expertise is impressive, Hetty," Mallory muttered. "You certainly command the data of your trade. . . ."

Hetty, who had been guzzling at another bottle of ale, laughed explosively. Foam splattered her chest. "Oh, Christ," she said, coughing, and smearing at her breasts. "Lor', Neddie, how you do talk. Look what you made me do."

"Sorry," Mallory said.

She gave him a fleering grin and picked her smoldering cigaretto from the edge of the bureau. "Get the rag and give 'em a good wash," she suggested. "I'll bet you'd like that, eh?"

Without a word, Mallory stooped to his work. He fetched the basin, and sopped the hand-towel, scrubbing the wet terry carefully over her breasts and the fat, navel-dimpled white rise of her belly. Hetty watched with hooded eyes, puffing at her cigaretto and flicking ashes on the floor, as if her flesh belonged to someone else. After a while, she silently gripped his prick, working it back and forth encouragingly as he wiped at her legs.

Mallory put on another sheath, with some clumsy fumbling, almost losing his erection as he did so. To his relief, he managed to enter her, where he soon regained stiffness in her welcoming flesh, and thumped hard at her, tired and drunk, with an ache in his arms and his wrists and his back, and a strange painful tingling at the root of his prick. The glans felt quite sore, almost painfully tender within its sheep-gut armor, and to spend seemed as hard and tricky as pulling a rusty nail. The bed-springs creaked like a field of metal crickets. Halfway through, Mallory felt as if he had run for miles, and Hetty, whose dead cigaretto had burnt the bureau, seemed entranced, or perhaps only stunned, or drunk. For a moment he wondered if he should simply stop, quit, tell her somehow that it simply wasn't working, but he could not even begin to find the words that would satisfactorily explain this situation, so he sawed on. His mind wandered, to another woman, a cousin of his, a red-haired girl whom he had seen being shagged behind a Sussex hedgerow, when he had been up a tree as a boy, hunting cuckoo's eggs. The red-haired cousin had married the man, and was forty years old now with grown children, a round little proper woman in a round little proper bonnet, but Mallory never met her without remembering the tortured look of pleasure on her freckled face. He clutched that secret image now like a galley-slave to his oar, and fought his way stubbornly toward a climax. Finally, there was that melting, cresting feeling in his loins that told him that he would, in fact, spend soon, that nothing would hold him back, and he shoved on with a new desperation, panting very hard, and the agonized rush of spending came up his aching spine like a rocket, a surge of shocking pleasure in his arms, in his legs, even in the naked soles of his cramping feet, and he cried out, a loud ecstatic bestial groan that surprised him.

"Lordy," Hetty commented.

Mallory collapsed off of her and lay blowing like a beached cetacean in the foetid air. His muscles felt like rubber, and he'd half-sweated the whiskey off with the sheer work of it. He felt utterly wonderful. He felt quite willing to die. If the tout had arrived and shot him on the spot he would somehow have welcomed it, welcomed the opportunity never to come back from that plateau of sensibility, the opportunity never to be Edward Mallory again, but only a splendid creature drowned in cunt and tea-rose.

But after a moment the feeling was gone and he was Mallory again. Too stupefied for any refinements of guilt or regret, Mallory nevertheless felt ready to leave. Some unspoken crisis had passed, and the episode was finished. He was simply too tired to move just yet, but he knew that he was about to. The whore's bedroom no longer felt like any kind of haven to him. The walls seemed unreal, mere mathematical abstractions, boundaries that could no longer restrain his momentum.

"Let's sleep a bit," Hetty said, her words blurred with drink and exhaustion.

"All right." He sensibly set the box of lucifers within convenient reach, turned out the lantern, and lay in the hot London dark like a suspended Platonic soul. He rested, eyes open, a flea feasting with leisurely precision on his ankles. He did not sleep, exactly, but rested for some indefinite time. When his mind began to run in circles, he lit and smoked one of Hetty's cigarettes, a pleasant ritual, though without much point as far as the proper use of tobacco went. Later he left the bed and pissed in the pot-de-chambre, by feel. Ale had spilled on the floor there, or perhaps it was something else. He would have liked to wipe his feet, but there seemed little point.

He waited for something akin to dawn to show at Hetty's bare and grimy casement, which gazed out gloomily at a nearby wall. At length there came a feeble glow, not much at all like honest daylight. He had sobered now, and lay there parched, his head feeling stuffed with gun-cotton. Not at all bad, really, if he didn't move it suddenly, but full of grim premonitory throbs.

He lit the bedside candle, found his shirt. Hetty woke with a groan, and stared at him, her hair snarled and sweaty, her eyes bulging with a look that almost frightened him—*ellynge*, they would have called it in Sussex—fey. "You're not going," she said.

"Yes."

"Why? It's so dark, still."

"I prefer an early start." He paused. "An old camp habit."

Hetty snorted. "Get back in bed, my brave soldier, don't be silly. Stay a bit. We'll wash and have breakfast. You can get that, can't you? A nice big breakfast?"

"I'd rather not. It's late, I must go, I have business."

"How late?" she yawned. "Not even dawn yet."

"It's late. I'm certain of it."

"What does Big Ben say?"

"I haven't heard Ben all night," Mallory said, the recognition surprising him. "Government have shut it down, I suppose."

This bit of speculation seemed to vaguely alarm Hetty. "French breakfast, then," she suggested, "sent up from downstairs. Pastry, pot o' coffee. It's cheap."

He shook his head.

Hetty paused, narrowed her eyes. The refusal seemed to have startled her. She sat up, the bed creaking, and tugged at her disordered hair. "Don't go out, the weather's dreadful. If you can't sleep, dear, then let's fuck."

"I don't think I can."

"I know you like me, Neddie." She raised the sweat-dampened sheet. "Come and feel me all over, that will make it stand." She lay there waiting, with the sheet up.

Mallory, unwilling to disappoint, came toward her, patted her lovely haunches, and groped about the luscious smoothness of her breasts. Her flesh delighted his touch, but his prick, though it stirred, did not stand. "I really must go," he said.

"It will stand again if you wait a bit."

"I can't stay anymore."

"I would not do this if you were not such a nice man," Hetty said slowly, "but I can make it stand right now if you like; *connaissez-vous la belle gamahuche?*"

"What's that, then?"

"Well," she said, "if you'd been with Gabrielle instead of me, you'd have had it by now; she always did it with her men, and said they were mad for it; it's what they call gamahuching, the French pleasure."

"I'm not sure I understand."

"Prick-sucking."

"Oh. That." He had heard the term, though only as the foulest kind of abusive curse, and was startled to find himself in a situation where it might be performed as a physical act. He tugged at his beard. "Ah . . . how much would that cost?"

"I wouldn't do it for any price, for some," she assured him, "but I do like you, Ned, and for you I'd do it."

"How much?"

She blinked. "Ten shillings?"

Half-a-pound. "I don't think so," he said.

"Well, all right, five shillings, if you don't finish there. But you have to promise that, and I mean it."

The implications of this proposal gave him an exquisite thrill of disgust. "No, I don't care for that." He began to dress.

"You'll come again then? When will you see me?"

"Soon."

She sighed, knowing he was lying. "Go then, if you must. But listen, Neddie, I do know you like me. And I don't remember your proper name exactly, but I know I've seen your portrait in the papers. You're a famous savant, and you have a deal of tin. I'm right about that, aren't I?"

Mallory said nothing.

She hurried on. "A fellow like you can get in bad trouble with the wrong sort of London girl. But you're safe as houses with Hetty Edwardes, for I only go with gentlemen, and I'm very discreet."

"I'm sure that you are," Mallory said, dressing hastily.

"I dance Tuesdays and Thursdays at the Pantascopic Theatre, down Haymarket. Will you come and see me?"

"If I'm in London."

He left her then, and felt his way out of the place. On his hasty way to the stairs he bloodily scraped his shin on the pedal of someone's chained bicycle.

The sky above the Hart was like nothing Mallory had ever seen, yet he knew it. He had seen such a sky with his mind's-eye, a lowering dome abrim with explosive filth, awash with obliterating dust—a sky that was the very harbinger of Catastrophe.

By the twilight blur of the fully risen sun he reckoned it near eight o'clock. Dawn had come, yet brought no day. The Land Leviathans had seen this very sky, he knew, after the earth-shaking shock of the Great Comet. For the scaly herds, ceaselessly progressing through the teeming jungles, driven always by a mighty hunger in their great fermenting bellies, this had been the sky of Armageddon. Storms of Cataclysm lashed the Cretaceous earth, vast fires raged, and cometary grit sifted through the roiling atmosphere, to blight and kill the wilting foliage, till the mighty Dinosauria, adapted to a world now shattered, fell in massed extinction, and the leaping machineries of Evolution were loosed in chaos, to re-populate the stricken Earth with strange new orders of being.

He scuffed down Flower-and-Dean Street, awestruck, coughing. He could see little more than thirty feet ahead, for the alley roiled with a low-lying yellow fog that blurred his eyes with its clinging acid tang.

More by luck than design, he emerged on Commercial Street, ordinarily a thriving Whitechapel avenue. Deserted now, its smooth tarmac was spread with fountained shards of shop-front glass.

He walked a block, then another. There was scarcely a window intact. Cobbles, grubbed up from side-streets, had been flung right and left like a shower of meteors. A seeming whirlwind had descended on a nearby grocery, leaving the street ankle-deep in dirty snow-drifts of flour and sugar. Mallory picked his way through battered cabbages, squashed greengages, crushed jars of syrupped peaches, and the booted footballs of whole smoked hams. Scatterings of damp flour showed a stampede of men's brogues, the small bare feet of street-urchins, the dainty trace of women's shoes, and the sweep of their skirt-hems.

Four mist-shrouded figures, three men and a woman, all dressed respectably, all carefully masked in thick cloth, came shuffling into view. Noticing him, they pointedly crossed the street. They moved slowly, unhurriedly, talking together in low tones.

Mallory moved on, splintered glass crunching under his shoe-heels. Meyer's Gent's Furnishings, Peterson's Haberdashery, LaGrange's Parisian Pneumatique Launderette, all presented disintegrated store-fronts and doors torn off their hinges. Their fronts had been thoroughly pelted with stones, with bricks, with raw eggs.

Now a more cohesive group appeared. Men and young boys, some rolling heaped barrows, though they were clearly not costers. In their masks, they seemed tired, bemused, somber, as though attending a funeral. In their aimless progress they slowed before a sacked cobbler's, picking over the scattered shoes with the limp enthusiasm of scavengers.

Mallory realized that he had been a fool. While he had wallowed in mindless dissipation, London had become a locus of anarchy. He should be home in peaceful Sussex now, with the family. He should be readying for little Madeline's wedding, in clean country air, with his brothers and sisters at hand, with decent home-cooked food and decent homely drink. A sudden agony of homesickness struck him, and he wondered what chaotic amalgam of lust and ambition and circumstance had marooned him in this dreadful, vicious place. He wondered what the family were doing at that very moment. What was the time, exactly?

With a jolt, Mallory remembered Madeline's clock. His sister's wedding-gift was sitting in its brass-hasped carry-case in the safety-box of the Palace of Paleontology. The lovely fancy clock for dear Madeline, now grotesquely out of his reach. The Palace was seven miles from Whitechapel. Seven miles of roiling chaos.

There must be some way back, some way to cross that distance, surely. Mallory wondered if any of the city's trains were running, or the omnibuses. Perhaps a hansom? Horses would choke in this foul mist. He was down to shank's mare. Likely any effort to cross London was foolish, and likely it would be wisest to cower in some quiet cellar like a rat, hoping for Catastrophe to pass him over. And yet Mallory found his shoulders squaring, his legs tramping forward of their own accord. Even the throbbing in his parched head began to pass as his wits focused on a goal. Back to the Palace. Back to his life.

"Hullo! Say there! Sir!" The voice echoed over Mallory's head like the cry of a bad conscience. He glanced up, startled.

From a third-floor window of Jackson Bros., Furriers & Hatters, protruded the black barrel of a rifle. Behind it, Mallory made out the balding head of a spectacled shopping-clerk, leaning from his open window now to reveal a striped shirt and scarlet braces.

"May I be of service?" Mallory called, the phrase emerging out of reflex.

"Thank you, sir!" the clerk cried, his voice cracking. "Sir, could you, please, have a look at our door there—just to the side, below the steps? I believe—there may be someone hurt!"

Mallory waved one hand in reply, walked to the shop's entrance. Its double-doors were intact but badly battered, dripping splattered eggs. A young man in a sailor's striped blouse and bell-bottomed trousers lay sprawled there, face-down, a pry-bar of forged iron near his hand.

Mallory seized the shoulder of the sailor's coarse blouse and turned him over. A bullet had taken him through the throat. He was quite dead, and his nose had been mashed to one side by the pavement, giving his bloodless young face a bizarre cast, so that he seemed to have come from some nameless country of sea-going albinos.

Mallory straightened. "You've shot him dead!" he shouted upward.

The clerk, seeming rattled, began coughing loudly, and made no reply.

Mallory spied the wooden butt of a pistol tucked in the dead sailor's intricately knotted sash; he tugged it out. A revolver of unfamiliar make, its massive cylinder curiously slotted and grooved. The long octagonal barrel, under-hung with a sort of piston, stank of black-powder. He glanced at the furrier's battered door. Clearly an entire mob had been at it, an armed mob, bent on the worst kind of mischief. The wretches must have scattered when the sailor had been shot.

He stepped into the street, waving the pistol. "The rascal was armed!" he shouted. "You did well to—"

A bullet from the clerk's rifle screamed off a cement stair-step, bleaching it white with impact and narrowly missing Mallory on the ricochet.

"God blame ye, ye cack-handed fool!" Mallory bellowed. "Stop that this instant!"

There was a moment's silence. "Sorry, sir!" the clerk cried.

"What in hell do you think you're doing?"

"I said I was sorry! You best throw away that gun, though, sir!"

"The hell I will!" Mallory roared, slipping the pistol into the waistband of his trousers. He meant to demand that the clerk come down and decently cover the dead man, but he thought better of it as other windows rattled up on their casters, four more rifle barrels appearing in defense of Jackson Bros.

Mallory backed up, showing empty hands and attempting to smile. When the fog had thickened around him, he turned and ran.

Now he moved more cautiously, keeping to the center of the street. He discovered a trampled cambric shirt and cut its baggy sleeve loose with the small saw-tooth blade of his Sheffield knife. It made a serviceable mask.

He examined the sailor's revolver, and plucked a blackened cartridge-case from the cylinder. It still held five shots. It was a clumsy thing, foreign, unevenly blued, though the mechanism looked to have been executed with a decent degree of accuracy. He made out BALLESTER-MOLINA, stamped faintly on the side of the octagonal barrel, but there were no other markings.

Mallory emerged on Aldgate High Street, recalling it from his walk with Hetty from the London Bridge pier, though it looked, if anything, more eerie and horrid than it had in the middle of the night. The mob did not seem to have touched it as yet, in the inherent vagary of Chaos.

A rhythmic clanging of alarm sounded from the fog behind him. He stepped aside to watch a fire-gurney steam past, its red-painted sides battered and dented. Some London mob had brutally attacked the firemen, attacked the trained men and machines that stood between the city and mass conflagration. This struck Mallory as the acme of perverse stupidity, yet somehow it failed to surprise him. Exhausted firemen clung to the gurney's running-boards, wearing bizarre rubber masks with gleaming eye-pieces and accordioned breathing-tubes. Mallory dearly wished for such a mask himself, for his eyes were misting so painfully now that he squinted like a pantomime pirate, but he tramped on.

Aldgate became Fenchurch, then Lombard, then Poultry Street, and still he was miles from his goal, if the Palace of Paleontology could be said to be one. His head pounded and swam with the sullen lees of bad whiskey and worse air, and he seemed to be nearer the Thames now, for a damp and viscous taint arose that sickened him.

On Cheapside, a city omnibus had been toppled on its side and set afire with its own boiler-coals. Every window in it had been shattered, and it had burnt to a blackened husk. Mallory hoped no one had died inside it. The smoking wreckage stank too fiercely for him to want to look more closely.

There were people in the churchyard of St. Paul's. The air seemed somewhat clearer there, for the dome was visible, and a large crowd of men and boys had collected among the church-yard trees. Unaccountably, they seemed in the highest spirits. Mallory perceived to his astonishment that they were brazenly tossing dice on the very steps of Wren's masterpiece.

A little farther on, and Cheapside itself was blocked by scat-tered crowds of eager and determined gamblers. Fairy-rings of rascals had sprouted left and right from the very pavement, men kneeling to guard their mounting stakes of coins and paper-money. Eager leaders in mischief, tough, squint-eyed cockneys who seemed to have leapt whole from the coagulated Stink of London, cried aloud, hoarsely, like patterers, as Mallory passed. "A shilling to open! Who'll shoot? Who will shoot, my lads?" From the scattered rings came cries of triumph at winning, angry groans muffled by masks.

For each man boldly gambling, there were three who timidly watched. A carnival attraction, it seemed, a stinking and criminal carnival, but a London lark nonetheless. There were no police in sight, no authority, no decency. Mallory edged warily through the thin, excited crowd, a cautious hand on the butt of the sailor's pistol. In an alley, two masked men booted a third, then relieved him of his watch and wallet. A crowd of at least a dozen watched the sight with only mild interest.

These Londoners were like a gas, thought Mallory, like a cloud of minute atomies. The bonds of society broken, they had simply flown apart, like the perfectly elastic gassy spheres in Boyle's Laws of Physics. Most of them looked respectable enough by their dress; they were merely reckless now, stripped by Chaos to a moral vacuity. Most of them, Mallory thought, had never seen any event remotely like this one. They had no proper standards left for judgment or comparison. They had become puppets of base impulse.

Like the Cheyenne tribesmen of Wyoming, dancing in the devil's grip of drink, the goodmen of civilized London had surrendered themselves to primitive madness. And by the patent look of surprised bliss on their shining faces, Mallory perceived that they enjoyed it. They enjoyed it very greatly indeed. It was exaltation to them, a wicked freedom more perfect and desirable than any they had ever known.

Along the edge of the crowd a line of gaudy handbills had been newly slapped-up across a formerly sacrosanct brick wall of Paternoster Row. They were adverts of the cheapest and most ubiquitous kind, the sort that pursued the eye all over London: PROFESSOR RENBOURNE'S MAGNETIC HEADACHE PILLS, BEARDSLEY'S SHREDDED CODFISH, MCKESSON & ROBBINS' TARTARLITHINE, ARNICA TOOTH SOAP . . . And some theatrical prints: MADAME SCAPIGLIONI at the Saville House in Leicester Square, a VAUXHALL PANMELODIUM SYMPHONY . . . Events, Mallory thought, that would surely never come off, and indeed the sheets had been posted with a careless haste that had badly wrinkled the paper. Fresh glue dripped from beneath the bills in rivulets of white ooze, a sight that perturbed Mallory in a way he could not define.

But slapped amid these mundane bills, as if it belonged there by right, was a great three-sheet broadside, a thing the size of a horse-blanket, Engine-printed, rumpled in the hasty plastering. Indeed, its very ink seemed still damp.

A mad thing.

Mallory stopped dead before it, stricken by its crude bizarrity. It had been done in three colors—scarlet, black, and an ugly greyish-pink that seemed a muddle of the two.

A scarlet blindfolded woman—a Goddess of Justice?—in a blurry scarlet toga brandished a scarlet sword labeled LUDD over the pinkish-grey heads of two very crudely rendered figures, a man and a woman depicted in busts—a king and queen? Lord and Lady Byron perhaps? The scarlet goddess trampled the midsection of a large two-headed snake, or scaly dragon, its writhing body labeled MERIT-LORDSHIP. Behind the scarlet woman, the skyline of London was vigorously aflame in scarlet tongues of fire, while the sky all about the various demented figures was full of stylized scrolls of thick black cloud. Three men, clergymen or savants apparently, dangled from a gallows in the upper-right-hand corner, and in the upper-left a confused mass of ill-formed gesticulating figures waved flags and Jacobin pikes, advancing toward some unknown goal under the bearded star of a comet.

And this was not the half of it. Mallory rubbed at his aching eyes. The vast rectangular sheet seethed with smaller images like a billiard-table littered with random pool-balls. Here a dwarfish wind-god blew out a cloud labeled PESTILENCE. There a cannon-shell, or bomb, exploded in stylized spiky fragments, small black misshapen imps being flung aside by the blast. A coffin heaped with flowers held a noose atop it. A nude woman crouched at the feet of a monster, a well-dressed man with the head of a reptile. A tiny praying man in epaulets stood on a gallows, while the hang-man, a little fellow with a hood and his sleeves rolled up, gestured brusquely at the noose. . . . More of the smudgy smoke-clouds, flung onto the image like mud, connected the whole business like the dough of a fruit-cake. And there was text, too, near the bottom. A title, in large smudgy Engine-type: "THE SEVEN CURSES OF THE WHORE OF BABYLONDON!!!"

Babylondon. Baby what? What "curses," and why "seven"? The sheet seemed flung together out of random chunks of Engine-imagery. Mallory knew that modern printers had special printers' punch-cards, clacked-up to print specific blocky pictures, much like the cheap woodcut-blocks on old murder-ballads. In the Engine-work of the catchpenny prints you might see the same hackneyed picture a hundred times. But here the colors were hideous, the images jammed hither and thither in apparent madness, and worst of all the broadsheet seemed to be attempting to *express* something, in however halting and convulsive a way, that was simply and truly unspeakable.

"Be ye talkin' a' me?" demanded a man next to Mallory.

Mallory jumped a bit, startled. "Nothing," he muttered.

The man loomed nearer at Mallory's shoulder, a very tall, gaunt cockney, with lank, filthy yellow hair under a towering stovepipe hat. He was drunk, for his eyes were maddened and bright. His face was masked securely in polka-dot fabric. His dirty clothes were near-rags—save the shoes, which were stolen and spanking-new. The cockney reeked with days of unwashed sweat, the stink of dereliction, madness. He squinted hard at the broadsheet, then at Mallory again. "Friends of yours, squire?"

"No," Mallory said.

"Tell me what it means!" the cockney insisted. "I heard you a-talking over it. You *do* know, don't you?"

The man's sharp voice trembled, and when he looked from the poster to Mallory again the bright accusing eyes above the mask seemed kindled with animal hate.

"Get away from me!" Mallory shouted.

"Blasphemin' Christ the Savior!" the tall man screeched, his voice rising, his gnarled hands kneading the air. "Christ's holy blood, what washed us free o' sin—"

He reached for Mallory. Mallory knocked the grasping hand away.

"*Kill 'im!*" an anonymous voice suggested eagerly. The gloating words charged the sullen air like a Leyden-jar. Suddenly, Mallory and his opponent were in the midst of a crowd—no longer random particles, but the focus of real trouble. The tall cockney, half-shoved perhaps, stumbled into Mallory. Mallory doubled him up with a punch to the bread-basket. Someone screamed then, a high hilarious bloodcurdling sound. A flung wad of mud missed Mallory's head and splattered against the picture. As if this were a signal, there was a sudden blinding melee of shrieks, thudding bodies, flung punches.

Mallory, shoving, swearing, dancing on his trampled feet, yanked the revolver from his waistband, pointed it in the air, and squeezed the trigger.

Nothing. An elbow caught him hard in the ribs.

He cocked the hammer with his thumb, squeezed again. The report was shocking, deafening.

In a split-second the melee was melting away from Mallory, men falling, billowing, scrambling away headlong on hands and knees in their utter beast-like eagerness to flee. Men were trampled before his eyes. Mallory stood for an instant, his jaw dropping in astonishment within his cambric mask, the gun still poised overhead.

Then a bolt of good sense struck him. He retreated. He tried to jam the pistol back into his waistband as he ran, but saw with shocked alarm that the hammer was cocked again, the gun ready to fire at any touch of the trigger. He dangled the treacherous thing at arm's-length as he fled.

At length he stopped, coughing bitterly. From behind him, wrapped in the roiling obscurity of fog, came scattered pistol-shots and bestial cries of rage, derision, glee.

"Dear Christ," Mallory muttered, and peered at the mechanism. The devilish thing had cocked itself automatically, channeling part of the powder-blast into the piston beneath the barrel, which shunted the grooved cylinder back against a stationary ratchet, spinning the next round into place and kicking the hammer back. Mallory hooked both thumbs over the hammer and worked at the trigger with care, until he could close the mechanism. He slid the pistol back into his waistband.

He had not outrun the line of pasted handbills. They

still ranged before him, apparently inexhaustible in number, slapped-up one after another in a ragged line. He followed them, through a street now seemingly empty. From somewhere came a distant crash of glass and whoops of boyish laughter.

SECRET KEYS made CHEAPLY, said a plastered bill. Handsome WATER-PROOFS for INDIA and the COLONIES. Apprentice CHYMISTS and DRUGGISTS Wanted.

Ahead he heard the quiet clop of slow hooves, the squeak of an axle. Emerging from the mist, then, the bill-sticker's van, a tall, black wagon, its towering sides mounted with great shouting billboards. A masked fellow in a loose grey raincoat was shoving a plastered bill against a wall. The wall was protected by a tall iron fence some five feet distant from the brick, but this bothered the sticker-man not at all, for he had a specialized roller-device on a kind of long broomhandle.

Mallory stepped nearer to watch. The bill-sticker did not look up, having reached a crucial moment of his work. The bill itself, which was tightly wrapped about a black rubber roller, was pressed and rolled, bottom-upward, against the wall; the sticker, at the same moment, deftly squeezing a hand-piston on the shaft of his device, which squirted out a gruelly mess of paste from twin spigots bracketed to the roller's ends. Another swipe downward to complete the pasting, and it was done.

The van moved on. Mallory stepped closer and examined the bill, which extolled, and depicted in an Engine-cut, the beautifying effects of Colgate's Clear Complexion Soap.

The sticker-man and his van moved on. Mallory followed it. The sticker-man noticed Mallory's attention, and it seemed to rattle him a bit, for he muttered something at the driver, and the van moved on a good ways.

Mallory followed discreetly. The van stopped now at a corner of Fleet Street, where the hoardings bore, by old tradition, the great shouting bills of the city's newspapers. But a bill was boldly slapped across the face of the *Morning Clarion*, and then another, and another.

More theatrical prints this time. DR. BENÉT of PARIS was to

lecture on the *"Therapeutic Value of Aquatic Sleep"*; The Chautauqua Society of the Susquehanna Phalanstery would present a symposium on *"The Social Philosophy of the Late Dr.
Coleridge"*; and a *Scientific Lecture with Kinotropy* would be presented by Dr. Edward Mallory . . .

Mallory halted, grinning behind his mask. Edward Mallory!
He had to admit that the name looked very well in eighty-point
Engine-Gothic. It was a great pity that the speech could not come
off, but clearly Huxley, or likely one of his staff-men, had placed
the order for bills with promptness, and there had been no can-
cellation.

A shame, Mallory thought, gazing at the departing bill-van
with a new proprietorial fondness. Edward Mallory. He would
have liked to keep the bill as a souvenir; and thought, indeed, of
peeling it loose, but the gobbets of paste dissuaded him.

He looked more closely, hoping to commit the text to memory.
At a second glance the printing-job was not all it might have been,
for the black lettering had, here and there, smudgy rims of
scarlet, as if the printing-pins had been soaked in red ink and not
properly cleaned.

"The Museum of Practical Geology, Jermyn Street, has the
honor to present to the London Public, for two shows only, Dr.
Edward Mallory. Dr. Mallory, F.R.S., F.R.G.S., will present the
thrilling history of his discovery of the famous Land Leviathan
in savage Wyoming; his theories of its milieu, habits, and suste-
nance; his encounters with the savage Cheyenne Indians; detailing with this the Melancholy and Hideous Murder of his closest
rival the late Professor Rudwich; Secrets of Professional Gambling, specifically that of Ratting-dens, to be imparted to those
eager to know the Technique of Odds-making, to be followed by
a most luscious Dance of the 7 Veils to be performed by the
several Misses Mallory, giving a Frank Account of their Several
Introductions to the Art of Love; only Gentlemen will be admitted; Price 2/6. Show to be accompanied by the advanced kinotropy of Mr. Keets."

Mallory gritted his teeth and broke into a sprint. He ran ahead of the van, which was moving on at foot-pace, and seized the bridle of the mule, two-handed. The animal stopped with a snort and a stumble. Its filthy head was swaddled in a canvas mask adapted from a feed-bag.

The coachman emitted a yelp from behind a smut-stained muffler. He leapt down from his wooden seat to land with a stagger, waving a hickory cudgel. "Hullo! Leave off!" he cried. "Bar that nonsense, Davey, and hook it sharp . . ." His voice trailed off as he took Mallory's measure, slapping the cudgel against his callused palm with an attempt at menace.

The second bill-sticker rushed up from behind the van to join his friend, brandishing his long-handled rig like a pitchfork.

"Hedge off, mister," the coachman suggested. "We ain't doin' you no harm."

"You most certainly are!" Mallory bellowed. "Where did you rascals obtain those bills? Tell me at once!"

The taller man defiantly shook the paste-smeared roller of his rig at Mallory's face. "London's wide-open today! You want to make a fight of where we dab our paper, then just you try us!"

One of the large advert-boards on the side of the van swung open suddenly, on squealing brass hinges. A carriage-door, it seemed, for a small stout balding man hopped through it, from within the van. He wore a neat red shooting-coat, and checkered trousers tucked into patent-leather walking-boots. He was bareheaded, his round, red-cheeked face was not masked, and to Mallory's astonishment, he was smoking a large, vilely fuming pipe.

"What's all this then?" he inquired mildly.

"A ruffian, sir!" the coachman declared. "Some villain bully-rock sent by Turkey-Legs!"

"What, all by hisself?" the stout man said, with a quizzical arch of his brows. "That don't seem right." He looked Mallory up and down. "You know who I am, son?"

"No," Mallory said. "Who are you?"

"I'm the gent they call the King of the Bill-Stickers, my boy! If you don't know that fact, you must be mighty green at this business!"

"I'm not in your business. I, sir, am Dr. Edward Mallory!"

The stout man folded his arms, and rocked a bit on his boot-heels. "So?"

"You just pasted-up a bill that grossly libeled me!"

"Oh," said the King. "So that's your bellyache, is it?" He grinned in evident relief. "Well, that's nothing to do with me, Dr. Edward Mallory. I just paste 'em; I don't print 'em. I ain't liable."

"Well, you're not putting up any more of those damnable libel-sheets!" Mallory said. "I want all the rest of them, and I demand to know where you obtained them!"

The King quieted his two bristling henchmen with a regal move of his hand. "I'm a very busy man, Dr. Mallory. If you'd care to step up in my van, and talk to me like a reasonable gentleman, then perhaps I'll listen, but I've no time for any bluster or threats." He fixed Mallory with a sharp squint of his little blue eyes.

"Well," Mallory blurted, taken aback. Though he knew he was in the right, the King's quiet retort had taken the steam out of his indignation; he felt rather foolish of a sudden, and rather out of his element, somehow. "Surely," he muttered. "Very well."

"Fair enough. Tom, Jemmy, let's back to work." The King clambered deftly into his van.

Mallory, after a moment's hesitation, followed him, heaving himself up into the body of the oddly made carriage. There were no seats inside; the flooring from wall to wall was dimpled and buttoned with thick maroon cushioning, like a Turkish ottoman. Slanted pigeon-holes of varnished wood lined the walls, stuffed with tightly rolled bills. A large trap-door in the ceiling had been flung open, admitting a gloomy light. It stank direly of paste and cheap, black, shag tobacco.

The King sprawled at his ease, propping himself on a fat tufted pillow. The mule brayed under the driver's whip-crack, and the van lurched into sluggish squeaking motion. "Gin and water?" the King offered, opening a cabinet.

"Plain water, if you please," Mallory said.

"Straight water it is." The King poured from a pottery canteen into a tin mug. Mallory tugged his frayed mask down below his chin, and drank with an aching thirst.

The King gave Mallory a second round, and then a third. "Perhaps a tasty squeeze o' lemon with that?" The King winked. "I do hope you know your limit."

Mallory cleared his slimy throat. "Very decent of you." His face felt oddly naked without the mask, and this show of civility within the King's van, together with its chemical stink of glue, almost worse than the Thames, had quite dizzied him. "I regret it if I, er, seemed a bit sharp earlier."

"Well, it's the lads, you know," said the King, with generous tact. "A cove must stand ready to handle his fists in the bill-sticking business. Just yesterday, my boys had to lay it on pretty brisk with old Turkey-Legs and his lads, over a matter of sticking-space within Trafalgar Square." The King sniffed in disdain.

"I've had certain sharp troubles of my own during this emergency," Mallory said hoarsely. "But basically, I'm a reasonable man, sir. Very rational—not the sort who looks for trouble; you mustn't think that."

The King nodded sagely. "I've never yet known Turkey-Legs to hire any scholar as a bully-rock. By your dress and manner I take you to be a savant, sir."

"You have a sharp eye."

"I like to think so," the King allowed. "So now that we have that matter clear, perhaps you'll informate me concerning this grievance you seem to hold."

"Those bills you've pasted are forgeries," Mallory said. "And libelous. They're certainly not legal."

"As I explained before, that's none of my affair," the King said. "Let me tell you a few facts of commerce, straight-out. For dabbing-up a hundred double-crown sheets, I expect to make one pound one shilling; which is to say tuppence and six-tenths of a penny per sheet; say three pence, rounded out. Now if you should care to purchase certain of my bills at that rate, I might be ready to talk business."

"Where are they?" Mallory said.

"If you'd care to have a look among the cubbyholes for the items in question I will oblige you."

When the crew had stopped to paste more bills, Mallory began to sort through the stock. The bills were tightly wrapped in neat thick perforated scrolls, as dense and hefty as bludgeons.

The King passed a scroll through the trap-door to the driver. Then he peaceably tapped out the dottle of his meerschaum, refilled it from a twist of coarse paper, and lit it with a German tinder-box. He blew a cloud of foulness with every appearance of satisfaction.

"Here they are," Mallory said. He peeled the outermost sheet from the roll and flapped it out within the van. "Have a look at this abomination, will you? It looks quite splendid at first, but the text is obscenely outrageous!"

"Standard roll o' forty; that'll be six shillings even."

"Read here," Mallory said, "where it as much as accuses me of murder!"

The King, politely, turned his eyes upon the sheet. His lips moved as he puzzled painfully over the title. "Ma Lorry," he said at length. "One of your lorry-shows, is it?"

"*Mallory*—that's my name!"

"It's a demi-sheet theatrical, no illos," the King said. "Bit smudgy . . . oh yes, I remember these." He sighed smoke. "I might 'a known no good would come of taking this consignment. Mind you, the rascal paid in advance though."

"Who? Whom?"

"Down in Limehouse, in the West India Docks," the King said. "A deal of commotion in that locale, Dr. Mallory. Rascals slapping brand-new bills up all over every wall and hoarding in sight, since yesterday. My boys were inclined to make a bit of trouble over that encroachment, till Captain Swing—that's what he calls hisself—saw fit to engage our services."

Mallory's armpits prickled with sweat. "Captain Swing, is it?"

"Sporting-fellow of some kind, to judge by his dress," the King said cheerfully. "Short, red-headed, squinty—had a bump on his head, just here. Crazy as a bedbug, I should say. He was polite enough though, not proposing to make any trouble for the bill-sticking trade once customary matters was explained to him. And he had him a sight of ready money."

"I know that man!" Mallory said, his voice trembling. "He's a violent Luddite conspirator. He may be the most dangerous man in England!"

"You don't say," the King grunted.

"He's a dire threat to public safety!"

"Fellow didn't look like much," the King said. "Funny little duck, wore spectacles and talked to hisself."

"The man is an enemy of the realm—a dark-lanternist of the most sinister description!"

"I don't much hold with politics, meself," said the King, leaning back quite at his ease. "The Bill-Sticking Regulatory Act—now that's politics for you, a doltish business! That blasted Act is mighty stiff, regarding where bills may be posted. Let me tell you, Dr. Mallory, I personally *know* the Member that got that Act passed in Parliament, for I was hired for his election campaign. *He* didn't mind where *his* bills went. It was all quite right-enough, so long as they was *his* bills!"

"My God!" Mallory broke in. "The thought of that evil man, loose in London—with money, from God only knows what source—fomenting riot and rebellion during a public emergency—and in control of an Engine-driven press! It's nightmarish! Horrible!"

"Pray don't fash yourself, Dr. Mallory," the King chided gently. "My dear old father, rest his soul, used to tell me: 'When all about you are losing their heads, son, just remember: there are still twenty shillings in a pound.'"

"That's as may be," Mallory said, "but—"

"My dear dad stuck bills in the Time of Troubles! Back in the thirties, when the cavalry charged on the working-people, and old Hooky-Nose Wellington got hisself blown to flinders. Hard times indeed, sir, much harder than soft modern days with this trifling Stink! Call this an emergency? Why, I call it opportunity, and have done with it."

"You don't seem to grasp the urgency of the crisis," Mallory said.

"The Time of Troubles—now that was when they printed the first four-sheet double-crowns! The Tory Government used to pay my old dad—my dad was Beadle and Bill-Sticker to the parish of St. Andrews, Holborn—to black-wash Radical bills. He had to hire women to do it, there was so much call for the job. He'd black-wash Rad bills by day, and stick up new ones by night! There's a deal of fine opportunity in your times of revolution."

Mallory sighed.

"My dad invented the device we call the Patent Extendable Dabbing-Joint—to which I myself have made a number of mechanical improvements. It serves to stick bills to the under-sides of bridges, for the water-trade. We are an entrepreneurial line in my family, sir. Not easily put out of countenance."

"A lot of good all that will do you when London's reduced to ashes," Mallory said. "Why, you're helping the scoundrel in his anarchistic plottings!"

"I should say you have that straight-backwards, Dr. Mallory," the King said, with an odd little chuckle. "Last I saw, the fellow was paying his money into my pockets, and not vice-versa. Now that I think on it, he's consigned a number of bills to my safe-keeping—right along the top row, here." The King stood, yanked the documents down, cast them onto his padded floor. "You see, sir, it don't really matter a hang what nonsense is blithered and babbled on these bills! The secret truth is, that bills is endless by their very nature, regular as the tides in the Thames, or the smoke of London. London's true sons call London 'The Smoke,' you know. She's an eternal city, like your Jerusalem, or Rome, or, some would say, Satan's Pandemonium! You don't see the King of the Bill-Stickers worrying for smoky London, do you? Not a bit of it!"

"But the people have fled!"

"A passing foolishness. They'll all be back," said the King, with sublime confidence. "Why, they have no place else to go. This is the center of the world, sir."

Mallory fell silent.

"So, sir," proclaimed the King, "if you was to take my advice, you'd spend six shillings on that roll of bills you're clutching. Why, for one pound even, I'll toss in these other misprinted bills of our friend Captain Swing's. Twenty simple shillings, sir, and you may leave these streets, and rest at home in peace and quiet."

"Some of these bills have already been posted," Mallory said.

"I could have the lads black-wash 'em—or paste 'em over, anyhow," the King mused. "If you was willing to make it worth their while, of course."

"Would that put an end to the matter?" said Mallory, reaching for his pocket-book. "I doubt it."

"A better end than any you can make with that pistol I see peeping from your trouser-band," said the King. "That is an item which cannot do a gentleman and scholar any credit."

Mallory said nothing.

"Heed my counsel, Dr. Mallory, and put that gun away before you do yourself a mischief. I do believe you might have hurt one of my lads, if I hadn't spied that gun through my peep-hole, and stepped out to set things right. Go home, sir, and cool your head."

"Why aren't *you* at home, if you truly mean that advice?" Mallory said.

"Why, this *is* my home, sir," said the King. He tucked Mallory's money into his shooting-jacket. "On pleasant days my old woman and I take our tea in here, and talk about old times . . . and walls, and embankments, and hoardings. . . ."

"I have no home in London; and in any case business calls me to Kensington," Mallory said.

"That's a distance, Dr. Mallory."

"Yes, it is," Mallory said, with a tug at his beard. "But it strikes me that there are any number of museums and savants' palaces in Kensington, which have never been touched by advert-paper."

"Really," mused the King. "Do tell."

Mallory bade the King farewell a good mile from the Palace of Paleontology; he was unable to bear the fumes of glue any longer, and the van's lurching had made him badly seasick. He staggered off with the heavy scrolls of libelous and anarchic bills bundled awkwardly in his sweating grip. Behind him, Jemmy and Tom set to eager glue-slapping on the virgin bricks of the Palace of Political Economy.

Mallory propped the rolled bills against an ornate lamp-post, and re-knotted his cloth mask over nose and mouth. His head spun evilly. Perhaps, he thought, that sticking-paste had had a bit of arsenic in it, or the ink some potent nauseous coal-derivative, for he felt poisoned, and weak in his very marrow. When he juggled up the bills again, their paper wrinkled in his sweating hands like the peeling skin of a drowned man.

He had, it seemed, frustrated a lashing bite of the tout's hydra-headed devilment. But this minor triumph seemed wretchedly small, when matched against the villain's seemingly endless reservoirs of wicked ingenuity. Mallory was stumbling in darkness—while torn at will by invisible fangs. . . .

And yet Mallory had discovered a crucial piece of evidence: the tout was gone to earth in the West India Docks! To be so close to a chance to grapple with the scoundrel, and yet so far—it was enough to madden a man.

Mallory stumbled badly on a slick lump of horse-dung, then swung the scrolls up onto his right shoulder, in an unstable heap. It was a useless fantasy to imagine confronting the tout—alone, unaided, while the man was miles away, back across the chaos of London. Mallory had almost reached the Palace now, and it had taken well-nigh all he had to manage the trick of it.

He forced himself to concentrate on the matters at hand. He

would haul the wretched bills to the Palace safety-box. They might prove useful as evidence someday, and they could take the place of Madeline's wedding-clock. He would take up the clock, he would find a way to flee this cursed London, and he would re-join his family, as he should have done. In green Sussex, in the bosom of the good auld clawney, there would be quiet, and sense, and safety. The gears of his life would begin to mesh once more in order.

Mallory lost his grip on the rolls of paper and they cascaded violently to the tarmac, one of them hitting him a smart blow across the shins as it bounded free. He gathered them up, groaning, and tried the other shoulder.

In the rancid mists down Knightsbridge a procession of some kind was moving steadily across the road. Ghost-like, blurred by distance and the Stink, they appeared to be military gurneys, the squat treaded monsters of the Crimean War. Fog muffled a heavy chugging and the faint repeated clank of jointed iron. One after another they passed, while Mallory peered forward, standing quite still and gripping his burden. Each gurney hauled a linked articulated caisson. These wains appeared to be canvas-shrouded cannon, with men, foot-soldiers in canvas-colored drab, clustered atop the cannons like barnacles, with a sea-urchin bristle of bayoneted rifles. At least a dozen war-gurneys, possible a score. Mallory rubbed his aching eyes in puzzled disbelief.

At Brompton Concourse he saw a trio of masked and hatted figures scamper off with light-foot tread from a broken doorway; but no one offered trouble to him.

Some civil authority had erected saw-horses at the gate of the Palace of Paleontology. But the barricades were not manned; it was a simple matter to slip past them and up the fog-slick stone stairs to the main entrance. The Palace's great double-doors were thickly curtained in a protective shroud of wet canvas, hung from the brick archway down to the very flagstones. The thick damp fabric smelled sharply of chloride of lime. Behind the canvas, the Palace doors were slightly ajar. Mallory eased his way inside.

Servants were draping the furniture of lobby and drawing-room with thin white sheets of muslin. Others, a peculiar crowd of them, swept, and mopped, and dabbled earnestly at the cornices with long jointed feather-dusters. London women, and a large number of children of all ages, bustled about wearing borrowed Palace cleaning-aprons, looking anxious but vaguely exalted.

Mallory realized at length that these strangers must be the families of the Palace staff, come to seek shelter and security within the grandest public building known to them. And someone—Kelly the major-domo, presumably, with help from whatever savants still remained on the premises—had pluckily organized the refugees.

Mallory strode toward the lobby-desk, lugging his paper burden. These were sturdy working-class folk, he realized. Their stations might be humble, but they were Britons through and through. They were not daunted; they had rallied in instinctive defense of their scientific institutions and the civil values of law and property. He realized, with a heart-lifting wash of patriotic relief, that the lurching madness of Chaos had reached its limit. Within the faltering maelstrom, a nucleation of spontaneous order had arisen! Now, like a cloudy muck resolving into crystals, everything would change.

Mallory flung his hated burden behind the deserted counter of the lobby-desk. In one corner, a telegraph was clacking fitfully, new punch-tape spooling by fits and starts upon the floor. Mallory observed this small but significant miracle, and sighed, like a diver whose head has broken water.

The Palace air was sharp with disinfectant, but blissfully breathable. Mallory stripped the filthy mask from his face and stuffed it in his pocket. Somewhere in this blessed shelter, he thought, there was food to be had. Perhaps a wash-basin, and soap, and sulphurated powder for the fleas that had been creeping about his waistband since morning. Eggs. Ham. Restorative wine. Postage-stamps, laundresses, shoe-blacking—the whole miraculous concatenated network of Civilization.

A stranger came marching toward Mallory across the lobby

floor: a British soldier, an Artillery subaltern, in elegant dress-gear. He wore a double-breasted blue coatee, bright with chevrons, brass buttons, and gold-braided epaulets. His sleek trousers had a red military stripe. He wore a round, gold-laced forage-cap, and a buttoned pistol-holster at his neat white waistbelt. With his shoulders square, spine straight, and head high, this handsome young man approached with a stern look of purpose. Mallory straightened quickly, taken aback, even vaguely shamed, to compare his rumpled, sweat-stained civilian garb to this crisp military paragon.

Then, with a leap of surprise, happy recognition dawned. "Brian!" Mallory shouted. "Brian, boy!"

The soldier quickened his pace. "Ned—why it *is* you, ain't it!" said Mallory's brother, a tender smile parting his new Crimean beard. He seized Mallory's hand in both his own, and shook it heartily, with a solid strength.

Mallory noted with surprise and pleasure that military discipline and scientific diet had put inches and pounds on the lad. Brian Mallory, the family's sixth-born child, had often seemed a bit quiet and timid, but now Mallory's little brother stood a good six-four in his military boots, and had the look in his creased blue eyes of a man who had seen the world.

"We've been a-waiting for you, Ned," Brian told him. His bold voice had slipped a bit, by some old habit, into the remembered tone of their childhood. For Mallory, it was a plaintive echo from deep memory: the demands of a crowd of little children upon their eldest brother. Somehow, this familiar call, far from tiring or burdening Mallory, rallied him immediately into a mental second-wind. Confusion vanished like a mist and he felt stronger, more capable; the very presence of young Brian had recalled him to himself. "Damme but it's good to see you!" Mallory blurted.

"It's good you're back at last," Brian said. "We heard tale of a fire in your room—and you vanished into London, none knew where! That put me and Tom in a very mizmaze!"

"Tom is here too, eh?"

"We both come into London in Tom's little gurney," Brian told him. His face fell. "With dire news, Ned, and no ways to tell it, save to your face."

"What is it?" Mallory said, bracing himself. "Is it . . . is it Dad?"

"No, Ned. Dad's all right; or right as he ever is, these days. It is poor Madeline!"

Mallory groaned. "Not the bride-to-be. What is it now?"

"Well, it's to do with my mate, Jerry Rawlings," Brian muttered, squaring his epauletted shoulders with a look of embarrassed pain. "Jerry wanted to do right by our Madeline, Ned, for he always talked of her, and lived very clean for her sake; but he's received such a *letter* at home, Ned, such a foul and dreadful thing! It quite knocked the heart out of him!"

"What letter, for God's sake?"

"Well, it warn't signed, 'cept 'One Who Knows'—but the writer knew so much about us, the family I mean, all our littlest doings, and said that Madeline had . . . been *unchaste*. 'Cept in rougher words."

Mallory felt a surge of hot fury rush to his face. "I understand," he said, in a quiet, choked voice. "Go on."

"Well, their engagement is broken, as you might guess. Poor Maddy has the vapors like she's never had them before. She liked to do herself an injury, and does nothing now but sit alone in the kitchen and cry rivers."

Mallory was silent, his mind grating over Brian's information.

"I've been away a deal of time, in India, and Crimea," Brian said, in a low halting voice. "I don't know how matters stand, exactly. Tell me true—you don't think there could be aught to what that wicked gossip told to Jerry? Do you?"

"What? Our own Madeline? My God, Brian, she's a Mallory girl!" Mallory slammed his fist on the counter. "No, it is slander; it's a foul deliberate attack on the honor of our family!"

"How . . . why would anyone do such a thing to us, Ned?" asked Brian, with a strange look of plaintive fury.

"I *know* why it was done—and I know the villain who did it."

Brian's eyes went wide. "You do?"

"Yes; he is the fellow who burnt my rooms. And I know where he is hiding, at this very moment!"

Brian gazed at him in astonished silence.

"I made an enemy of him, in a dark affair-of-state," Mallory said, measuring his words. "I'm a man of some influence now, Brian; and I've uncovered the kind of secret, silent plottings that a man like yourself, an honest soldier of the Crown, could scarcely credit!"

Brian shook his head slowly. "I've seen pagan vileness done in India to make strong men sick," he said. "But to see it done in England is more than I can bear!" Brian tugged at his whiskers, a gesture Mallory found oddly familiar. "I knew it was right to come to you, Ned. You always seem to see straight through things, the way none else can. Say on, then! What shall we do about this horrid business? What *can* we do?"

"That pistol in your holster—is it in working order?"

Brian's eyes brightened. "Truth to tell, 'tisn't regulation! A war trophy, gotten off a dead Tzarist officer . . ." He began to unlatch his holster-flap.

Mallory shook his head quickly, looking about the lobby. "You're not afraid to use your pistol, if you have to do so?"

"Afraid?" Brian said. "If you warn't a civilian, Ned, I might take that question ill."

Mallory stared at him.

Brian met his eyes boldly. "It's for the family, ain't it? That's what we fought the Russkies for—for the sake of the folks at home."

"Where is Thomas?"

"He's eating in the—well, I'll show you."

Brian led the way into the Palace saloon. The scholarly pre-cincts were crowded with babbling, raucous diners, working-folk mostly, forking up potatoes off the Palace china as if famished. Young Tom Mallory, dressed rather flash in a short linen coat and checked trousers, sat at table with a companion, over the remains of fried fish and lemonade.

The other man was Ebenezer Fraser.

"Ned!" cried Tom. "I knew you'd come!" He rose, and seized another chair. "Sit down with us, sit down! Your friend Mr. Fraser here has been kind enough to buy us lunch."

"And how are you, Dr. Mallory?" Fraser inquired glumly.

"A bit fatigued," Mallory told him, sitting, "but nothing a bite of food and a huckle-buff wouldn't set to rights. How are you, Fraser? Quite recovered, I hope?" He lowered his voice. "And what line of clever nonsense have you been telling my poor brothers, pray?"

Fraser said nothing.

"Sergeant Fraser's a London policeman," Mallory said. "Of the dark-lantern variety."

"Truly?" Tom blurted, alarmed.

A waiter worked his way toward the table, one of the regular staff, looking harried and apologetic. "Dr. Mallory—the Palace larder's a bit low, sir. Simple fish-and-taters would be best, sir, if you don't mind it."

"That will be fine. And if you could mix a huckle-buff—well, never mind. Bring me coffee. Strong and black."

Fraser watched the waiter leave, with melancholy patience. "You must have had a lively night," Fraser remarked, when the man was out of ear-shot. Both Tom and Brian were watching Fraser with a new, half-resentful suspicion.

"I have discovered that the tout—Captain Swing, that is—has gone to earth in the West India Docks," Mallory said. "He's attempting to incite a general insurrection!"

Fraser's lips tightened.

"He has an Engine printing-press, and a rabble of confederates. He's printing seditious documents by the scores and hundreds. I confiscated a few specimens this morning—obscene, libelous, Luddite filth!"

"You've been industrious."

Mallory snorted. "I'll shortly be a deal busier yet, Fraser. I mean to hunt the wretch down directly and put a sharp end to this!"

Brian leaned forward. "It was this 'Captain Swing' who wrote that lying slander against our Maddy, then, was it?"

"Yes."

Tom sat up straight in his chair, with a flush of excitement. "West India Docks. Where's that, then?"

"Down on the Limehouse Reach, clear across London," Fraser said.

"That don't matter a hang," Tom said quickly. "I've my *Zephyr*!"

Mallory was startled. "You brought the Brotherhood's racer?"

Tom shook his head. "Not that old banger, Ned, but the latest model! She's a spanking-new little beauty, sitting in your Palace stables. Took us all the way from Sussex in a morning, and would have gone faster yet, if I hadn't had a coal-wain hitched to her." He laughed. "We can go wherever we like!"

"Let's not lose our heads, gentlemen," Fraser warned.

They fell unwillingly silent for a moment, as the waiter deftly set Mallory's food before him. The sight of fried plaice and sliced potatoes made Mallory's stomach knot with a famished pang. "We are free British subjects and may go as we please," Mallory said firmly, then seized his silverware and fell to at once.

"I can only call that foolish," said Fraser. "Riotous mobs are roaming the streets, and the man you seek is as cunning as an adder."

Mallory grunted derisively.

Fraser was dour. "Dr. Mallory, it is my duty to see that you don't come to harm! We can't have you stirring up dangerous serpent's-nests in the vilest slums in London!"

Mallory gulped hot coffee. "You know that he means to destroy me," he told Fraser, locking eyes with him. "If I don't finish him now, while I've the chance, he'll slowly peck me into pieces. There's not a dashed thing you can do that can protect me! This man is not like you and I, Fraser! He is beyond the pale! The stakes are life and death—it is him, or me! You know that is the truth."

Fraser, struck by Mallory's argument, looked shaken. Tom and

Brian, even more alarmed at this new revelation of the depth of their troubles, glanced at one another in confusion, then turned to glare angrily at Fraser.

Fraser spoke reluctantly. "Let's not act hastily! Once the fog lifts, and law and order have returned—"

"Captain Swing lives within a fog that never lifts," Mallory said.

Brian broke in, with a swipe of his gilded sleeve. "I see *no point* in this, Mr. Fraser! You have deliberately *deceived* my brother Thomas and myself! I can put no credit in any of your counsel!"

"Brian's right!" said Tom. He regarded Fraser with a mingled scorn and wonder. "This man claimed he was a friend of yours, Ned, and got me and Brian to talking free-and-easy about you! Now he's a-trying to order us about!" Tom shook his clenched fist, sinewy and work-hardened. "I mean to teach this Captain Swing a sharp lesson! If I need to start with *you*, Mr. Fraser, then I stand a-ready!"

"Softly now, lads," Mallory told his brothers. Other diners nearby had begun to stare. Mallory deliberately wiped his mouth with a napkin. "Fortune favors us, Mr. Fraser," he said quietly. "I have acquired a pistol. And young Brian is also armed."

"Oh, dear," said Fraser.

"I'm not afraid of Swing," Mallory told him. "Remember, I knocked him flat at the Derby. Face-to-face, he's nought but a yellow cur."

"He is at the Docks, Mallory!" Fraser said. "D'ye think you're going to waltz and polka through a riot in the hardest part of London?"

"We Mallory lads aren't fancy-jacks from any dancing academy," Mallory told the policeman. "D'ye think the London poor more frightful to face than Wyoming savages?"

"Actually, yes," Fraser said slowly. "*Considerably* worse, I should judge."

"Oh, for Heaven's sake, Fraser! Don't waste our time with this trifling! We must grapple once and for all with this slippery phantom, and a better chance will never come! In the name of sanity and justice, put an end to your useless, officious grizzling!"

Fraser sighed. "And suppose, in this brave expedition, that you are cunningly trapped and murdered, like your colleague Rudwick? What then? How would I answer to my superiors?"

But now Brian fixed Fraser with a soldier's steely eye. "Did you ever have a little sister, Mr. Fraser? Did you ever have to watch that girl's happiness shattered like a china cup, trampled by a monster? And with her broken heart, the honest heart of a Crimean hero, whose simple, manly intention was to make her his bride—"

Fraser groaned aloud. "Enough!"

Brian leaned back, looking somewhat crestfallen at the interruption.

Fraser smoothed his dark lapels with both hands. "It seems the fated time for risks," he admitted, with a lopsided shrug, and a passing wince. "I haven't had a bit of luck since I met you, Dr. Mallory, and I daresay I'm due for a change of fortune." Suddenly, his eyes glittered. "Who's to say that we might not bag the scoundrel, eh? Arrest him! He's clever, but four brave men might catch the nasty wretch with his guard down, whilst he swaggers about in poor stricken London like some Jacobin prince." Fraser scowled, his lean face twisting with genuine anger. It was an unexpectedly fearsome sight.

"Fortune favors the brave," Brian said.

"And God looks after fools," muttered Fraser. He leaned forward intently, plucking his trouser-legs from his bony knees. "This is no light matter, gentlemen! No lark for amateurs. This is dire work! We shall be taking the law, and our lives, and our honor, into our own hands. If it is to be done at all, it must be done in the strictest and most permanent secrecy."

Mallory, sensing victory, spoke up with an adroitness that surprised even himself. "My brothers and I respect your special expertise, Sergeant Fraser! If you will guide us toward justice, then we will gladly place ourselves at your command. You need never doubt our discretion or our resolve. The sacred honor of our own dear sister is at stake."

Tom and Brian seemed taken aback at this sudden change of tack, for they still distrusted Fraser, but Mallory's somber pledge brooked no objection from them. They followed his lead.

"You'll never see me peaching!" Tom declared. "Not to my grave!"

"I should think the sworn word of a British soldier still accounts," Brian said.

"Then we shall try the venture," Fraser said, with a wry look of fatalism.

"I must get steam up in the *Zephyr*!" Tom said, rising from his chair. "Half-an-hour my little beauty takes, from a cold start."

Mallory nodded. He would put every minute to good use.

Outside the Palace, washed, combed, and intimately dusty with flea-powder, Mallory sought a lumpy purchase atop the *Zephyr*'s wooden coal-wain. The chugging little gurney had barely room for two men within its line-streamed tin shell. Tom and Fraser had taken those seats. They were arguing now over a London street-map.

Brian stamped out a rude nest within the wain's flabby canvas, stretched atop a diminishing heap of coal. "They take a deal of shoveling, your modern gurneys," Brian observed, with a stoic smile. He sat across from Mallory. "Tom does take-on about this precious machine of his; talked my ear off about *Zephyrs*, all the way from Lewes."

The gurney and wain lurched into motion, the coal-wain's wooden-spoked rubbered wheels turning with a rhythmic creak. They rolled down Kensington Road with a startling celerity. Brian brushed a flaming smokestack spark from his dapper coat-sleeve.

"You need a breathing-mask," Mallory said, offering his

brother one of the makeshift masks the ladies had sewn within the Palace: a neatly stitched ribboned square of gingham, stuffed with cheap Confederate cotton.

Brian sniffed at the rushing air. "Ain't so bad."

Mallory knotted the ribbons of his own mask neatly behind his head. "Miasma will tell against your health, lad, in the long run."

"This don't compare to the pong of an Army transport boat," said Brian. The absence of Fraser seemed to have relaxed him. There was something more of the Sussex lad about him, and less of the stern young subaltern. "Coaly fumes pouring out our engine-room," Brian reminisced, "and the lads tossing-up their rations from the mal-de-mer, right and left! We steamed through that new Frenchy canal in Suez, straight from Bombay. We lived in that bloody transport for weeks! Rotten Egyptian heat— straight through to hard Crimean winter! If the cholery, or the quartan fever, didn't carry me off from that, then I needn't worry over any little mist in London." Brian chuckled.

"I often thought of you, in Canada," Mallory told his brother. "You, with a five-year enlistment—and a war on! But I knew you'd do the family proud, Brian. I knew you'd do your duty."

"We Mallory lads are all over the world, Ned," said Brian, philosophically. His voice was gruff, but his bearded face had colored at Mallory's praise. "Where's brother Michael right now, eh? Good old Mickey?"

"Hong Kong, I think," Mallory said. "Mick would be here today with us surely, if luck had put his ship in port in England. He was never the sort to flinch from a proper fight, our Michael."

"I've seen Ernestina and Agatha, since I was back," Brian said. "And their dear little ones." He said nothing about Dorothy. The family did not talk about Dorothy anymore. Brian shifted on the lumpy canvas, turning a wary eye on the looming crenellations of a palace of savantry. "Don't care much for a fight in the streets," he remarked. "That was the only place the Russkies really stung us, in the streets of Odessa. Scrapping and sniping house-to-house in the city, like bandits. That's no civilized war." He frowned.

"Why didn't they stand up straight, and give you an honest battle?"

Brian glanced at him in surprise, then laughed, a bit oddly. "Well, they surely tried that at first, at Alma and Inkermann. But we gave 'em such a hell of a toweling that it knocked 'em into a panic. You might call that partly my doing, I suppose. The Royal Artillery, Ned."

"Do tell," Mallory said.

"We're the most scientific of the forces. They love the Artillery, your military Rads." Brian snuffed another fat smokestack spark with a spit-dampened thumb. "Special military savantry! Dreamy little fellers with specs on their noses, and figures in their heads. Never seen a sword drawn, or a bayonet. Don't need to see such things to win a modern war. 'Tis all trajectories, and fuse-timings."

Brian watched with alert suspicion as a pair of men in baggy raincoats sidled down the road. "The Russkies did what they could. Huge redoubts, at the Redan, and Sevastopol. When our heavy guns opened up, they came apart like cracker-boxes. Then they fell back into trench-works, but the grapeshot from the mortar-organs worked like a marvel." Brian's eyes were distant now, focused on memory. "You could see it, Ned, white smoke and dirt flying up at the head of the barrage-line, every round falling neat and true as the trees in an orchard! And when the shelling stopped, our infantry—French allies mostly, they did a deal of the foot-work—would trot in over the palisades, and finish poor Ivan off with wind-up rifles."

"The papers said the Russians fought with no respect for military decency."

"They got mortal desperate when they found they couldn't touch us," Brian said. "Took to partisan work, fighting from ambush, firing on white flags and such. Ugly business, dishonorable. We couldn't put up with that. Had to take measures."

"At least it was all over swiftly," Mallory said. "One doesn't like war, but it was time to teach Tsar Nicholas a lesson. I doubt the tyrant will ever tug the Lion's tail again."

Brian nodded. "It's right astonishing, what those new incendiary shells can do. You can lay 'em down in a grid-work, neat as pie." His voice fell. "You should have seen Odessa burning, Ned. Like a flaming *hurricane*, it was. A giant hurricane . . ."

"Yes—I read about that," Mallory nodded. "There was a 'storm-fire' in the siege of Philadelphia. Very similar business, very remarkable principle."

"Ah," said Brian, "that's the problem with the Yankees—no military sense! To think of doing that to your own cities! Why, you'd have to be a cack-handed fool!"

"They're a queer folk, the Yanks," Mallory said.

"Well, some folk are too chuckleheaded to manage themselves, and that's a fact," Brian said. He glanced about warily as Tom piloted the *Zephyr* past the smoldering wreckage of an omnibus. "Did you take to the Yankees, at all, in America?"

"Never saw Americans, just Indians." And the less said about that the better, thought Mallory. "What did you think of India, by the way?"

"It's a dreadful place, India," Brian said readily, "brim-full of queer marvels, but dreadful. There's only one folk in Asia with any sense, and that's the Japanese."

"I heard you took part in an Indian campaign," Mallory said. "But I never was quite sure who those 'Sepoys' were, exactly."

"Sepoys are native troops. We had a rash of trouble with mutineers, Moslem nonsense, about pig-fat in their rifle-cartridges! It was sheer native foolishness, but Moslems don't care to eat pork, you know, all very superstitious. It looked dicey, but the Viceroy of India hadn't given the native regiments any modern artillery. One battery of Wolseley mortar-organs can send a Bengali regiment straight to hell in five minutes."

Brian's gold-braided shoulders glittered as he shrugged. "Still, I saw barbarities at Meerut and Lucknow, during the rebellion . . . . You'd not think any man could do such vile, savage things. Especially our own native soldiers, that we ourselves had trained."

"Fanatics," Mallory nodded. "Your common Indian, though, must be surely grateful for a decent civil government. Railroads, telegraphs, aqueducts, and such."

"Oh," said Brian, "when you see some Hindu fakir a-sitting in a temple niche, filthy naked with a flower on his hair, who's to say what goes on in that queer headpiece of his?" He fell silent, then pointed sharply over Mallory's shoulder. "Over there—what are those rascals doing?"

Mallory turned and looked. In the mouth of an adjoining street, the paving had been taken over by a large and thriving ring of gamblers. "They're tossing dice," Mallory explained. A knot of shabby, disheveled men—scouts of some primitive kind, lawless pickets—were standing look-out under an awning, passing a bottle of gin. One fat ruffian gestured obscenely as the *Zephyr* chugged past, and his startled companions hooted disbelieving taunts from behind their rag-masks.

Brian flung himself full-length across the coal-wain, and peered over the wooden wall. "Are they armed?"

Mallory blinked. "I don't think they mean us any harm—"

"They're a-going to rush us," Brian announced. Mallory glanced at his brother in surprise, but to his greater astonishment he saw that Brian was quite right. The shabby men were capering after the *Zephyr*, almost skipping down the empty street, with a shake of their fists and a slosh of their gin-bottle. They seemed possessed with an angry yapping energy, like farm-dogs pursuing a carriage. Brian rose to one knee, untoggled his holster-flap, set his hand to the large queer pistol-butt within it—

He was almost flung from the wain as Thomas hit the *Zephyr*'s throttle. Mallory grabbed his brother's belt and hauled him back to sprawling safety. The *Zephyr* racketed smoothly up the street, a small cascade of coal pattering out the back with the shock of acceleration. Behind them the pursuers stopped short in disbelief, then stooped like idiots to pick at the fallen coals, as if they were emeralds.

"How did you know they would do that?" Mallory asked.

Brian knocked coal-dust from his trouser-knees with a pocket-kerchief. "I knew it."

"But why?"

" 'Cause we're here, and they're there, I suppose! 'Cause we ride and they walk!" He looked at Mallory red-faced, as if the question were more trouble to him than a gun-fight.

Mallory sat back, looking away. "Take the mask," he said mildly, holding it out. "I brought it just for you."

Brian smiled then, sheepish, and knotted the little thing about his neck.

There were soldiers with bayoneted rifles on the street-corners in Piccadilly, in modern speckled drab and slouch hats. They were eating porridge from mess-kits of stamped tin. Mallory waved cheerily at these minions of order, but they glared back at the *Zephyr* with such militant suspicion that he quickly stopped. Some blocks on, at the corner of Longacre and Drury Lane, the soldiers were actively bullying a small squad of bewildered London police. The coppers milled about like scolded children, feebly clutching their inadequate billy-clubs. Several had lost their helmets, and many bore rude bandages on hands and scalps and shins.

Tom stopped the *Zephyr* for coaling, while Fraser, followed by Mallory, sought intelligence from the London coppers. They were told that the situation south of the river was quite out of control. Pitched battles with brickbats and pistols were raging in Lambeth. Many streets were barricaded by pillaging mobs. Reports had it that the Bedlam Hospital had been thrown open, its unchained lunatics capering the streets in frenzy.

The police were sooty-faced, coughing, exhausted. Every able-bodied man in the force was on the streets, the Army had been called in by an emergency committee, and a general curfew declared. Volunteers of the respectable classes were being deputized in the West End, and equipped with batons and rifles. At least, Mallory thought, this litany of disaster crushed any further doubts about the propriety of their own venture. Fraser made no comment; but he returned to the Zephyr with a look of grim resolution.

Tom piloted on. Beyond authority's battered boundary, things grew swiftly more grim. It was noonday now, with a ghastly amber glow at the filthy zenith, and crowds were clustering like flies in the crossroads of the city. Clumps of masked Londoners shuffled along, curious, restless, hungry, or desperate—unhurried, and conspiring. The *Zephyr*, with merry toots of its whistle, passed through the amorphous crowd; they parted for it reflexively.

A pair of commandeered omnibuses patrolled Cheapside, crammed with hard-faced bruisers. Men waving pistols hung from the running-boards, and the roofs of both steamers were piled high and bristling with stolen furniture. Thomas easily skirted the wallowing 'buses, glass crunching beneath the *Zephyr*'s wheels.

In Whitechapel there were dirty, shoeless children clambering like monkeys, four stories in the air, on the red-painted arm of a great construction-crane. Spies of a sort, Brian opined, for some were waving colored rags and screeching down at people in the street. Mallory thought it more likely that the urchins had clambered up there in hope of fresher air.

Four dead and bloating horses, a team of massive Percherons, lay swollen in Stepney. The stiffened carcasses, shot to death, were still in their harness. A few yards on, the dray itself appeared, sacked, its wheels missing. Its dozen great beer-casks had been rolled down the street, then battered open, each site of rapturous looting now surrounded by a pungent, fly-blown stickiness of spillage. There were no revelers left now, their only evidence being shattered pitchers, dirty rags of women's clothing, single shoes.

Mallory spotted a leprous plague of bills, slapped-up at the site of this drunken orgy. He hit the top of the *Zephyr* with a flung lump of coal, and Tom stopped.

Tom decamped from the gurney, Fraser following him,

stretching cramps from his shoulders and favoring his wounded ribs. "What is it?"

"Sedition," Mallory said.

The four of them, with a wary eye for interference, marched with interest to the wall, an ancient posting-surface of plastered timber, so thick with old bills that it seemed to be made of cheese-rind. Some two dozen of Captain Swing's best were freshly posted there, copies of the same gaudy, ill-printed broadside. The bill featured a large winged woman with her hair afire, surmounting two columns of dense text. Words, apparently at random, had been marked out in red. They stood silently, attempting to decipher the squirming, smudgy print. After a moment, young Thomas, with a shrug and a sneer, excused himself. "I'll see to the gurney," he said.

Brian began to read aloud, haltingly.

" 'AN APPEAL TO THE PEOPLE! Ye are all free Lords of Earth, and need only COURAGE to make triumphant WAR on the Whore of Babylondon and all her learned thieves. Blood! Blood! Vengeance! Vengeance, vengeance! Plagues, foul plagues, et cetera, to all those that harken not to universal justice! BROTHERS, SISTERS! Kneel no more before the vampyre capitalist and the idiot savantry! Let the slaves of crowned brigands grovel at the feet of Newton. WE shall destroy the Moloch Steam and shatter his rocking iron! Hang ten score tyrants from the lamp-posts of this city, and your happiness and liberty be guaranteed forever! Forward! Forward!!! We take hope in the human Deluge, we have no recourse but a general war! We crusade for the REDEMPTION, of the oppressed, of the rebels, of the poor, of the criminals, all those who are TORMENTED by the Seven-Cursed Whore whose body is brimstone and who rides the nightmare horse of iron. . . .' "

There was much more. "What in the name of heaven is the wretch trying to *say*?" asked Mallory, his head buzzing.

"I've never seen the like of this," murmured Fraser. "It's the ranting of a criminal lunatic!"

Brian pointed at the bottom of the bill. "I cannot understand about these so-called 'Seven Curses'! He refers to them as if they were dreadful afflictions, and yet he never names and numbers them. He never makes them clear. . . ."

"What can it be that he wants?" Mallory demanded. "He can't think that a general massacre is any answer to his grievances, whatever they may be. . . ."

"There's no reasoning with this monster," Fraser said grimly. "You were quite right, Dr. Mallory. Come what may—no matter what risk—we must be rid of him! There is no other way!"

They returned to the *Zephyr*, where Tom had finished the coaling. Mallory glanced at his brothers. Above their masks, their reddened eyes shone with all the stern courage of manly resolution. Fraser had spoken for them all; they were united; there was no more need of words. In the very midst of this low squalor, it seemed to Mallory a moment of true splendor. Touched to the core, he felt his heart soar within him. For the first time in seeming ages, he felt redeemed, clean, utterly purposeful, utterly free of doubt.

As the *Zephyr* rolled on through Whitechapel, the exaltation began to fade, replaced with a heightened attention and a racing pulse. Mallory adjusted his mask, checked the workings of the Ballester-Molina, exchanged a few words with Brian. But with all doubt resolved, with life and death awaiting the coming roll of the die, there seemed little enough to say. Instead, like Brian, Mallory found himself inspecting every passing door and window with a nervous care.

It seemed that every wall in Limehouse was spattered with the wretch's outpourings. Some were vivid madness pure and simple: many others, however, were cunningly disguised. Mallory noted five instances of the lecture-posters that had libeled him. Some might have been genuine, for he did not read the text. The sight of his own name struck his heightened sensibilities with a shock almost painful.

And he had not been the only victim of this queer kind of forgery. An advert for the Bank of England solicited deposits of pounds of flesh. A seeming offer of first-class railway excursions incited the public to rob the wealthy passengers. Such was the devilish mockery of these fraudulent bills that even quite normal adverts began to seem queer. As he scanned the bills, searching for double-meanings, every posted word seemed to decay into threatening nonsense. Mallory had never before realized the ubiquity of London's advertisements, the sullen omnipresence of insistent words and images.

An inexplicable weariness of soul struck him, as the *Zephyr* rumbled on unchallenged through the macadamed streets. It was a very weariness of London, of the city's sheer physicality, its nightmare endlessness, of streets, courts, crescents, terraces, and alleys, of fog-shrouded stone and soot-blackened brick. A nausea of awnings, a nastiness of casements, an ugliness of scaffoldings lashed together with rope; a horrible prevalence of iron street-lamps and granite bollards, of pawn-shops, haberdashers, and tobacconists. The city seemed to stretch about them like some pitiless abyss of geologic time.

An ugly shout split Mallory's reverie. Masked men had scuttled into the street before them, shabby, threatening, blocking the way. The *Zephyr* braked to a sudden stop, the coal-wain lurching.

Mallory saw at a glance that these were rascals of the roughest description. The first, an evil youngster with a face like dirty dough, in a greasy jacket and corduroy trousers, had a mangy fur cap pulled low, but not low enough to hide the prison-cut of his hair. The second, a sturdy brute of thirty-five, wore a tall grease-stiffened hat, checked trousers, and brass-toed lace-up boots. The third was thick-set and bow-legged, with leather knee-breeches and soiled stockings, a long muffler wrapped round and round his mouth.

And then, rushing from inside a plundered ironmonger's, two more confederates—hulking, idle, slouching young men, with short baggy shirt-sleeves and trousers too tight. They had armed themselves with spontaneous weapons—a goffering-iron, a yard-long salamander. Homely items these, but unexpectedly cruel and frightening in the ready hands of these bandits.

The brass-booted man, their leader, it seemed, tugged the

kerchief from his face with a sneering yellow grin. "Get out of that kerridge," he commanded. "Get the hell out!"

But Fraser was already in motion. He emerged, with quiet assurance, before the five jostling ruffians, for all the world like a school-teacher calming an unruly class. He announced, quite clearly and firmly: "Now *that's* no use, Mr. Tally Thompson! I know *you*—and I should think you know *me*. You are under arrest, for felony."

"That be damned!" blurted Tally Thompson, turning pale with astonishment.

"It's Sergeant Fraser!" shouted the dough-faced boy in horror, falling back two steps.

Fraser produced a pair of blued-iron handcuffs.

"No!" Thompson yelped, "none o' that! I won't stand *them!* I won't bear none o' that!"

"You *will* clear the way here, the rest of you," Fraser announced. "You, Bob Miles—what are you creeping round here for? Put away that silly ironware, before I take you in."

"For Christ's sake, Tally, *shoot him!*" shouted the mufflered ruffian.

Fraser deftly snapped his cuffs on Tally Thompson's wrists. "So we have a gun, do we, Tally?" he said, and yanked a derringer from the man's brass-studded belt. "That's a shame, that is." He frowned at the others. "*Are* you going to hook it, you lads?"

"Let's hook it," whined Bob Miles. "We should hook it, like the sergeant says!"

"*Kill him,* you jolterheads!" shouted the mufflered man, pressing his mask to his face with one hand, and pulling a short, broad-bladed knife with the other. "He's a fucking *copper,* you idiots—*do* for him! Swing'll choke you if we don't!" The mufflered man raised his voice. "Coppers here!" he screeched, like a man selling hot chestnuts. "Everybody, come up and do for these copper sons-of-bitches—"

Fraser lashed out deftly with the butt of the derringer, cracking it against the mufflered man's wrist; the wretch dropped his knife with a howl.

The three other ruffians took at once to their heels. Tally Thompson also tried to flee, but Fraser snagged the man's cuffed wrists left-handed, yanked him off-balance and spun him to his knees.

The man with the muffler hopped and hobbled back several paces, as if dragged against his will. Then he stopped, stooped over, picked up a heavy toppled flat-iron by its mahogany handle. He cocked his hand back, to throw.

Fraser leveled the derringer, and fired. The mufflered man doubled over, his knees buckling, and fell to the street, writhing in a fit. "He's killed me," the ruffian squawked. "I'm gut-shot, he's killed me!"

Fraser gave Tally Thompson an admonitory cuff on the ear. "This barker of yours is rubbish, Tally. I aimed for his bloody legs!"

"He didn't mean no harm," Tally sniveled.

"He'd a five-pound flat-iron." Fraser glanced back at Mallory and Brian, where they stood astonished in the coal-wain. "Come down, you lads—look sharp now. We'll have to leave your gurney. They'll be looking for it. We have to hoof it now."

Fraser yanked Tally Thompson to his feet, with a cruel jerk of the cuffs. "And you, Tally, you'll lead us to Captain Swing."

"I won't, Sergeant!"

"You will, Tally." Fraser hauled Tally forward, with a sharp beckoning glance back at Mallory.

The five of them picked their way around the squealing, choking ruffian, who rolled in his spreading blood on the pavement, his dirty bow-legs trembling in spasm. "Damme if he don't take on," Fraser said coldly. "Who is he, Tally?"

"Never knew his name."

Without breaking step, Fraser slapped Tally's battered top-hat from his head. The wrinkled topper seemed glued to the ruffian's scalp with grime and macassar-oil. "Of course you know him!"

"No name!" Tally insisted, looking back at his lost hat with a leer of despair. "A Yankee, inne?"

"What sort of Yankee, then?" asked Fraser, scenting deceit. "Confederate? Unionist? Texian? Californian?"

" 'E's from New York," Tally said.

"What," Fraser said in disbelief, "you'd tell me he was a Manhattan Communard!" He glanced back once at the dying man as they walked on, then recovered himself swiftly and spoke with tepid skepticism. "He didn't talk like any New York Yankee."

"I don't know nothing 'bout any commoners. Swing liked 'im, is all!"

Fraser led them down an alleyway crossed with rusty elevated cat-walks, its towering brick walls glistening with greasy damp. "Are there more like that one, in Swing's counsel? More men from Manhattan?"

"Swing's got a deal of friends," Tally said, seeming to recover himself, "and he'll do for you, he will, you trifle wi' him!"

"Tom," said Fraser, turning his attention to Mallory's brother, "can you handle a pistol?"

"A pistol?"

"Take this one," said Fraser, handing over Tally's derringer. "There's but one shot left. You musn't use it lest your man is close enough to touch."

Having rid himself of the derringer, Fraser then reached, without pause, into his coat-pocket, pulled out a small leather blackjack, and commenced, while still walking steadily, to batter Tally Thompson, with numbing accuracy, on the thick meat of his arms and shoulders.

The man flinched and grunted under the blows, and finally began to howl, his flat nose running snot.

Fraser stopped, pocketed his truncheon. "Damn ye for a fool, Tally Thompson," he said, with a queer kind of affection. "Know you nothing of coppers? I've come for your precious Swing all by meself, and brought these three jolly lads just to see the fun! Now where's he lurking?"

"A big warehouse in the docks," Tally sniveled. "Full of loot—wonders! And guns, whole cases of fancy barkers—"

"Which warehouse, then?"

"I dunno," Tally wailed, "I never been inside the bloody gates before! I don't know the bloody names of all them fancy go-downs!"

"What's the name on the door? The owner!"

"I can't read, Sergeant, you know that!"

"Where is it, then?" Fraser asked relentlessly. "Import docks or export?"

"Import . . ."

"South side? North side?"

"South, about middle-ways . . ." From the street behind them came distant shouts, a frenzied shattering of glass, and drum-like echoed booms of battered sheet-metal. Tally fell silent, his head cocked to listen. His lips quirked. "Why, that's your kerridge!" he said, the whine gone from his voice. "Swing's lads a-come back hotfoot, and found yer kerridge, Sergeant!"

"How many men in this warehouse?"

"Listen to 'em breaking 'er up!" said Tally. A queer variety of child-like wonder had chased all fear from his sullen features.

"How many men?" Fraser barked, boxing Tally's ear.

"They're knocking 'er to smithers!" Tally declared cheerily, shrugging from the blow. "Ludd's work on your pretty gurney!"

"Shut yer trap, ye bastard!" young Tom burst out, his voice high with rage and pain.

Startled, Tally regarded Tom's masked face with a dawning leer of satisfaction. "What's that, young mister?"

"Shut up, I told ye!" Tom cried.

Tally Thompson leered like an ape. "It ain't me hurting your precious gurney! Yell at them, boy! Tell 'em to stop, then!" Tally lurched backward suddenly, snatching his manacled hands from Fraser's grip. The policeman staggered, almost knocking Brian from his feet.

Tally turned and screeched through his cupped hands. "Stop that fun, my hearties!" His howl echoed down the brick-work canyon. "Ye're hurtin' private property!"

Tom pounced on the man like lightning, with a wild spinning swing of his fist. Tally's head snapped back, and the breath left him in a ragged gasp. He tottered a step, then dropped to the cobbled floor of the alley like a sack of meal.

There was a sudden silence.

"Damme, Tom!" said Brian. "Ye knocked his lights out!"

Fraser, his truncheon drawn now, stepped across the supine ruffian, and peeled one eyelid back with his thumb. Then he glanced up at Tom, mildly. "You've a temper, lad. . . ."

Tom tugged his mask free, breathing shakily. "I could have shot him!" he blurted, his voice thin. He looked to Mallory, with a strange confused appeal. "I could ha', Ned! Shot him down dead!"

Mallory nodded shortly. "Easy, lad. . . ."

Fraser fumbled to unlock the handcuffs; they were slick with blood from Tally's lacerated wrists.

"That was mortal strange, what the rascal just did!" Brian marveled, in a hushed Sussex drawl. "Are they bedlam crazy here, Ned? Have they all gone ellynge, these London folk?"

Mallory nodded soberly. Then he raised his voice. "But nowt that a good right arm don't cure!" He whacked Tom's shoulder with an open palm. "Ye're a boxer, Tommy lad! Ye blowed him down like a slaughtered ox!"

Brian snorted laughter. Tom smiled shyly, rubbing his knuckles.

Fraser rose, pocketing truncheon and cuffs, and set off up the alley, at a half-trot. The brothers followed him. "It warn't so much," Tom said, his voice giddy.

"What," Mallory objected, "a mere lad of nineteen, layin' out that brassy-boots brawler? It's a marvel surely!"

"It warn't any fair fight, with his hands bound," Tom said.

"One punch!" Brian gloated. "Ye stretched him flat as an oaken plank, Tommy!"

"Stow it!" Fraser hissed.

They fell silent. The alley ended by the vacant ground of a demolished building, its cracked foundation strewn with bits of red brick and greying spars of splintered lumber. Fraser picked his way forward. The sky rolled yellow-grey overhead, the haze breaking here and there to reveal thick greenish clouds like rotting curd.

"Hell's bells," Tom declared, in a tone of thin jollity. "They can't a-heard us talking, Mr. Fraser! Not with that almighty rucket they were making on my gurney!"

"It isn't that lot worries me now, lad," Fraser said, not unkindly. "But we might meet more pickets."

"Where are we?" Brian asked, then stumbled to a halt. "God in heaven! *What* is that smell?"

"The Thames," Fraser told him.

A thick wall of low brick stood at the end of the vacant plot. Mallory hoisted himself up and stood, breathing very shallowly, his mask pressed hard to his bearded lips. The far side of the brick wall—it was part of the Thames embankment—sloped down ten feet to the river-bed. The tide was out, and the shrunken Thames was a sluggish gleam between long plazas of cracked muddy shore.

Across the river stood the steel navigation-tower of Cuckold's Point, adorned with nautical warning-flags. Mallory could not recognize the signals. Quarantine, perhaps? Blockade? The river seemed nigh deserted.

Fraser looked up and down the mud-flats at the foot of the embankment. Mallory followed his gaze. Small boats were embedded in the grey-black mud as if set in cement. Here and there along the bend of the Limehouse Reach, rivulets of viridian slime reached up through the gouged tracks of channel-dredgers.

Something like a river-breeze—not a breeze at all, but a soft liquid ooze of gelatinous Stink—rose from the Thames and spilled over them where they stood. "Dear God!" Brian cried in weak amazement, and knelt quickly behind the wall. With a sympathetic ripple of queasiness, Mallory heard his brother retch violently.

With a stern effort, Mallory mastered the sensation. It was not easy. Clearly, the raw Thames surpassed even the fabled stench in the holds of Royal Artillery transports.

Young Thomas, though he'd also gone quite pale, seemed of

tougher stuff than Brian—inured, perhaps, by the chugging exhaust of steam-gurneys. "Why, look at this nasty business!" Tom suddenly declared, in a muffled, dreamy voice. "I knew we'd a drought upon the land, but I never dreamt of this!" He looked to Mallory with astonished, reddened eyes. "Why, Ned— the air, the water—there's never been such a dreadfulness, surely!"

Fraser seemed pained. "London's never what she might be, in summer. . . ."

"But look at the river!" Tom cried innocently. "And look, look, yonder comes a ship!" A large paddle-steamer was working her way up the Thames, and a very queer-looking craft she was indeed, with her hull flat as a raft's, and a cheese-box cabin of sloping, riveted iron, the walls of black armor patched bow-to-stern with large white squares: cannon-hatches. On her bow, two sailors, in rubber gloves and nozzled rubber helmets, took soundings with a leaded line.

"What sort of vessel is that?" asked Mallory, wiping his eyes.

Brian rose unsteadily, leaned across the wall, wiped his mouth, and spat. "Pocket ironclad," he announced hoarsely. "A river gunship." He pinched his nose shut and shuddered from head to foot.

Mallory had read of such craft, but had never seen one. "From the Mississippi campaign, in America." He stared beneath a shading hand, wishing for a spyglass. "Does she fly Confederate colors, then? I didn't know we'd any of her class here in England. . . . No, I see she flies the Union Jack!"

"See what her paddle-wheels do!" Tom marveled. "That river-water must be thick as neat's-foot jelly. . . ."

No one saw fit to remark on this observation. Fraser pointed downstream. "Listen, lads. Some rods away lies a deep-dredged channel. It leads into the moorings for the West India Docks. With the river this low, with luck, a man might creep through that channel, to emerge within the docks unseen."

"Walk o'er the mud o' the shore, you mean to say," Mallory said.

"No!" Brian cried. "There must be another stratagem!"

Fraser shook his head. "I know those docks. They've an eight-foot wall about 'em, topped by a very sharp cheval-de-frise. There are loading-gates, and a rail-head, too, but they'll be close-guarded sure. Swing chose well. The place is nigh a fortress."

Brian shook his head. "Won't Swing guard the river, too?"

"Doubtless," Fraser said, "but how many men will stand sharp lookout over this stinking mud, for Swing or anyone else?"

Mallory nodded, convinced. "He's right, lads."

"But it'll daub us neck to foot with smeechy filth!" Brian protested.

"We're not made o' sugar," Mallory grunted.

"But my uniform, Ned! D'ye know what this dress-coatee cost me?"

"I'll swap ye my gurney for that shiny gold braid," Tom told him.

Brian stared at his younger brother, and winced.

"Then we must strip for it, lads," Mallory commanded, shrugging out of his jacket. "Like we were farm-hands, a-pitching sweet hay on a nice Sussex morn. Hide that city finery in the rubble, and be quick about it."

Mallory stripped to the waist, tucked his pistol in the belt of his rolled-up trousers, and lowered himself down the embankment wall. He half-slid, half-hopped to the evil mud below.

The river-bank was as hard and dry as brick. Mallory laughed aloud. The others joined him, Brian coming last. Brian kicked a cracked dinner-plate of mud with his waxed and polished boot. "Damme for a fool," he said, "to let you talk me out of uniform!"

"Pity!" Tom taunted. "Ye'll never launder the sawdust out o' that fancy forage-cap."

Fraser, removing his collar now, was in white shirt and braces—surprisingly dandyish items, of watered scarlet silk. A new shoulder-holster of pale chamois held a stout little pepperbox pistol. Mallory noted the bulge of a neat padded bandage beneath the shirt and strap. "Don't go griping, lads," Fraser said, leading the way. "Some folk pass their very lives in the mud of the Thames."

"Who's that then?" asked Tom.

"Mudlarks," Fraser told him, picking his way. "Winter and summer, they slog up to their middles, in the mud o' low tide. Hunting lumps o' coal, rusty nails, any river-rubbish that will fetch a penny."

"Are you joking?" Tom asked.

"Children mostly," Fraser persisted calmly, "and a deal of feeble old women."

"I don't believe you," Brian said. "If you told me Bombay or Calcutta, I might grant it. But not London!"

"I didn't say the wretches were British," Fraser said. "Your mudlarks are foreigners, mostly. Poor refugees."

"Well, then," Tom said, relieved.

They tramped on silently, breathing as best they could. Mallory's nose had clogged solid and his throat was thick with phlegm. It was a relief of sorts, to be spared the sense of smell.

Brian was still muttering, a monotone to match their tramping step. "Britain's a sight too hospitable to all these damn foreign refugees. If I'd my way, I'd transport the lot to Texas. . . ."

"All the fish here must be dead, eh?" said Tom, stooping to rip up a china-hard platter of mud. He showed Mallory a mash of flattened fish-bones embedded in it. "Look, Ned—the very image of your fossils!"

They reached an obstacle a few yards on, a dredger's muddy hollow, half-filled with black silt, marbled with veins of vile pale grease like the lees from a pan of bacon. There was no help for it but to leap and dodge and splash across the ditch, and Brian had the evil luck to miss his footing. He came up foully smeared, flicking muck from his hands and cursing wildly in what Mallory took to be Hindustani.

Beyond the ditch, the crust grew treacherous, plates of dried mud skidding or crumbling underfoot, over a pitchy, viscous muck full of ooze and bubbling gas-pockets. But there was worse luck yet at the entrance-channel to the Docks. Here the channel's banks were close-packed tarred pilings, slick with greenish fur and oily damp, rising fifteen feet above the water-line. And the water itself, which filled the broad channel from bank to bank, was a chilly grey sump, seemingly bottomless, writhing with leg-thick wads of viridian slime.

It was an impasse. "Now what's our course?" asked Mallory grimly. "Swim?"

"Never!" Brian shouted, his eyes reddened and wild.

"Scale the walls, then?"

"We can't," Tom groaned, with a hopeless look at the slimy pilings. "We can scarcely breathe!"

"I wouldn't wash my *hands* in that damn water!" Brian cried. "And *my* hands are caked in stinking muck!"

"Stow it!" Fraser said. "Swing's men will hear you sure. If they catch us down here, we'll be shot like dogs! Stow it, and let me think!"

"My God, the *Stink!*" Brian cried, ignoring him. He seemed near panic. "It's worse than a transport—worse than a Russki trench! Christ Jesus, I saw 'em bury week-old *pieces* of Russki at Inkermann, and *that* smelled better than *this!*"

"Knife it!" Fraser whispered. "I hear something."

Footsteps. The tramp of a group of men, coming nearer. "They've got us," Fraser said in sharp desperation, gazing up the sheer wall and putting a hand to his pistol. "Our number's up—sell your lives dear, lads!"

But in one moment—a series of instants shaved so thin as to be normally useless to the human mind—inspiration blew through Mallory like a gust of Alpine wind.

"Don't," he commanded the others, in a voice of iron conviction. "Don't look up. Do as I do!"

Mallory began to sing a chantey, loudly, drunkenly.

> " 'At Santiago love is kind,
>   And we'll forget those left behind—
>   So kiss us long, and kiss us well,
>   Polly and Meg and Kate and Nell—'

"C'mon, you lads!" he urged cheerily, with a boozy wave of his arm. Tom and Brian, direly puzzled, chimed in the chorus, faltering and belated.

> " 'Farewell, farewell, you jolly young girls,
>   We're off to Rio Bay!' "

"Next verse!" Mallory crowed.

> " 'At Vera Cruz the days are fine,
>   Farewell to Jane and Caroline . . .' "

"Ahoy!" came a brusque shout from the top of the wall. Mallory glanced up, in feigned surprise, to see foreshortened bodies. Half-a-dozen marauders were looming over them, rifles slung over their backs. The speaker crouched at the top of the pilings, his head and face swathed in kerchiefs of knotted silk paisley. He held a gleaming, long-barreled pistol, with seeming carelessness, across his knee. His trousers, of white duck, looked immaculate.

"Ahoy the shore!" Mallory shouted, craning his neck. He flung his arms wide in jovial greeting, and almost toppled backward. "How might we be o' service to you flash gentlemen?"

"Here's a conundrum!" the leader announced, in the elaborate tone of a man casting pearls of wit before swine. "Just how very lushed, how utterly well-pissed indeed, can four London pigeons be?" He raised his voice. "Can't you smell that dreadful stench down there?"

"Surely!" Mallory said. "But we want to see the India Docks!"

"Why?" The word was cold.

Mallory laughed harshly. "Because it's full of things we want, ain't it? Stands to reason, don't it?"

"Things like clean linen?" said one of the other men. There was laughter, mixed with grunts and coughing.

Mallory laughed too, and slapped his naked chest. "Why not! Can you lads help us? Throw us down a rope or the like!"

The leader's eyes narrowed between his paisley wraps, and he tightened his grip on the pistol-butt. "You're no sailor! A jack-tar never says 'rope.' Rather, he always says 'line'!"

"What's it to you, what I am?" Mallory shouted, scowling up at the man. "Throw us a rope! Or a ladder! Or a bleeding balloon! Or else go to hell!"

"Jolly right!" Tom chimed in, his voice shaking. "Who needs you lot, anyway!"

The leader turned, his men vanishing with him. "Hurry up!" Mallory bellowed, as a parting shot. "You can't keep all that fancy swag to yourselves, you know!"

Brian shook his head. "Jesus, Ned," he whispered. "This is a damn tight pinch!"

"We'll pass as looters," Mallory said quietly. "We'll pose as drunken rascals, primed for any kind of mischief! We'll join their ranks, and make our way to Swing!"

"What if they ask us questions, Ned?"

"Act stupid."

"Halloo!" came a shrill voice from above.

"What's that?" Mallory cried roughly, looking up. It was a masked and scrawny boy of fifteen years or so, balanced atop the pilings with a rifle in his hands.

"Lord Byron's dead!" the boy yelled.

Mallory was dumbstruck.

Tom shrilled out in the silence. "Who *says* he is?"

"It's true! Old bastard's kicked the bucket, he's dead as mutton!" The boy laughed in giddy delight, and capered along the edge of the pilings with his rifle waggling over his head. He vanished with a leap.

Mallory found his voice. "Surely not."

"No," Fraser agreed.

"Not likely, anyway."

"Wishful thinking on the part of these anarchists," Fraser suggested.

There was a long, empty silence.

"Of course," Mallory said, tugging his beard, "if the Great Orator truly is dead, then that means . . ." Words failed him in a foundering rush of confusion, but the others watched Mallory for guidance, silent and expectant. "Well . . . ," Mallory said, "the death of Byron would mark the end of an age of greatness!"

"It needn't mean much at all," Fraser objected, his voice under firm control. "There are many men of great talent in the Party. Charles Babbage yet lives! Lord Colgate, Lord Brunel . . . the Prince Consort for instance. Prince Albert is a sound and thoughtful man."

"Lord Byron *can't* be dead!" Brian burst out. "We're standing in stinking mud, believing a stinking lie!"

"Quiet!" Mallory commanded. "We'll simply have to suspend any judgment on this matter until we have firm evidence!"

"Ned's right," nodded Tom. "The Prime Minister would have wanted it that way! That's the scientific method. That was what Lord Byron always taught us. . . ."

A thick, tarred rope, its end knotted in a fat noose, came snaking down the wall. The anarchist lieutenant—the dainty man with the paisley kerchiefs—posed one bent leg atop the wall, with his elbow on his knee and his chin in his hand. "Put your arse in that, my friend," he suggested, "and we'll hoist you up in a trice!"

"I thank you kindly!" Mallory said. He waved with cheery confidence and stepped into the noose.

When the tug came, he braced his mud-caked shoes against the slick and nasty timbers, and stamped his way up, and over the top.

The leader tossed the emptied noose back down, with a kid-gloved hand. "Welcome, sir, to the august company of the vanguard of mankind. Permit me, under the circumstances, to introduce myself. I am the Marquess of Hastings." The self-styled Marquess bowed slightly, then struck a pose, chin cocked, one gloved fist poised on his hip.

Mallory saw that the fellow was in earnest.

The title of Marquess was a relic from the years before the Rads, yet here was a young pretender of some sort, a living fossil, alive and in command of this vipers' crew! Mallory could scarcely have been more startled to see a young plesiosaur lift its snaky head from the depths of the stinking Thames.

"Lads," drawled the young Marquess, "pour some of that co-logne over our pungent friend! If he does anything stupid, you know what to do."

"Shoot him?" someone blurted, idiotically.

The Marquess winced elaborately—an actor's gesture indicating a breach of taste. A boy in a stolen copper's helmet and a ripped silk shirt slopped chill cologne from a cut-glass bottle over Mallory's bare neck and back.

Brian rose next, at the end of the rope. "Those are soldier's trousers, under that muck," the Marquess observed. "Absent without leave, comrade?"

Brian shrugged mutely.

"Enjoying your little holiday in London?"

Brian nodded like a fool.

"Give this filthy personage new trousers," the Marquess commanded. He looked about his little troupe of six, who were once again lowering the line with the clumsy enthusiasm of a May Day tug-o'-war. "Comrade Shillibeer! You're about this man's size—give him your trousers."

"Aw, but Comrade Markiss—"

"To each according to his needs, Comrade Shillibeer! Doff the garment at once."

Shillibeer climbed clumsily out of his trousers and proffered them up. He wore no undergarments, and he tugged nervously at his shirt-tails with one hand.

"For heaven's sake," the Marquess said quizzically, "must I tell you sheepish dullards every little thing?" He pointed sharply to Mallory. "You! Take Shillibeer's place and haul that line. You, soldier—no longer the oppressor's minion, but a man entirely free!—put on Shillibeer's trousers. Comrade Shillibeer, quit that wriggling. You have nothing of which to be ashamed. You may go at once to the general depot for fresh garments."

"Thank you, sir!"

" 'Comrade,' " the Marquess corrected. "Get something nice, Shillibeer. And bring more cologne."

Tom came up next, Mallory helping with the heaving. The

bandits were badly hampered by their clattering, poorly slung rifles. These were general-issue Victoria carbines, heavy single-shot relics now consigned to native troops in the Colonies. The rioters were rendered yet more clumsy by fearsome kitchen-knives and home-made truncheons, stuffed at random into their looted finery. They wore gaudy scarves, sweaty silks, Army ban-doliers, and more resembled Turkish bashi-bazouks than any kind of Briton. Two of them were scarcely more than boys, while another pair were thick-set, lumpish, thievish rascals, sodden with drink. The last, to Mallory's continued surprise, was a slen-der, silent Negro, in the quiet dress of a gentleman's valet.

The Marquess of Hastings examined Tom. "What is your name?"

"Tom, sir."

The Marquess pointed. "What's *his* name?"

"Ned."

"And him?"

"Brian," Tom said. "I think . . ."

"And what, pray, is the name of that grim-looking cove below, looking so awfully much like a copper?"

Tom hesitated.

"Don't you know?"

"He never gave us any proper name," Mallory broke in. "We just call him the Reverend."

The Marquess glared at Mallory.

"We only met the Reverend today, sir," Tom apologized glibly. "We ain't what you'd call bosom pals."

"Suppose we leave him down there, then," the Marquess sug-gested.

"Haul him up," Mallory countered. "He's clever."

"Oh? And what of you, Comrade Ned? You're not half so stupid as you pretend, it seems. And you're not very drunk."

"Then give me a drink," Mallory said boldly. "And I could do with one of them carbines too, if you're divvying loot."

The Marquess took note of Mallory's pistol, then cocked his masked head and winked, as if they were sharing a joke.

"All things in time, my eager friend," he said. He waved his neat gloved hand. "Very well. Haul him."

Fraser rose within the noose. "So, 'Reverend,' " said the Marquess, "what, pray, might be your denomination?"

Fraser shook the rope loose and stepped out. "What do you think, guv'nor? I'm a bleedin' Quaker!"

There was evil laughter. Fraser, pretending a loutish pleasure at the others' fun, shook his gingham-masked head. "No," he rasped, "no Quaker I, for I'm a Panty-sucker!"

The laughter stopped short.

"Panty-sucker," Fraser insisted, "one o' them yellow-back Yankee ranters—"

The Marquess broke in with chill precision. "A Pantisocrat, do you mean? That is to say, a lay preacher of the Susquehanna Phalanstery?"

Fraser stared dumbly at the Marquess.

"I refer to the utopian doctrines of Professor Coleridge and Reverend Wordsworth," the Marquess persisted, with gentle menace.

"Right," Fraser grunted, "one o' them."

"That seems to be a copper's sling and pistol that you carry, my pacifistic Pantisocrat friend."

"Got it from a copper, didn't I?" He paused. "A dead'un!"

There was laughter again, broken with coughs and grunts.

The boy standing next to Mallory elbowed one of the older louts. "This Stink's turning me head, Henry! Can't we hook it?"

"Ask the Marquess," Henry said.

"You ask 'im," the boy wheedled, "he always makes such fun o' me. . . ."

"Harken, now!" said the Marquess. "Jupiter and I shall escort the new recruits to the general depot. The rest of you shall continue shore patrol."

The remaining four groaned in dissent.

"Don't deviate," the Marquess chided, "you know that all the comrades get a turn at river-duty, same as you."

The Marquess, followed closely by the Negro, Jupiter, led the way along the embankment. It astonished Mallory that the fellow would turn his back on four armed strangers, an act of either arrant foolishness or sublimely careless bravery.

Mallory traded silent glances, full of meaning, with Tom, Brian, and Fraser. All four still bore their weapons, the anarchists having not even troubled to confiscate them. It would be the work of moments to shoot their guide in the back, and perhaps the Negro too, though the black was unarmed. A vile business, though, striking from behind, though perhaps a necessity of war. But the others were shifting itchily as they walked, and Mallory realized that they looked to him to do the deed. This venture had become his, now, and even Fraser had bet his life on the fortunes of Edward Mallory.

Mallory edged forward, matching his stride with that of the Marquess of Hastings. "What's in this depot of yours, Your Lordship? A deal of fine loot, I should hope."

"A deal of fine hope, my looting friend! But never you mind that. Tell me this, Comrade Ned—what would you do with loot, if you had it?"

"I suppose that might depend on what it was," Mallory ventured.

"You'd carry it back to your rat-warren," the Marquess surmised, "and sell it for a fraction of its worth to a fencing-Jew, and spend the lot of that on drink, to wake, in a day or two, in a filthy station-house, with a copper's foot on your neck."

Mallory stroked his chin. "What would you do with it, then?"

"Put it to use, of course! We shall use it in the cause of those who gave it value. By that, I mean the common-folk of London, the masses, the oppressed, the sweated labor, those who produce all the riches of this city."

"That's a queer sort of talk," Mallory said.

"The revolution does not loot, Comrade Ned. We sequester, we commandeer, we liberate! You and your friends were drawn here by a few imported gewgaws. You think to carry off what your hands can clutch in a few moments. Are you men, or magpies? Why settle for a pocketful of dirty shillings? You could own London, the modern Babylon herself! You could own futurity!"

" 'Futurity,' eh?" said Mallory, glancing back at Fraser. Above his gingham mask the policeman's eyes showed unmitigated loathing.

Mallory shrugged. "How much tin will a quart of 'futurity' fetch, Yer Lordship?"

"I'll thank you not to call me that," the Marquess said sharply. "You address a veteran of popular revolution, a people's soldier who takes pride in the simple title of 'comrade.' "

"Begging your pardon, I'm sure."

"You're not a fool, Ned. You can't mistake me for a Rad Lord. I'm no bourgeois meritocrat! I am a revolutionary, and a mortal enemy by blood and conviction of the Byron tyranny and all its works!"

Mallory coughed harshly, cleared his throat. "All right then," he said in a new and sharper voice. "What's all this talk about? Seizing London—you can't be serious! That hasn't been done since William the Conqueror."

"Read your history, friend!" the Marquess retorted. "Wat Tyler did it. Cromwell did it. Byron himself did it!" He laughed. "The People Risen have seized New York City! The working-people rule Manhattan as we walk and speak here! They have liquidated the rich. They have burned Trinity! They have seized the means of information and production. If mere Yankees can do that, then the people of England, far more advanced along the course of historical development, can do it with even greater ease."

It was clear to Mallory that the man—the lad, rather, for beneath that mask and swagger he was very young—believed this evil madness with a whole heart. "But the Government," Mallory protested, "will send in the Army."

"Kill their officer-class, and the Army rank-and-file will rise with us," the Marquess said coolly. "Look at your soldier-friend Brian there. He seems happy enough in our company! Aren't you, Comrade Brian?"

Brian nodded mutely, waving a filth-smeared hand.

"You don't yet grasp the genius of our Captain's strategy," the Marquess said. "We stand in the heart of the British capital, the one area on Earth that Britain's imperial elite are unwilling to devastate in the pursuit of their evil hegemony. The Rad Lords will not shell and burn their own precious London to quell what they falsely think a period of passing unrest. But!" He raised one gloved forefinger. "When we mount the barricades throughout this city, then they will have to struggle hand-to-hand with an aroused working-class, men nerved to the marrow with the first true freedom they have ever known!"

The Marquess stopped a moment, wheezing for breath at the foetid air. "Most of the oppressor-class," he continued, coughing, "have already fled London, to escape the Stink! When they attempt to return, the risen masses will meet them with fire and steel! We will fight them from the roof-tops, from doorways, alleyways, sewers, and rookeries!" He paused to dab his nose with a snotty kerchief from his sleeve. "We will sequester every sinew of organized oppression. The newspapers, the telegraph lines and pneumatic tube-ways, the palaces and barracks and bureaux! We will put them all to the great cause of liberation!"

Mallory waited, but it seemed that the young fanatic had at last run out of steam. "And you want us to help you, eh? Join this people's army of yours?"

"Of course!"

"What's in it for us, then?"

"Everything," the Marquess said. "Forever."

There were handsome ships moored inside the West India Docks, tangled rigging and steamer-stacks. The water within the Docks, a byway from the sewage-flow of the Thames, did not seem quite so foul to Mallory, until he saw, floating amid thin wads of slime, the bodies of dead men. Murdered sailors, the skeleton crews that shipping-lines left to guard their ships in harbor. The corpses floated like driftwood, a sight to chill the marrow. Mallory counted fifteen bodies, possibly sixteen, as he followed the Marquess along the gantry-shrouded wooden dock-way. Perhaps, he theorized, most of the crews had been killed elsewhere, or else recruited to swell the ranks of Swing's piracy. Not all sailors were loyal to order and authority. The Ballester-Molina pistol was a cold weight against Mallory's gut.

The Marquess and his black led them blithely on. They passed a deserted ship where an ugly vapor, steam or smoke, curled up ominously from the hatches below-decks. A quartet of anarchist guards, their carbines propped in a crude stack, played cards atop a barricade of bales of looted calico.

Other guards, drunken, whiskered wretches in bad plug-hats and worse trousers, armed derelicts, slept in toppled barrows and loading-sledges, amid a swelling debris of barrels, baskets, hawser-coils and loading-ramps, heaps of black coal for the silenced steam-derricks. From the warehouses across the water, to the south, came a ragged volley of distant popping gunshots. The Marquess showed no interest, did not break stride, did not even look.

"You overpowered all these ships?" Mallory inquired. "You must have a deal of men, Comrade Marquess!"

"More by the hour," the Marquess assured him. "Our men are combing Limehouse, rousing every working family. Do you know the term 'exponential growth,' Comrade Ned?"

"Why, no," Mallory lied.

"Mathematical clacking-term," the Marquess lectured absently. "Very interesting field, Engine-clacking, no end of use in the scientific study of socialism. . . ." He seemed distracted now, nervous. "Another day of Stink like this and we'll have more men than the London police-force! You're not the first coves I've recruited, you know! I'm quite an old hand at it, by now. Why, I wager even my man Jupiter could do it!" He slapped the shoulder of the Negro's livery-coat.

The Negro showed no reaction. Mallory wondered if he were deaf-and-dumb. He wore no breathing-mask. Perhaps he did not need one.

The Marquess led them to the greatest among a series of warehouses. Even among the stellar names of commerce: Whitby's, Evan-Hare, Aaron's, Madras & Pondicherry Co., this was a very palace of mercantile modernity. Its vast loading-doors had risen on a clever system of jointed counter-weights, re-vealing an interior of steel-frame construction, with translucent plate-glass vaulting a roof that stretched wide and long as a soccer-green. Below this roof grew a maze of steel braces, a fret-work of ratchets and wheeled tracking, where Engine-driven pulley-carts could run along like spiders. Somewhere pistons chugged, with the familiar popping racket of an Engine printing-press.

But the press was hidden somewhere behind a maze of booty to stupefy a Borgia. Merchandise lay in heaps, haystacks, moun-tains: brocades, lounge-chairs, carriage-wheels, epergnes and chandeliers, tureens, mattresses, iron lawn-dogs and Parian bird-baths, billiard-tables and liquor-cabinets, bedsteads and stair-newels, rolled rugs and marble mantlepieces. . . .

" 'Struth!" Tom cried. "How did you do all this?"

"We've been here for days now," the Marquess said. He tugged the kerchief from his face, revealing a pale visage of almost girlish beauty, with a downy blond mustache. "There are goods in plenty, still, in the other godowns, and you shall all have a chance for a turn at the sledge and barrow. It's grand fun. And it's yours, for it belongs to all of us, equally!"

"All of us?" Mallory said.

"Of course. All the comrades."

Mallory pointed at the Negro. "What about him?"

"What, my man Jupiter?" The Marquess blinked. "Jupiter be-longs to all of us too, of course! He's not my servant alone, but the servant of the common good." The Marquess mopped his drip-ping nose on a kerchief. "Follow me."

The heaping of booty had made a monster rat's-nest of the warehouse's scientific storage-plan. Following the Marquess, they picked their way across shoals of broken crystal, puddles of cooking-oil, a crunchy alleyway littered with peanut-hulls.

"Odd," the Marquess muttered, "when last I was here, the comrades were all about the place. . . ."

The heaps of goods dwindled toward the rear of the warehouse. They passed the whacking printing-press, hidden from sight in a cul-de-sac of towering bundles of news-print. Someone threw a bundle of wet printing-bills over the barricade, almost striking the Marquess, who hopped deftly over it.

Mallory became aware of a distant voice, high-pitched and shrill.

At the very rear of the warehouse, a large section of floor-space had been made into an impromptu lecture-hall. A chalkboard, a table piled with glassware, and a lectern, all sat unsteadily on a stage of close-packed soap-crates. Mismatched sets of cheap dining-chairs, in pressed oak and maple veneer, served as seating for a silent audience of perhaps three score.

"So here they are," said the Marquess, with an odd quaver in his voice. "You're in luck! Dr. Barton is favoring us with an exposition. Seat yourselves at once, comrades. You will, I assure you, find this well worth your attention!"

To his vast surprise, Mallory found himself and his companions forced to join the audience, in the final row of chairs. The Negro remained standing, hands clasped behind his back, at the rear of the hall.

Mallory, seated next to the Marquess, rubbed his smarting eyes in disbelief. "This speaker of yours is wearing a dress!"

"Hush," the Marquess whispered urgently.

The female lecturer, brandishing a chalk-tipped ebony pointer, was hectoring the seated crowd in a voice of shrill but closely measured fanaticism. The strange acoustics of the make-shift hall warped her words as if she were speaking through a drumhead. Some kind of queer temperance lecture it seemed, for she was decrying "the poison alcohol" and its threat to the "revolutionary spirit of the working-class." She had flasks, great glass-stoppered carboys, full of liquor on her table. They were labeled with the skull-and-crossbones, amid a truck of distillation-flasks, red rubber-tubing, wire cages, and laboratory gas-rings.

Tom, at Mallory's right, tapped Mallory's arm and whispered in a voice of near-terror, "Ned! Ned! Is that Lady Ada?"

"My God, boy," Mallory hissed, the hair prickling in fear all across his arms and neck, "what makes you think that? Of course it isn't she!"

Tom looked relieved, puzzled, vaguely offended. "Who is it, then?"

The lecturing female turned to the chalkboard, and wrote, in a ladylike cursive, the words "Neurasthenic Degeneracy." She turned, aimed a false and brilliant smile at the audience over her shoulder, and for the first time Mallory recognized her.

She was Florence Russell Bartlett.

Mallory stiffened in his chair with a half-stifled gasp of shock. Something—a fleck of dry cotton from within his mask—lodged like a barb in his throat. He began coughing. And he could not stop. His slimy throat was lacerated. He tried to smile, to whisper a word of apology, but his windpipe seemed pinched in iron bands. Mallory fought the racking spasms with all his strength, hot tears gushing freely, but he could not stop himself, nor even muffle the nightmare hacking. It called a deadly attention to him like a costermonger's bellow. At last Mallory jerked to his feet, knocking his chair back with a clatter, and staggered away half-bent, half-blinded.

He tottered, arms outstretched, through the blurry wilderness of booty, his feet tangling in something, some wooden object falling with a clatter. Somehow he found a spot of shelter, and bent there shaking violently, his breath choked now by a loathsome bolus of phlegm and vomit. I could die from this, he thought in desperation, his eyes bulging in their sockets. Something will rupture. My heart will burst.

Then somehow the clog was gone, the fit defeated. Mallory drew a ragged squeak of air, coughed, found his wind and began to breathe. He wiped foul spittle from his beard with his bare hand, and found himself leaning against a piece of statuary. It was a life-sized Hindu maiden in Coate's patent artificial stone, half-nude, with a water-jug poised on her draperied hip. The jug was solid stone, of course, though every atom in him cried out for a cleansing sip of water.

Someone clapped him firmly on the back. He turned, expecting Tom or Brian, and found the Marquess there.

"Are you quite all right?"

"A passing fit," Mallory croaked. He waved one hand, unable to straighten.

The Marquess slipped a curved silver flask into his hand. "Here," he said. "This will help."

Mallory, expecting brandy, tilted the flask to his lips. A treacly concoction, tasting vaguely of licorice and elm, flooded his mouth. He swallowed reluctantly. "What—what is this?"

"One of Dr. Barton's herbal remedies," the Marquess told him, "a specific against the foetor. Here, let me soak your mask in it; the fumes will clear your lungs."

"I'd rather you didn't," Mallory rasped.

"Are you fit then to return to the lecture?"

"No! No."

The Marquess looked skeptical. "Dr. Barton is a medical genius! She was the first woman ever to graduate with honors from Heidelberg. If you knew the wonders she's worked among the sick in France, the poor wretches given up for dead by the so-called experts—"

"I know," Mallory blurted. Something like strength returned to him, and with it a strong urge to throttle the Marquess, shake this damned and dangerous little fool till the nonsense squeezed out of him like paste. He felt a suicidal urge to blurt out the truth, that he knew this Barton to be a poisoner, an adulteress, a vitrioleuse, wanted by police in at least two countries. He could whisper that confession, then kill the Marquess of Hastings and stuff his wretched body under something.

The fit left him, replaced with a rational cunning cold and brittle as ice. "I should rather talk with you, comrade," said Mallory, "than listen to any lecture."

"Really?" said Hastings, brightening.

Mallory nodded earnestly. "I . . . I find I always profit by listening to a man who truly knows his business."

"I cannot make you out, comrade," the Marquess said. "Sometimes you seem to me a typical self-seeking fool, but then again you seem a man of quite sophisticated understanding—certainly a cut above those friends of yours!"

"I've traveled a bit," Mallory said slowly. "I suppose it broadens a man."

"Traveled where, comrade?"

Mallory shrugged. "Argentina. Canada. On the Continent, here and there."

The Marquess glanced about them, as if looking for spies a-lurk in the birdbaths and chandeliers. When none showed, he seemed to relax a bit, then spoke with a renewed but quiet urgency. "Might you know the American South at all? The Confederacy?"

Mallory shook his head.

"There's a city called Charleston, in South Carolina. A charming town. It has a large community of well-born British exiles, who fled the Rads. Britain's ruined cavaliers."

"Very nice," Mallory grunted.

"Charleston is as refined and cultured a city as any in Britain."

"And you were born there, eh?" Mallory had blundered to speak this deduction aloud, for Hastings was sensitive about it, and frowned. Mallory hastened on. "You must have prospered in Charleston, to own a Negro."

"I do hope you are not an anti-slavery bigot," the Marquess said. "So many Britons are. I suppose you would have me pack poor Jupiter off to one of those fever-ridden jungles in Liberia!"

Mallory restrained his nod of agreement. He was in fact an abolitionist, and a supporter of Negro repatriation.

"Poor Jupiter wouldn't last a day in the Liberian Empire," the Marquess insisted. "Do you know he can read and write? I myself taught him. He even reads poetry."

"Your Negro reads verse?"

"Not 'verse'—poesy. The great poets. John Milton—but you've never heard of him, I wager."

"One of Cromwell's ministers," Mallory said readily, "author of the *Areopagitica*."

The Marquess nodded. He seemed pleased. "John Milton wrote an epic poem, *Paradise Lost*. It's a Biblical story, in blank verse."

"I'm an agnostic myself," Mallory said.

"Do you know the name of William Blake? He wrote and illustrated his own books of poems."

"Couldn't find a proper publisher, eh?"

"There are still fine poets in England. Did you ever hear of John Wilson Croker? Winthrop Mackworth Praed? Bryan Waller Procter?"

"I might have," Mallory said. "I read a bit—penny-dreadfuls, mostly." He was puzzled by the Marquess's strange interest in this arcane topic. And Mallory was worried about Tom and the others—what they must be thinking as they sat and waited for him. They might lose all patience and try something rash, and that wouldn't do.

"Percy Bysshe Shelley was a poet, before he led the Luddites in the Time of Troubles," the Marquess said. "Know that Percy Shelley lives! Byron exiled him to the island of St. Helena. He remains a prisoner there, in the manse of Napoleon the First. Some say he's since written whole books of plays and sonnets there."

"Nonsense," Mallory said, "Shelley died in prison ages ago."

"He lives," the Marquess said. "Not many know that."

"Next you'll be saying that Charles Babbage wrote poetry," Mallory said, his nerves raw. "What's the point of this?"

"It's a theory of mine," the Marquess said. "Not so much a proper theory, as a poetic intuition. But since studying the writings of Karl Marx—and of course the great William Collins—it has come to me that some dire violence has been done to the true and natural course of historical development." The Marquess paused, smirked. "But I doubt you can understand me, my poor fellow!"

Mallory shook his head roughly. "I understand well enough. A Catastrophe, you mean."

"Yes. You might well call it that."

"History works by Catastrophe! It's the way of the world, the

only way there is, has been, or ever will be. There is no history—
there is only contingency!"

The Marquess's composure shattered. "You're a liar!"

Mallory felt the foolish insult gall him to the quick. "Your
head's full of phantoms, boy! 'History'! You think you should have
a title and estates and I should rot in Lewes making hats. There's
nothing more to it than that! You little fool, the Rads don't care
tuppence for you or Marx or Collins or any of your poetic mum-
meries! They'll kill the lot of you here like rats in a sawdust pit."

"You're not what you seem," the Marquess said. He had gone as
white as paper. "Who are you? *What* are you?"

Mallory tensed.

The boy's eyes widened. "A spy." He went for his gun.

Mallory punched him full in the face. As the Marquess reeled
back, Mallory caught his arm and clubbed him, once, twice,
across the head, with the heavy barrel of the Ballester-Molina.
The Marquess fell bleeding.

Mallory snatched up the second pistol, rose, glanced about him.

The Negro stood not five yards away.

"I saw that," Jupiter said quietly.

Mallory was silent. He leveled both guns at the man.

"You struck my master. Have you killed him?"

"I think not," Mallory said.

The Negro nodded. He spread his open palms, gently, a gesture like a blessing. "You were right, sir, and he was quite wrong.
There is nothing to history. No progress, no justice. There is
nothing but random horror."

"That's as may be," Mallory said slowly, "but if you cry out I will
have to shoot you."

"If you had killed him, I should have certainly cried out," the
Negro said.

Mallory glanced back. "He's still breathing."

There was a long silence. The Negro stood quite still, his
posture stiff and perfect, undecided, unmoving, like a Platonic
cone balanced perfectly upon its needle tip, waiting for some
impetus beyond causality to determine the direction of its fall.

The Negro sighed. "I'm going back to New York City," he said. He turned on one polished heel and walked away, unhurried, vanishing into the looming barricades of goods.

Mallory felt quite certain that the man would not cry out, but he waited a few moments for the evidence that would confirm that belief. The Marquess stirred where he lay, and groaned. Mallory whipped the paisley kerchief from the man's curly head and gagged him with it.

It was the work of a moment to shove him behind a massive terra-cotta urn.

The shock of action had left Mallory dry. His throat felt like bloodied sandpaper. There was nothing to drink—except of course that silver flask of quack potion. Mallory dragged it by feel from the Marquess's jacket-pocket, and wet his throat. It left a numbing tingle at the back of his palate, like dry champagne. It was vile, but it seemed to be bracing him, somehow. He helped himself to a number of swallows.

Mallory returned to the lecture-area and took a seat beside Fraser. The policeman lifted one brow in silent query. Mallory patted the butt of the Marquess's pistol, lodged within his waistband opposite the Ballester-Molina. Fraser nodded, by a fraction.

Florence Russell Bartlett was continuing her harangue, her stage-manner seeming to afflict her audience with an occult paralysis. Mallory saw to his shock and disgust that Mrs. Bartlett was displaying quack devices intended to avert pregnancy. A disk of flexible rubber, a wad of sponge with a thread attached. Mallory could not avoid the dark imagining of coitus involving these queer objects. The thought made his gut lurch.

"She killed a rabbit a moment ago," Fraser hissed from the corner of his mouth. "Dipped its nose in essence of cigar."

"I didn't kill the boy," Mallory whispered in return. "Concussed, I think. . . ." He watched Bartlett as her rant drifted into queer plans for selective breeding to improve the stock of humanity. In her futurity, it seemed, proper marriage would be abolished. "Universal free love" would replace chastity. Reproduction would be a matter for experts. The concepts swam like dark

shadows at the shore of Mallory's mind. It struck him then, for no
seeming reason, that this day—this very afternoon in fact—was
the time specified for his own triumphant lecture on the Brontosaurus, with kinotrope accompaniment by Mr. Keats. The fear-
ful coincidence sent a queer shiver through him.

Brian leaned suddenly across Fraser, seizing Mallory's bare
wrist in a grip of iron. "Ned!" he hissed. "Let's get out of this
damned place!"

"Not yet," Mallory said. But he was shaken. A mesmeric flow of
sheer panic seemed to jolt into him, through Brian's grip. "We
don't know yet where Swing is hiding; he could be anywhere in
this warren—"

"Comrades!" Bartlett sang out, in a voice like an iced razor.
"Yes, you four, in the back! If you *must* disturb us—if you have
news of such *pressing* interest—then surely you should share it
with the other comrades in the Chautauqua!"

The four of them froze.

Bartlett raked them with a Medusa glare. The other listeners,
freed somehow from their queer bondage, turned to glare backward with bloodthirsty glee. The eyes of the crowd glowed with a
nasty pleasure, the relief of wretches who find their own destined
punishment falling elsewhere—

Tom and Brian spoke both at once, in frenzied whispers.

"Does she mean *us*?"

"My God, what do we do?"

Mallory felt trapped in nightmare. A word would break it,
he thought. "She's just a woman," he said, quite loudly and
calmly.

"Knife it!" Fraser hissed. "Be still!"

"Nothing to tell us?" Bartlett taunted. "I thought not—"

Mallory rose to his feet. "I do have something to say!"

With the speed of jack-in-the-boxes, three men rose from
within the audience, their hands raised. "Dr. Barton! Dr. Barton?"

Bartlett nodded graciously, gestured with the chalk-wand.
"Comrade Pye has the floor."

"Dr. Barton," cried Pye, "I do not recognize these comrades. They are behaving regressively, and I—I think they should be *criticized*!"

A fierce silence wrapped the crowd.

Fraser yanked at Mallory's trouser-leg. "Sit down, you fool! Have you lost your mind?"

"I do have news!" Mallory shouted, through his gingham mask. "News for Captain Swing!"

Bartlett seemed shocked; her eyes darted back and forth. "Tell it to all of us, then," she commanded. "We're all of one mind here!"

"I know where the Modus is, Mrs. Bartlett!" Mallory shouted. "Do you want me to tell that to all these dupes and slaveys?"

Chairs clattered as men leapt to their feet. Bartlett shrieked something lost in the noise.

"I want Swing! I must speak to him alone!" As chaos rose, Mallory kicked the empty chair before him into skidding flight, and yanked both pistols from his belt. "Sit down, you bastards!" He leveled his pistols at the audience. "I'll blow daylight through the first coward that stirs!"

His answer was a fusillade of shots.

"Run!" Brian screeched. He, Tom, and Fraser fled at once.

Chairs splintered, toppling, on either side of Mallory. The audience was shooting at him, ragged popping shots. Mallory leveled both his pistols at Bartlett at her podium, and squeezed the triggers.

Neither gun fired. He had neglected to cock the hammers. The Marquess's gun seemed to have some kind of nickeled safety-switch.

Someone nearby threw a chair at Mallory; he fended it off, absently, but then something struck him hard in the foot. The blow was sharp enough to numb his leg, and knock him from his stance; he took the opportunity to retreat.

He could not seem to run properly. Perhaps he had been crippled. Bullets sang past him with a nostalgic drone from far Wyoming.

Fraser beckoned at him from the mouth of a side-alley. Mallory ran to him, turned, skidded.

Fraser stepped coolly into the open, raising his copper's pepperbox in a dueling stance, right arm extended, body turned to present a narrow target, head held keen-eyed and level. He fired twice, and there were screams.

Fraser took Mallory's arm. "This way!" Mallory's heart was jumping like a rabbit, and he could not get his foot to work.

He limped down the alley. It ended abruptly. Fraser searched frantically for a crawl-way. Tom was boosting Brian atop a great unsteady heap of cartons.

Mallory stopped beside his brothers, turned, raised both pistols. He glanced down swiftly at his foot. A stray bullet had knocked the heel from his shoe. He looked up an instant later to see half-a-dozen screaming bandits approaching in hot pursuit.

A vast concussion shook the building. Heaps of tinned goods clattered to the floor in a billow of powder-smoke. Mallory gaped.

All six of the wretches lay sprawled and blasted in the alley, as if lightning-struck.

"Ned!" shouted Brian, from atop his heap of cartons. "Get their weapons!" He crouched there on one knee, the Russian pistol gushing smoke from its opened loading-chamber. He loaded a second cartridge of brass and red waxed-paper, as thick as a copper's baton.

Mallory, ears ringing, lunged forward, then slipped and almost fell headlong in the spreading blood. He grabbed right-handed for support and the Ballester-Molina went off, its bullet whanging from an iron beam overhead. Mallory paused, uncocked it carefully, uncocked the Marquess's pistol as well, stuck them both into his belt, precious seconds ticking as he dithered.

The alley was awash with blood. The blunderbuss blast of the Russian hand-cannon had lacerated the men hideously. One poor devil was still gurgling as Mallory pried a Victoria carbine from beneath him, its stock dripping red. He struggled with the fellow's bandolier, but gave that up for another's wooden-handled

Yankee revolver. Something stung his palm as he snatched up the pistol. Mallory looked stupidly at his wounded hand, then at the pistol-butt. There was a corkscrewed bit of hot shrapnel embedded in the wood, a razored thing like a big metal-shaving.

Rifles began to crack from a distance, slugs plowing into the bounty around them with odd crunches and a musical tinkling of glass. "Mallory! This way," Fraser shouted.

Fraser had uncovered a crevice along the warehouse wall. Mallory turned to sling the carbine and look for Brian, seeing the young artilleryman leap across the alley for another vantage-point.

He followed Fraser into the crevice, grunting and heaving, for several yards along the wall. Bullets began whacking into the brick, before them and behind them, but well above their heads. Ill-aimed shots burst the tin-sheet roof with drum-like metal bangs. Mallory emerged to find Tom working like a demon in an open cul-de-sac, flinging up a barricade of spindle-legged ladies' vanity-tables. The things lay piled in a white-lacquered heap like dead tropical spiders.

The cracking of rifles, sharper now, made the warehouse a cacophony. From behind them Mallory heard shouts of rage and fear over the dead.

Tom drove a length of iron bedstead into a heap of crates, put his back into it, and toppled the mess with a crash. "How many?" Tom panted.

"Six."

Tom smiled like a madman. "That's more than they'll ever kill of us. Where's Brian now?"

"I don't know." Mallory unslung the carbine, handed it to Tom. Tom took it by the barrel and held it at arm's-length, surprised by its caking of gore.

Fraser, maintaining close watch at the crevice, fired his pepper-box. There was an awful, girlish scream and a thrashing, like a poisoned rat in a wall.

Bullets began to plunge into the rubble around them with

somewhat greater accuracy, attracted by the scream. A thumb-sized conical slug fell from nowhere at Mallory's feet and spun like a top on the floor-boards.

Fraser tapped his shoulder. Mallory turned. Fraser had tugged the mask from his face; his eyes glittered and stubble showed black on his pale chin. "How now, Dr. Mallory? What new inspired maneuver?"

"That might well have worked, you know," Mallory protested. "She might have taken us straight to Swing if she'd believed me. There's no accounting for women. . . ."

"Oh, she believed you right-enough," said Fraser, and suddenly he laughed, a strange dry chuckling like the rubbing of resined wood. "Well, what do you have there?"

"Pistol?" Mallory offered Fraser the salvaged revolver. "Mind that bit of shrapnel in it."

Fraser scraped the embedded barb free on his boot-heel. "Never saw the like of that lad's barker! I rather doubt it's legal, even for one of your gallant Crimea heroes."

A rifle-shot knocked a spinning chunk from one of the vanity-tables, narrowly missing Fraser. Mallory looked up, startled. "Damn!" A distant sniper clung monkey-like to one of the iron rafters, fitting another round into his rifle.

Mallory snatched the Victoria from Tom, braced the bloodied strap around his forearm, and took close aim. He squeezed the trigger. To no effect, for the single-shot had been fired already. But the sniper's mouth opened in an O of terror and he leapt from his perch with a distant crash.

Mallory yanked the bolt back, flinging the dead cartridge. "I should have taken that damned bandolier—"

"Ned!" Brian appeared suddenly to their left, crouched at the top of a heap. "Over here—cotton-bales!"

"Right!" They followed Brian's lead, scrambling and heaving atop the booty in a cascade of whalebone and candlesticks. Bullets whizzed and thwacked around them—more men in the rafters, Mallory thought, too busy to look. Fraser rose once and took a pot-shot, to no apparent effect.

Dozens of hundred-weight bales of Confederate ginned cotton, wrapped in rope and burlap, had been stacked almost to the rafters.

Brian gestured wildly, then vanished over the far side of the cotton-stack. Mallory understood him: it was a natural fortress, with a little work.

He and Tom heaved and toppled one of the bales free from the top of the stack, stepping into the cavity. Bullets thumped with gentle huffs into the cotton as Fraser rose and returned fire.

They kicked out another bale, and then a third. Fraser joined them in the excavation, with a leap and a stumble. In a frantic, heaving minute they had burrowed their way into the thick of it, like ants amid a box of cube sugar.

Their position was obvious now; bullets popped and thudded into the cotton fortress, but to no effect. Mallory yanked a great clean wad and wiped sweat and blood from his face and arms. It was dire hard work, hauling cotton-bales; no wonder the Southrons had relegated it to their darkeys.

Fraser cleared a narrow space between two bales. "Give me another pistol." Mallory handed him the Marquess's long-barreled revolver. Fraser squeezed off a shot, squinted, nodded. "Fine piece . . ." A volley of futile shots came in reply. Tom, grunting and heaving, cleared more space by lifting and dropping a bale off the back of the heap; it struck something with a crash like a splintering pianola.

They took inventory. Tom had a derringer with one loaded chamber; useful, perhaps, if the anarchists swarmed in like boarding pirates, but not otherwise. Mallory's Ballester-Molina had three rounds. Fraser's pepperbox had three caps left, and the Marquess's gun five rounds. And they had an empty Victoria carbine, and Fraser's little truncheon.

There was no sign of Brian.

There were angry, muffled shouts in the depths of the warehouse—orders, Mallory thought. The gunfire died away quite suddenly, replaced by an ominous silence, broken by rustling and what seemed to be hammering. He peered up over the edge of a forward bale. There was no visible enemy, but the doors of the warehouse had been shut.

Gloom flew across the warehouse in a sudden wave. Beyond the glazed vaulting of the ceiling, it had grown swiftly and astonishingly dark, as if the Stink had thickened further.

"Should we make a run for it?" whispered Tom.

"Not without Brian," Mallory said.

Fraser shook his head dourly—not speaking his doubt, but it was clear enough.

They worked in the gloom for a while, clearing space, digging in deeper, heaving up some of the bales to serve as crenellations. At the sound of their activity, more shots came, muzzle-flashes savagely lighting the darkness, bullets screaming off iron braces overhead. Here and there in the heaps of merchandise, the kindled light of lanterns glowed.

More shouted orders, and the firing ceased. There was a flurry of pattering on the metal roof, swiftly gone.

"What was that?" Tom asked.

"Sounded like rats scampering," Mallory said.

"Rain!" Fraser suggested.

Mallory said nothing. Another ash-fall seemed far more likely.

The gloom lightened again, quite suddenly. Mallory peered over the edge. A crowd of the rascals were creeping forward, almost to the foot of the ramparts, barefoot and in hushed silence, some with knives in their teeth. Mallory bellowed in alarm and began firing.

He was blinded at once by his own muzzle-flashes, but the Ballester-Molina, kicking and pumping, seemed to have a life of its own; in an instant the three remaining rounds were gone. Not wasted, though; at such short range he had not been able to miss. Two men were down, a third crawling, and the rest fleeing in terror.

Mallory could hear them re-grouping out of sight, milling, cursing each other. Mallory, his gun empty, grasped its hot barrel like a club.

The building shook with the awful roar of Brian's pistol.

The silence afterward was broken by agonized screams. A long and harrowing minute passed then, filled with infernal yells from the wounded and dying, with a crashing, a cursing and clattering.

Suddenly a dark form came catapulting into their midst, stinking of gunpowder.

Brian.

"Good job you didn't shoot me," he said. "Damme, it's dark in here, ain't it?"

"Are ye all right, lad?" Mallory said.

"Nicks," Brian said, getting to his feet. "Look what I brought ye, Ned."

He passed the thing into Mallory's hands. The smooth heavy form of stock and barrel fit Mallory's grip like silk. It was a buffalo-rifle.

"They've a whole crate of such beauties," Brian said. "Out in a pokey little office, across the way. And munitions with it, though I could only carry two boxes."

Mallory began loading the rifle at once, round after brassy round clicking into the spring-loader with a ticking like fine clockwork.

"Queer business," Brian said. "Don't think they knew I was loose among them. No proper sense of strategy. Don't seem to be any Army traitors among this rabble, I'll tell you that!"

"That barker of yours is a marvel, lad," Fraser said.

Brian grunted. "Not anymore, Mr. Fraser. I'd only two rounds. Wish I'd held back, but when I saw that lovely chance for enfilading-fire, I'd got to take it."

"Never you mind," Mallory told him, caressing the rifle's walnut stock. "If we'd four of these, we could hold 'em back all week."

"My apologies!" Brian said. "But I won't be doing much more of a proper reconnaisance-in-force. They winged me a bit."

A stray bullet had seared across the front of Brian's shin. White bone showed in the shallow wound and his filth-caked boot was full of blood. Fraser and Tom wadded clean cotton against the wound while Mallory kept watch with the rifle.

"Enough," Brian protested at last, "you fellows carry on to beat Lady Nightingale. D'ye see anything, Ned?"

"No," Mallory said. "I hear them plotting mischief, though."

"They're back in three mustering-grounds," Brian said. "They had a rally-point just out of your line-of-fire, but I raked 'em there with the Tsar's slag-shot. I doubt they'll rush us again. They've not got the nerve for it now."

"What will they do, then?"

"Some sort of sapper's work, I'd wager," Brian said. "Advancing barricades, perhaps something on wheels." He spat dryly. "Damme, I need a drink. I haven't been this dry since Lucknow."

"Sorry," Mallory said.

Brian sighed. "We had a very pukka water-boy with the regiment in India. That bleeding little Hindu was worth any ten of these buggers!"

"Did you see the woman?" Fraser asked him. "Or Captain Swing?"

"No," Brian said. "I was staying to cover, creeping about. Looking for a better class of firearm, mostly, something with a range. Queer things I saw, too. Found Ned's game-rifle in a little office-room, not a soul in it but a little clerky chap, writing at a desk. Pair of candles burning, papers all scattered about. Full of crated guns for export, and why they're keeping those fine rifles back with some clerk, and passing out Victorias, is beyond my professional understanding."

A wave of drowned and greenish light passed into the building—outlining, as it passed, an armed man rising up a pulley-line, seated in a noose. Swift as thought, Mallory centered his bead on the man, exhaled, fired. The man flopped backward, dangled from his knees, hung limp.

Rifle-fire began to smack into the cotton. Mallory ducked down again.

"Fine emplacements, cotton-bales," said Brian with satisfaction, patting the burlapped floor. "Hickory Jackson hid behind 'em in New Orleans, and gave us a toweling, too."

"What happened in the office-room, Brian?" Tom asked.

"Fellow rolled himself a sort of papirosi," Brian said. "Know those? Turkish baccy-wraps. 'Cept the bugger took an eye-dropper from a little medical vial, dribbled it about on the paper first, then wrapped some queer leaf from a candy jar. I'd a proper look at his face when he lit his smoke from the candle, and he'd a very absent look, deluded you might say, rather like brother Ned here with one of his scholarly problems!" Brian laughed drily, meaning no harm. "Scarcely seemed right to disturb his fancy then, so I took a rifle and a box or two real quiet-like, and left!"

Tom laughed.

"You'd a good look, eh?" Mallory asked.

"Surely."

"Fellow had a bump on his forehead, right here?"

"Damme if he didn't!"

"That was Captain Swing," Mallory said.

"Then I'm a chuckleheaded fool!" Brian cried. "Didn't seem right to shoot a man in the back, but if I'd knowed it was him I'd have blowed his lumpy headpiece off!"

"Doctor Edward Mallory!" a voice cried, from the darkened floor below.

Mallory rose, peered around a bale. The Marquess of Hastings stood below them, his head bandaged and a lantern in one hand. He waved a white kerchief on a stick.

"Leviathan Mallory, a parley with you!" the Marquess shouted.

"Speak up then," Mallory said, careful not to show his head.

"You're trapped here, Dr. Mallory! But we've an offer for you. If you'll tell us where you've hidden a certain object of value, which you stole, then we'll let you and your brothers go free. But your police-spy from the Special Bureau must stay. We have questions for him."

Mallory laughed him to scorn. "Hear me, Hastings, and all the rest of you! Send us that maniac Swing and his murdering tart, with their hands bound! Then we'll let the rest of you creep out of here before the Army comes!"

"A show of insolence avails you nothing," the Marquess said. "We shall fire that cotton, and you'll roast like a brace of rabbits!"

Mallory turned. "Can he do that?"

"Cotton won't burn worth a hang when it's packed tight as this," Brian theorized.

"Surely, burn it!" Mallory shouted. "Burn down the whole godown and smother to death in the smoke."

"You've been very bold, Dr. Mallory, and very lucky. But our choicest men patrol the streets of Limehouse now, liquidating the police! Soon they shall return, hardened soldiers, veterans of Manhattan! They'll take your little hideaway by storm, at the point of the bayonet! Come out now, while you've yet a chance to live!"

"We fear no Yankee rabble! Bring 'em on, for a taste of grape-shot!"

"We've made our offer! Reason it through, like a proper savant!"

"Go to hell," Mallory said. "Send me Swing; I want to talk to Swing! I've had my fill of you, you poncey little traitor."

The Marquess retreated. After some moments, a desultory firing began. Mallory expended half a box of cartridges, returning fire at the muzzle-flashes.

The anarchists then commenced the painful work of advancing a siege-engine. It was an improvised phalanx of three heavy dolly-carts, their fronts lashed with a sloping armor of marbled table-tops. The rolling armor was too wide to fit down the crooked alley to the cotton-bales, so the rebels dug their way through the heaps of goods, piling them up by the flanks of the freight-dollies. Mallory wounded two of them at their work, but they grew wiser with experience, and soon had erected a covered walkway behind the advancing siege-works.

There seemed to be far more men in the warehouse now. It had grown darker yet, but lantern-light showed here and there and the iron beams were full of snipers. There was loud talk— argument it seemed—to add to the groans of the wounded.

The siege-works crept closer yet. They were now below Mallory's best line-of-fire. If he exposed himself in an attempt to lean over the ramparts, without doubt the snipers would hit him.

The siege-works reached the base of the cotton-bales. There was a sound of shredding at the base of the wall.

A warped and muffled voice—assisted perhaps by a megaphone—sounded from within the siege-works. "Dr. Mallory!"

"Yes?"

"You asked for me—here I am! We are toppling the wall of your palace, Dr. Mallory. Soon you will be quite exposed."

"Hard work for a professional gambler, Captain Swing! Don't blister your delicate hands!"

Tom and Fraser, who had been working in tandem, toppled a heavy cotton-bale onto the siege-works. It bounced off harmlessly. Well-concerted fire raked the fortress, sending the defenders diving for cover.

"Cease fire!" Swing shouted, and laughed.

"Have a care, Swing! If you shoot me, you'll never learn where the Modus is hidden."

"Still the blustering fool! You stole the Modus from us at the Derby. You might have returned it to us, and spared yourself certain destruction! You stubborn ignoramus, you don't even have a notion of the thing's true purpose!"

"It belongs by right to the Queen of Engines, and I know that well enough."

"If you think that, you know nothing."

"I know it is Ada's, for she told me so. And she knows where it is hidden, for I told her where I keep it!"

"Liar!" Swing shouted. "If Ada knew, we would have it already. She is one of us!"

Tom groaned aloud.

"You are her tormentors, Swing!"

"I tell you Ada is ours."

"The daughter of Byron would never betray the realm."

"Byron's dead!" Swing cried, with the terrible conviction of truth. "And all that he built, all that you believe in, will now be swept away."

"You're dreaming."

There was a long silence. Then Swing spoke again, in a new and coaxing voice. "The Army now fires upon the people, Dr. Mallory."

Mallory said nothing.

"The British Army, the very bulwark of your so-called civilization, now shoots your fellow citizens dead in the streets. Men and women with stones in their hands are being murdered with rapid-fire weapons. Can you not hear it?"

Mallory made no reply.

"You have built on sand, Dr. Mallory. The tree of your prosperity is rooted in dark murder. The masses can endure you no longer. Blood cries out from the seven-cursed streets of Babylondon!"

"Come out, Swing!" Mallory cried. "Come out of your darkness, let me see your face!"

"Not likely," Swing said.

There was another silence.

"I intended to take you alive, Dr. Mallory," Swing said, in a voice of finality. "But if you have truly confessed your secret to Ada Byron, then I have no more need of you. My trusted comrade, my life's companion—she holds the Queen of Engines in a perfect net! We shall have Lady Ada, and the Modus, and futurity as well. And you shall have the depths of the poisoned Thames for your sepulchre."

"Kill us then, and stop your damned blather!" Fraser shouted suddenly, stung beyond endurance. "Special Branch will see you kicking at a rope's end if it takes a hundred years."

"The voice of authority!" Swing taunted. "The almighty British Government! You're fine at mowing down poor wretches in the street, but let us see your bloated plutocrats take this warehouse, when we hold merchandise worth millions hostage here."

"You must be completely mad," Mallory said.

"Why do you suppose I chose this place as my headquarters? You are governed by shopkeepers, who value their precious goods more than any number of human lives! They will never fire on their own warehouses, their own shipping. We are impregnable here!"

Mallory laughed. "You utter jolterhead! If Byron's dead, then the Government is in the hands of Lord Babbage and his emergency committees. Babbage is a master pragmatist! He'll not be stayed by concern for any amount of merchandise."

"Babbage is the pawn of the capitalists."

"He's a visionary, you deluded little clown! Once he learns you're in here, he'll blast this place into the heavens without a second thought!"

Thunder shook the building. There was a pattering against the roof.

"It's raining!" Tom cried.

"It's artillery," Brian said.

"No, listen—it's raining, Brian! The Stink is over! It's blessed rain!"

An argument had broken out beneath the shelter of the siege-works. Swing was snarling at his men.

Cool water began dripping through the ragged fret-work of bullet-holes in the roof.

"It's rain," Mallory said, and licked his hand. "Rain! We've won, lads." Thunder rolled. "Even if they kill us here," Mallory shouted, "it's over for them. When London's air is sweet again, they'll have no place to hide."

"It may be raining," Brian said, "but those are ten-inch naval guns, off the river. . . ."

A shell tore through the roof in a torrent of blazing shrapnel.

"They've got our range now!" Brian shouted. "For God's sake, take cover!" He began to struggle desperately with the cotton-bales.

Mallory watched in astonishment as shell after shell punched through the roof, the holes as neatly spaced as the stabs of a shoemaker's awl. Whirlwinds of blazing rubbish flew, like the impact of iron comets.

The glass vaulting burst into a thousand knife-edged shards.

Brian was screaming at Mallory, his voice utterly drowned by the cacophony. After a stunned moment, Mallory bent to help his brother, heaving up another cotton-bale and crouching within the trench.

He sat there, the rifle across his knees. Blasts of light sheeted across the buckling roof. Iron beams began to twist under pressure, their rivets popping like gunshots. The noise was hellish, supernatural. The warehouse shook like a sheet of beaten tin.

Brian, Tom, and Fraser crouched like praying Bedouins, their hands clamped to their ears. Bits of flaming wood and fabric fell gently onto the bales around them, jumping a bit with each repeated concussion, smoldering into the cotton where they lay. The warehouse billowed with air and heat.

Mallory absently plucked two wads of cotton and stuffed them into his ears.

A section of roofing collapsed, quite slowly, like the wing of a dying swan. Rain in torrents fought the fires below.

Beauty entered Mallory's soul. He stood, the rifle like a wand in his hands. The shelling had stopped, but the noise was incessant, for the building was on fire. Tongues of dirty flame leapt up in a hundred places, twisted fantastically by gusts of wind.

Mallory stepped to the edge of the cotton parapet. The shelling had knocked the covered walkway into fragments, like a muddy crawl-way of termites, crushed by a boot. Mallory stood, his head filled with the monotone roaring of absolute sublimity, and watched as his enemies fled screaming.

A man stopped amid the flames, and turned. It was Swing. He gazed up at Mallory where he stood. His face twisted with a desperate awe. He screamed something—screamed it louder still—but he was a little man, far away, and Mallory could not hear him. Mallory slowly shook his head.

Swing raised his weapon then. Mallory saw, with a glow of pleased surprise, the familiar outlines of a Cutts-Maudslay carbine.

Swing aimed the weapon, braced himself, and pulled the trigger. Pleasantly tenuous singing sounds surrounded Mallory, with a musical popping from the perforating roof behind him. Mallory, his hands moving with superb and unintentioned grace, raised his rifle, sighted, fired. Swing spun and fell sprawling. The Cutts-Maudslay, still in his grasp, continued its spring-driven jerking and clicking even after its drum of cartridges was empty.

Mallory watched, with tepid interest, as Fraser, leaping through the wreckage with a spidery agility, approached the fallen anarchist with his pistol drawn. He handcuffed Swing, then lifted him limply over one shoulder.

Mallory's eyes smarted. Smoke from the flaming warehouse was gathering under the wreckage of its roof. He looked down, blinking, to see Tom lowering a limping Brian to the floor.

The two joined Fraser, who beckoned sharply. Mallory smiled, descended, followed. The three then fled through the whipping, thickening fires, with Mallory strolling after them.

Catastrophe had knocked Swing's fortress open in a geyser of shattered brick dominos. Mallory, blissful, the nails of his broken shoe-heel grating, walked into a London reborn.

Into a tempest of cleansing rain.

On April 12, 1908, at the age of eighty-three, Edward Mallory died at his house in Cambridge. The exact circumstances of his death are obscured, steps having apparently been taken to preserve the proprieties incumbent on the decease of a former President of the Royal Society. The notes of Dr. George Sandys, Lord Mallory's friend and personal physician, indicate that the great savant died of a cerebral hemorrhage. Sandys also noted, apparently for purposes of his own, that the deceased had seemingly taken to his death-bed while wearing a patent set of elasticated underwear, socks with braces, and fully laced leather dress-shoes.

The doctor, a thorough man, also noted an item discovered beneath the deceased's flowing white beard. About the great man's neck, on a fine steel chain, was strung an antique lady's signet-ring which bore the crest of the Byron family and the motto CREDE BYRON. The doctor's ciphered note is the only known evidence of this apparent bequest, possibly a token of appreciation. Very probably, Sandys confiscated the ring, though a thorough catalogue of Sandys' possessions, made after his own death in 1940, makes no mention of it.

There is no mention of any such ring in the Mallory will, a very elaborate document of otherwise impeccable specificity.

Envision Edward Mallory in the scholarly office of his palatial Cambridge home. It is late. The great paleontologist, his field-days long behind him and his Presidency resigned, now devotes the winter of his life to matters of theory, and to the subtler outreaches of scientific administration.

Lord Mallory has long since modified the radical Catastrophist doctrines of his youth, gracefully abandoning the discredited notion that the Earth is no more than three hundred thousand years old—radioactive dating having proven otherwise. It is enough, for Mallory, that Catastrophism proved a fortunate road to higher geological truth, leading him to his greatest personal triumph: the discovery, in 1865, of continental drift.

More than the Brontosaurus, more than the ceratopsian eggs of the Gobi Desert, it is this astonishing leap of reckless insight that has assured his immortal fame.

Mallory, who sleeps little, seats himself at a curvilinear Japanese desk of artificial ivory. Past the open curtains, incandescent bulbs gleam beyond the polychrome, abstractly patterned windows of his nearest neighbor. The neighbor's house, like Mallory's own, is a meticulously orchestrated riot of organic forms, roofed with iridescent ceramic dragon-scales—England's dominant style of modern architecture, though the mode itself has its turn-of-the-century origins in the thriving Republic of Catalonia.

Mallory has only recently dismissed a purportedly clandestine meeting of the Society of Light. As the final Hierarch of this dwindling confraternity, tonight he wears the formal robes of office. His woolen chasuble of royal indigo is fringed in scarlet. A floor-length indigo skirt of artificial silk, similarly fringed, is decorated with concentric bands of semi-precious stones. He has set aside a domed crown of beaded gold-plate, with a neck-guard of overlapping gilt scales; this rests now upon a small desk-printer.

He dons his spectacles, loads a pipe, fires it. His secretary, Cleveland, is a most punctilious and orderly man, and has left him two sets of documents, neatly squared atop the desk in folders of brass-clasped manila. One folder lies to his right, the other to his left, and it cannot be known which he will choose.

He chooses the folder to his left. It is an Engine-printed report from an elderly officer of the Meirokusha, a famous confraternity of Japanese scholars which serves, not incidentally, as the foremost Oriental chapter of the Society of Light. The precise text of the report cannot be found in England, but is preserved in Nagasaki along with an annotation indicating that it was wired to the Hierarch via standard channels on April 11. The text indicates that the Meirokusha, suffering a grave decline in membership and a growing lack of attendance, have voted to indefinitely postpone further meetings. It is accompanied by an itemized bill for refreshments, and rental fees for a small upstairs room in the Seiyoken, a restaurant in the Tsukiji quarter of Tokyo.

Lord Mallory, though this news is not unexpected, is filled with a sense of loss and bitterness. His temper, fierce at the best of times, has sharpened with old-age; his indignation swells to helpless rage.

An artery fails.

That chain of events does not occur.

He chooses the folder to his right. It is thicker than the one to his left, and this intrigues him. It contains a detailed field report from a Royal Society paleontological expedition to the Pacific coast of Western Canada. Pleased by an awakened nostalgia for his own expedition days, he studies the report closely.

The modern labor of science can scarcely be more different from that of his own day. The British scientists have flown to the mainland from the flourishing metropolis of Victoria, and have motored at their ease into the mountains from a luxurious base in the coastal village of Vancouver. Their leader, if he can be given this title, is a young Cambridge graduate named Morris, whom Mallory remembers as a queer, ringleted fellow, given to wearing velvet capes and elaborate Modernist hats.

The strata under examination are Cambrian, dark shale of a near-lithographic quality. And, it seems, they teem with a variety of intricate forms, the paper-thin and thoroughly crushed remnants of an ancient invertebrate fauna. Mallory, a vertebrate specialist, begins to lose interest; he has seen, he thinks, more trilobites than anyone ever should have to, and in truth he has always found it difficult to conjure up enthusiasm for anything less than two inches in length. Worse yet, the report's prose strikes him as unscientific, marked by a most untoward air of radical enthusiasm.

He turns to the plates.

There is a thing in the first plate that possesses five eyes. It has a long clawed nozzle instead of a mouth.

There is a legless, ray-like thing, all lobes and jelly, with a flat, fanged mouth that does not bite but irises shut.

There is a thing whose legs are fourteen horny, pointed spikes—a thing which has no head, no eyes, no gut, but does have seven tiny pincered mouths, each at the tip of a flexible tentacle.

These things bear no relation to any known creature, from any known period whatever.

A rush of blood and wonder mounts within Mallory's skull. A vortex of implications begins to sort itself within him, mounting step-by-step to a strange and numinous glow, an ecstatic rush toward utter comprehension, ever brighter, ever clearer, ever closer—

His head strikes the table as he slumps forward. He sprawls upon his back at the foot of the chair, limbs numb and airy, still soaring, wrapped within the light of marvel, the light of an awesome knowledge, pushing, pushing at the borders of the real—a knowledge that is dying to be born.

FIFTH ITERATION

The All-Seeing Eye

A N AFTERNOON IN Horseferry Road, twelfth of November, 1855, image recorded by A. G. S. Hullcoop of the Department of Criminal Anthropometry.

The shutter of Hullcoop's Talbot "Excelsior" has captured eleven men descending the broad steps from the entrance of the Central Statistics Bureau. Triangulation locates Hullcoop, with his powerful lens, concealed atop the roof of a publishers' offices in Holywell Street.

Foremost among the eleven is Laurence Oliphant. His gaze, beneath the black brim of his top-hat, is mild and ironical.

The tall, dull-surfaced hats create a repeated vertical motif common to images of the period.

Like the others, Oliphant wears a dark frock-coat above narrow trousers of a lighter hue. His neck is wrapped in a high choker of dark silk. The effect is dignified and columnar, though something in Oliphant's manner manages to suggest the sportsman's lounging stroll.

The other men are barristers, Bureau functionaries, a senior representative of the Colgate Works. Behind them, above Horse-ferry Road, swoop the tarred copper cables of the Bureau's tele-graphs.

Processes of resolution reveal the pale blurs dotting these lines to be pigeons.

Though the afternoon is unseasonably bright, Oliphant, a frequent visitor to the Bureau, is opening an umbrella.

The top-hat of the Colgate's representative displays an elon-gated comma of white pigeon-dung.

Oliphant sat alone in a small waiting-room, which communicated by a glazed door with a surgery. The buff-colored walls were hung with colored diagrams depicting the ravages of hideous diseases. A bookcase was crammed with dingy medical volumes. There were carved wooden pews that might have come from a wrecked church, and a coal-dyed woolen drugget in the middle of the floor.

He looked at a mahogany instrument-case and a huge roll of lint occupying places of their own on the bookcase.

Someone called his name.

He saw a face through the panes of the surgery door. Pallid, the bulging forehead plastered with drenched strands of dark hair.

"Collins," he said. " 'Captain Swing.' " And other faces, legion, the faces of the vanished, names suppressed from memory.

"Mr. Oliphant?"

Dr. McNeile regarded him from the doorway. Vaguely embar-rassed, Oliphant rose from his pew, automatically straightening his coat.

"Are you entirely well, Mr. Oliphant? Your expression was most extraordinary, just then." McNeile was slender and neatly bearded, with dark brown hair, his grey eyes so pale as to suggest transparency.

"Yes, thank you, Dr. McNeile. And yourself?"

"Very well, thank you. Some remarkable symptoms are emerg-ing, Mr. Oliphant, in the wake of recent events. I've one gentleman who was seated atop an omnibus, Regent Street, when that vehicle was struck broadside by a steam-gurney traveling at an estimated twenty miles per hour!"

"Really? How dreadful . . ."

To Oliphant's horror, McNeile actually rubbed his long white hands together. "There was no evident *physical* trauma as a result of the collision. *None.* None whatever." He fixed Oliphant with that bright, nearly colorless gaze. "Subsequently, we have observed insomnia, incipient melancholia, minor amnesiac episodes—numerous symptoms customarily associated with latent hysteria." McNeile smiled, a quick rictus of triumph. "We have observed, Mr. Oliphant, a remarkably pure, that is to say, a clinical progression of railway spine!"

McNeile bowed Oliphant through the doorway, into a handsomely paneled room, which was sparsely furnished with ominous electro-magnetic appliances. Oliphant removed his coat and waistcoat, arranging them upon a mahogany valet-stand.

"And your . . . 'spells,' Mr. Oliphant?"

"None, thank you, since the last treatment." Was this true? It was difficult to say, really.

"And your sleep has been undisturbed?"

"I should say so. Yes."

"Any dreams of note? Waking visions?"

"No."

McNeile stared with his pale eyes. "Very well."

Oliphant, feeling utterly foolish in his braces and starched shirt-front, climbed upon McNeile's "manipulation table," a curiously articulated piece of furniture that in equal parts resembled a chaise-longue and a torturer's rack. The thing's various segments were upholstered in a stiff, Engine-patterned brocade, smooth and cold to the touch. Oliphant attempted to find a comfortable position; McNeile made this impossible, spinning one or another of several brass wheels. "Do be still," McNeile said.

Oliphant closed his eyes. "This fellow Pocklington," McNeile said.

"I beg your pardon?" Oliphant opened his eyes. McNeile stood above him, positioning a coil of iron on an adjustable armature.

"Pocklington. He's attempting to take credit for the cessation of the Limehouse cholera."

"The name isn't familiar. A medical man?"

"Hardly. The fellow's a *works-engineer*. He claims to have ended the cholera by the simple expedient of removing the handle from a municipal water-pump!" McNeile was screwing a braided copper cable in place.

"I'm afraid I don't follow you."

"Little wonder, sir! The man's either a fool or the worst sort of charlatan. He's written in the *Times* that the cholera is nothing more than the result of contaminated water."

"Is that entirely unreasonable, do you think?"

"Utterly counter to enlightened medical theory." McNeile set to work with a second length of copper. "This Pocklington, you see, is something of a favorite of Lord Babbage's. He was employed to remedy the ventilation troubles of the pneumatic trains."

Oliphant, detecting the envy in McNeile's tone, felt a slight and spiteful satisfaction. Babbage, speaking at Byron's state funeral, had regretted the fact that modern medicine remained more an art than a science. The speech, naturally, had been most widely published.

"Do close your eyes, please, in the event of a spark being discharged." McNeile was pulling on a pair of great, stiff, leather gauntlets.

McNeile connected the copper cables to a massive voltaic cell. The room filled with the faint eerie odor of electricity.

"Please try to relax, Mr. Oliphant, so as to facilitate the polar reversal!"

Half-Moon Street was illuminated by a massive Webb lamp, a fluted Corinthian column fueled by sewer-gas. Like the rest of London's Webbs, it had remained unlit, during the summer's emergency, for fear of leaks and explosions. Indeed, there had been at least a dozen pavement-ripping blasts, most attributed to the same firedamp that powered the Webb. Lord Babbage was an outspoken supporter of the Webb method; as a result, every school-boy knew that the methane potential from a single cow was adequate for an average household's daily heating, lighting, and cooking requirements.

He glanced up at the lamp as he neared his own Georgian facade. Its light was another apparent token of returning normalcy, but he took little comfort in tokens. The physical and more crudely social cataclysm was past now, certainly, but Byron's death had triggered successive waves of instability; Oliphant imagined them spreading out like ripples in a pond, overlapping with others that spread from more obscure points of impact, creating ominously unpredictable areas of turbulence. One such, certainly, was the business of Charles Egremont and the current Luddite witch-hunt.

Oliphant knew with absolute professional certainty that the Luddites were defunct; despite the best efforts of a few manic anarchists, the London riots of the past summer had shown no coherent or organized political agenda. All reasonable aspirations of the working-class had been successfully subsumed by the Radicals. Byron, in his vigorous days, had tempered justice with a well-dramatized show of mercy. Those early Luddite leaders who had made their peace with the Rads were now the tidy, comfortably well-to-do leaders of respectable trades-unions and craft-guilds. Some were wealthy industrialists—though their peace of mind was severely perturbed by Egremont's systematic disinterment of old convictions.

A second wave of Luddism had arisen in the turbulent forties, aimed, this time, directly against the Rads, with a charter of popular rights and a desperate zest for violence. But it had crumbled in a welter of internecine treachery, and its boldest spirits, such as Walter Gerard, had met a distressingly public punishment. Today, such groups as the Manchester Hell-Cats, to which Michael Radley had belonged as a boy, were mere youth-gangs, quite devoid of political purpose. Captain Swing's influence might still be felt occasionally in rural Ireland, or even in Scotland, but Oliphant attributed this to the Rads' agricultural policies, which tended to lag behind their brilliance in industrial management.

No, he thought, as Bligh opened the door at his approach, the spirit of Ned Ludd was scarcely abroad in the land, but what was one to make of Egremont and his furious campaign?

"Good evening, sir."

"Good evening, Bligh." He gave Bligh his top-hat and umbrella.

"Cook has a cold joint, sir."

"Very good. I'll dine in the study, thank you."

"Feeling well, sir?"

"Yes, thank you." Either McNeile's magnets or the devilishly uncomfortable manipulation table had set his back aching. McNeile had been recommended to him by Lady Brunel, Lord Brunel's spine being assumed to have suffered an inordinate amount of railway-shock in the course of his famous career. Dr. McNeile had recently diagnosed Oliphant's "numinous spells," as he insisted on calling them, as symptoms of railway-spine, a condition in which the magnetic polarity of the patient's vertebrae was assumed to have been reversed by trauma. It was McNeile's thesis that this condition might be corrected by the application of electro-magnetism, and to this end Oliphant now paid weekly visits to the Scot's Harley Street premises. McNeile's manipulations reminded Oliphant of his own father's unhealthily keen interest in mesmerism.

Oliphant senior, having served as Attorney-General of the Cape Colony, had subsequently been appointed Chief Justice of Ceylon. Consequently, Oliphant had received a private and necessarily rather fragmentary education, one to which he owed both his fluency in modern languages and his extraordinary ignorance of Greek and Latin. His parents had been Evangelicals of a markedly eccentric sort, and though he himself retained, however privately, certain aspects of their faith, he recalled with an odd dread his father's experiments: iron wands, spheres of crystal . . .

And how, he wondered, climbing the carpeted stairs, would Lady Brunel be adjusting to life as the Prime Minister's wife?

His Japanese wound began to throb as he gripped the banister.

Taking out a triple-splined Maudslay key from his waistcoat-pocket, he unlocked the door to his study. Bligh, who held the key's only duplicate, had lit the gas and banked the coals.

The study, paneled in oak, overlooked the park from a shallow triple-bay. An ancient refectory-table, quite plain, running very nearly the length of the room, served as Oliphant's desk. A very modern office-chair, mounted on glass-wheeled patent casters, regularly migrated around the table as Oliphant's work took him from one stack of folders to the next, then back again. The casters, in the chair's daily peregrinations, had begun to wear away the nap of the blue Axminster.

Three Colt & Maxwell receiving-telegraphs, domed in glass, dominated the end of the table nearest the window, their tapes coiling into wire baskets arranged on the carpet. There was a spring-driven transmitter as well, and an encrypting tape-cutter of recent Whitehall issue. The various cables for these devices, in tightly woven sleeves of burgundy silk, snaked up to a floral eyebolt suspended from the central lavalier, where they then swung to a polished brass plate, bearing the insignia of the Post Office, which was set into the wainscoting.

One of the receivers began immediately to hammer away. He walked the length of the table and read the message as it emerged from the machine's mahogany base.

VERY BUSY WITH PARTICULATE FOULING BUT YES DO VISIT
STOP WAKEFIELD ENDIT

Bligh entered with a tray of sliced mutton and pickle. "I've brought a bottle of ale, sir," he said, setting out linen and silverware on a section of the table kept cleared for this purpose.

"Thank you, Bligh." Oliphant raised the tape of Wakefield's

message with his fingertip, then let it droop back toward its wire basket.

Bligh poured the ale, then departed with his tray and the empty ceramic bottle. Oliphant trundled the office-chair around the table and sat down to spread his mutton with Branston pickle.

He was startled from his solitary meal by the clatter of one of his three receivers. He glanced down the table and saw the tape beginning to unspool in the machine to the right. The machine to the left, on which Wakefield's invitation to lunch had arrived, was on his personal number. Right meant police business of some kind, likely Betteredge, or Fraser. Putting down knife and fork, he rose.

He watched the message emerge from its brass slot.

RE F B YOU ARE REQUIRED AT ONCE STOP FRASER ENDIT

He took his father's German hunter from his waistcoat to note the time. Tucking it away, he touched the glass that domed the centermost of the three receiving-telegraphs. There had been no message on that one since the death of the late Prime Minister.

The address to which the cab carried him was in Brigsome's Terrace, off a thoroughfare of the sort that speculative builders delighted in carving through the ancient and still largely unexplored wilderness that was East London.

The terrace itself, Oliphant decided as he alighted from his hansom, was as dismal a block of buildings as had ever been composed of brick and mortar. The builder who had speculated on these ten dreary prison-houses, he thought, had likely hung himself behind the parlor door of some adjacent tavern before the hideous things were finished.

The streets through which the cab had conveyed him had been those one seemed to traverse at times such as these—all those thoroughfares seemingly unknown to day and the ordinary pedestrian. A thin rain was falling now, and Oliphant momentarily regretted not having accepted the water-proof that Bligh had offered at the door. The two men before No. 5 wore long drooping black cape-like articles of waxed Egyptian cotton. A recent innovation from New South Wales, Oliphant knew, much praised in the Crimea and precisely the thing for concealing weapons of the sort that these two most certainly concealed.

"Special Bureau," Oliphant said, briskly climbing past the guards. Abashed by his accent and manner, they let him pass. It would be necessary to report that to Fraser.

He entered the house, finding himself in a parlor lit by a powerful carbide-lantern, atop a tripod, its merciless white glare magnified by a concave round of polished tin. The parlor was furnished with scraps salvaged from the ruins of gentility. There was a cottage-piano, and a chiffonier several sizes too large for the room. The latter struck him as pathetically gorgeous, with its tarnished gilt moldings. A threadbare patch of Brussels carpet swarmed with roses and lilies, amid a desert of colorless drugget. Knitted curtains shaded the windows overlooking Brigsome's Terrace. Beside the glass, two hanging wire baskets were festooned with plants of the cactus species, which grew in prickly and spider-like profusion.

Oliphant noted an acrid stench, more penetrating than the reek of carbide.

Betteredge emerged from the rear of the house. He wore a high-crowned derby hat that made him seem altogether American, so that he might easily have been mistaken for one of the Pinkerton operatives he shadowed daily. Likely the effect was deliberate, down to the patent boots with their elasticated side-gores. His expression, quite uncharacteristically, was one of grave anxiety. "I'll take full responsibility, sir," he stammered. Something was very wrong. "Mr. Fraser's waiting for you, sir. Nothing's been moved."

Oliphant allowed himself to be led through the doorway, and up a narrow, perilously steep flight of stairs. They emerged in a barren hallway, illuminated by a second carbide-lantern. Great spreading continents of niter marred the bare plaster walls. The burnt smell was stronger here.

Through another doorway, into yet brighter glare, and Fraser's dour face looking up from where he knelt beside a sprawled body. Fraser seemed about to speak; Oliphant silenced him with a gesture.

Here, then, was the source of the reek. Upon an old-fashioned coaching-case stood a compact modern Primus stove of the sort intended for camp, its brass fuel-canister gleaming bright as a mirror. Upon its ring rested a pannikin of black cast-iron. Whatever had been cooking in this vessel was now a charred and bitterly odorous residue.

He turned his attention to the corpse. The man had been a giant; in the small room, it was necessary to step over his outspread limbs. Oliphant bent to study the contorted features, the death-dulled eyes. He straightened, facing Fraser. "And what do you make of this?"

"He was warming tinned beans," Fraser said. "Eating them straight out of the pot there. With this." With the toe of his shoe, Fraser indicated a kitchen-spoon of chipped blue enamel. "I'd say he was alone. I'd say he managed to choke down a good third of the tin before the poison felled him."

"This poison," Oliphant said, taking his cigar-case and sterling cutter from his coat, "what do you suppose it was?" He extracted a cheroot, clipped and pierced it.

"Something potent," Fraser said, "by the look of him."

"Yes," Oliphant agreed. "Big chap."

"Sir," Betteredge said, "you'd best see this." He displayed a very long knife, sheathed in sweat-stained leather. A sort of harness dangled from the sheath. The weapon's handle was of dull horn, its hilt of brass. Betteredge drew the thing from its sheath. It was something on the order of a sailor's dirk, though single-edged, with a peculiar reverse curve at the tip.

"What is that bit of brass along the top?" Oliphant asked.

"To parry another man's blade," Fraser said. "Soft stuff. Catches the edge. American business."

"Maker's mark?"

"No, sir," Betteredge said. "Hand-forged by a smith, from the look of it."

"Show him the pistol," Fraser said.

Betteredge sheathed the knife, set it atop the coaching-case. He produced a heavy revolver from beneath his coat. "Franco-Mexican," he said, sounding remarkably like a salesman, "Ballester-Molina; cocks itself automatically, after the first shot."

Oliphant raised an eyebrow. "Military issue?" The pistol was somewhat crude in appearance.

"Cheap stuff," Fraser said, with a glance for Oliphant. "For the American war trade, evidently. The Metropolitans have been confiscating them from sailors. Too many of them about."

"Sailors?"

"Confederates, Yanks, Texians . . ."

"Texians," Oliphant said, and tasted the end of his unlit cheroot. "I take it we agree in assuming our friend here is of that nationality?"

"He'd a sort of nest, in the garret, reached by a trap-door." Betteredge was wrapping the pistol back into its oilcloth.

"Terribly cold, I imagine?"

"Well, he'd blankets, sir."

"The tin."

"Sir?"

"The tin that contained the man's last meal, Betteredge."

"No, sir. No tin."

"Tidy," Oliphant said to Fraser. "She waited for the poison to do its work, then returned, removing the evidence."

"The surgeon will have our evidence out for us, never you fear," Fraser said.

Oliphant was overtaken by an abrupt nausea—at Fraser's manner, at the proximity of the corpse, at the pervading stink of burnt beans. He turned and stepped out into the hallway, where another of Fraser's men was adjusting the carbide-lantern.

What a foul house this was, in a foul street, harboring the foulest sort of business. A wave of loathing overtook him, a fierce hopeless detestation of the secret world, its midnight journeys, labyrinthine lies, its legions of the damned, the lost.

His hands were trembling as he struck a lucifer to light his cheroot.

"Sir, the responsibility—" Betteredge was at his elbow.

"My friend at the corner of Chancery Lane hasn't given me such a good leaf as usual," Oliphant said, frowning at the tip of his cheroot. "One must be very careful how one chooses one's cigars."

"We've been over the place top-to-bottom, Mr. Oliphant. If she was living here, there's no trace of her."

"Really? And to whom does that handsome chiffonier downstairs belong? Who waters the cacti? Does one water cacti? Perhaps they reminded our Texian friend of his homeland. . . ." He puffed resolutely on his cheroot and descended the stairs, with Betteredge on his heels like an anxious young setter.

A prim-looking sort from Criminal Anthropometry was lost in thought in front of the piano, as though trying to recall a tune. Of the various articles carried in this gentleman's black case, Oliphant knew, the least unpleasant were the calibrated linen tapes employed in taking Bertillon measurements of the skull.

"Sir," Betteredge said, when the anthropometrist had moved upstairs, "if you feel I was responsible, sir . . . For losing her, I mean—"

"I believe, Betteredge, that I dispatched you earlier to a matinee, at the Garrick, to report on the acrobatic ladies of Manhattan, did I not?"

"Yes, sir. . . ."

"You saw the Manhattan troupe, then?"

"Yes, sir."

"But—do let me suppose—you saw *her* there, as well?"

"Yes, sir! And Mackerel and his two as well!"

Oliphant removed his spectacles and polished them.

"The acrobats, Betteredge? To attract such an audience they must have been quite remarkable."

"Lord, sir, they batter one another with brickbats! The women run about in their dirty bare feet, and, well, scarves, sir, bits of gauze, no proper garments to speak of. . . ."

"And you enjoyed yourself, Betteredge?"

"Quite honestly, sir, no. Like a panto in Bedlam, it was. And I'd the job of it, with the Pinkers there. . . ."

"Mackerel" was their name for the senior Pinkerton agent, a side-whiskered Philadelphian who most frequently presented himself as Beaufort Kingsley DeHaven, though sometimes as Beaumont Alexander Stokes. He was Mackerel by virtue of his seemingly invariable choice of breakfast, as reported by Betteredge and the other watchers.

Mackerel and two subordinates had been regular London fixtures for some eighteen months now, and Oliphant found them remarkably interesting, and a solid pretext for his own Government funding. The Pinkerton organization, while ostensibly a private firm, served as the central intelligence-gathering organ of the embattled United States. With networks in place throughout the Confederate States, as well as in the Republics of Texas and California, the Pinkertons were often privy to information of considerable strategic importance.

With the arrival in London of Mackerel and his cohorts, certain voices in Special Branch had argued for the various classic modes of coercion. Oliphant had quickly moved to quash this suggestion, arguing that the Americans would be of inestimably greater value if they were allowed to operate freely—under, he made it clear, the constant surveillance of both the Special Branch and his own Special Bureau of the Foreign Office. In practice, of course, the Special Bureau utterly lacked the manpower for any such undertaking, which had resulted in Special Branch assigning Betteredge to the task, along with a steady rota of nondescript Londoners, all of them experienced watchers, personally vetted by Oliphant. Betteredge reported directly to

Oliphant, who assessed the raw material before passing it on to Special Branch. Oliphant found the arrangement thoroughly agreeable; Special Branch had so far refrained from comment.

The movements of the Pinkertons had gradually revealed minor but hitherto unsuspected sub-strata of clandestine activity. The resultant information constituted a rather mixed bag, but this was all the more to Oliphant's liking. The Pinkertons, he had happily declared to Betteredge, would provide the equivalent of geological core-samples. The Pinkertons would plumb the depths, and Britain would reap the benefits.

Betteredge, almost immediately and to his considerable pride, had discovered that one Mr. Fuller, the Texian legation's sole and woefully overworked clerk, was in Pinkerton pay. In addition, Mackerel had demonstrated a profound curiosity about the affairs of General Sam Houston, going so far as to personally burglarize the country estate of the exiled Texian President. Some months subsequently, the Pinkertons had shadowed Michael Radley, Houston's flack, whose murder in Grand's Hotel had led directly to a number of Oliphant's current lines of inquiry.

"And you saw our Mrs. Bartlett, attending the Communard performance? You're entirely positive?"

"No question, sir!"

"Mackerel and company were aware of her? She of them?"

"No, sir—they were watching the Communard panto, hooting and jeering. Mrs. Bartlett crept back-stage between acts! She kept well in the rear, afterwards. Applauding, though." Betteredge frowned.

"The Pinkertons made no attempt to follow Mrs. Bartlett?"

"No, sir!"

"But you did."

"Yes, sir. When the show was done, I left Boots and Becky Dean to ghost our chaps, and set out to dog her alone."

"You were very foolish, Betteredge." Oliphant's tone was exceptionally mild. "You should rather have dispatched Boots and

Becky. They're far more experienced, and a team is invariably more efficient than a single watcher. You might easily have lost her."

Betteredge winced.

"Or she might have killed you, Betteredge. She's a murderess. Quite appallingly accomplished. Known to conceal vitriol about her person."

"Sir, I take full—"

"No, Betteredge, no. None of it. She'd already killed our Texian Goliath. Highly premeditated, no doubt. She was in a position to provide him food, aiding and abetting him, just as she and her friends did, during that night of terror at Grand's Hotel. . . . She'd bring him round his tinned beans, you see. He depended on her; he'd gone to ground in a garret. Simply a matter of doctoring a tin."

"But why should she turn on him now, sir?"

"A question of loyalties, Betteredge. Our Texian was a nationalist zealot. Patriots may league with the very devil in pursuit of a nation's interest, but there are matters at which they balk. Likely she demanded some deadly service from him, and he refused." He knew as much from the confession of Collins; the nameless Texian had been a fractious ally. "The fellow crossed her, spurned her schemes; as did the late Professor Rudwick. So he met the same fate as the man he killed."

"She must be desperate."

"Perhaps. . . . But we have no reason to believe you alerted her by following her here."

Betteredge blinked. "Sir, when you sent me to see the Communards, did you suspect she might be there?"

"Not at all. I confess, Betteredge, I was indulging a whim. Lord Engels, an acquaintance of mine, is fascinated by this fellow Marx, the Commune's founder. . . ."

"Engels the textile magnate?"

"Yes. He's quite eccentric about it, actually."

"About those Communard women, sir?"

"About Mr. Marx's theories in general, and the fate of the Manhattan Commune in particular. Friedrich's generosity, in fact, made this current tour possible."

"The richest man in Manchester, funding that sort of tripe?" Betteredge seemed genuinely disturbed by the revelation.

"Peculiar, yes. Friedrich is himself the son of a wealthy Rhineland industrialist. . . . In any case, I was curious for your report. And, of course, I did rather expect our Mr. Mackerel to put in an appearance. The United States take the dimmest possible view of the Red revolution in Manhattan."

"One of the women gave a sort of, well, sermon, sir, before the panto, and ranted like sixty! Some business about 'iron laws'—"

" 'The iron law of history,' yes. All very doctrinaire. But Marx has borrowed much of his theory from Lord Babbage—so much so, that his doctrine may one day dominate America." Oliphant's nausea had passed. "But consider, Betteredge, that the Commune was founded during city-wide anti-war riots, protesting the Union conscription. Marx and his followers seized power during a period of chaos, somewhat akin to last summer's affliction in London. Here, of course, we've come through in good form, and that in spite of having lost our Great Orator in the very midst of the emergency. Proper succession of power is everything, Betteredge."

"Yes, sir." Betteredge nodded, distracted from the matter of Lord Engel's Communard sympathies by Oliphant's patriotic sentiments. Oliphant, suppressing a sigh, rather wished that he himself believed them.

Oliphant nodded and napped, on the journey home. He dreamed, as he often did, of an omniscient Eye in whose infinite perspectives might be sorted every least mystery.

Upon arrival, he found, to his ill-concealed chagrin, that Bligh had drawn a bath for him in the collapsible rubber tub recently prescribed by Dr. McNeile. In robe and nightshirt, slippered in embroidered moleskin, Oliphant examined the thing with resigned distaste. It stood, steaming, before the perfectly good and perfectly empty tub of white porcelain which dominated his bath-room. It was Swiss, the rubber bath, its slack black trough gone taut and bulbous with the volume of water it presently contained. Supported by an elaborately hinged frame of black-enameled teak, it was connected to the geyser with a worm-like hose and several ceramic petcocks.

Removing his robe, and then his nightshirt, he stepped from his slippers, then from the chill of octagonal marble tiles, into the soft, warm maw. It very nearly overturned as he struggled to sit. The elastic material, supported on all sides by the frame, gave distressingly beneath one's feet. And was, he discovered, quite horrid in its embrace of one's buttocks. He was, according to McNeile's prescription, to recline for a quarter-hour, his head supported on the small pneumatic pillow of rubberized canvas supplied for this purpose by the manufacturer. McNeile maintained that the cast-iron body of a porcelain tub confused the spine's natural attempts to return to its correct magnetic polarity. Oliphant shifted slightly, grimacing at the obscene sensation of the clinging rubber.

Bligh had arranged a sponge, pumice, and a fresh bar of French-milled soap in the little bamboo basket attached to the side of the tub. Bamboo, Oliphant supposed, must also lack magnetic properties.

He groaned, then took up sponge and soap and began to wash himself.

Released from the pressing business of the day, Oliphant, as he often did, undertook a detailed and systematic act of recollection. He had a natural gift for memory, greatly aided in youth by the educational doctrines of his father, whose ardent interest in mesmerism and the tricks of stage-magic had introduced his son to the arcane disciplines of mnemonics. Such accomplishments had been of great use to Oliphant in later life, and he practiced them now with a regularity he had once devoted to prayer.

Almost a year had passed since his search through the effects of Michael Radley, in Room 37, Grand's Hotel.

Radley had owned a modern steamer-trunk of the sort that, upended and opened, served as a compact combination of wardrobe and bureau. This, along with a scuffed leather hat-case and a brass-framed Jacquard satchel, constituted the whole of the publicist's luggage. Oliphant had found the intricacy of the trunk's fittings depressing. All these hinges, runners, hooks, nickeled catches, and leather tabs—they spoke of a dead man's anticipation of journeys that were never to be. Equally pathetic were the three gross of fancily stippled cartes-de-viste, with Radley's Manchester telegraph-number arranged in the French manner, still wrapped in printer's-tissue.

He began by unpacking each section in turn, laying Radley's clothing out on the hotel bed with a valet's precision. The publicist had entertained a fondness for silk nightshirts. As he worked, Oliphant examined maker's labels and laundry-marks, turning out pockets and running his fingers over seams and linings.

Radley's toilet articles were secured in a removable envelope of water-proofed silk.

Oliphant examined the contents, handling each object in turn: a badger shaving-brush, a self-stropping safety-razor, a toothbrush, a tin of tooth-powder, a sponge-bag . . . He rapped the ivory handle of the brush against the foot of the bedstead. He opened the razor's leatherette case: nickel-plate gleamed against a bed of violet velour. He emptied the tooth-powder out on a sheet of Grand's engraved stationery. He looked in the sponge-bag—and found a sponge.

The glitter of the razor drew his eye. Dumping its various components atop the starched bib of an evening-shirt, he used the penknife on his watch-chain to pry the fitted velour nest from the case. It came away easily, revealing a tightly folded sheet of foolscap.

Upon this sheet, in pencil, quite smudged with frequent erasure and re-erasure, was written what appeared to be the start of a draft letter. Undated, lacking any term of address, it was unsigned:

I trust you recall our two Conversations of th past Aug, during 2nd of which you so kindly entrusted me w yr Conjectures. I am pleased to inform you that cert manipulations have yielded a version—a *true* vers of yr orig—which I feel most confidently can at last be run, thereby demonstrating that Proof so long sought & expected.

The remainder of the sheet was blank, with the exception of three faintly penciled rectangles, containing the Roman capitals ALG, COMP, and MOD.

ALG, COMP, and MOD had subsequently become a fabulous three-headed beast, frequent visitor to the higher fields of Oliphant's imagination. His discovery of the probable meaning of this cipher, while examining transcripts of the interrogation of William Collins, had failed to dispel the image; Alg-Comp-Mod was with him still, a serpent-necked chimera, its heads nastily human. Radley's face was there, quite dead, mouth agape, eyes blank as fog, and the cool marble features of Lady Ada Byron, aloof and impassive, framed by curls and ringlets that were proofs of a pure geometry. But the third head, sinuously swaying, evaded Oliphant's gaze. He sometimes imagined its face was Edward Mallory's, resolutely ambitious, hopelessly frank; at other times he took it to be the pretty, poisonous visage of Florence Bartlett, wreathed in fumes of vitriol.

And sometimes, particularly as now, in the rubber bath's cloying embrace, drifting toward the continent of sleep, the face was his own, its eyes filled with a dread he could not name.

The following morning, Oliphant slept in, then kept to his bed, Bligh supplying him with files from the study, strong tea, and anchovy toast. He read a Foreign Office dossier on one Wilhelm Stieber, a Prussian agent posing as an émigré newspaper editor named Schmidt. With considerably more interest, he read and annotated a Bow Street file detailing several recent attempts to smuggle munitions, each incident involving cargo destined for Manhattan. The next file consisted of Engine-printed copies of several letters from a Mr. Copeland, of Boston. Mr. Copeland, who traveled in lumber, was in British pay. His letters described the system of forts defending the island of Manhattan, with extensive notes on ordnance. Oliphant's gaze, from long practice, slid lightly over Copeland's account of the south battery on Governor's Island, something of a relic by the sound of it, and quickly arrived at a report of rumors that the Commune had strung a chain of mines from the Romer Shoals to the Narrows.

Oliphant sighed. He very much doubted that the channel had been mined, but the leaders of the Commune would certainly wish it to be thought to have been mined. As indeed it might soon be, if the gentlemen of the Commission for Free Trade were to have their way.

Bligh was at the door.

"You've an appointment with Mr. Wakefield, sir, at the Central Statistics Bureau."

An hour later, Betteredge greeted him from the open door of a cab. "Good afternoon, Mr. Oliphant." Oliphant climbed in and settled himself. Pleated shades of black-proofed canvas were drawn firmly across either window, shutting out Half-Moon Street and the stark November sun. As the driver urged the cab-horse forward, Betteredge opened a case at his feet, took out a lamp, which he lit in a rapid and dextrous fashion, and fixed, with a brass apparatus of screws and bolts, to the arm of the seat. The interior of the case glittered like a miniature arsenal. He passed Oliphant a crimson file-folder.

Oliphant opened the file, which detailed the circumstances of the death of Michael Radley.

He had himself been in the smoking-room with the General and poor doomed Radley, the both of them awash with drink. Of their respective styles of drunkenness, Radley's had been the more presentable, the least predictable, the more dangerous. Houston, in his cups, delighted in playing the barbarous American; red-eyed, perspiring, foul-mouthed, he lounged with one great coarse boot propped muddily atop an ottoman. As Houston spoke, and smoked, and spat, roundly cursing Oliphant and Britain, he sullenly shaved curls from a bit of pine, periodically pausing to strop the jack-knife on the edge of his boot-sole. Radley, in contrast, had positively quivered with the liquor's stimulant effect, cheeks flushed and eyes flashing.

Oliphant's visit had been intended deliberately to disturb Houston on the eve of his departure to France, but the display of ill-concealed mutual hostility evident between the General and his publicist had been quite unexpected.

He had hoped to sow seeds of doubt with regard to the French tour; to this end, and primarily for Radley's benefit, he had managed to imply an exaggerated degree of cooperation on the parts of the intelligence services of Britain and France. Oliphant had suggested that Houston already possessed at least one powerful enemy among the Police des Châteaux, the bodyguard and secret personal agency of the Emperor Napoleon. While the Police des Châteaux were few in number, Oliphant insinuated, they were utterly without legal or constitutional restraint; Radley, at least, in spite of his condition, had obviously taken note of the implied threat.

They had been interrupted by a page, who brought a note for Radley. As the door opened to admit the man, Oliphant had glimpsed the anxious face of a young woman. Radley had stated, as he excused himself, that it was necessary that he speak briefly with a journalistic contact.

Radley had returned to the smoking-room some ten minutes later. Oliphant then took his leave, having endured an extended and particularly florid tirade from the General, who had consumed the better part of a pint of brandy during Radley's absence.

Summoned back to Grand's by telegram in the early hours of dawn, Oliphant had immediately sought out the hotel-detective, a retired Metropolitan named McQueen, who had been called to Houston's room, number 24, by the desk clerk, Mr. Parkes.

While Parkes attempted to calm the hysterical wife of a Lancashire paving-contractor, resident in number 25 at the time of the disturbance, McQueen had tried the knob of Houston's door, discovering it to be unlocked. Snow was blowing in through the demolished window, and the air, already chilled, stank of burnt gunpowder, blood, and, as McQueen delicately put it, "the contents of the late gentleman's bowel." Spying the scarlet ruin that was Radley's corpse, all too visible in the cold light of dawn, McQueen had called to Parkes to telegraph the Metropolitans. He then used his passkey to lock the door, lit a lamp, and blocked the view from the street with the remains of one of the window-curtains.

The condition of Radley's clothing indicated that the pockets had been gone through. Sundry personal objects lay in the pool of blood and other matter surrounding the corpse: a repeating match, a cigar-case, coins of various denominations. Lamp in hand, the detective surveyed the room, discovering an ivory-handled Leacock & Hutchings pocket-pistol. The weapon's trigger was missing. Three of its five barrels had been discharged— very recently, McQueen judged. Continuing his search, he had discovered the gaudy gilded head of General Houston's stick, awash in splintered glass. Nearby lay a bloodied packet, tightly wrapped in brown paper. It proved to contain a hundred kinotrope-cards, their intricate fretting of punch-holes ruined by the passage of a pair of bullets. The bullets themselves, of soft lead and much distorted, fell into McQueen's palm as he examined the cards.

Subsequent examination of the room by specialists from Central Statistics—the attention of the Metropolitan Police, at Oliphant's request, having been swiftly deflected from the matter—added little to what the veteran McQueen had observed. The trigger of the Leacock & Hutchings pepperbox was recovered from beneath an armchair. A more peculiar discovery consisted of a square-cut white diamond, of fifteen carats and very high quality, which was found firmly wedged between two floor-boards.

Two men from Criminal Anthropometry, no more than usually

cryptic about their purposes, employed large squares of tissue-thin adhesive grid-paper to capture various hairs and bits of fluff from the carpet; they guarded these specimens jealously, and took them away promptly, and nothing was ever heard of them again.

"Are you done with that one, sir?"

He looked up at Betteredge, then down at the file, seeing Radley's blood spread in a tacky pool.

"We're in Horseferry Road, sir."

The cab came to a halt.

"Yes, thank you." He closed the file and handed it to Betteredge. He descended from the cab and mounted the broad stairs.

Regardless of the circumstances surrounding a given visit, he invariably felt a peculiar quickening upon entering the Central Statistics Bureau. He felt it now, certainly: a sense of being observed, somehow—of being known and numbered. The Eye, yes . . .

As he spoke to the uniformed clerk at the visitor's-desk, a gang of journeymen mechanics emerged from a hallway to his left. They wore Engine-cut woolen jackets and polished brogues soled with creped rubber. Each man carried a spotless tool-satchel of thick white duck, cornered with bronze rivets and brown hide. As they moved toward him, conversing among themselves, some drew pipes and cheroots from their pockets in anticipation of a shift's-end smoke.

Oliphant experienced a sharp pang of tobacco-hunger. He had often had call to regret the Bureau's necessary policy regarding tobacco. He looked after the mechanics as they passed, out between the columns and the bronze sphinxes. Married men, assured of a Bureau pension, they would live in Camden Town, in New Cross, in any respectable suburb, and would furnish their tiny sitting-rooms with papier-mâché side-boards and ornate Dutch clocks. Their wives would serve tea on gaudily japanned tin trays.

Passing an irritatingly banal quasi-biblical bas-relief, he made his way to the lift. As the attendant bowed him in, he was joined by a glum gentleman who was daubing with a handkerchief at a pale streak on the shoulder of his coat.

The articulated bars of the brass cage rattled shut. The lift ascended. The gentleman with the soiled coat made his exit at the third stop. Oliphant rode on to the fifth, the home of Quantitative Criminology and Non-Linear Analysis. While he found the latter infinitely more compelling than the former, it was Q C he needed today, most particularly in the person of Andrew Wakefield, the departmental Under-Secretary.

The clerks of Q C were individually walled into neatly cramped cells of rolled-steel, asbestos, and veneer. Wakefield presided over them from a grander version of the same scheme, his sparse sandy head framed by the brass-fitted drawers of a multitude of card-files.

He glanced up as Oliphant approached, prominent front teeth displayed against his lower lip. "Mr. Oliphant, sir," he said. "A pleasure as ever. Pardon me." He shuffled a number of punch-cards into a sturdy blue envelope lined with tissue-paper, and meticulously wound the little scarlet string about the two halves of the patent-clasp. He set the envelope aside, in an asbestos-lined hutch containing several other envelopes of identical hue.

Oliphant smiled. "Fancy I can read your punch-holes, Andrew?" He levered a spring-loaded stenographer's-chair up from its ingenious housing and took a seat, his furled umbrella balanced across his knees.

"Know what a blue envelope's about, do you?" Springs clanged as Wakefield folded his articulated writing-desk into its narrow slot.

"Not a *specific* one, no, but I rather imagine that's the trick of it."

"There *are* men who can read cards, Oliphant. But even a junior clerk can read the directive primaries as easily as you read the kinos in the underground."

"I never read the kinos in the underground, Andrew."

Wakefield snorted. Oliphant knew this to be his equivalent of laughter. "And how are things among the *corps diplomatique*, Mr. Oliphant? Coping with our 'Luddite conspiracy,' are we?" It would have been impossible to mistake the man's sarcasm, but Oliphant pretended to take him quite literally.

"It really hasn't had too great an effect, as yet. Not among my own areas of special interest."

Wakefield nodded, assuming that Oliphant's "areas of special interest" were limited to the activities of foreign nationals on British soil. On Oliphant's request, Wakefield regularly ordered the files spun on groups as diverse as the Carbonari, the Knights of the White Camellia, the Fenian Society, the Texas Rangers, the Greek Hetairai, the Pinkerton Detective Agency, and the Confederate Bureau of Scientific Research, all of whom were known to be operative in Britain.

"I trust that the Texian material we provided has been of some use?" Wakefield inquired, coil-springs creaking behind him as he leaned forward.

"Quite," Oliphant assured him.

"You wouldn't know," Wakefield began, taking a gold-plated propelling-pencil from his pocket, "if their legation intends a change of premises?" He tapped the pencil against his front teeth, producing a loud clicking sound that Oliphant found repulsive.

"From their present location in St. James's? 'Round from Berry's the wine-merchant?"

"Precisely."

Oliphant hesitated, seeming to weigh the matter. "I shouldn't think so. They haven't any money. I suppose it would depend upon the good-will of the landlord, finally. . . ."

Wakefield smiled, his teeth dimpling his lower-lip.

"Wakefield," Oliphant said, "do tell me—who wishes to know?"

"Criminal Anthropometry."

"Really? Are *they* involved in surveillant activities?"

"I gather it's technical, actually. Experimental." Wakefield put his pencil away. "Your savant chap—Mallory, was it?"

"Yes?"

"Saw a review of his book. Off to China, is he?"

"Mongolia. Heading up an expedition for the Geographical Society."

Wakefield pursed his lips and nodded. "Out from underfoot, I should think."

"Out of harm's way, one should hope. Not a bad sort, really. Seemed to keenly appreciate the technical aspects of your Bureau's work. But I've a technical matter for you myself, Andrew."

"Really?" Wakefield's springs creaked.

"Having to do with Post Office procedure."

Wakefield made a small, entirely noncommittal sound in his throat.

Oliphant took an envelope from his pocket and passed it to the Under-Secretary. It was unsealed. Wakefield took a pair of white cotton gloves from a wire basket at his elbow, drew them on, extracted a white telegraphic address-card from the envelope, glanced at it, then met Oliphant's gaze.

"Grand's Hotel," Wakefield said.

"Quite." The establishment's crest was printed on the card. Oliphant watched as Wakefield automatically ran a gloved fingertip across the lines of punch-holes, checking for indications of wear that might cause mechanical difficulties.

"You wish to know who sent it?"

"That information is in my possession, thank you."

"Name of addressee?"

"I am aware of that as well."

The springs creaked—nervously, it seemed to Oliphant. Wakefield rose, with a twanging of steel, and carefully inserted the card in a brass slot set into the face of a glass-fronted instrument which overhung a bank of card-files. With a glance at Oliphant, he reached up a gloved hand and cranked down an ebony-handled lever. On the down-stroke, the device thumped like a shopman's credit-press. As Wakefield released the lever, it began to slowly right itself, humming and clicking like a publican's wagering-machine. Wakefield watched as the whirling character-wheels ticked and slowed. Abruptly, the device was silent.

"Egremont," Wakefield read aloud, but quietly, " 'The Beeches,' Belgravia."

"Indeed." Oliphant watched as Wakefield extracted the card from the brass slot. "I require the text of that telegram, Andrew."

"Egremont," Wakefield said, as though he hadn't heard. He took his seat again, replaced the card in its envelope, and removed his gloves. "He seems to be everywhere, our Right Honorable Charles Egremont. No end of work he's making for us here, Oliphant."

"The text of the message, Andrew, is here in the Bureau. It exists physically, I believe, as however many inches of telegrapher's tape."

"Do you know I've fifty-five miles' gear-yardage under me, still fouled from the Stink? Aside from the fact that your request is rather more than usually irregular . . ."

" 'Usually irregular'? That's rather good. . . ."

"And your friends from the Special Branch trooping in hourly, demanding that our brass be spun and spun again, in hope of shaking loose these Luddites alleged to be lodged in the nation's rafters! Who *is* this bloody man, Oliphant?"

"A rather junior Rad politician, I understand. Or was, till the Stink and the resulting disorders."

"Till Byron's death, rather."

"But we've Lord Brunel now, haven't we?"

"Indeed, and bloody madness under him in Parliament!"

Oliphant let the silence lengthen. "If you could obtain the text of the telegram, Andrew," he said at last, very quietly, "I should be very grateful."

"He's a very *ambitious* man, Oliphant. With ambitious friends."

"You are not alone in that assessment."

Wakefield sighed. "Under the circumstances, extreme discretion—"

"By all means!"

"Aside from which our yardage is filthy. Condensed particulate matter. We're working the mechanics on triple-shifts, and having some success with Lord Colgate's aerosol applications, but I sometimes despair of ever having the system properly up and spinning!" He lowered his voice. "Do you know that the finer functions of the Napoleon have been unreliable for months?"

"The Emperor?" Oliphant pretended to misunderstand.

"The Napoleon's gear-yardage, in equivalent terms, is very nearly double ours," Wakefield said. "And it simply isn't functioning!" The thought seemed to fill him with a special horror.

"Had a Stink of their own, have they?"

Wakefield grimly shook his head.

"There you are, then," said Oliphant, "most likely the gears are jammed on a bit of onion-skin. . . ."

Wakefield snorted.

"Do find me that telegram? At your earliest convenience, of course."

Wakefield inclined his head, but only very slightly.

"Good fellow," Oliphant declared. He saluted the Under-Secretary with his furled umbrella and rose, to retrace his steps through Q C's cubbies and the bowed and patient heads of Wakefield's clerks.

Oliphant had made his professionally circuitous way to Dean Street from the Soho tavern where he had instructed Betteredge to deposit him. Now he entered a soot-streaked house, its door unlatched. Latching it carefully behind him, he climbed two flights of uncarpeted stairs. The chill air smelled of cooked cabbage and stale tobacco.

He rapped twice at a door, then twice again.

"Come in, come in, you'll let in the cold. . . ." The heavily bearded Mr. Hermann Kriege, late of the New York *Volks Tribüne*, appeared to be wearing every article of clothing he possessed, as though he had wagered that he could all at once don the entire contents of a ragman's barrow.

He locked and chained the door behind Oliphant.

Kriege had two rooms, the one with the view of the street being the drawing-room, and behind it a bedroom. Everything broken and tattered, and in the greatest disorder. A large, old-fashioned table, covered with wax-cloth, stood in the middle of the drawing-room. On it lay manuscripts, books, newspapers, a doll with a Dresden head, bits and pieces of a woman's sewing things, chipped teacups, dirty spoons, pens, knives, candlesticks, an inkpot, Dutch clay pipes, tobacco-ash.

"Sit, sit, please." More ursine than ever in his bundled attire, Kriege waved vaguely toward a chair with only three legs. Blinking through a haze of coal- and tobacco-smoke, Oliphant made out a chair that seemed whole, though Kriege's daughter had been playing kitchen on it. Choosing to risk a pair of trousers, Oliphant swept jammy crumbs aside and sat, facing Kriege across the sad domestic litter of the crowded table-top.

"A small gift for your little Traudl," Oliphant said, taking a tissue-wrapped parcel from his coat. The tissue was secured with a self-adhesive rectangle, embossed with the initials of an Oxford Street toy-emporium. "A doll's tea things." He placed the parcel on the table.

"She calls you 'Uncle Larry.' She shouldn't know your name."

"Many's the Larry about Soho, I should imagine." Oliphant produced a plain envelope, unsealed, and placed it beside the parcel, precisely aligned with the table's edge. It contained three well-circulated five-pound notes.

Kriege said nothing. A silence lengthened.

"The Manhattan Women's Red Pantomime Troupe," Oliphant said at last.

Kriege snorted derisively. "The Bowery's Sapphic best, come to London? I remember them in Purdy's National. They wooed and won the Dead Rabbits to the cause, whose sole previous involvement with politics had consisted of rock-fights and punch-ups in municipal elections. The butcher-boys, the bootblacks, the prostitutes of Chatham Square and the Five Points, that was their audience. Sweaty proletarians, come to see a woman shot out of a gun, flattened against a wall, and peeled off like paper. . . . I tell you, sir, your interest is misplaced."

Oliphant sighed. "My friend, it is my job to ask questions. You must understand that I cannot tell you my reasons for asking a given question. I know that you have suffered. I know that you suffer now, in exile." Oliphant glanced meaningfully about the tragic room.

"What then do you wish to know?"

"It has been suggested that among the various criminal elements, active during the recent civil disruptions, were agents of Manhattan." Oliphant waited.

"I find that unlikely."

"On what basis, Mr. Kriege?"

"To my knowledge, the Commune has no interest in disturbing the British status-quo. Your Rads have shown themselves to be benevolent bystanders, with regard to America's class-struggle. Indeed, your nation has behaved as an ally of sorts." There was much bitterness in Kriege's tone, a curdled cynicism. "One imagines it was in Britain's own interest to see the Northern Union lose its greatest city to the Communards."

Oliphant shifted cautiously on the uncomfortable chair. "You knew Mr. Marx intimately, I believe." In order to extract a given piece of information from Kriege, he knew, it was necessary to engage the man's dominant passion.

"Knew him? I was there to greet him off the boat. He embraced me, and not a minute later had borrowed twenty gold dollars, to pay his rent in the Bronx!" Kriege assayed a sort of laugh, strangled with abiding rage. "He'd his Jenny with him, then, though the marriage didn't survive the revolution. . . . But he'd a Brooklyn Irish factory-girl in his bed when he expelled me from the Commune, sir, for preaching 'religionism and free-love'! Free-love indeed!" Kriege's large pale hands, with their unkept nails, plucked abstractedly at a sheaf of papers.

"You have been badly used, Mr. Kriege." Oliphant thought of his friend, Lord Engels; it did seem extraordinary, that the brilliant textile-manufacturer should involve himself, however distantly, with people of this sort. Kriege had been a member of the Commune's so-called "Central Committee," before Marx had sent him packing. With a price on his head in the Northern

Union, he had sailed in steerage from Boston, penniless, under an assumed name, with his wife and child, to join London's thousands of American refugees.

"These Bowery pantomimes . . ."

"Yes?" Oliphant leaned forward.

"There are factions within the Party . . ."

"Do go on."

"Anarchists disguising themselves as communists; feminists, all manner of incorrect ideologies, you see, covert cells not under Manhattan's control . . ."

"I see," Oliphant said, thinking of the reams of yellow fan-fold representing the confession of William Collins.

Again on foot, Oliphant made his roundabout way through Soho, to Compton Street, where he paused before the entrance of a public house known as the Blue Boar.

"A SPORTING-GENTLEMAN," he was informed by a large bill, "a Staunch Supporter of the destruction of these Vermin," would give "A GOLD REPEATER-WATCH TO BE KILLED FOR BY DOGS under 13¾ pounds weight." Below the smudged bill, a painted wooden placard advertised "Rats always on hand for the accommodation of Gentlemen to try their dogs."

He entered, and shortly was greeting Fraser in the rank smell of dogs, tobacco-smoke, and hot penny-gin.

The long bar was crowded with men of every grade of society, many with their animals under their arms. There were bull-dogs, Skye terriers, small brown English terriers. The room was low-ceilinged and quite unadorned. About the walls were hung clusters of leather collars.

"You came by cab, sir?" Fraser inquired.

"On foot, from a previous appointment."

" 'Ere now," cried the barman, "don't block up the bar!" There was a general movement toward the parlor, where a young waiter now shouted, "Give your orders, gentlemen!" With Fraser at his side, Oliphant followed the crowd of sporting-men and their dogs. Above the parlor fireplace were glass-fronted cases displaying the stuffed heads of animals famous in their day. Oliphant noticed the head of a bull-terrier, its glass eyes bulging hugely.

"Looks as though this one died of strangulation," Oliphant remarked, pointing the thing out to Fraser.

"They've spoilt her in the stuffing, sir," said the waiter, a fair-haired boy in a greasy striped apron. "Good as any in England, she was. I've seen her kill twenty at a go, though they killed her at the last. Your sewer-rats are dreadful for giving a dog canker, though we'd always rinse her mouth out well with peppermint and water."

"You're Sayers' boy," Fraser said. "We want a word with him."

"Why, I know you, sir! You were 'ere about that savantry gent—"

"Your old dad, Jem, and brisk about it," Fraser interjected, preventing the boy from announcing the arrival of a copper to the assembled sportsmen.

" 'E's upstairs lighting the pit, sir," the boy said.

"Good chap," Oliphant said, giving the boy a shilling.

Oliphant and Fraser mounted a broad wooden staircase, which led to what had once been the drawing-room. Opening a door, Fraser led the way into the rat-killing apartment.

"Pit's not bloody open," bellowed a fat man with ginger side-whiskers. Oliphant saw that the pit consisted of a wooden circus, some six feet in diameter, fitted with a high rim at elbow-height. Above it branched the arms of an eight-mantle gas-light, brightly illuminating the white-painted floor of the little arena. Mr. Sayers, the Blue Boar's proprietor, in a bulging silk waistcoat, stood with a live rat in his left hand. "But it's you, Mr. Fraser. My apologies, sir!" Having caught the creature somehow by the throat, he deftly prized out its larger teeth with no more implement than his strong thumbnail. "Order for a dozen with their teeth drawed." He dropped the mutilated rat into a rusted wire cage with several others and turned to face his visitors. " 'Ow might we be of service, Mr. Fraser?"

Fraser took out an Engine-stippled morgue-portrait.

"Aye, 'e's your man," Sayers said, his brows rising. "Big chap, long in the leg. And a dead'un, by the look of 'im."

"You're quite positive?" Oliphant could smell the rats now. "This is Professor Rudwick's murderer?"

"Aye, sir. We gets all sorts 'ere, but none too many Argentine giants. I recall 'im quite plain."

Fraser had taken out his notebook and was writing in it.

"Argentine?" Oliphant asked.

" 'E spoke Spanish," Sayers said, "or so I took it to be. Now mind you, we none o' us saw 'im do the deed, but 'e was on the premises that night, so 'e was."

"Cap'an's here," Sayers' son called from the doorway.

" 'Ell! And I've not drawed the teeth of 'alf 'is rats!"

"Fraser," Oliphant said, "I fancy a warm gin. Let us retire to the bar and allow Mr. Sayers to complete arrangements for the evening's sport." He bent to examine a larger cage, this one of iron bands. It seemed to contain a solid mound of rats.

"Mind your fingers there," Sayers said. "For believe me, you get a bite and you'll not forget it. These 'ere are none o' the cleanest. . . ."

In the parlor, a young officer, evidently the Captain, was threatening to leave the place if he were kept waiting any longer.

"I shouldn't drink that if I were you," Fraser said, looking at Oliphant's noggin of warm gin. "Almost certainly adulterated."

"Actually it's quite good," Oliphant said. "It has a very faint after-taste, rather like bitter wormwood."

"An intoxicant poison."

"Quite. The French use it in the preparation of herbals. What do you make of our good Captain here?" Oliphant gestured with his gin, indicating the man in question, who was pacing about in an agitated fashion, examining the paws of various animals as their owners presented them, all the while shouting that he should depart immediately if the pit weren't opened.

"Crimea," Fraser said.

The Captain bent to peer at the claws of a young terrier in the arms of a swarthy, rather portly man whose pomaded spit-curls protruded like wings from beneath his high-crowned derby.

"Velasco," Fraser said, as if to himself, something nastily akin to pleasure in his tone, and was instantly beside the fellow.

The Captain started, his handsome young face convulsed with a violent tic, and Oliphant's eye abruptly filled with all the red Crimea—whole cities aflame like bonfires, and shell-churned wastes of jellied filth sprouting white flowers that were men's hands. He shuddered with the intensity of the vision, then forgot it utterly.

"Do I *know* you, sir?" the Captain inquired of Fraser, with a brittle murderous jollity.

"Gentlemen!" Mr. Sayers cried from the stairs. Led by the Captain, the entire company, save only Oliphant, Fraser, the swarthy man, and a fourth man, made for the pit above. The fourth man, perched on the arm of a ragged brocade armchair, began to cough. Oliphant saw Fraser's grip tighten about his prey's upper arm.

"Shouldn't bloody ought to do that, Fraser," the man on the chair-arm said, unfolding his legs and standing. Oliphant noted a certain calculation evident in his tone. Like the swarthy man, he was newly and nattily kitted out, all in Oxford Street's latest, his coat of Engine-cut gabardine dyed a blue that verged on lavender. Oliphant saw that his lapel, like that of his companion, was decorated with a gleaming cloisonné badge in the shape of the Union Jack.

" 'Bloody,' Mr. Tate?" Fraser said, a schoolmaster about to deliver a tongue-lashing or worse.

"Fair warning, Fraser," the swarthy man said, his dark eyes protruding. "We're about Parliamentary business!" The little brown terrier shivered in his arms.

"Are you, then?" Oliphant inquired mildly, "and what business has Parliament in a rat-pit?"

"Might ask the same of you, eh?" the taller man said insolently, then coughed. Fraser glared at him.

"Fraser," Oliphant said, "are these gentlemen the confidential agents you mentioned in regard to Dr. Mallory?"

"Tate and Velasco," Fraser said grimly.

"Mr. Tate," Oliphant said, stepping forward, "a pleasure, sir. I am Laurence Oliphant, journalist." Tate blinked, confused by Oliphant's cordiality. Fraser, rather reluctantly taking Oliphant's cue, released Velasco's arm. "Mr. Velasco." Oliphant smiled.

Velasco's face clouded with suspicion. "Journalist? What sort of journalist?" he demanded, glancing from Oliphant to Fraser and back.

"Travel pieces, primarily," Oliphant said, "though I'm currently engaged, with Mr. Fraser's able help, in compiling a popular history of the Great Stink."

Tate peered narrowly at Oliphant. "Mallory, you said. What about 'im?"

"I interviewed Dr. Mallory prior to his departure for China. His experiences during the Stink were most remarkable, and highly illustrative of the perils that might befall anyone during such a chaotic period."

" 'Befall anyone'?" Velasco challenged. "Rubbish! Mallory's trouble was savantry trouble and your *Mr.* Fraser knows it well enough!"

"Yes, yes, quite," Oliphant agreed. "And that is why I am delighted to have encountered you gentlemen tonight."

Velasco and Tate glanced uncertainly at one another. "You are?" Tate ventured.

"Utterly. You see, Dr. Mallory explained to me the unfortunate contretemps with his rival and fellow savant, Peter Foulke. It seems, you see, that even in the most rarified circles, during a period of such unprecedented stress—"

"You'll not see Peter bloody Foulke moving in your rarified bloody circles now," Velasco interjected, "not for all his gentry posing." He paused for effect. "He was discovered in bed with a girl not twelve years old!"

"No!" Oliphant feigned shock. "Foulke? But surely—"

"He was," Tate affirmed, "in Brighton, and those as found him beat the bugger silly and flung him stark-naked into the street!"

"But it wasn't *us* did that," Velasco stated flatly, "and you'll not prove it was."

"There's a new trend of thought about," Tate said, thrusting his shallow chest forward so as to better display his Union Jack insignia, the gin-reddened tip of his button-nose glinting wetly, "such as doesn't tolerate decadence," giving equal stress to the word's three syllables, "be it in the savantry or however high at all. Hidden wickedness ran rife under Byron, all manner of it, and well you know it, Fraser!" Fraser's eyes widened at this effrontery, as Tate turned in his excitement to Oliphant. "That Stink was Ned Ludd's work, mister, and there's your history of it!"

"Sabotage on a titanic scale," Velasco pronounced darkly, as if quoting from a speech, "abetted by conspirators in the highest ranks of society! But there are true patriots among us, sir, patriots at work to root that evil out!" The terrier growled in Velasco's arms, and Fraser looked on the verge of throttling man and dog alike.

"We're Parliamentary investigators," Tate said, "about a Member's business, and I'm sure you'd not care to detain us."

Oliphant put his hand upon Fraser's sleeve.

With a smirk of triumph, Velasco soothed his little dog and sauntered to the stairs. Tate followed. From overhead came the mad yapping of dogs and the hoarse cries of sportsmen.

"They're working for Egremont," Oliphant said.

Fraser's face twisted with disgust. Disgust and something akin to amazement.

"There seems nothing more to be done here, Fraser. I take it you arranged for a cab?"

Mr. Mori Arinori, Oliphant's favorite among his young Japanese "pupils," took a fierce delight in all things British. Oliphant, who customarily breakfasted lightly if at all, would sometimes subject himself to massively "English" breakfasts to please Mori, who on this particular occasion wore the burliest of golfing-tweeds and a scarf in the tartan of the Royal Hibernian Order of Steam Engineers.

There was a certain enjoyably melancholy sense of paradox, Oliphant mused, in watching Mori spread a slice of toast with marmalade, while he himself indulged a nostalgia for his own days in Japan, where he had served as first-secretary under Rutherford Alcock. His stay in Edo had nurtured in him a passionate regard for the muted tones and subtle textures of a world of ritual and shadow. He longed now for the rattle of rain blown against oiled paper, for flowering weeds a-nod down tiny alleys, the glow of rush-lamps, for scents and darknesses, the shadows of the Low City . . .

"Oriphant-san, toast is very good, is most excellent! You are sad, Oriphant-san?"

"No, Mr. Mori, not at all." He helped himself to bacon, though he wasn't hungry in the least. He put aside a sudden intrusive memory of the morning's hideous bath, the black clinging rubber. "I was recalling Edo. That city possessed great charm for me."

Mori chewed bread and marmalade, regarding Oliphant steadily with his bright dark eyes, then dabbed expertly at his lips with a linen napkin. " 'Charm.' Your word for the old ways. The old ways hinder my nation. Only this week have I posted to Satsuma an argument against the wearing of swords." The bright eyes darted, for a fractional moment, toward the crooked fingers of Oliphant's left hand. As if stung by the pressure of Mori's awareness, the scar beneath Oliphant's cuff began a slow ache.

"But, Mr. Mori," Oliphant said, setting his silver fork aside to abandon the unwanted bacon, "the sword, in your country, is in many respects the focal symbol of the feudal ethic and the sentiments attaching to it—an object of reverence second only to one's own lord."

Mori smiled, pleased. "Odious custom of rude and savage age. This is *good* to be rid of, Oriphant-san. This is modern *day*!" This latter a favorite and frequent expression.

Oliphant returned the smile. Mori combined boldness and compassion with a certain problematical brashness that Oliphant found most appealing. More than once, to Bligh's dismay, Mori had paid some cockney cabman, full fare plus tip, and then invited the fellow into Oliphant's kitchen for a meal. "But you must learn to proceed apace, Mr. Mori. While you yourself may regard the wearing of swords as a primitive custom, to openly oppose this minor matter might well provoke resistance to other, more important reforms, the deeper changes you wish to implement in your society."

Mori nodded gravely. "Your policy no doubt has merit, Oriphant-san. Far better, for example, if all Japanese were taught English. Our meager tongue is of no use in the great world beyond our islands. Soon power of steam and the Engine must pervade our land. English language, following such, must suppress any use of Japanese. Our intelligent race, eager in pursuit of knowledge, cannot depend on weak and uncertain medium of communication. We must grasp principal truths from precious treasury of Western science!"

Oliphant tilted his head to one side, considering Mori carefully. "Mr. Mori," he said, "pardon me if I misunderstand you, but am I correct in assuming that you are proposing nothing less than the deliberate abolition of the Japanese language?"

"This is modern *day*, Oriphant-san, modern *day*! All reasons support our tongue's disuse."

Oliphant smiled. "We must arrange to discuss this at length, Mr. Mori, but now I must ask if you are engaged this evening. I propose an entertainment."

"By all means, Oriphant-san. English social festivities are ever gratifying." Mori beamed.

"We shall go then, to Whitechapel, to the Garrick Theatre, for what I understand is a most unusual pantomime."

According to the spottily stippled program, the Clown was known as "Jackdaw Jaculation," though this was perhaps the least peculiar aspect of that evening's performance, by the Manhattan Women's Red Pantomime Troupe, of *Mazulem the Night Owl*. Other characters included "Freedman Bureau Bill, a black boy," "Levy Stickemall, a merchant, offering two segars for five cents," "a Yankee Peddler," "a Lady Shop-Lifter," "a Roast Turkey," and the eponymous "Mazulem."

All of the players, to judge by the program, were female, though in several cases this would otherwise have been quite impossible to determine. The Clown, ornate with frills, in elaborately spangled satin, boasted an egg-bald shaven pate and the sinister white-face of the Pierrot, touched with color only in the outlined lips.

The performance had been preceded by a brief, ranting address from one "Helen America," her heaving, apparently unconstrained bosom, through layers of diaphanous scarves, serving to hold the attention of the predominantly masculine audience. Her speech had consisted of slogans Oliphant found rather more cryptic than rousing. What exactly did it mean, for instance, when she declared that "We have nothing to wear but our chains . . ."?

Consulting the program, he was informed that Helen America was in fact the authoress of *Mazulem the Night Owl*, as well as *Harlequin Panattahah* and *The Genii of the Algonquins*.

Musical accompaniment was provided by a moon-faced organist—her eyes, it seemed to Oliphant, glinting either with lunacy or laudanum.

The pantomime had opened in what Oliphant supposed was meant to be taken as a hotel dining-room, with the peripatetic Roast Turkey—apparently played by a dwarf—attacking the diners with a carving-knife. Oliphant had very quickly lost track of the narrative, if indeed there were one, which he doubted. Scenes were punctuated repeatedly by characters firing stuffed bricks at one another's heads. There was kinotropic accompaniment, of a sort, though it consisted of crudely polemical cartoons that seemed to bear little relationship to the action.

Oliphant stole a glance at Mori, who sat beside him, his treasured topper upright on his lap, his face expressionless. The audience was howlingly rowdy, though less in response to the substance of the pantomime, whatever that might be, than to the whirling, curiously formless dances of the Communard women, their bare shins and ankles plainly visible beneath the ragged hems of their flowing garments.

Oliphant's back began to ache.

The choreography accelerated into a sort of balletic assault, the air thick with brickbats, until, quite abruptly, *Mazulem the Night Owl* was ended.

The crowd hooted, applauded, jeered. Oliphant noted a hulking, gaunt-jawed man with a stout rattan over his shoulder, lounging beside the entrance to the pit. The fellow was watching the crowd through narrowed eyes.

"Come then, Mr. Mori. I sense a journalistic opportunity."

Mori stood, hat and evening-cane in hand. He followed Oliphant toward the pit.

"Laurence Oliphant, journalist." He presented his card to the hulking man. "If you would be so kind, you might convey this to Miss America with my request for an interview."

The man took the card, glanced at it, and let it fall to the floor. Oliphant saw the knobby fist tighten around the rattan. Mori emitted a brief hiss, as if of steam; Oliphant turned; Mori, his top-hat jammed firmly forward on his head, had assumed the pose of the samurai warrior, the handle of his evening-cane grasped in both his hands. Immaculate linen and gold links glinted at his supple wrists.

The untidily coiffed, extravagantly hennaed head of Helen America appeared. Her eyes were ringed with kohl.

Mori held his pose.

"Miss Helen America?" Oliphant produced a second card. "Allow me to introduce myself. I am Laurence Oliphant, journalist. . . ."

Helen America performed a rapid manipulation before the stony face of her compatriot, as though she were conjuring something from the air. The man lowered his length of rattan, still glowering fiercely at Mori. The stick, Oliphant saw, was obviously weighted. "Cecil's a deaf mute," she said, pronouncing the name with a case-hardened American *e*.

"I'm very sorry. I offered my card—"

"He can't read. You say you're a newspaper-man?"

"An occasional journalist. And you, Miss America, are an authoress of the first-water. Allow me to introduce my good friend, Mr. Mori Arinori, an envoy of the Mikado of Japan."

With a deadly glance at Cecil, Mori reversed his cane with admirable grace, removed his hat, and bowed in the European fashion. Helen America, wide-eyed, regarded him as one might a trained dog. She wore a neatly mended military cloak, threadbare but apparently clean, in the shade of grey the Confederates called butternut, though the original regimental buttons had been replaced with plain round horn.

"I haven't ever seen a Chinaman dress like that," she said.

"Mr. Mori is Japanese."

"And you're a newspaper-man."

"After a fashion, yes."

Helen America smiled, revealing a gold tooth. "And did you enjoy our show?"

"It was extraordinary, quite extraordinary."

Her smile widened. "Then come to Manhattan, mister, for the People Risen have the old Olympic, east of Broadway, over Houston Street. We're best appreciated in our own venue." Thin bands of silver pierced her ears, amid a tangled cloud of hennaed curls.

"It would be my great pleasure. As it would be my pleasure to conduct an interview with the authoress of—"

"I didn't write that," she said, "Fox did."

"Pardon me?"

"George Washington Lafayette Fox—the Marxian Grimaldi, the Tamla of socialist pantomime! It was the Troupe's decision to put that I wrote it, though I continue to argue against it."

"But your prefatory message . . ."

"Now I did write that, sir, and am proud of it. But poor Fox . . ."

"I hadn't heard," Oliphant submitted, somewhat baffled.

"It was the terrible pressure of toil," she said. "The great Fox, who'd single-handedly elevated socialist pantomime to its present level of revolutionary importance, was sweated mad by one-night stands, sir; driven to sheer exhaustion at having to contrive sharper tricks and quicker transformations. He slid into dementia then, his grimaces hideous to behold." She had assumed her stage delivery; now she lapsed back into a more confidential tone. "He'd lapse into the crudest indecency, mister, so we kept his dresser in a monkey-suit, to run out and belabor him, if he got too obscene."

"I'm very sorry—"

"Manhattan's no place for the mad, sir, sad to say. He's in the asylum in Somerville, Massachusetts, and if you'd care to publish that, be my guest."

Oliphant found that he was staring at her, entirely at a loss for words. Mori Arinori had retired somewhat, and seemed to be watching the crowd as it made its way out of the Garrick. The deaf-mute Cecil had vanished, taking with him his shot-loaded length of rattan.

"I could eat a horse," Helen America said cheerfully.

"Allow me, please, to provide you with a meal. Where do you wish to dine?"

"There's a place around the corner." As she stepped from the topmost of the steps that ascended the pit, Oliphant saw that she wore a pair of the rubber boots Americans called Chickamaugas, great clumsy things of military origin. With Mori at his side, he followed her out of the Garrick. She had not waited for him to offer his arm.

She led them down the street, and as she had said, around a corner. Gas-light flared, before a clacking kino-sign that checkered from MOSES & SONS AUTOCAFÉ into CLEAN MODERN RAPID and back again. Helen America glanced back with an encouraging smile, her callipygian hips swaying beneath the Confederate cloak and the tattered muslin of her remarkable stage-garment.

The Autocafé was crowded and noisy, packed with Whitechapel locals. Its iron-mullioned windows were opaque with steam. Oliphant had seen nothing like it before.

Helen America demonstrated how business was conducted here, taking up a rectangular gutta-percha tray from a stack of the things, and pushing it along a ledge of shining zinc. Above the ledge were several dozen miniature windows, trimmed with brass. Oliphant and Mori followed her example. Behind each window, a different dish was displayed. Oliphant, noting the coin-slots, fumbled for his change-purse. Helen America chose a slice of shepherd's pie, a helping of toad-in-the-hole, and fried chips, Oliphant providing the requisite coinage. An additional tuppence produced a copious quantity of very dubious-looking brown gravy, from a spigot. Mori chose a baked potato, a particular favorite of his, but declined the gravy-spigot. Oliphant, disoriented by the oddness of the place, opted for a pint of machine-made ale, from another spigot.

"Clystra's liable to kill me for this," Helen America remarked, as they arranged their trays on a ridiculously small cast-iron table. The table, like the four chairs around it, was bolted into the concrete floor. "Doesn't hold with us talking to gentlemen of the press." She shrugged, beneath her butternut cloak. She smiled happily and began to sort a small pile of cheap tin-ware, giving Mori a knife and dinner-fork. "Have you been to a town called Brighton, mister?"

"Yes, actually, I have."

"What kind of place is that?"

Mori was examining, with keen interest, the rectangular dish of coarse grey cardboard beneath his potato.

"It's very pleasant," Oliphant said, "very picturesque. The Hydropathic Pavilion is quite famous—"

"Is it in England?" Helen America asked, around a mouthful of toad-in-the-hole.

"It is, yes."

"Lot of working-folks?"

"Perhaps not, in the sense I take you to mean, though the various facilities and attractions employ a great many people."

"Haven't seen a real factory-crowd since we got here. Well— let's eat!" And with that, Helen America bent to the task. Dinner-conversation, Oliphant gathered, was not highly valued in Red Manhattan.

She left the cardboard "dishes" utterly devoid of scraps or crumbs, contriving to sop up the last dross of gravy with a chip she had carefully retained for this purpose.

Oliphant took out his notebook. Opening it, he removed a plain white card stippled with Florence Bartlett's Bow Street portrait. "Are you familiar at all with Flora Barnett, the American actress, Miss America? She's enormously popular in Manhattan, or so I was recently told. . . ." Oliphant displayed the card.

"She's no actress, mister. Nor an American either. She's a Southron, if you can even call her that; next thing to a damn' Frenchie. The People Risen don't need her kind. Hell, we've already hung our share of 'em!"

"Her kind?"

Helen America met his gaze with a defiant stare. "In a pig's eye, you're a journalist. . . ."

"I'm sorry if—"

"Sorry like the rest of 'em. You give just about that much of a damn. . . ."

"Miss America, please, I wish only to—"

"Thanks for the feed, mister, but you can't pump me, understand? And that brontosaur, that's got no damn' business over here in the first place! You got no right to it, and one day it'll sit in the Manhattan Metropolitan, for it belongs to the People Risen! And what makes you limeys think you can come digging up the People's natural treasures?"

And in through the door, as if on cue, marched the very formidable Clown of the Manhattan Women's Red Pantomime Troupe, her bald pate hugely bonneted in polka-dot gingham, and her Chickamauga boots even larger than Helen America's.

"Coming right this minute, Comrade Clystra," Helen America said.

The Clown fixed Oliphant with a murderous glare, and then the two were gone.

Oliphant looked at Mori. "A peculiar evening, Mr. Mori."

Mori, apparently lost in contemplation of the Autocafé's clatter and bustle, took a moment to respond.

"We will have places such as this in my country, Oriphant-san! Clean! Modern! Rapid!"

Bligh, upon Oliphant's return to Half-Moon Street, followed him upstairs to the door of the study. "May I come in for a moment, sir?" Locking the door behind them with his own key, Bligh crossed to a miniature parquet bureau that supported Oliphant's smoking-things; unsealing the top of a humidor, he reached inside and removed a squat little cylinder of black-japanned tin. "This was brought 'round to the kitchen door by a young man, sir. He wouldn't give his name, when asked. I took the liberty of opening it myself, sir, recalling some of the more heathen attempts, abroad. . . ."

Oliphant took the cannister and unscrewed its lid. Perforated telegraph-tape.

"And the young man?"

"A junior Engine-clerk, sir, to judge by the state of his shoes. Aside from the fact that he wore a clerk's cotton gloves, which he didn't remove."

"And there was no message?"

"There was, sir. 'Tell him,' he said, 'that we can do no more, there is great danger, he mustn't ask again.' "

"I see. Would you mind bringing up a pot of strong green-tea?"

Alone, Oliphant set about removing the heavy glass from his personal receiving-telegraph, a matter of loosening four brass wing-screws. Placing the tall vitrine-like dome out of harm's way, he spent some minutes consulting the maker's instructional manual. After rummaging through several drawers, he located the requisite implements: a walnut-handled brass hand-crank and a small gilt screw-driver embossed with the monogram of the Colt

& Maxwell Company. He located the knife-switch at the base of the instrument and severed the electrical connection with the Post Office. He then used the screw-driver to make the necessary adjustments, carefully threaded the end of the tape onto the bright steel sprockets, locked the guide-plates into position, and took a deep breath.

He was all at once aware of the beating of his own heart, and of the night's silence pressing in from the darkness of Green Park, and of the Eye. He took up the crank, thrust its hexagonal tip into the mechanism's socket, and began, steadily but slowly, to turn it clockwise. The character-hammers began to rise and fall, rise and fall, deciphering the punch-code of the Post Office tape. He refused to look at it, as it emerged from the slot.

It was done. With scissors and paste-pot, he assembled the message on a sheet of foolscap:

DEAR CHARLES COMMA NINE YEARS AGO YOU PUT ME TO THE WORST DISHONOR THAT A WOMAN CAN KNOW STOP CHARLES COMMA YOU PROMISED ME THAT YOU WOULD SAVE MY POOR FA- THER STOP INSTEAD YOU CORRUPTED ME COMMA BODY AND SOUL STOP TODAY I AM LEAVING LONDON COMMA IN THE COM- PANY OF POWERFUL FRIENDS STOP THEY KNOW VERY WELL WHAT A TRAITOR YOU WERE TO WALTER GERARD COMMA AND TO ME STOP DO NOT ATTEMPT TO FIND ME COMMA CHARLES STOP IT WOULD BE USELESS STOP I DO HOPE THAT YOU AND MRS EGRE- MONT WILL SLEEP SOUNDLY TONIGHT STOP SYBIL GERARD ENDIT

Only barely aware of Bligh arriving with the tea, he sat unmoving for the better part of an hour, the message before him. Then, after pouring himself a cup of luke-warm tea, he gathered stationery, took out his reservoir-pen, and began to compose, in his flawless diplomat's French, a letter to a certain Monsieur Arslau, of Paris.

*   *   *

Flash-powder still stank in the air.

The Prince Consort turned, with his full Teutonic gravity, from an elaborate stereoptic camera, of Swiss manufacture, and greeted Oliphant in German. He wore aquamarine spectacles, their circular lenses no larger than florins, and was draped in a photographer's smock of spotless white duck. His fingers were stained with silver nitrate.

Oliphant bowed, wishing His Highness a good afternoon in what amounted to the Royal Family's language of choice, and pretended to examine the Swiss camera, an intricate creation whose stereoptic lenses, like eyes, stared from beneath a smooth brass brow. Like the eyes of Mr. Cart, the Consort's muscular Swiss valet, they struck Oliphant as being set rather too widely apart.

"I've brought Affie a little gift, Your Highness," Oliphant said. His German, like the Prince Consort's, had the accent of Saxony—the legacy of a prolonged and delicate mission Oliphant had undertaken there at the behest of the Royal Family. Prince Albert's Coburg relatives, ever ingenious at the ancient craft of marriage-politics, were eager to expand their tiny domain—a delicate matter indeed, when the policy of the British Foreign Office was to keep the German mini-states as fragmented as politically possible. "Has the young Prince concluded his day's lessons?"

"Affie is ill today," Albert said, peering through his tinted spectacles at one of the camera's lenses. He produced a small brush and lightly whisked at the surface of the lens. He straightened. "Do you think the study of statistics too much a burden for a tender young mind?"

"My opinion, Your Highness?" Oliphant said. "Statistical analysis is indeed a powerful technique. . . ."

"His mother and I disagree on the matter," the Prince confided mournfully. "And Alfred's progress in the subject is far from satisfactory. Nevertheless, statistics is the key to the future. Statistics are everything in England."

"Does he progress well in his other studies?" Oliphant hedged.

"Anthropometry," the Prince suggested absently. "Eugenics. Powerful fields of learning, but less taxing, perhaps, to the youthful brain."

"Perhaps I might have a word with him, Your Highness," Oliphant said. "I know the lad means well."

"He is in his room, no doubt," the Prince said.

Oliphant made his way through the drafty glamor of the Royal Apartments to Alfred's room, where he was greeted with a whoop of glee, the Prince scrambling in bare-feet from mounded bedclothes and hopping nimbly across the tracks of a most elaborate miniature railway. "Uncle Larry! Uncle Larry! Brilliant! What have you brought for me?"

"Baron Zorda's latest."

In Oliphant's pocket, wrapped in green tissue and smelling strongly of cheap fresh ink, was a copy of *Paternoster the Steam Bandit*, by one "Baron Zorda," the third volume in the popular series, young Prince Alfred having expressed his unbridled enthusiasm for the two previous numbers, *The Skeleton Army* and *Wheelmen of the Tsar*. The book's garishly colored cover depicted the daring Paternoster, pistol in hand, climbing from the cabin of a hurtling vehicle one took to be a gurney in the latest style—sheathed in tin, bulbous at the prow, and very narrow in the rear. The frontispiece, which Oliphant had examined in the Piccadilly news-agent's where he had purchased the volume, offered Baron Zorda's raffish highwayman in rather more detail, particularly in regard to his dress, which included a broad belt of studded leather and bellbottomed trousers with buttoned vents at the cuffs.

"Super!" The boy eagerly tore the green tissue from *Paternoster the Steam Bandit*. "Look at his gurney, Uncle Larry! It's linestreamed like sixty!"

"Nothing but the swiftest for wicked Paternoster, Affie. And see the frontispiece. He's got up like Smashjaw Ned."

"Look at his narrow-go-wides," Alfred said admiringly. "And his bloody great belt!"

"And how have you been, Affie," Oliphant asked, ignoring the boy's lapse in language, "since my last visit?"

"Very well, Uncle Larry"—and a shadow of anxiety crossed the young face—"but I'm afraid I—I'm afraid she—she's broken, you see—" The Prince pointed to where the Japanese tea-doll slumped disconsolately against the foot of the massive four-poster, surrounded by a tumbled sea of lithographed tin and painted lead. A long sharp sliver of some translucent material protruded grotesquely from her gorgeous robe. "It's the spring, you see. I think it was wound too tightly, Uncle Larry. It sprang right out, on the tenth turn."

"The Japanese power their dolls with springs of baleen, Affie. 'Whale-whiskers,' they call the stuff. They haven't yet learned from us the manufacture of proper springs, but soon they shall. When they do, their dolls shan't break so easily."

"Father says you're too keen on your Japanese," Alfred said. "He says you think them the equal of Europeans."

"And I do, Affie! Their mechanical appliances are presently inferior, due to their lack of knowledge in the applied sciences. Some day, in futurity, they may lead civilization to heights yet untold. They, and perhaps the Americans . . ."

The boy regarded him dubiously. "Father wouldn't like that at all, what you said."

"No, I rather doubt he would."

Oliphant then spent half-an-hour, down on his knees upon the carpet, watching Alfred demonstrate a toy French Engine—operated, as was its cousin the Great Napoleon, by compressed air. The little Engine employed lengths of telegraph-tape, rather than cards, reminding Oliphant of his letter to M. Arslau. Bligh would have taken it 'round to the French Embassy by now; very likely it was already on its way to Paris by diplomatic pouch.

Alfred was connecting his Engine to a miniature kinotrope. There came a ceremonious rattle at the door-knob; the doors of Buckingham Palace were never knocked. Oliphant rose, and opened the tall white portal, to discover the well-known face of Nash, a palace valet-de-chambre, whose unwise speculations in railway shares had briefly made him the unwilling intimate of the Metropolitan Fraud Bureau. Oliphant's politesse had successfully smoothed the matter—a kindness well-invested, he saw now, by Nash's unfeigned air of respectful attention. "Mr. Oliphant," Nash announced, "a telegram has come, sir. Most urgent."

The velocity of the Special Branch vehicle contributed in no small part to Oliphant's general sense of unease. Paternoster himself could have asked for nothing faster, or more radically line-streamed.

They flew past St. James's Park with the speed of dream, the bare black branches of the lime-trees flashing by like wind-driven smoke. The driver wore leather goggles with round lenses, and plainly relished their headlong flight, periodically sounding a deep-throated whistle that sent horses rearing and pedestrians scurrying. The stoker, a burly young Irishman, was grinning maniacally as he shoveled coke into the burner.

Oliphant had no idea of their destination. Now, as they neared Trafalgar, the traffic caused the driver to yank the whistle-cord continually, steadily, setting up a mournful bellowing ululation, like the grief of some marine behemoth. The traffic, at this sound, parted like the Red Sea before Moses. Helmeted police-men saluted smartly as they sped past. Urchins and crossing-sweepers turned cartwheels of delight, at the sight of a sleek tin fish racketing down the Strand.

The evening had grown quite dark. As they entered Fleet Street, the driver applied the brake and worked a lever that released a mighty gout of uprushing steam. The line-streamed gurney bumped to a halt.

"Well, sir," the driver commented, raising his goggles to peer through the fretted glass of the vehicle's prow, "would you look at that."

Traffic, Oliphant saw, had been halted completely by the erec-tion of wooden barricades hung with lanterns. Behind these stood grim-faced soldiers in combat drab, Cutts-Maudslay car-bines unslung and at the ready. Beyond them, he saw sheets of canvas, loosely hung from raw timber uprights, as though someone were attempting to erect stage-scenery in the middle of Fleet Street.

The stoker swabbed his face with a polka-dot kingsman. "Something here the press aren't meant to see."

"They've put it in the wrong street, then," the driver said, "haven't they?"

As Oliphant climbed from the gurney, Fraser came walking quickly toward him. "We've found her," Fraser said glumly.

"And seem to have attracted considerable publicity in the process. Perhaps a few less infantry would be in order?"

"It isn't a matter for levity, Mr. Oliphant. You'd best come with me."

"Is Betteredge here?"

"Haven't seen him. This way, please." Fraser led the way between a pair of barricades. A soldier curtly nodded them past.

Oliphant glimpsed a mustachioed gentleman in urgent conversation with two Metropolitans. "That's Halliday," he said, "chief of Criminal Anthropometry."

"Yes, sir," Fraser said. "They're all over this one. The Museum of Practical Geology has been broken into. The Royal Society is angry as a nest of hornets, and bloody Egremont will be in every first-edition, calling it a Luddite outrage. Our only bit of luck would seem to be that Dr. Mallory is well away in China."

"Mallory? Why is that?"

"The Land Leviathan. Mrs. Bartlett and her cohorts attempted to make away with the thing's skull."

They rounded one of the makeshift barriers, its coarse fabric stamped at intervals with the broad-arrow mark of the Army Ordnance Department.

A cab-horse lay on its side in a great pool of darkening blood. The cab, a common one-horse fly, was overturned nearby, its dull black-lacquered panels stitched with bullet-holes.

"She was with two men," Fraser said. "Three if you count a corpse they left behind in the Museum. The hack was driven by a Yankee exile called Russell, a bully-rock bruiser living in Seven Dials. The other man was Henry Dease of Liverpool, quite the accomplished cracksman. I'd our Henry in dock ten times, when I was on the force, but no more. They're laid out there, sir." He pointed. "Russell, the driver, evidently got into a shouting match with a real cabman, over who should give way. A Metropolitan on traffic-duty attempted to intervene, at which point Russell produced a pistol."

Oliphant was staring at the overturned cab.

"The traffic officer was unarmed, but a pair of Bow Street detectives happened to be passing. . . ."

"But this cab, Fraser . . ."

"That's the work of an Army-gurney, sir. The last of the temporary garrisons is just by the Holborn viaduct." He paused. "Dease had a Russian shotgun. . . ."

Oliphant shook his head in disbelief.

"Eight civilians taken to hospital," Fraser said. "One detective dead. But come along, sir—best we get this done with."

"What is the meaning of these canvas screens?"

"Criminal Anthropometry ordered them."

Oliphant felt as though he were moving through a dream, his limbs numb and without volition. He allowed himself to be led to where three canvas-draped bodies were arranged upon stretchers.

The face of Florence Bartlett was a hideous ruin.

"Vitriol," Fraser said. "A bullet shattered whatever container she employed."

Oliphant turned quickly away, retching into his handkerchief.

"Sorry, sir," Fraser said. "No point in you seeing the other two."

"Betteredge, Fraser—have you seen him?"

"No, sir. Here's the skull, sir, or what remains of it."

"The skull?"

Perhaps half-a-dozen massive fragments of petrified bone and ivory-tinted plaster were neatly arranged atop a varnished trestle-table. "There's a Mr. Reeks here, from the Museum, come to take it back," Fraser said. "Says it isn't as badly damaged as we might think. Would you like to sit down, sir? I could find you a folding-stool—"

"No. Why does there seem to be fully half of Criminal Anthro-pometry about, Fraser?"

"Well, sir, you're in a better position to determine that than I," Fraser said, lowering his voice, "though I've heard it said that Mr. Egremont and Lord Galton have recently discovered they've much in common."

"Lord Galton? The eugenics theorist?"

"Lord Darwin's cousin, that is. He's Anthropometry's man in the House of Lords. Has a deal of influence in the Royal Society." Fraser brought out his notebook. "You'd best see why I thought it urgent you come here, sir." He led Oliphant back around the ruin of the cab. Glancing about for possible observers, he passed Oliphant a fold of blue flimsy. "I took it from the Bartlett woman's reticule."

The note was undated, unsigned:

> That which you so persistently desire has been located, albeit in a most peculiar hiding-place. I am informed, by our mutual acquaintance of the Derby, Dr. Mallory, that it has been sealed up within the skull of his Land Leviathan. I would hope that you will consider this crucial intelligence a full repayment of all my debts to you. I am in some peril now, from recent political developments, and certainly I am observed by elements of Government; pray consider that in any further attempt to com-municate. I have done all that I can, I swear it.

The elegant hand, as familiar to Oliphant as it was to Fraser, was Lady Ada Byron's.

"The two of us alone have seen that," Fraser said.

Oliphant folded the paper in quarters before putting it away in his cigar-case. "And what exactly was it, Fraser, that was hidden in the skull?"

"I'll escort you back through the line, sir."

Reporters surged forward as Fraser and Oliphant emerged from the barricades. Fraser took Oliphant's arm and led him into a cluster of helmeted Metropolitans, some of whom he greeted casually by name. "To answer your question, Mr. Oliphant," Fraser said, the policemen walling off the shouting crowd behind blue serge and brass buttons, "I don't know. But we have it."

"You do? By whose authority?"

"None but my own lights," Fraser said. "Harris here, he found it in the cab, before Anthropometry arrived." Fraser very nearly smiled. "The boys on the force aren't too keen on Anthropometry. Bloody-minded amateurs, aye, Harris?"

"Aye, sir," said a Metropolitan with blond side-whiskers, "they are that."

"Where is it, then?" Oliphant asked.

"Here, sir." Harris produced a cheap black satchel. "Just as we found it, in this."

"Mr. Oliphant, sir, I think you'd best take that straight away," Fraser said.

"Indeed, Fraser, I agree. Tell the Special Branch chap in the fancy gurney that I won't be needing him. Thank you, Harris. Good evening." The policemen parted smoothly. Oliphant, satchel in hand, strode smartly out through the throng who jostled for a better view of the soldiers and the canvas screens.

"Pardon, guv, but couldyer spare a copper?"

Oliphant looked down into the squinting brown eyes of little Boots, every inch the crippled jockey. He was neither. Oliphant threw him a penny. Boots caught it adroitly, then edged forward on his cut-down crutch. He stank of damp fustian and smoked mackerel. "Trouble, guv. Becky'll tell yer." Boots wheeled about on his crutch and hobbled determinedly away, muttering as he went, a beggar intent upon finding a better pitch.

He was one of Oliphant's two most talented watchers.

The other, Becky Dean, kept pace beside Oliphant as he neared the corner of Chancery Lane. She was gotten up as a rather successful tart, brass-heeled and brazen.

"Where has Betteredge got to?" Oliphant asked, as if talking to himself.

"Taken," Becky Dean said. "Not three hours ago."

"Taken by whom?"

"Two men in a hack. They'd been following you. Betteredge got on to them, then set us to watching the watchers."

"I knew nothing of this."

"Day before yesterday, he came to us."

"And who were these men?"

"One's a greasy little ponce of a private detective. Velasco his name is. The other was Government by the look of him."

"He was taken in broad daylight? By force?"

"You know well enough how it's done," Becky Dean said.

In the soothing reek of his tobacconist's quiet stock-room, at the corner of Chancery Lane and Carey Street, Oliphant held the corner of the blue flimsy above the concise jet of a bronze cigar-lighter in the shape of a turbaned Turk.

He watched the paper reduce itself to delicate pinkish ash.

The satchel had contained a Ballester-Molina automatic revolver, a silvered-brass pocket-flask filled with some sickly, sweet-scented decoction, and a wooden case. This last was plainly the object in question, encrusted as it was with raw white plaster. It held a very large number of Engine-cards in the Napoleon gauge, cut from a novel material, milky and very smooth to the touch.

"The parcel," he said to Mr. Beadon, the tobacconist, "is to be held for me alone."

"Certainly, sir."

"My man Bligh to be the sole exception."

"As you wish, sir."

"If any inquiry at all should be made, Beadon, please send a boy 'round to advise Bligh."

"Our pleasure, sir."

"Thank you, Beadon. Could you possibly give me forty pounds cash, against my account?"

"*Forty*, sir?"

"Yes."

"Yes I could, sir. With pleasure, Mr. Oliphant." Mr. Beadon

took a ring of keys from his coat and went to unlock an admirably modern-looking safe.

"And a dozen prime *habanas*. And Beadon?"

"Yes, sir?"

"I think it might be a very good idea if you were to keep the parcel in your safe there."

"Of course, sir."

"I believe that the Lambs is nearby, Beadon, the dining-club?"

"Yes, sir. Holborn, sir. A short walk."

The year's first snow began to fall, as he made his way up Chancery Lane, a dry gritty stuff that seemed unlikely to adhere to the paving.

Boots and Becky Dean were nowhere to be seen, which could reliably be taken to mean that they were about their customarily invisible business.

You know well enough how it's done.

And didn't he? How many had been made to vanish, vanish utterly, in London alone? How could one sit among friends at pleasant little dinners, sipping Moselle, listening to kind and careless talk, yet carry in one's mind the burden of such knowledge?

He'd meant Collins to be the last, absolutely the last; now Betteredge had gone, and at the hands of another agency.

In the beginning, it had made so horribly elegant a sort of sense.

In the beginning, it had been his idea.

The Eye. He sensed it now—yes, surely, its all-seeing gaze full upon him as he nodded to the tasseled doorman and entered the marbled vestibule of the Lambs, Andrew Wakefield's dining club.

Brass letter-boxes, a telegraph-booth, an excess of French-polished veneer, all thoroughly modern. He glanced back, through glass doors, to the street. Opposite the Lambs, beyond twin streams of snow-dusted traffic, he glimpsed a solitary figure in a tall derby hat.

A page directed him to the grill-room, which was done in dark oak, with an enormous fireplace topped with a mantel of carved Italian stone. "Laurence Oliphant," he told the tightly jacketed head-waiter, "for Mr. Andrew Wakefield."

A look of unease crossed the man's face. "I'm sorry, sir, but he isn't—"

"Thank you," Oliphant said, "but I believe I see Mr. Wakefield."

With the head-waiter at his heels, Oliphant marched between the tables, diners turning as he passed.

"Andrew," he said, arriving at Wakefield's table, "how very fortunate to find you here."

Wakefield was dining alone. He seemed to experience a temporary difficulty in swallowing.

"Mr. Wakefield, sir," the head-waiter began.

"My friend will be joining me," Wakefield said. "Sit down, please. We're attracting attention."

"Thank you." Oliphant took a seat.

"Will you be dining, sir?" the head-waiter asked.

"No, thank you."

When they were alone, Wakefield sighed loudly. "Damn it all, Oliphant, but didn't I make my terms clear?"

"What exactly is it, Andrew, of which you've become so frightened?"

"It should be fairly obvious."

"Should it?"

"Lord Galton's in league with your bloody Mr. Egremont. He's the great patron of Criminal Anthropometry. Always has been. Their virtual founder. He's Charles Darwin's *cousin*, Oliphant, and he wields great influence in the House of Lords."

"Yes, and in the Royal Society, and in the Geographical as well. I'm thoroughly familiar with Lord Galton, Andrew. He espouses the systematic breeding of the human species."

Wakefield put down his knife and fork. "Criminal Anthropometry have effectively taken over the Bureau. For all intents and purposes, the Central Statistics Bureau is now under Egremont's control."

Oliphant watched as Wakefield's upper teeth began to worry at his lower-lip.

"I've just come from Fleet Street," Oliphant said. "The level of violence in this society"—and he drew the Ballester-Molina from within his coat—"or rather, I should say, the level of *unacknowledged* violence, has become remarkable, don't you think, Andrew?" He placed the revolver on the linen between them. "Take this pistol as an example. All too readily obtainable, I'm told. It is of Franco-Mexican manufacture, though the invention of Spaniards. Certain of its internal parts, I am informed, springs and whatnot, are actually British, available on the open market. It becomes rather difficult, then, to say where a weapon like this *comes from.* Emblematic of something in our current situation, don't you think?"

Wakefield had gone quite white.

"But I seem to have upset you, Andrew. I'm sorry."

"They'll *erase* us," Wakefield said. "We'll cease to exist. There'll be nothing left, nothing to prove either of us ever lived. Not a check-stub, not a mortgage in a City bank, nothing whatever."

"Exactly what I'm on about, Andrew."

"Don't take that moral tone with me, sir," Wakefield said. "*Your* lot began it, Oliphant—the disappearances, the files gone missing, the names expunged, numbers lost, histories edited to suit specific ends. . . . No, don't take that tone with *me.*"

Oliphant could think of nothing to say. He rose, leaving the pistol on the table-cloth, and left the grill-room without looking back.

"Pardon me," he said, in the marbled vestibule, to a burgundy-jacketed bellman who was sifting cigar-ends from a sand-filled marble urn, "but could you please direct me to the office of the club steward?"

"You bet," the bellman said, or some similar bit of American dialect, and led Oliphant smartly away, down a corridor lined with mirrors and rubber-plants.

Fifty-five minutes later, having toured the club's premises at some length, having been shown a photographic album of the Lambs' annual "gambols," having applied for membership, and having paid a not inconsiderable initiation fee, non-refundable, via his own number in the National Credit, Oliphant shook hands with the pomaded steward, gave the man a pound-note, and requested that he be let out by the club's most obscure trade-entrance.

This proved to be a scullery-door which opened on exactly the sort of dank and narrow passage he had hoped for.

Within a quarter-of-an-hour, he stood at the public bar of a crowded house in Bedford Road, reviewing the text of the tele-gram that one Sybil Gerard had once dispatched to Mr. Charles Egremont, M.P., of Belgravia.

"Lost both me boys o' sickness in the Crimea, squire, an' innit allus the tele-gram comes—innit?"

Oliphant folded the sheet of foolscap into his cigar-case. He watched his dim reflection in the polished zinc of the bar. He looked at his empty tumbler. He looked up at the woman, a raddled harridan in rags gone a color that had no name, her cheeks roseate with gin-blossoms under a patina of grime.

"No," he said, "that tragedy is not mine."

"Me Roger it was," she said, " 'n' Tommy-lad too. An' not a rag come 'ome, squire—not a bloody rag. . . ."

He handed her a coin. She thanked him, mumbling, and retreated.

He seemed to have thoroughly slipped the traces for the mo-ment. He was entirely alone. It was time to find a cab.

In the dim, high hollow of the great station a thousand voices seemed to mingle, the constituent elements of language reduced to the aural equivalent of fog, homogeneous and impenetrable.

Oliphant went about his business below at a measured and deliberate pace, purchasing a first-class railway ticket to Dover, reserved, for the ten o'clock evening-express. The ticket-clerk seated Oliphant's National Credit plate in the machine and cranked hard on the lever.

"There you are, sir. Reserved in your name."

Thanking the clerk, Oliphant made his way to a second wicket, where he again produced his plate. "I wish to book a cabinette on the morning mail-boat to Ostend." Apparently as an after-thought, as he was putting the boat-tickets and his National Credit plate into his note-case, he requested a second-class ticket on the midnight boat to Calais.

"Would that be this evening, sir?"

"Yes."

"That would be the *Bessemer*, sir. On National Credit, sir?"

Oliphant paid for the ticket to Calais with pound-notes from Mr. Beadon's safe.

Ten till nine, by his father's gold hunter.

At nine o'clock he boarded a departing train at the last possible moment, paying the first-class fare to Dover directly to the conductor.

The swinging-saloon ship *Bessemer*, her twin turtle-decks awash with Dover spray, steamed for Calais sharp on the midnight. Oliphant, having visited the purser with his second-class ticket and his pound-notes, was seated in a brocade armchair in the saloon cabin, sipping mediocre brandy and taking the measure of his fellow passengers. They were, he was pleased to note, a thoroughly unremarkable lot.

He disliked swinging-saloons, finding the Engine-controlled movements of the cabin, intended to compensate for the vessel's pitch and roll, somehow more unsettling than the ordinary mo-tion of a ship at sea. In addition, the cabin itself was effectively windowless. Swung on gimbals in a central well, the cabin was mounted so deeply in the hull that its windows, such as they were, were located high up along the walls, well above one's line of sight. All in all, as a remedy for mal-de-mer, Oliphant thought it exces-sive. The public, however, were apparently fascinated by the novel employment of a small Engine, somewhat on the order of a gunnery Engine, whose sole task consisted of maintaining as near a level footing in the cabin as was deemed possible. This was accomplished via something the press referred to, in clacker's argot, as "back-feed." Still, with twin paddles fore and aft, the *Bessemer* customarily performed the distance of twenty-one miles between Dover and Calais in an hour and thirty minutes.

He would rather have been above-decks, now, facing into the wind; able then, perhaps, to imagine himself steaming toward some grander, more accessible goal. But the promenade of a swinging-saloon offered no bulwark, only an iron railing, and the Channel wind was damp and cold. And he had, he reminded himself, only the one goal now, and it, in all likelihood, a fool's errand.

Still: Sybil Gerard. He had decided, upon reading the telegram to Egremont, against having her number spun. He had expected it might attract unwanted attention; with Criminal Anthropometry holding sway at Central Statistics, of course, he had been proven correct. And he rather suspected that Sybil Gerard's file might no longer exist.

Walter Gerard of Manchester, sworn enemy of progress, agitator for the rights of man. Hanged. And if Walter Gerard had had a daughter, what might have become of her? And if she had been ruined, as she claimed to have been, by Charles Egremont?

Oliphant's back began to ache. Beneath the chair's stiff brocade, Jacquard-woven with repeated images of the *Bessemer*, the horsehair stuffing held a chill.

But if nothing else, he reminded himself, he at least had temporarily escaped the soft black pit of Dr. McNeile's patent Swiss bath-tub.

Putting his brandy aside unfinished, he nodded then, and napped.

And dreamed, perhaps, of the Eye.

The *Bessemer* docked at Calais at half past one.

*   *   *

Monsieur Lucien Arslau's apartments were in Passy. At noon, Oliphant presented his card to the concierge, who conveyed it via pneumatic tube to Monsieur Arslau's establishment. Almost immediately, the whistle attached to a nickeled speaking-tube peeped twice; the concierge bent his ear to the funnel; Oliphant made out faint tones of shouted French.

The concierge showed Oliphant to the lift.

He was admitted, on the fifth floor, by a liveried man-servant wearing an ornate Corsican stiletto through a pleated sash of gros de Naples. The young man managed to bow without taking his eyes from Oliphant. Monsieur Arslau regretted, the servant said, that he was unable at the moment to receive Monsieur Oliphant; in the meantime, would Monsieur Oliphant care for any sort of refreshment?

Oliphant declared that he would very much appreciate an opportunity to bathe. He would also find a pot of coffee most agreeable.

He was led through a broad drawing-room, rich in satin and ormolu, buhl cabinets, bronzes, statuettes, and porcelain, where the lizard-eyed Emperor and his dainty Empress, the former Miss Howard, gazed from twin portraits in oil. And then through a morning-room hung with proof-engravings. A graceful curve of stairway mounted from an octagonal anteroom.

Some two hours later, having bathed in a marble-rimmed tub of gratifying solidity, having taken strong French coffee and lunched upon cutlets à la Maintenon, and wearing borrowed linen with far more starch than he cared for, he was ushered into the study of Monsieur Arslau.

"Mr. Oliphant, sir," Arslau said, in his excellent English, "it is a great pleasure. I regret not having been able to see you earlier, but . . ." He gestured toward a broad mahogany desk littered with files and papers. From behind a closed door came the steady clatter of a telegraph. On one wall hung a framed engraving of the Great Napoleon, its mighty gear-towers rising behind a grid-work of plate-glass and iron.

"Not at all, Lucien. I'm grateful to have had the time to take advantage of your hospitality. Your chef has an extraordinary way with mutton; a sublimated meat that could scarcely have grown on any mundane sheep."

Arslau smiled. Nearly Oliphant's height, broader in the shoulders, he was some forty years of age and wore his greying beard in the Imperial fashion. His cravat was embroidered with small golden bees. "I've had your letter, of course." He returned to his desk and settled himself in a high-backed chair upholstered in dark-green leather. Oliphant took a seat in an armchair opposite.

"I must admit my curiosity, Laurence, as to what it is you are currently about." Arslau made a steeple of his fingers and peered over them, raising his eyebrows. "The nature of your request would hardly seem to warrant the precautions you deem necessary. . . ."

"On the contrary, Lucien, you must know that I would not presume in this way upon our acquaintance for any but the most pressing of reasons."

"But no, my friend," Arslau said, with a dismissive little wave of his hands, "you have asked the merest of favors. Among colleagues, men such as ourselves, it is nothing. I am simply curious; it is one of my many vices. You convey to me a letter by Imperial diplomatic pouch—no mean feat in itself, for an Englishman, though I know that you are familiar with our friend Bayard. Your letter requires my help in locating a certain English adventuress, no more. You believe she may be resident in France. Yet you stress the need for very great secrecy; you warn me particularly against communicating with you either by telegraph or by the regular post. You instruct me to await your arrival. What am I to make of this? Have you succumbed at last to the wiles of some woman?"

"Alas, I have not."

"Given the current model of English womanhood, my friend, I find that entirely understandable. Far too many of your gentlewomen aspire to be elevated to the level of masculine intellectuality—superior to crinoline, superior to pearl-powder, above taking the pains to be pretty, above making themselves agreeable in any way! What a dreary, utilitarian, entirely *ugly* life an Englishman shall eventually lead, if this trend continues! So why then, I ask, have you crossed the Channel to find an *English* adventuress? Not that we haven't our share of them. They're rather thick upon the ground, actually, not to mention the origin"—Arslau smiled—"of our own Empress."

"You yourself have never married, Lucien," Oliphant remarked, attempting to deflect Arslau from his purpose.

"But look at matrimony! Who is to say which shall be the one judicious selection out of the nine hundred and ninety-nine mistakes? Which is to be the one eel out of the barrel of snakes? The girl on the kerbstone may be the one woman out of every female creature in this universe capable of making me a happy man, my friend, yet I pass her by, and bespatter her with the mud from my wheels, in my utter ignorance!" Arslau laughed. "No, I have not married, and your mission is a political one."

"Of course."

"Things are not well with Britain. I don't need my British sources to tell me that, Oliphant. The papers suffice. The death of Byron . . ."

"Great Britain's political direction, Lucien—indeed, her ultimate stability as a nation—may even now be at stake. I need not remind you of the paramount importance of our two nations' continued mutual recognition and support."

"And the matter of this Miss Gerard, Oliphant? Shall I take it you suggest she is somehow pivotal in the situation?"

Oliphant took out his cigar-case and selected one of Beadon's *habanas*. His fingers brushed the folded text of Sybil Gerard's telegram. He closed the case. "Do you mind if I smoke?"

"Please do."

"Thank you. The matters which hinge upon Sybil Gerard are entirely British, entirely domestic. They may stand, ultimately, to affect France, but in a most indirect way." Oliphant clipped and pierced his cigar.

"Are you entirely sure of that?"

"I am."

"I am not." Arslau rose to bring Oliphant a copper ash-tray

atop a walnut stand. He returned to his desk but remained standing. "What do you know of the Jacquardine Society?"

"They are the approximate equivalent of our Steam Intellect Society, are they not?"

"Yes and no. There is another, a secret society, within the Jacquardines. They style themselves Les Fils de Vaucanson. Certain of them are anarchists, others in league with the Marianne, others with the Universal Fraternity, others with any sort of rabble. Class-war conspirators, you understand? Others are simply criminals. But you know this, Laurence."

Oliphant took a lucifer from a box emblazoned with a stippled image of the *Bessemer*, and struck it. He lit his cigar.

"You tell me that the woman you know as Sybil Gerard is of no concern to France," Arslau said.

"You think otherwise?"

"Perhaps. Tell me what you know of our difficulties with the Great Napoleon."

"Very little. Wakefield of Central Statistics mentioned it to me. The Engine is no longer functioning accurately?"

"*Ordinateurs*, thank the good God, are not my specialty. The Napoleon performs with its accustomed speed and accuracy in most instances, I am informed, but an outré element of inconstancy presently haunts the machine's higher functions. . . ." Arslau sighed. "Those higher functions being deemed a matter of considerable national pride, I have myself been forced to peruse reams of the most abstruse technical prose in the Empire. To no ultimate avail, it now seems, as we've had the culprit in hand."

"The culprit?"

"An avowed member of Les Fils de Vaucanson. His name is of no importance. He was arrested in Lyons in connection with an ordinary case of civil fraud involving a municipal *ordinateur.* Elements of his subsequent confession brought him to the attention of the Commission of Special Services, and hence to ours. During interrogation, he revealed his responsibility for the current lamentable state of our Great Napoleon."

"He confessed to *le sabotage*, then?"

"No. He would not confess to that. He refused, until the end. With regard to the Napoleon, he would admit only to having run a certain sequence of punch-cards, a mathematical formula."

Oliphant watched the smoke from his cigar spiral toward the high ceiling's ornate plaster rosette.

"The formula came from London," Arslau continued. "He obtained it from an Englishwoman. Her name was Sybil Gerard."

"Have you attempted analysis of this formula?"

"No. It was stolen, our Jacquardine claimed, spirited away by a woman he knew as Flora Bartelle, apparently an American."

"I see."

"Then tell me what you see, my friend, for I myself am very much in the dark."

The Eye. All-seeing, the sublime weight of its perception pressing in upon him from every direction.

Oliphant hesitated. Ash from his cigar fell unnoticed to Arslau's rich carpet. "I have yet to meet Sybil Gerard," he said, "but I may be able to offer you information regarding this formula you've mentioned. It may even be possible to obtain a copy. I can promise nothing, however, until I myself am allowed to interview the lady in question, privately and at some length."

Arslau fell silent. He seemed to look through Oliphant. At last he nodded. "We can arrange that."

"She is not, I take it, in custody?"

"Let us say that we are aware of her movements."

"You allow her apparent freedom, yet observe her closely?"

"Precisely that. If we take her now, and she reveals nothing, the trail goes cold."

"As ever, Arslau, your technique is impeccable. And when might it be arranged for me to meet with her?"

The Eye, the pressure, the pounding of his heart.

"This evening, if you so desire," said Monsieur Arslau of the Police des Châteaux, adjusting his gold-embroidered cravat.

*   *   *

The walls of the Café de l'Univers were hung with paintings, etched mirrors, and enamel plaques advertising the ubiquitous product of Pernod Fils. The pictures, if one could call them that, were either grotesque daubs, seemingly executed in a messy imitation of Engine-stippling, or queer geometric formulations suggesting the restless motion of kinotrope-bits. In some cases, Oliphant supposed, the painters themselves were present—or such he took them to be, these long-haired fellows in velvet caps, their corduroy trousers smeared with pigment and tobacco-ash. But the majority of the clientele—according to his companion, one Jean Beraud—consisted of *kinotropistes.* These gentlemen of the Latin Quarter sat and drank with their black-clad *grisettes* at the round marble tables, or held forth on theoretical matters before small groups of their peers.

Beraud, in an unseasonable boater and a brown suit of intensely Gallic cut, was one of Arslau's *mouchards,* a professional informer who referred to the kinotropists as members of *"le milieu."* He was fresh and rosy as a young pig, he drank Vittel and peppermint, and Oliphant had taken an immediate dislike to him. The kinotropists seemed to favor the absinthe of Pernod Fils; Oliphant, sipping a glass of red wine, watched the ritual of glass and water-decanter, of sugar-lump and trowel-shaped spoon.

"Absinthe is the bed of tuberculosis," Beraud said.

"Why do you suppose that Madame Tournachon would choose to appear tonight in this café, Beraud?"

The *mouchard* shrugged. "She is a familiar of *le milieu,* monsieur. She goes to Madelon's, also to Batiffol's, but it is here, in l'Univers, that she most nearly finds companionship."

"And why is that, do you think?"

"Because she was Gautier's mistress, of course. He was a kind of prince here, monsieur, it must be understood. Her relationship with Gautier has necessarily limited her contacts with ordinary society. He taught her French, or such French as she has."

"What sort of woman, exactly, do you take her to be?"

Beraud smirked. "She is perhaps attractive, but cold. Unsympathetic. In the manner of Englishwomen, you understand."

"When she arrives, Beraud—if she arrives, I should say—you are to take your leave immediately."

Beraud raised his eyebrows. "On the contrary, monsieur—"

"You are to go, Beraud. Take your leave." A measured pause. "Vanish."

The sharply padded shoulders of Beraud's brown suit rose at the word.

"You will instruct the cab to wait, and the stenographer as well. The stenographer, Beraud—his English is adequate? My friend—my very good friend, Monsieur Arslau—has assured me that this is the case. . . ."

"Entirely adequate, yes! And monsieur"—getting up so quickly that he nearly overturned his bentwood chair—"it is she. . . ."

The woman now entering l'Univers might easily have been mistaken for a modish *Parisienne* of more than common means. Slender and blond, she wore a somber merino crinoline with matching cloak and bonnet, narrowly trimmed in mink.

As Beraud continued his hasty retreat into the depths of the café, Oliphant rose. Her eyes, very alert, very blue, met his. He approached her, hat in hand, and bowed. "Forgive me," he said in English. "We have not been introduced, but I must speak with you regarding a matter of great urgency."

Recognition dawned in the wide blue eyes, and fear.

"Sir, you mistake me for another."

"You are Sybil Gerard."

Her lower-lip was trembling now, and Oliphant experienced an abrupt, powerful, and entirely unexpected sympathy. "I am Laurence Oliphant, Miss Gerard. You are presently in terrible danger. I wish to help you."

"That is not my name, sir. Pray let me pass. My friends are waiting."

"I know that Egremont betrayed you. I understand the nature of his betrayal."

She started at the name, Oliphant in terror of her swooning on the spot, but then she gave a little shudder and seemed to study him quietly for a moment. "I saw you in Grand's, that night," she said. "You were in the smoker with Houston and . . . Mick. You had a gammy arm, up in a sling."

"Please," he said, "join me."

Seated opposite her at his table, Oliphant listened as she ordered *absinthe de vidangeur* in quite passable French.

"Do you know Lamartine, the singer?" she asked.

"I'm sorry, no."

"He invented it, 'scavenger's absinthe.' I can't drink it otherwise."

The waiter arrived with the drink, a mixture of absinthe and red wine.

"Theo taught me to order it," she said, "before he . . . went away." She drank, the wine red against her painted lips. "I know you've come to take me back. Don't gull me otherwise. I know a copper when I meet one."

"I have no desire to see you return to England, Miss Gerard—"

"Tournachon. I'm Sybil Tournachon. French by marriage."

"Your husband is here in Paris?"

"No," she said, lifting an oval locket of cut-steel on its black ribbon. She snapped it open, displaying a daguerreotyped miniature of a handsome young man. "Aristide. He fell at Philadelphia, in the great inferno. He volunteered, to fight on the Union side. He was real, you know; I mean, he actually existed, and wasn't just one of them the clackers make up. . . ." She gazed at the little image with a look of mingled longing and sadness, though Oliphant understood that she had never in her life set eyes upon Aristide Tournachon.

"It was a marriage of convenience, I take it."

"Yes. And you've come to take me back."

"Not at all, Miss . . . Tournachon."

"I don't believe you."

"You must. A great deal depends upon it, not least your own safety. Since you departed London, Charles Egremont has become a very powerful, a very dangerous man. As dangerous to the well-being of Great Britain as he is no doubt dangerous to you."

"Charles? Dangerous?" She seemed suddenly on the verge of laughter. "You're gulling me."

"I need your help. Desperately. As desperately as you need mine."

"Do I, then?"

"Egremont has powerful resources at his command, branches of Government easily capable of reaching you here."

"You mean the Specials, and that lot?"

"More to the point, I must inform you that your activities are even now monitored by at least one secret agency of Imperial France. . . ."

"Because Theophile chose to help me?"

"Indeed, that seems to be the case. . . ."

She drank off the last of the vile-looking concoction in her glass. "Dear Theophile. What a lovely, silly sort of cove he was. Always in his scarlet waistcoat, and madly clever at clacking. I gave him Mick's set of fancy cards, and he was terribly kind to me then. Spun me up a marriage-license and a French citizen-number rat-tat-tat. Then, one afternoon, I was to meet him here . . ."

"Yes?"

"He never came." She lowered her eyes. "He used to boast of having a 'gambling modus.' They all do, but he talked as if he meant it. Someone might have believed him. It was foolish of him. . . ."

"Did he ever speak with you about his interest in the Engine known as the Great Napoleon?"

"Their monster, you mean? Your Paris clacker speaks of little else, sir! They're mad for the thing!"

"The French authorities believe that Theophile Gautier damaged the Great Napoleon with Radley's cards."

"Is he dead, then, Theo?"

Oliphant hesitated. "Alas, I believe so, yes."

"That's so vicious bloody cruel," she said, "to spirit a man away like a rabbit in a conjuring trick, and leave his loved-ones ever to wonder, and worry, and never rest! It's *vile.*"

Oliphant found that he could not meet her eyes.

"There's a deal of that about in this Paris, there is," she said. "The things I've heard their clackers jest about . . . And London, they say, is no better, really, to them as know. Do you know they say the Rads murdered Wellington? They say the sappers, the sand-hogs, hand-in-glove with the Rads, cut a tunnel beneath that restaurant, and the master sapper himself tamped the powder and set the fuses. . . . Then the Rads lay the blame on men like . . ."

"Your father. Yes. I know."

"And knowing that, you'd ask me to trust *you*?" There was defiance in her eyes, and perhaps a pride long-buried.

"Knowing that Charles Egremont betrayed your father, Walter Gerard, unto his destruction; that he betrayed you as well, bringing about your ruin in the eyes of society; yes, I must ask that you trust me. In exchange, I offer you the complete, utter, and virtually instantaneous negation of your betrayer's political career."

She lowered her eyes again, and seemed to consider. "Could you do that, really?" she asked.

"Your testament alone will serve. I shall be merely the instrument of its delivery."

"No," she said at last, "if I were to denounce him publicly, then I would expose myself as well. Charles isn't the only one I need to fear, as you yourself have said. Remember, I was there that night, in Grand's; I know how long an arm revenge can have."

"I've not suggested denouncing him publicly. Blackmail will suffice."

Now her eyes were far away, as if she walked the distant pavements of memory. "They were so close, Charles and my father, or so it seemed. . . . Perhaps if things had taken a different turn . . ."

"Egremont lives daily with that betrayal. It is the crucial grain of constant irritation around which his depraved politics have been allowed to form. Your telegram galvanized his guilt—his terror of those early Luddite sympathies being revealed. Now he would tame the beast, make political terror his constant ally. But you and I stand in his way."

The blue eyes were strangely calm. "I find I wish to believe you, Mr. Oliphant."

"I will keep you safe," Oliphant said, quite startled by his own intensity. "So long as you choose to remain in France, you shall do so under the protection of powerful friends, colleagues of mine, agents of the Imperial court. A cab awaits us, and a stenographer, to take down the details of your testimony."

With a tortured, flatulent wheeze of compressed air, a small panmelodium was activated at the rear of the café. Oliphant, turning, caught the eye of the *mouchard* Beraud, who was smoking a Dutch clay pipe amid a cluster of chattering *kinotropistes*.

"Madame Tournachon," Oliphant said, rising, "may I offer you my arm?"

"It's healed, has it?" She rose in a rustle of crinoline.

"Entirely," Oliphant said, remembering the lightning-stroke of the samurai's sword, in Edo, amid the shadows. He had been attempting to hold the fellow off with a riding-crop.

As the Engine-driven music of the grand panmelodium brought the *grisettes* from their chairs, she took his arm.

A girl burst in, then, from the street, her naked breasts daubed with green. About her waist were strung angular constructs of copper-foil, like the leaves of a date-palm approximated by a kinotrope. She was followed by two boys in a similar lack of attire, and Oliphant felt utterly lost.

"Come then," Sybil said, "don't you know they're art students, and been to a *bal*? It's Montmartre, you know, and the art students, they've such a mad and lovely time."

Oliphant had entertained the gallant notion of personally delivering to Charles Egremont a transcript of Sybil Gerard's testimony. But upon his return to England, those symptoms of advanced syphilis which Dr. McNeile had incorrectly diagnosed as railway-spine temporarily overcame him. Disguised as a commercial traveler from M. Arslau's native Alsace, Oliphant went to ground in Brighton's hydropathic spa, to take the waters and dispatch a number of telegrams.

*   *   *

Mr. Mori Arinori arrives in Belgravia at a quarter past four, driving a new-model *Zephyr* gurney leased from a commercial garage in Camden Town, just as Charles Egremont is departing for Parliament and a most important speech.

Egremont's body-guard, on assignment from the Central Statistics Bureau's Department of Criminal Anthropometry, a machine-carbine slung beneath his coat, watches as Mori descends from the *Zephyr*, a diminutive figure in evening-clothes.

Mori marches straight across the new-fallen snow, his boots leaving perfect prints upon the black macadam.

"For you, sir," Mori says and bows, handing Egremont the stout manila envelope. "Very good day to you, sir." Donning round goggles with an elasticated band, Mori returns to his *Zephyr*.

"What an extraordinary little personage," Egremont says, looking down at the envelope. "One hasn't seen a Chinaman, got up like that . . ."

Recede.

Reiterate.

Rise above these black patterns of wheel-tracks,

These snow-swept streets,

Into the great map of London,

forgetting

MODUS

The Images Tabled

The Language of Signs

THE CIRCULAR ARRANGEMENT of the axes of the Difference Engine 'round large central wheels led to the most extended prospects. The whole of arithmetic now appeared within the grasp of mechanism. A vague glimpse even of an Analytical Engine opened out, and I pursued with enthusiasm the shadowy vision.

The drawings and the experiments were of the most costly kind. Draftsmen of the highest order were engaged, to economize the labor of my own head; whilst skilled workmen executed the experimental machinery.

In order to carry out my pursuits successfully, I had purchased a house with about a quarter of an acre of ground, in a very quiet locality in London. My coach-house was converted into a forge and foundry, whilst my stables were transformed into a workshop. I built other extensive workshops myself, and had a fire-proof building for my drawings and draftsmen.

The complicated relations amongst the various parts of the machinery would have baffled the most tenacious memory. I overcame that difficulty by improving and extending a language of signs, the Mechanical Notation, which in 1826 I had explained in a paper printed in the *Philosophic Transactions of the Royal Society*. By such means I succeeded in mastering a train of investigation so vast in extent that no length of years could otherwise have enabled me to control it. By the aid of the language of signs, the Engine became a reality.

—LORD CHARLES BABBAGE,
Passages in the Life of a Philosopher, 1864.

Letters from Our Readers

[*From* The Mechanics Magazine, *1830*.]

To judge by readers' letters we receive, certain among our public would doubt that political matters come within the province of this journal. But the interests of science and manufacturing are inextricably mixed with a nation's political philosophy. How then can we be silent?

We look with delight for a grand new age for Science, as well as to every other PRODUCTIVE interest of this country, from the election to Parliament of a man of Mr. Babbage's eminence in the scientific world, his tried independence of spirit, his very searching and business-like habits.

Therefore we say forthrightly to every elector of Finsbury who is a reader of this journal—go and vote for Mr. Babbage. If you are an inventor, whom the ubiquitous and oppressive TAX ON PATENTS shuts out from the field of fair competition, and desire to see that TAX replaced by a wise and deliberate system of PUBLIC SUBSIDIES—go and vote for Mr. Babbage. If you are a manufacturer, harassed and obstructed in your operations by the fiscal stupidities of the present Government—if you would see British industry become as free as the air you breathe—go and vote for Mr. Babbage. If you are a mechanic, and depend for your daily bread on a constant and steady demand for the products of your skill, and are aware of the influence of free trade on your fortunes—go and vote for Mr. Babbage. If you are a devotee of Science and Progress—principle and practice united as bone and sinew—then meet us today on Islington Green, and VOTE FOR MR. BABBAGE!

In the Time of Troubles

The results of the general election of 1830 made public feeling obvious. Byron and his Radicals had captured the tone of the day, and the Whig Party were an utter shambles. Lord Wellington's Tories, however, resenting the threat to aristocratic privilege posed by Radical proposals of "merit-lordship," took a hard line. The Commons procrastinated on the Radical Reform Bill, and on 8 October the Lords threw it out. The King refused to create new Radical peers who might force the Bill through; on the contrary, the Fitzclarences were ennobled instead, leading Byron to comment bitterly: "How much better it is to be a *Royal bastard* than a *philosopher* in England at present. But a mighty change is at hand."

Popular pressure mounted swiftly. In Birmingham, Liverpool, and Manchester, the working-class, inspired by Babbage's ideals of union ownership and mutual co-operatives, took to the streets in massive torchlight parades. The Industrial Radical Party, disdaining violence, called for moral suasion and a peaceful mass-campaign for redress of legitimate grievances. But the Government remained stubborn, and events took an ugly turn. In a rising crescendo of random outrage, violent rural "Swing bands" and proletarian Luddites attacked aristocratic homes and capitalist factories alike. Mobs in London shattered the windows in the house of the Duke of Wellington and other Tory peers, and, cobblestones in hand, lay sullenly in wait for the passing carriages of the elite. The Anglican bishops, who had voted against Reform in the Lords, were burned in effigy. Ultra-radical conspirators, fired to frenzy by the furious polemics of the atheist P. B. Shelley, attacked and looted Establishment churches.

On 12 December Lord Byron introduced a new Reform Bill, more radical yet, proposing outright disfranchisement of the hereditary British aristocracy, including himself. This was more than the Tories could bear, and Wellington involved himself in covert planning for a military coup.

The crisis had polarized the nation. At this juncture, the middle-classes, terrified of the prospect of anarchy, made their own move and came down on the side of the Radicals. A tax-strike was declared, to force Wellington from office; there was a deliberate run on the banks, in which merchants demanded and hoarded gold specie, bringing the national economy to a grinding halt.

In Bristol, after three days of major riots, Wellington ordered the Army to put down "Jacobinism" by any means necessary. In the resulting massacre three hundred people, including three prominent Radical M.P.'s, lost their lives. When the news of the massacre reached him, a furious Byron, now calling himself "Citizen Byron," and appearing without coat or necktie at a London rally, called for a general strike. This rally was also attacked by Tory cavalry, with bloody results, but Byron eluded capture. Two days later the nation was under martial-law.

In future, the Duke of Wellington would turn his considerable military genius against his own countrymen. The first uprisings against the Tory Regime—as it must now be called—were swiftly and efficiently put down, while garrison troops ruled all major cities. The Army remained loyal to the victor of Waterloo, and the aristocracy, to their discredit, also threw in their lot with the Duke.

But the Radical Party elite had escaped apprehension, abetted by a well-organized covert network of Party faithful. By the spring of '31, any hope of a swift military solution was over. Mass hangings and deportations were answered by sullen resistance and vicious guerrilla reprisals. The Regime had destroyed any vestige of popular support, and England was in the throes of class-war.

—*The Time of Troubles: A Popular History, 1912,*
BY W. E. PRATCHETT, PH.D., F.R.S.

Somber Melodies of the Automatic Organs

[*This private letter of July 1855 conveys Benjamin Disraeli's eye-witness impressions of the funeral of Lord Byron. The text derives from a tape-spool emitted by a Colt & Maxwell Typing Engine. The addressee is unknown.*]

Lady Annabella Byron entered on the arm of her daughter, looking very frail. She seemed a little dazed. Both mother and daughter were very worn and white, at the end of their forces. Then a funeral march was played—very fine—the panmelodium sounding splendid amid the somber melodies of the automatic organs.

Then the processions arrived. The Speaker first, preceded by heralds with white staves but in mourning-dress. The Speaker was quite splendid. He walked slowly and firmly, very impassive and dignified; an almost Egyptianate face. The mace was carried before him, and he wore a gold-laced gown, very fine. Then the Ministers; Colonial Secretary, very dapper indeed. Viceroy of India looks quite recovered from his malaria. Chairman of the Commission on Free Trade looked the wickedest of the human race, as if writhing under a load of disreputable guilt.

Then the House of Lords. The Lord Chancellor absolutely grotesque, and made more so by the tremendous figure of the Sergeant-at-Arms with a silver chain and large, white silk bows on his shoulders for mourning. Lord Babbage, pale and upright, most dignified. Young Lord Huxley, lean, light on his feet, very splendid. Lord Scowcroft, the shiftiest person I ever saw, in threadbare clothes like a sexton.

The coffin came solemnly along, the bearers holding feebly onto it. The Prince Consort Albert foremost among them, with the oddest gnawing look—duty, dignity, and fear. He was kept waiting, I hear, just in the doorway, and muttered in German about the Stink.

When the coffin entered, the widowed Iron Lady looked a thousand years old.

The Widowed Iron Lady

So now the world falls into the hands of the little men, the hypocrites and clerks.

Look at them. They have not the mettle for the great work. They will botch it.

Oh, even now I could set it all to rights, if only the fools would listen to sense, but I could never speak as you did, and they do not listen to women. You were their Great Orator, a puffed and painted mountebank, without one real idea in your head—no gift for logic, nothing but your posturing wickedness, and yet they listened to you; oh, how they did listen. You wrote your silly books of verse, you praised Satan and Cain and adultery, and every kind of wicked foolishness, and the fools could not get enough of it. They knocked down the bookshop doors. And women threw themselves at your feet, armies of them. I never did. But then, you married me.

I was innocent then. From the days of our courtship, some moral instinct in me revolted at your sly teasing, your hateful double-entendres and insinuations, but I did see qualities of promise in you, and ignored my doubts. How swiftly you revived them, as my husband.

You cruelly used my innocence; you made me a party to sodomy before I even knew the nature of that sin; before I learned the hidden words for the unspeakable. *Pederastia, manustupration, fellatio*—you were so steeped in unnatural vice that you could spare not even the marriage-bed. You polluted me, even as you had polluted your own hare-brained fool of a sister.

If society had learned the tenth of what I knew, you would have been driven from England like a leper. Back to Greece, back to Turkey and your catamites.

How easily, then, might I have ruined you, and very nearly did, to spite you, for it vexed me sorely that you did not know, or care to know, the depth of my conviction. I sought refuge in my mathematics, then, and kept to silence, wishing still to be a good wife in the eyes of society, for I had uses to which to put you, and great work to do, and no means with which to do it, save through my husband. For I had glimpsed the true path toward the greatest good for the greatest number, a good so great it made a trifle of my own humble wishes.

Charles taught it me. Decent, brilliant, unworldly Charles, your opposite in every way; so full of great plans, and the pure light of mathematical science, but so utterly impolitic, so entirely unable to suffer fools gladly. He had the gifts of a Newton, but he could not *persuade*.

I brought you together. At first you hated him, and mocked him behind his back, and me as well, for showing you a truth beyond your comprehension. I persisted; begged you to think of honor, of service, of your own glory, of the future of the child in my womb, Ada, that strange child. (Poor Ada, she does not look well, she has too much of you in her.)

But you cursed me for a cold-hearted shrew and retired in a drunken temper. For the sake of that greater good, I painted a smile on my face and descended open-eyed into the very Pit. How it pained me, that vile greasy probing and animal nastiness; but I let you do as you liked, and forgave you for it, and petted and kissed you for it, as if I liked it. And you wept like a child, and were grateful, and talked of love undying and united souls, until you tired of that sort of talk. And then, to hurt me, you told me dreadful, shocking things, to disgust me and frighten me away, but I would no longer allow you to frighten me; I was steeled to anything, that night. So I forgave you, forgave and forgave, until at last you could find no further confession even in the foulest dregs of your soul, and at last you had no pretense left, nothing left to say.

I imagine that after that night you became frightened of me, perhaps, a little frightened, and that did you a great deal of good, I think. It never hurt me so again, after that night. I taught myself to play all your "pretty little games," and to win them. That was the price I paid, to put your beast in harness.

If there is a Judge of Men in another world, though I no longer believe that, no, not in my heart, and yet at times, evil times, times like these—I fancy I sense a never-closing, all-embracing Eye, and feel the awful pressure of its dreadful comprehension. And if there be a Judge, milord husband, then do not think to gull him. No, do not boast of your magnificent sins and demand damnation—for how little you knew, over the years. You, the greatest Minister of the greatest Empire in history—you flinched, you were feeble, you dodged every consequence—

Are these tears?

We should not have killed so many. . . .

We, I say, but it was I, I who sacrificed my virtue, my faith, my salvation, all burnt to black ashes on the altar of your ambition. For all your bold trumpery talk of Corsairs and Bonaparte, you had no iron in you; you wept even at the thought of hanging miserable Luddites, and could not bear to chain away vicious mad Shelley, until I forced your hand. And when reports came from our bureaux, hinting, requesting, then demanding the right to eliminate the enemies of England, it was I who read them, I who covertly weighed lives in the balance, and I who signed your name, while you ate and drank and joked with those men you called your friends.

And now these fools who bury you will brush me aside as if I were nothing, had accomplished nothing, simply because you are gone. You, their sounding-brass, their idol of paint and dyed hair. The truth, the dreadful slime-entangled roots of history, vanish now without trace. The truth is buried with your gilt sarcophagus.

I must stop thinking in this manner. I am weeping. They think me old and foolish. Was not every civil evil we committed repaid, repaid ten-fold for the public good?

Oh Judge, hear me. Oh Eye, search the depths of my soul. If I am guilty, then you must forgive me. I took no pleasure in what I had to do. I swear unto you: I took no pleasure in it.

The Master Emeritus Recalls Wellington

The reddish glow of enfeebled gas-light. The rhythmic, echoing clank and screech of the Brunel Tunneling Torpedo. Thirty-six cork-screw teeth of best Birmingham steel gnaw with relentless vigor into a reeking seam of ancient London clay.

Master Sapper Joseph Pearson, at his ease at the mid-day meal, feeds himself a congealed wedge of gravy-thick meat-pie from a hinged tin box. "Aye, I met the great Mallory," he says, voice echoing from arching whale-ribs of riveted cast-iron. "We warn't exactly introduced, like, but he was Leviathan Mallory, right-enough, for I seen his phiz in the penny-papers. He stood as close to me as I am to you now, lad. 'Lord Jefferies?' the Leviathan says to me, all surprised and angry, 'I know Jefferies! The fookin' bastard should be censured for fraud!' "

Master Pearson grins in triumph, red light glinting from a gold earring, a gold tooth. "And damme if that savant Jefferies didn't catch every kind of hell, once the Stink had passed. Leviathan Mallory took a proper hand in that chastisement, sure enough. He's one of Nature's noblemen, Leviathan Mallory is."

"I seen that brontosaur," says 'Prentice David Waller, nodding, eyes bright. "That's a fine thing!"

"I myself was workin' the shaft in '54, when they dug up them elephant teeth." Master Pearson, rubber-booted feet dangling from the second-story platform of the excavation-shaft, shifts on his damp-proofed mat of coir and burlap, and yanks a split of champagne from a pocket of his excavation-gear. "French fizz, Davey-lad. Your first time down; ye got to have a taste of this."

"That ain't proper, is it, sir? 'Gainst the book."

Pearson wrenches the cork loose, no pop, no gush of foam. He winks. "Hell, lad, it's your first time down; won't never be another first time." Pearson tosses sugary dregs of strong tea from his tin cup, fills it to the brim with champagne.

"It's gone flat," 'Prentice Waller mourns.

Pearson laughs, rubbing a burst vein in his fleshy nose. "It's the pressure, lad. Wait till ye get topside. It goes off right inside yer. You'll fart like an ox."

'Prentice Waller sips, with some caution. An iron bell rings, above them. "Chamber coming down," Pearson says, hastily corking the bottle. He stuffs it back into a pocket, gulps the rest of the cup, wipes his mouth.

A bullet-shaped cage descends, passing with cloacal slowness through a membrane of heavy waxed leather. There are hisses, creaks, as the cage touches bottom.

Two men emerge. The Chief Foreman wears a helmet, digging-gear, and leather apron. With him, carrying a brass dark-lantern, is a tall, white-haired man in a black tailcoat and black satin cravat, a kerchief of black silk crepe about his polished top-hat. In the red light of the tunnel, a pigeon's-egg diamond, or perhaps a ruby, glints at the old man's throat. Like the Chief Foreman, his trousered legs are swathed in knee-high boots of india-rubber.

"The Grand Master Miner Emeritus," Pearson gasps in a single breath, and scrambles at once to his feet. Waller leaps up as well.

The two of them stand at attention as the Grand Master strolls beneath them, up the tunnel toward the Torpedo's massive digging-face. He does not glance up, takes no notice of them, but speaks with cool authority to the Foreman. He examines bolts, seams, and grouting with the stabbing beam of his bull's-eye lantern. The lantern has no handle, for the Grand Master carries the hot brass caught in a sleek iron hook which protrudes from an empty sleeve.

"But that's a queer way to dress, ain't it?" whispers young Waller.

"He's still in mourning," Pearson whispers.

"Ah," says the 'prentice. He watches the Grand Master walk on a bit. "Still?"

"He knew Lord Byron dead-familiar like, the Grand Master did. Knew Lord Babbage too! In the Time o' Troubles—when they was running from Wellington's Tory police! They warn't no Lordships then—not proper Rad Lords, anyway, just rebels and agitators, like, with a price on their heads. The Grand Master hid 'em out down a digging once—a reg'lar Party headquarters, it was. The Rad Lords never forgot the great favors he done for 'em. That's why we're the greatest of Radical unions."

"Ah."

"That's a great man, Davey! Master of iron, a great master of blasting-powder. . . . They don't make 'em like him, today."

"So—he must be nigh eighty now, eh?"

"Still hale and hearty."

"Could we get down, sir, d'ye think—could I see him up close, like? Maybe shake his famous hook!"

"All right, lad—but on your dignity now. No bad words."

They climb down to the bare planks at the base of the tunnel.

As they follow the Grand Master, the gnawing rumble of the Torpedo changes abruptly. The Torpedo's crew leaps up, for such a change means trouble—quicksand, a vein of water, or worse. Pearson and his 'prentice break into a shuffling run toward the digging-face.

Shavings of soft black filth begin to pour from the sharp iron spirals of the thirty-six twisting teeth, falling in greasy clods to the flat-carts of the carriage-ramp. From within the black soil of the digging-face come little muffled pops of old embedded gas-pockets, weak as Pearson's enfeebled champagne-cork. No deadly rush of water, though; no slurry of quicksand. They inch forward warily, gazing after the sharp white beam of the Grand Master's lantern.

Knobs of hardened yellow show amid greenish-black muck. "Bones, is it?" says a workman, wiping his nose at a smell of soured dust. "Fossils, like . . ."

Bones pour forth in a broken torrent as the Torpedo's hydraulics lurch in reaction, pressing it forward into the softening mass. Human bones.

"A cemetery!" Pearson cries. "We've hit a churchyard!"

But the tunnel is too deep for that, and there are too many bones, bones tangled thick as the branches of a fallen forest, in a deep promiscuous mass, and mixed of a sudden with a thin and deadly reek, of long-buried lime and sulphur.

"Plague pit!" the Chief Foreman cries in terror, and the men fall back, stumbling. There is a lurch, and a hiss of steam as the Foreman shuts down the Torpedo.

The Grand Master has not moved.

He stands quietly, regarding the work of the teeth.

He puts his lamp aside, and reaches into the heap of spoil. He dabbles in it with his shining hook, and has something up by one eyehole. A skull.

"Ah, then," he says, his deep voice ringing in the sudden utter silence, "ye poor damn' bastard."

The Gaming Lady Is Bad Luck

"The Gaming Lady is bad luck to those that know her. When a poor night at the wagering-machines has emptied her purse, her jewels are carried privately into Lombard Street, and Fortune is tempted yet again with a sum from my lady's pawnbroker! Then she sells off her wardrobe as well, to the grief of her maids; stretches her credit amongst those she deals with, pawns her honor to her intimates, in vain hope to recover her losses!

"The passions suffer no less by this gaming-fever than the understanding and the imagination. What vivid, unnatural hope and fear, joy and anger, sorrow and discontent, burst out all at once upon a roll of the dice, a turn of the card, a run of the shining gurneys! Who can consider without indignation that all those womanly affections, which should have been consecrated to children and husband, are thus vilely prostituted and thrown away. I cannot but be grieved when I see the Gaming Lady fretting and bleeding inwardly from such evil and unworthy obsessions; when I behold the face of an angel agitated by the heart of a fury!

"It is divinely ordered that almost everything which corrupts the soul, must also decay the body. Hollow eyes, haggard looks, and pale complexion are the natural indications of a female gamester. Her morning sleeps cannot repair her sordid midnight watchings. I have looked long and hard upon the face of the Gaming Lady. Yes, I have watched her well. I have seen her carried off half-dead from Crockford's gambling-hell, at two o'clock in the morning, looking like a specter amid a flare of wicked gas-lamps—

"Pray resume your seat, sir. You are in the House of God. Is that remark to be taken as a threat, sir? How dare you. These are dark times, grave times indeed! I tell you, sir, as I tell this congregation, as I will tell all the world, that I *have* seen her, I have witnessed your Queen of Engines at her vile dissipations—

"Help me! Stop him! Stop him! Oh dear Jesus, I am shot! I am undone! Murder! Can none of you stop him?"

Gentlemen, The Choice Is Yours

[*At the height of the Parliamentary crisis of 1855, Lord Brunel assembled and addressed the members of his Cabinet. His remarks were recorded by his private secretary, using the Babbage shorthand notation.*]

"Gentlemen, I cannot call to mind a single instance in which any individual in the Party or the Ministry has spoken, even casually, in my defense within the walls of Parliament. I have waited patiently, and I hope uncomplainingly, doing what little I could to protect and extend the wise legacy of the late Lord Byron, and to heal the reckless wounds inflicted on our Party by over-zealous juniors.

"But there has been no change in the contempt in which you honorable gentlemen seem to hold me. On the contrary, the last two nights have been taken up with a debate on a vote of want-of-confidence, directed, obviously and especially, against the head of the Government. The discussion has been marked with more than usual violence against my office, and there has been no defense from any of you—the members of my own Cabinet.

"How, under these circumstances, are we to successfully resolve the matter of the murder of the Reverend Alistair Roseberry? This shameful, atavistic crime, brutally perpetrated within a Christian church, has blackened the reputation of Party and Government, and cast the gravest doubts on our intentions and integrity. And how are we to root out the murderous dark-lantern societies whose power, and provocative daring, grows daily?

"God knows, gentlemen, that I never sought my present office. Indeed, I would have done anything, consistent with honor, to avoid assuming it. But I must be master in this House, or else resign my office—abandoning this nation to the purported leadership of men whose intentions are increasingly stark in their clarity. Gentlemen, the choice is yours."

Death of the Marquess of Hastings

Yes, sir, two-fifteen to be quite exact, sir—and no other way to be, as we're on the Colt & Maxwell system of patent punch-clocks.

Just a sort of dripping sound, sir.

For a moment I took it to be a leakage, forgetting the night was clear. Rain, I thought, and that was all my anxiety, sir, thinking the Land Leviathan would be damaged by damp, so I flung my lantern's beam up quick, and there the poor rascal hung, and blood all down the Leviathan's neck-bones, sir, and all on the—what d'ye call 'em?—the armatures, what hold the beast upright. And his head a bloody ruin, sir—no longer as you'd call a head at all. Dangling there by his ankles from this manner of harness, and I saw the ropes and pulleys going straight up, taut, into the dark of the great dome, and the sight struck me so, sir, that it wasn't till I'd sounded the alarm that I saw the Leviathan's head was missing too.

Yes, sir, I do believe that to be the case—the manner in which it was done. He was lowered down from the dome and did the job up there, in the dark, and paused when he'd hear my footsteps, and then continue his work. The work of some hours, for they'd had to rig their lines and pulleys. Likely I passed beneath them several times, on my watch. And when he'd got it free, the head, sir, someone else winched it up, and took it away through that panel they'd unbolted. But something must have given, sir, or slipped, for down he came, square into the floor, best Florentine marble that is. We found where his brains had been dashed, sir, though I'd as soon forget it. And I did then recall a sound, sir, likely of him striking, but no outcry.

If I may say, sir, what strikes me as vilest, in the whole business, must be the cool way they hauled him back up, quiet as spiders, and left him slung there, like a coney in a butcher's window, and stole away across the roof-top with their booty. There's a deal of meanness in that, isn't there?

—KENNETH REYNOLDS,
night watchman, the Museum of Practical Geology,
in deposition before Magistrate G. H. S. Peters,
Bow Street,
Nov. 1855.

Believe Me Always

MY DEAR EGREMONT,

I write to you to express my profound regret that the circumstances of the moment should deprive me of the opportunity and hope of enlisting your great capacity in the further service of Party and Government.

You will well understand that my recognition of your difficult personal circumstances is absolutely separate from any want of confidence in you as a statesman; this is the last idea I should wish to convey.

How can I close without fervently expressing to you my desire that there may be reserved for you a place of permanent public distinction?

Believe me always,
Yours sincerely,
I. K. BRUNEL

—*Ministerial letter to Charles Egremont, M.P.,
Dec. 1855.*

Memorandum to the Foreign Office

On this occasion, our distinguished guest, the ex-President of the American Union, Mr. Clement L. Vallandigham, got as drunk as a fiddle. The eminent Democrat showed that he could be as profligate as any English Lord. He fumbled Mrs. A., kissed the shrieking Miss B., pinched the plump Mrs. C. black and blue, and ran at Miss D. with flagrant intent to ravish her!

Finally, after throwing our female guests into hysterics by behaving like an elephant in must, the noble beast was captured by main force, and carried upstairs, all four feet in the air, by our

household staff. Within his room, Mrs. Vallandigham was awaiting him, in shift and mobcap. There and then, to our considerable amazement, this remarkable man satiated his baffled lust on
the unresisting body of his legitimate spouse, and copiously vom-
ited during the operation. Those who have seen Mrs. Vallandigham would not think this latter incredible.

News has now reached me that the former President of Texas,
Samuel Houston, has died in Veracruz, in his Mexican exile. He
was, I believe, awaiting any call to arms that might have brought
him back to eminence; but the French *alcaldes* were likely too wily
for him. Houston had his faults, I know, but he was easily worth
ten of Clement Vallandigham, who made a shrinking peace with
the Confederacy, and has allowed the vultures of Red Manhattan
Communism to gnaw the carcass of his dishonored country.

—LORD LISTON, *1870.*

Before the Rads

[*The following testament is a sound-recording inscribed on wax. One of
the earliest such recordings, it preserves the spoken reminiscences of
Thomas Towler (b. 1790), grandfather of Edward Towler, inventor of
the Towler Audiograph. Despite the experimental nature of the apparatus employed, the recording is of exceptional clarity. 1875.*]

I remember one winter and it was a very long cold winter, and
there was dire poverty in England then, before the Rads. Me
brother Albert, he used to get some bricks and cover them with
bird-lime, and set 'em by the stables to catch sparrows. And he'd
pluck them, clean them, him and me together, I helped him. Our
Albert would make a fire and get the oven hot and we used to cook
those little sparrows in Mother's roasting-tin, with a big lump of
dripping in it. And me mother'd make a big jug of tea for us and
we'd have what we'd call a tea-party, eating those sparrows.

Me father . . . he went to all the shopkeepers on Chatwin Road and got scrap-meat. Bones, you know, lamb-bones, all sorts of things, dried peas, beans, and left-over carrots and turnips and . . . he got some oatmeal promised him and a baker gave him stale bread. . . . Me father had a big iron boiler . . . that he used to make gruel for the horses and he cleaned it all out and they made soup in this big horse-boiler. I can remember seeing the poor people come. They came twice a week, that winter. They had to bring their own jugs. They was that hungry, before the Rads.

And Eddie, did you ever hear tell of the Irish Famine, in the forties? I thought not. But the 'tater crop failed then, two, three years in a row, and it looked mighty dire for the Irish. But the Rads, they wouldn't stand for that, and declared an emergency, and mobilized the nation. Lord Byron made a fine speech, in all the papers. . . . I signed aboard one of the relief-boats, out of Bristol. All day, all night, we'd load big gantry-crates, with bills-of-lading from the London Engines; trains come day and night from all over England, with every kind of food. "God Bless Lord Babbage," the poor Irish would cry to us, with tears in their eyes, "Three cheers for England and the Rad Lords." They have long memories, our own loyal Irish . . . they don't never forget a kindness.

John Keats in Half-Moon Street

I was ushered by a man-servant into Mr. Oliphant's study. Mr. Oliphant greeted me cordially, and noted that my telegram had mentioned my association with Dr. Mallory. I told Mr. Oliphant that it had been my pleasure to accompany Dr. Mallory's triumphant lecture on the Brontosaurus with a highly advanced kinotropic program. *The Monthly Review of the Steam Intellect Society* had run a most gratifying review of my efforts, and I offered Mr.

Oliphant a copy of the magazine. He glanced within it, but it seemed that his grasp of the intricacies of clacking was amateurish at best, for his reaction was one of polite puzzlement.

I then informed him that Dr. Mallory had led me to his door. In one of our private conversations, the great savant had seen fit to tell me of Mr. Oliphant's daring proposal—to employ the Engines of the police in the scientific exploration of previously hidden patterns underlying the movements and occupations of the metropolitan population. My admiration for this bold scheme had brought me directly to Mr. Oliphant, and I stated my willingness to assist in the implementation of that vision.

He interrupted me, then, in a markedly distracted manner. We are numbered, he declared, each of us, by an all-seeing eye; our minutes, too, are numbered, and each hair upon our heads. And surely it was God's will, that the computational powers of the Engine be brought to bear upon the great commonality, upon the flows of traffic, of commerce, the tidal actions of crowds—upon the infinitely divisible texture of His work.

I waited for a conclusion to this extraordinary outburst, but Mr. Oliphant seemed quite lost in thought, of a sudden.

I then explained to him, as nearly as possible in layman's terms, how the nature of the human eye necessitates, in kinotropy, both remarkable speed and remarkable complexity. For this reason, I concluded, we kinotropists must be numbered among Britain's most adept programmers of Enginery of any sort, and virtually all advances in the compression of data have originated as kinotropic applications.

At this point, he interrupted again, asking if I had indeed said "the compression of data," and was I familiar with the term "algorithmic compression"? I assured him that I was.

He rose, then, and going to a bureau near at hand, he brought out what I took to be a wooden box of the sort used to transport scientific instruments, though this was partially covered, it seemed, with remnants of white plaster. And would I be so kind, he requested, as to examine the cards within, copy them for safe-keeping, and privately report to him upon the nature of their content?

He had no idea of their astonishing import, you see, no idea whatever.

—JOHN KEATS,
quoted in an interview conducted by H. S. Lywood, for
The Monthly Review of the Steam Intellect Society,
May 1857.

The Grand Panmelodium Polka

Oh! Sure the world is all run mad,
The lean, the fat, the old, the Rad,
All swear such pleasure they ne'er had,
As the Grand Panmelodium Polka.

First cock up your right leg so,
Balance on your left great toe,
Stamp your heels and off you go,
The Grand Panmelodium Polka.

Quadrilles and waltzes all give way,
Machine-made music bears the sway.
The chimney-sweeps on the first of May,
In London dance the Polka.

If a pretty girl you meet,
With sparkling eyes and rosy cheek,
She'll say, young man we'll have a treat,
If you can dance the Polka.

Professors swarm in every street,
To hear the Panmelodium sweet,
And every friend you chance to meet,
Asks if you dance the Polka.

And so the row-de-dow we dance,
And in short skirts and brass-heels prance,
Ladies won't you spare a glance,
For the boys what spin the Polka.

The Tatler

We learn with mingled regret and amazement of the recent
departure, aboard the *Great Eastern*, of the well-liked and many-
talented Mr. Laurence Oliphant—author, journalist, diplomat,
geographer, and friend of the Royal Family—for America, with
the stated intention of residing in the so-called Susquehanna
Phalanstery established by Messrs. Coleridge and Wordsworth,
thereby to pursue the utopian doctrines espoused by these worthy expatriates!

—" 'ROUND TOWN," *a column, September 12, 1860.*

A London Playbill, 1866

THE GARRICK THEATRE, Whitechapel, Newly Rebuilt and Refur-
bished, Under the Management of J. J. TOBIAS, Esq., presents

˙The First Nights of a New Kinotropic Drama
Monday, Nov. 13 and During the Week

The performance will commence with (FIRST TIME!) an entirely
new national, local, characteristic, metropolitan, melo-dramatic,
kinotropic drama of the day, in five acts, correctly exhibiting
modern life and manners in innumerable novel and interesting
phases, called the

CROSSROADS OF LIFE!!
or
THE CLACKERS OF LONDON

The Groundwork of the drama founded on the celebrated play, "Les Fils de Vaucanson," now attracting the attention of all France, and applied to the circumstances and realities of the present moment.

With kinotropic scenery by MR. JJ TOBIAS *and Assistants*

The New Flash Medley Orchestra, led by MR. MONTGOMERY

The Action of the Piece arranged by MR. CJ SMITH

The Dresses by MRS. HAMPTON *and* MISS BAILEY

The Whole Produced Under the Direction of MR. JJ TOBIAS

Dramatis Personae

Mark Riddley, alias Fox Skinner, (*a swell cove, and King of the London Clackers*) . . . . MR. H.L. MARSTON.

Mr. Dorrington (*a wealthy Liverpool Merchant, on a visit to London*) . . . . MR. J. ROMER.

Frank Danvers (*a British Naval Officer, just arrived from the Indies*) . . . . MR. WM. BIRD.

Robert Danvers (*his younger brother, a ruined roué, pigeoned by the clackers*). . . . . MR. L. MELVIN.

Mr. Hawksworth Shabner (*Principal Proprietor of a West-End Clacking-Hall, Bill-Discounter, and Anythingarian where there is Anything to be Got*). . . . . MR. P. WILLIAMS.

Bob Yorkner (*a Duffer, tired of the Lay*) . . . . MR. W. JONES.

Ned Brindle (*the Magsman, a half-and-half cove*) . . MR C. AUBREY.

Tom Fogg, alias Old Deady, alias The Animal, (*a laudanum fiend suffering under delirium-tremens*). . . . . MR. A. CORENO.

Joe Onion, alias The Crocodile, (*a bully-rock, and creature of Shabner's*) . . . . MR. G. VELASCO.

Dickey Smith (*the Wakeful Bird, a young Engine-clerk in no ways particklar, pecking out a living as best he can*) . . MR. G. MASKELL.
Ikey Bates (*Landlord of Rat's Castle, proprietor of two-penny dabs and a scandalous bagatelle board, having cut the bumblepuppy as too low!*). . . . . MR. GOTOBED.
Waiter at the Cat-and-Bagpipes Tavern . . . . . . MR. SMITHSON.
The Bow Street Special Inspector. . . . . MR. FRANKS.
Louisa Truehart (*the Victim of an ill-requited attachment*)
. . . . MISS CAROLINE BARNETT.
Charlotte Willers (*a young lady with her cat from the country*)
. . . . MISS MARTHA WELLS.

DRESS CIRCLE, 3S. BOXES, 2S. PIT, 5D. GALLERY 2D.

BOX OFFICE OPEN DAILY FROM TEN O'CLOCK UNTIL FIVE.

A Poem of Farewell

[*Mori Yujo, a samurai and classical scholar of Satsuma Province, wrote the following ceremonial poem upon his son's departure for England, in 1854. It is translated from Sinicized Japanese.*]

My child rides the unfathomable deep,
In pursuit of noble ambition;
Far must he sail—ten thousand leagues—
Outpacing the breezes of spring.
Some say that East and West
Have naught in common;
But I say the same heaven
Overarches both.
His own life he risks, on command of his *han*.
Braving great danger to learn from far places;
For family's sake, he spares no effort,
Seeking for wisdom in face of great hardship.
He travels far beyond

The fabled rivers of China;
His scholarly labors shall someday
Bear fruit in splendid achievement.

A Letter Home

As always, I searched that day for land, in all four directions, but could still find none. How melancholy it was! Then by chance, with the Captain's permission, I climbed up one of the masts. From the great height, with sails and smokestack far below me, I was amazed to make out the coast of Europe—a mere hair's-breadth of green, above the watery horizon. I shouted down to Matsumura: "Come up! Come up!" And up he came, very swiftly and bravely.

Together atop the mast, we gazed upon Europe. "Look!" I told him. "Here is our first proof that the world is really round! While we were standing down there on deck we could not see a thing; but up here, land is distinctly visible. This is proof that the surface of the sea is curved! And if the sea is curved, why, then, so is the whole earth!"

Matsumura exclaimed, "It's fantastic—it's just the way you say! The Earth indeed is round! Our first real proof!"

—MORI ARINORI, *1854.*

Modus

It seemed that Her Ladyship had been ill-served by the Paris publicists, for the lecture-hall, modest as it was, was less than half-filled.

Dark folding-seats, in neat columnar rows, were precisely dotted by the shiny pates of balding mathematicians. Here and there among the savants sat shifty-eyed French clackers in middle-age, the summer linen of their too-elegant finery looking rather past the mode. The last three rows were filled by a Parisian women's club, fanning themselves in the summer heat and chattering quite audibly, for they had long since lost the thread of Her Ladyship's discourse.

Lady Ada Byron turned a page, touched a gloved finger to her bifocal pince-nez. For some minutes, a large green bottle-fly had been circling her podium. Now it broke the intricacy of its looping flight to alight on the bulging archipelago of Her Ladyship's padded, lace-trimmed shoulder. Lady Ada took no apparent notice of the attentions of this energetic vermin, but continued on gamely, in her accented French.

The Mother said:

"Our lives would be greatly clarified if human discourse could be interpreted as the exfoliation of a deeper formal system. One would no longer need ponder the grave ambiguities of human speech, but could judge the validity of any sentence by reference to a fixed and finitely describable set of rules and axioms. It was the dream of Leibniz to find such a system, the *Characteristica Universalis*. . . .

"And yet the execution of the so-called Modus Program demonstrated that any formal system must be both *incomplete* and *unable to establish its own consistency*. There is no finite mathematical way to express the property of 'truth.' The *transfinite* nature of the Byron Conjectures were the ruination of the Grand Napoleon; the Modus Program initiated a series of nested loops, which, though difficult to establish, were yet more difficult to extinguish. The program ran, yet rendered its Engine useless! It was indeed a painful lesson in the halting abilities of even our finest *ordinateurs*.

"Yet I do believe, and must assert most strongly, that the Modus technique of *self-referentiality* will someday form the bedrock of a genuinely transcendent meta-system of calculatory mathematics.

The Modus has proven my Conjectures, but their practical exfoliation awaits an Engine of vast capacity, one capable of iterations of untold sophistication and complexity.

"Is it not strange that we mere mortals can talk about a concept—*truth*—that is infinitely complicated? And yet—is not a closed system the essence of the mechanical, the unthinking? And is not an open system the very definition of the organic, of life and thought?

"If we envision the entire System of Mathematics as a great Engine for proving theorems, then we must say, through the agency of the Modus, that such an Engine *lives*, and could indeed *prove* its own life, should it develop the capacity to look upon itself. The Lens for such a self-examination is of a nature not yet known to us; yet we know that it exists, for we ourselves possess it.

"As thinking beings, we may envision the universe, though we have no finite way to sum it up. The term, 'universe,' is not in fact a rational concept, though it is something of such utter immediacy that no thinking creature can escape a pressing knowledge of it, and indeed, an urge to know its workings, and the nature of one's own origin within it.

"In his final years, the great Lord Babbage, impatient of the limits of steam-power, sought to harness the lightning in the cause of calculation. His elaborate system of 'resistors' and 'capacitors,' while demonstrative of the most brilliant genius, remains fragmentary, and is yet to be constructed. Indeed, it is often mocked by the undiscerning as an old man's hobby-horse. But history shall prove its judge, and then, I profoundly hope, my own Conjectures will transcend the limits of abstract concept and enter the living world."

Applause was thin and scattered. Ebenezer Fraser, watching from the shelter of the wings, in the shadow of ropes and sandbags, felt his heart sink. But at least it was over. She was leaving the podium to join him.

Fraser opened the nickeled catches of Her Ladyship's traveling-bag. Lady Ada dropped her manuscript within it, followed it with her kid gloves and her tiny ribboned hat.

"I think they understood me!" she said brightly. "It sounds quite elegant in French, Mr. Fraser, does it not? A very rational language, French."

"What next, milady? The hotel?"

"My dressing-room," she said. "This heat is rather fatiguing. . . . Will you hail the gurney for me? I'll join you presently."

"Certainly, milady." Fraser, the bag in one hand, his sword-cane in another, led Lady Ada to the cramped little dressing-room, opened the door, bowed her within, set her bag at her neatly slippered feet, and closed the door firmly. Within the room, he knew, Her Ladyship would seek the consolation of the silvered brandy-flask she had hidden in the left-hand lower drawer of her dressing-table—wrapped, with pathetic duplicity, in a shroud of tissue-paper.

Fraser had taken the liberty of providing seltzer-water in a bucket of ice. He hoped she would water the liquor a bit.

He left the lecture-hall by a rear door, then circled the building warily, from old habit. His bad eye ached below the patch, and he made some use of the stag-handled sword-cane. As he had fully expected, he saw nothing resembling trouble.

There was also no sign of the chauffeur for Her Ladyship's hired gurney. Doubtless the frog rascal was nursing a bottle somewhere, or chatting-up a *soubrette*. Or he might, perhaps, have mistaken his instructions, for Fraser's French was none of the best. He rubbed his good eye, examining the traffic. He would give the fellow twenty minutes, then hail a cab.

He saw Her Ladyship standing, rather uncertainly, at the lecture-hall's rear door. She had put on a day-bonnet, it seemed— and forgotten her traveling-bag, which was very like her. He hurried, limping, to her side. "This way, milady—the gurney will meet us at the corner. . . ."

He paused. It was not Lady Ada.

"I believe you mistake me, sir," the woman said in English, and lowered her eyes, and smiled. "I am not your Queen of Engines. I am merely an admirer."

"I beg your pardon, madame," Fraser said.

The woman glanced down shyly at the intricate Jacquard patterning of her white-on-white skirt of fine muslin. She wore a jutting French bustle, and a stiff high-shouldered walking-jacket, trimmed with lace. "Her Ladyship and I are dressed quite alike," she said, with a wry half-smile. "Her Ladyship must shop at Monsieur Worth's! That's quite a tribute to my own taste, sir, *n'est-ce pas?*"

Fraser said nothing. A light tingle of suspicion touched him. The woman—a trim little blonde, in her forties perhaps—wore the dress of respectability. Yet there were three gold-banded brilliants on her gloved fingers, and showy little stems of filigreed jade dangled at her delicate earlobes. There was a killing beauty-patch—or a black sticking-plaster—at the corner of her mouth, and her wide blue eyes, for all their look of seasoned innocence, held the gleam of the *demi-mondaine*—a look that somehow said, *I know you, copper.*

"Sir, may I wait for Her Ladyship with you? I hope I will not intrude if I request her autograph."

"At the corner," Fraser nodded. "The gurney." He offered her his left arm, tucked the sword-cane in the pit of his right, his hand resting easy on the handle. It would not hurt to get a bit of distance down the pavement, before Lady Ada approached; he wanted to watch this woman.

They stopped at the corner, beneath an angular French gas-lamp. "It's so good to hear a London voice," said the woman, coaxingly. "I have lived so long in France that my English has grown quite rusty."

"Not at all," Fraser said. Her voice was lovely.

"I am Madame Tournachon," she said, "Sybil Tournachon."

"My name is Fraser." He bowed.

Sybil Tournachon fidgeted with her kid-skin gloves, as though her palms were perspiring. The day was very hot. "Are you one of her paladins, Mr. Fraser?"

"I'm afraid I fail to take your meaning, madame," Fraser said politely. "Do you live in Paris, Mrs. Tournachon?"

"In Cherbourg," she said, "but I came all that way, by the morning express, simply to see her speak." She paused. "I scarcely understood a word she said."

"No harm in that, madame," Fraser said, "neither do I." He had begun to like her.

The gurney arrived. The chauffeur, with a bold wink at Fraser, hopped from behind the wheel and whipped a dirty chamois from his pocket. He applied it to the tarnished trim of a scalloped fender, whistling.

Her Ladyship emerged from the lecture-hall. She had remembered her hand-bag. As she approached, Mrs. Tournachon went a bit pale with excitement, and took a lecture-program from her jacket.

She was quite harmless.

"Your Ladyship, may I present Mrs. Sybil Tournachon," Fraser said.

"How do you do?" Lady Ada said.

Mrs. Tournachon curtsied. "Will you sign my program? Please."

Lady Ada blinked. Fraser, adroitly, handed her the pen from his notebook. "Of course," Lady Ada said, taking the paper. "I'm sorry—what was the name?"

" 'To Sybil Tournachon.' Shall I spell it?"

"No need," said Her Ladyship, smiling. "There's a famous French aeronaut named Tournachon, isn't there?" Fraser offered his back to the flourish of Her Ladyship's pen. "A relation of yours, perhaps?"

"No, Your Highness."

"I beg your pardon?" Lady Ada said.

"They call you Queen of Engines. . . ." Mrs. Tournachon, smiling triumphantly, plucked the inscribed program from Her Ladyship's unresisting fingers. "The Queen of Engines! And you're just a funny little grey-haired blue-stocking!" She laughed. "This lecture-gull you're running, dearie—does it pay at all well? I do hope it pays!"

Lady Ada regarded her with unfeigned astonishment.

Fraser's grip tightened on the cane. He stepped to the curb, swiftly opened the gurney door.

"One moment!" The woman tugged with sudden energy at one gloved finger, came up with a gaudy ring. "Your Ladyship—please—I want you to have this!"

Fraser stepped between them, lowering the cane. "Leave her alone."

"No," Mrs. Tournachon cried, "I've heard the tales, I know she needs it. . . ." She pressed against him, stretching out her arm. "Your Ladyship, please take this! I shouldn't have wounded your feelings, it was low of me. Please take my gift! Please, I *do* admire you, I sat through that whole lecture. Please take it, I brought it just for you!" She fell back then, her hand empty, and smiled. "Thank you, Your Ladyship! Good luck to you. I shan't trouble you again. *Au revoir! Bonne chance!*"

Fraser followed Her Ladyship into the gurney, shut the door, rapped the partition. The chauffeur took his post.

The gurney pulled away.

"What a queer little personage," Her Ladyship said. She opened her hand. A fat little diamond gleamed in its filigreed setting. "Who was she, Mr. Fraser?"

"I should guess an exile, ma'am," Fraser said. "Very forward of her."

"Was it wrong of me to take this?" Her breath smelled of brandy and seltzer. "Not really proper, I suppose. But she would have made a scene, otherwise." She held the gem up, in a sheet of dusty sunlight through the window. "Look at the size of it! It must be very dear."

"Paste, Your Ladyship."

Swift as thought, Lady Ada pinched the ring in her fingers like a bit of chalk, and ran the stone along the gurney's window. There was a thin grating shriek, almost inaudible, and a shining groove appeared across the glass.

They sat in companionable silence, then, on their way to the hotel.

Fraser watched Paris through the window and recalled his instructions. "You may let the old girl drink as she likes," the Hierarch had told him, with his inimitable air of mincing irony, "talk as she likes, flirt as she likes, saving open scandal, of course. . . . You may take your mission as fulfilled if you can keep our little Ada from the wagering-machines." There had been small chance of that disaster, for her purse held nothing but tickets and small-change, but the diamond had rather changed matters. He would have to keep a closer eye, now.

Their rooms in the Richelieu were quite modest, with a connecting-door he had not touched. The locks were sound enough, and he had found and plugged the inevitable spy-holes. He kept the keys.

"Is there anything left of the advance?" Lady Ada asked.

"Enough to tip the chauffeur," Fraser said.

"Oh dear. That little?"

Fraser nodded. The French savants had paid little enough for the pleasure of her learned company, and her debts had swiftly eaten that. The meager takings at the ticket-booth would scarcely have paid their passage from London.

Lady Ada opened the curtains, frowned at summer daylight, closed them again. "Then I suppose I shall have to take on that tour in America."

Fraser sighed, inaudibly. "They say that continent boasts many natural wonders, milady."

"Which tour, though? Boston and New Philadelphia? Or Charleston and Richmond?"

Fraser said nothing. The names of the alien cities struck him with a leaden gloom.

"I shall toss a coin for it!" Her Ladyship decided brightly. "Have you a coin, Mr. Fraser?"

"No, milady," Fraser lied, searching his pockets with a muted jingle, "I'm sorry."

"Don't they pay you at all?" Her Ladyship inquired, with a hint of temper.

"I have my police pension, milady. Quite generous, promptly

paid." The promptness part was true, at least.

She was concerned now, hurt. "But doesn't the Society pay you a proper salary? Oh dear, and I've put you to so much trouble, Mr. Fraser! I had no idea."

"They recompense me in their own way, ma'am. I am well rewarded."

He was her paladin. It was more than enough.

She stepped to her bureau, searching among papers and receipts. Her fingers touched the tortoise-shell handle of her traveling-mirror.

She turned then, and caught him with a woman's look. Under its pressure, he lifted his hand, quite without volition, and touched his bumpy cheek below the eye-patch. His white side-whiskers did not hide the scars. A shotgun had caught him there. It still ached sometimes, when it rained.

She did not see his gesture, though, or did not choose to see it. She beckoned him nearer. "Mr. Fraser. My friend. Tell me something, won't you? Tell me the truth." She sighed. "Am I nothing but a funny little grey-haired blue-stocking?"

"Madame," Fraser said gently, "you are *la Reine des Ordinateurs.*"

"Am I?" She lifted the mirror, gazed within it.

In the mirror, a City.

It is 1991. It is London. Ten thousand towers, the cyclonic hum of a trillion twisting gears, all air gone earthquake-dark in a mist of oil, in the frictioned heat of intermeshing wheels. Black seamless pavements, uncounted tributary rivulets for the frantic travels of the punched-out lace of data, the ghosts of history loosed in this hot shining necropolis. Paper-thin faces billow like sails, twisting, yawning, tumbling through the empty streets, human faces that are borrowed masks, and lenses for a peering Eye. And when a given face has served its purpose, it crumbles, frail as ash, bursting into a dry foam of data, its constituent bits and motes. But new fabrics of conjecture are knitted in the City's shining cores, swift tireless spindles flinging off invisible loops in their millions, while in the hot unhuman dark, data melts and mingles, churned by gear-work to a skeletal bubbling pumice, dipped in a dreaming wax that forms a simulated flesh, perfect as thought—

It is *not* London—but mirrored plazas of sheerest crystal, the avenues atomic lightning, the sky a super-cooled gas, as the Eye chases its own gaze through the labyrinth, leaping quantum gaps that are causation, contingency, chance. Electric phantoms are flung into being, examined, dissected, infinitely iterated.

In this City's center, a *thing* grows, an auto-catalytic tree, in almost-life, feeding through the roots of thought on the rich decay of its own shed images, and ramifying, through myriad lightning-branches, up, up, toward the hidden light of vision,

Dying to be born.
The light is strong,
The light is clear;
The Eye at last must see itself

Myself . . .
I see:
I see,
I see
I
!

About the Authors

WILLIAM GIBSON is the Hugo and Nebula award-winning author of the *Cyberspace* trilogy: *Neuromancer, Count Zero,* and *Mona Lisa Overdrive*. His widely acclaimed short stories are collected in *Burning Chrome*. He lives in Vancouver, British Columbia, with his family.

BRUCE STERLING is the author of *Involution Ocean, The Artificial Kid, Schismatrix, Islands in the Net,* and the short-story collection *Crystal Express*. He edited *Mirrorshades,* the definitive "cyberpunk" anthology. He lives with his wife and daughter in Austin, Texas.